Haunted West

by

Nathan Wright

Nathan Wright

This is a work of fiction. All of the characters, organizations, and events portrayed in this novel are either products of the author's imagination or are used fictitiously.

ISBN: 9781723982309

Haunted West

Rusty was a bit more cautious this morning, more so than usual which was unlike the big horse. It seemed every few steps he wanted to stop and look around, sniff the air and perk his ears up to listen. His was the personality that usually forged ahead as if he were in a hurry to get somewhere fast, but not today. On this day he picked his steps with great care. I noticed the change starting to take place a couple of days back, extreme caution; it could almost be described as fear. Rusty was four and a half years old but as horses go he was intelligent as if he had lived a hundred previous years and remembered everything he had ever experienced. He was descended from fine Kentucky stock of which my father was famous, he was a Conley horse and there were none better in all the country as far as I was concerned. This view was also held by many others.

My father, William Haskel Conley, is a hardworking man from Southeastern Kentucky. He raises horses for fun and cattle for profit and is quite good at both. Rusty was a gift from my father on my eighteenth birthday. I had been planning on heading west as soon as I came of age and Paw couldn't talk me out of it, finally realizing that the more he talked against it the more I was determined to go. Rusty was my going away present. The second day after my birthday was the day I had chosen to leave the coal fields of Kentucky and make my way west. It was both a sad and a happy day for me. I loved my family but adventure was waiting and any young man who has ever wanted to seek fame and fortune in the world will tell you that it is an itch that can never truly be scratched.

The year is 1887 and it's late fall. I turned nineteen on the trail and celebrated the occasion alone with only Rusty and the dusty plains as my party guests. That was a little over a month ago and to tell you the truth; if a man were ever happier then I tip my hat to him. I had grown so accustomed to sleeping under the stars or the thunderstorms, whichever happened to be the case; that the thought of sleeping in a house again with a roof over my head seemed to make me lose my breath, almost as if smothering. I truly doubted if I would ever be as happy in a town as I was in the wilds.

Today I wasn't sure where I was and that really didn't matter much. I was where I was and that was a fact. For the life of me I couldn't figure out what had Rusty so spooked. His ears had been up and he held his head high and it seemed nothing was going to change that. He sniffed the air as if something were lurking, something that might just jump out and eat us both alive. After a few hours of this, I started to get a little spooked myself. One thing I learned when I was younger was that the senses of an animal were much more keen than that of a man. If your horse was spooked then he probably had a damn good reason for it.

We rode for another hour and I was starting to look for a place to rest a while and have a piece of jerky when Rusty stopped dead in his tracks. I quickly looked around not knowing what to expect. Nothing seemed to be out of the ordinary. There was no sound or smell that would indicate why Rusty was acting so fidgety. I prodded the big horse but he refused to move. Now this was starting to present a problem. If Rusty was unsure and afraid of his surroundings then I should also be taking notice.

I decided to step down and lead the horse through the scattered brush and trees. It might be safer on the ground and then again it might not. Being on the ground made me less of a target if this unseen danger was a man with a rifle bent on mischief. Being on the ground would be a lot less safe if it was a bear or a wolf on the hunt for food. I guessed I would find out soon enough.

I decided to leave my rifle in its scabbard and instead drew my Colt, checking the loads and action before moving forward. Rusty seemed more willing to move now that I was on the ground and had my gun out. The two of us walked as quietly as possible. I paid close attention to where Rusty was looking as we walked and decided to head in that direction. We had gone maybe a thousand feet when Rusty stopped again. I scanned the area but still couldn't see anything that would explain the sudden change of attitude in my horse. Maybe he was just going trail crazy and this was how a horse acted when he got that way.

Now I had a problem, I couldn't tie him up and proceed alone. If it was a bear or wolf then either could kill Rusty before I got back. We would have to proceed together until we found out what the problem was or until we were past it. I rubbed the big horse's neck and then led the way again. He followed, but reluctantly.

By the looks of things there was a small clearing ahead with a few trees scattered about. As we cleared the brush and got a better look I could see what appeared to be a campsite. There was a fire that had grown cold and a pair of saddle bags thrown over a low hanging tree limb. A big horse was tied to a tree and it stood motionless, staring at me and Rusty. I had known for years that to walk into a man's camp unannounced was a good way to get a gun pointed at you. I hadn't really walked into this camp though, more like stumbled into it.

"Hello the camp," I shouted. There wasn't a reply.

"Hello the camp, anybody here?" I again shouted, still no reply.

As I waited for a response I looked over the situation at hand. The fire was out completely, not even the slightest wisp of smoke. There were no tracks that I could make out which was odd. The ground looked like it had been rained on recently which had settled the dust but it looked like the rain had been at least twenty four hours ago and the ground had dried completely, if anyone had been here today they would have left fresh tracks, there were none.

I eased a little closer still holding the Colt. The camp's only occupant, the horse, pulled on its reins as it tried to back away. The ground where it was tethered indicated the horse had been tied there for at least a full day, probably longer. Everything within reach had been picked clean and even the bark of the tree showed signs of being gnawed on. This poor horse was hungry and probably extremely thirsty.

I decided to invade this camp and find out what was going on. As I got closer I saw a saddle leaning against the opposite side of a tree. The horse looked at me and I could tell it was frightened; whether that was because of me or something else was yet to be seen. I walked up and slowly rubbed the horse's nose, it was dry. By the looks of the animal's mouth it hadn't had water in at least a day. I looked around again to see if anyone was about and saw nothing.

There was a small stream just below the campsite and I quickly untied the horse and led her down to the water. She tried to bolt but I had expected this and held the bridle tightly as we made our way. Once at the stream the horse bent and began to frantically drink. I looked the animal over. The bridle had been stretched and was starting to pull apart at the joints. It was well made and I wondered if the powerful horse could have actually broken free before it died of thirst. After a couple of minutes I pulled her away from the stream and headed back up to the camp. I would bring her back to the stream after she settled down a bit, didn't want her to drink too much this soon after being denied water for so long.

I found a spot with suitable grass and tied her out with a long lead. She immediately went to pulling grass. The poor animal had suffered from both thirst and hunger. By the looks of it she might have been two years old but I doubted it, more like a year and a half. She was in good shape other than the effects brought on by lack of food and water. I tied Rusty nearby and he also went to cropping grass. I pulled the Winchester and decided to have a better look around. At this point I was fairly certain that whoever owned the horse and had occupied the camp was either dead or in some sort of trouble, no man just walks away like that.

I checked out the saddle first and found it to be a well-made affair, same as the bridle. I pulled the saddle bags from the tree limb and sat them near the saddle. They were heavy. I didn't want to look inside until

I found out if the owner was nearby. I doubted if they were close though, who would leave a horse tied out this long if all they had to do was lead it thirty feet to water? The best thing to do at this point was to scout the surrounding area to find any sign of what might have happened here. I had heard of men dying of natural causes out in the wilderness, maybe that was what had happened here. If it had been a robbery and murder then I am sure they would have taken the horse and all the belongings. Everything was here though as if the owner had just made camp and was getting ready to sleep by his fire for the night.

I ratcheted a round into the Winchester, better to stay on the careful side of caution. Rusty was looking at me as I headed into the surrounding brush. He had calmed significantly, either due to me having a rifle in hand or to the presence of the new horse. As he looked at me he chomped on his snack of prairie grass as if it were the best thing in the world.

As I circled the camp I kept a close eye on the horses. After two complete trips I decided that if anything happened here then the sign was long gone. As I walked back to the horses I noticed the blankets not far from the cold fire. It looked like whoever had been here had actually slept here. I walked over and with the toe of my boot I tossed the top blanket over. Next to the bottom blanket was a rifle, a big rifle. Again I looked around to see if anyone was about, they were not.

I bent at the knees and retrieved the weapon. It was a Winchester .45.75. I had heard of these before but never seen one other than at my paw's farm back in Kentucky, it was truly a magnificent weapon. It looked as if it had been well taken care of. The stock was dark and polished to a brilliant shine. The barrel was well oiled and dried. Whoever owned this gun was proud of it and would never have wandered out of camp without it.

I held the gun by the stock as I stood and then with my boot tossed the rest of the blanket away. There on the ground was a rolled up gun belt and holster, inside was a revolver. Again I surveyed my surroundings. I expected to see someone run from the brush and demand to know what I was doing in his camp. All was quiet, not a soul around, just me and the two horses. I slowly picked up the gun and belt. The gun was loaded with five rounds; the cylinder under the hammer was empty. Whoever owned the gun hadn't expected any trouble or he would have had all six chambers loaded. The belt contained cartridges for the revolver and all were filled except eight. This man hadn't used a lot of ammunition while on the trail. Cartridges for the big rifle were not in the pistol belt. I would probably find them when I inspected the saddle bags. I checked the action of the revolver and found it to be smooth. The owner had taken as good a care of his pistol as he had his rifle.

There were five small notches on the outside handle of the Colt. I took this to mean the owner had taken the lives of five men. I had never met anyone who had killed five men before, for that matter I had never met a man who had killed more than two. I suspected whoever owned this gun was either an outlaw or a lawman.

Carrying the two saddlebags, I went to the big tree that more or less defined the camp. It was where the missing rider had put his saddle and was a good landmark if he got lost, the tree was huge. I sat down and put my back to the tree, letting the sun warm my left hand side. Maybe the contents of the two bags could shed some light on who they belonged to.

I opened the first leather flap and peered inside. There were the usual saddle bag contents, tobacco, matches, and rolling paper. There was also chewing tobacco and a pipe with the makings for a pipe smoke. Whoever owned this stuff was a tobacco connoisseur. Anyone who smoked cigarettes, chewed tobacco and also smoked a pipe was bound to spend half his day coughing. I dug deeper and found cartridges for the .45 .75 rifle. There were thirty two bullets and twelve empty brass cartridges. It was apparent by the empty brass cartridges that shells for the big rifle were hard to find, the man kept up with his brass.

The second bag contained reloading tools for the empty cartridges. There were also two small dime novels and a pair of reading spectacles, the owner of the saddlebags could read but needed glasses to enjoy his hobby. There was twenty two dollars and some coins, not much else. I reclosed the two bags and tied the flaps shut. This was truly becoming a mystery with not much to go on in the way of answers.

I checked my pocket watch and looked up at the position of the sun. One-thirty, that was about right. I decided to scout around the camp again, maybe find something I might have missed earlier. With my Winchester in hand I retraced my path of earlier that day with the same disappointing results as before, nothing.

I had a decision to make, if I left now and did nothing then the camp would still be here if whoever owned the horse came back. If I stayed and the missing camper came back then I would have the burden of explaining what I was doing in his camp. Those were the two scenarios that would take place if the man came back.

If I left and the owner never came back then the big horse would wander around here and probably perish when the harsh winter set in. If I took the horse and all the other stuff with me then I would appear to be a horse thief. The authorities would assume I had killed the owner of the horse and stolen all his belongings. What a mess this was turning out to be.

After some careful thought I decided to leave the camp as I had found it. The big horse though was a different story. I couldn't re-tie the horse and just leave, that might prove to be a death sentence on the poor animal. I couldn't stay in camp because the missing rider might return in the night and kill me in my sleep.

There was another option, I could ground hitch the horse and then move off into the brush; far enough away to keep an eye on the camp but not close enough to be spotted. After I found a suitable spot I tied Rusty nearby and decided to stay awake the entire night. I really didn't like the thoughts of being surprised in my sleep.

The night was long, cold, and difficult. Staying awake was nearly impossible. When the sun finally came up I stood and stretched. I walked over and looked around. Nothing had changed; of course not, I had kept a close watch the entire night. I led the big horse down to the stream and then went back for Rusty. With both horses down by the water I stood and looked at the abandoned campsite, I now had a decision to make. There was no way I was going to spend another night here, it was just too spooky. I would load up the man's belongings and head for the nearest town. Let the local law deal with it.

By seven-thirty I had everything loaded and was ready to leave. I thought about nailing a note to the tree, but then thought better. If the owner of the horse had been bushwhacked then I really didn't want whoever had done it to track me down and do the same thing to me. I pulled out of camp with the rider less horse tethered to my saddle horn and all the missing man's belongings securely placed about the horse where they would have been if the man who owned them was here. The only thing missing was the man and after more than two days it was looking real doubtful if he was ever going to show up.

Rusty, me, and the second horse, traveled the rest of the day in a southerly direction trying to put as many miles as possible between us and that spooky camp site. I looked back at the horse that was tied to my saddle. She was sure a fine looking animal, sleek and powerful with the brightest hazel green eyes I had ever seen, especially on a horse. Hazel, for lack of a better name I would call her Hazel.

"Hazel, you hear that? What do you think?"

The big horse snorted and done a quick two step.

"Well Rusty, I think Hazel likes her new name."

Rusty snorted and slung his head up and down.

"That looks like a yes from both of you, its unanimous then, Hazel it is."

We rode on until about an hour before dark. We would have ridden another thirty minutes but I came across the greatest campsite I believe I had ever seen. There was good water and grass for the horses and a fresh deadfall for firewood. The spot was sheltered by spruce trees on all sides with a small clearing in the center. I just couldn't pass up a spot like that.

By dark I had both horses stripped of their saddles and rubbed down. They were both watered and happily cropping grass at the edge of the clearing where I had picketed both. I had a small fire going and bacon and beans in the skillet. The coffee was about to boil and I could hardly wait.

"Crunch!"

I looked in the direction of sound. The noise made a cold shiver run down my spine. "What the hell?" I said to myself.

"Crunch!"

Twice. What in the world could have made that sound? Both horses had taken notice and had turned to face the noise. I grabbed the Winchester and went to a crouching position facing in the general direction from where I thought the sound had come from.

"Crunch!"

This time the sound was directly behind me in the timber. Whatever it was couldn't have made it that far in so short a time. The sounds must have been playing tricks on my senses. I had drawn my revolver and pointed it behind me while still holding the Winchester in the direction of the first noise. The sound had stopped. I stayed there in my crouching position holding a gun in both directions. After enough time for my arms to start to hurt I holstered the Colt and slowly stood holding the Winchester at the ready.

I looked at the horses and found Rusty to be mostly curious but Hazel, well that was a different story. She looked to be terrified. Her ears were perked up and her eyes were wide with fear. Her right front leg shook and she rocked back and forth as if she wanted to run, but she didn't want to run. The lead I tied her out with was limp; she wasn't trying to pull away. I think as scared as she was she still would rather be here with Rusty and me than running around in the dark with whatever it was out there on the loose.

It was now completely dark, even if it wasn't I didn't want to break camp and leave, not until I found out what was happening and what was out there.

Before long the two horses had grown silent, they never made a sound, never even moved. I continued to scan the area but saw nothing. The noise had stopped.

"Hello out there. You better show yourself before I start shootin." I waited but there was no response. After a few minutes with no more noise I decided to put out the fire. The darkness was actually a welcome addition to my situation. If I couldn't see what was out there then whatever was out there couldn't see me either. The horses seemed to have settled down a mite which made me feel a little better.

As I lay in my blankets and replayed the frightful noise I had heard I kept coming back to the same belief; the noise was something chewing on bones. The crunch was that of a large animal eating the carcass of another animal, that had to be it. Nothing else could have made a noise like that. Whatever it was must have been big and I surely didn't want the next crunching sound to be that of my leg. I cocked the Colt and kept it in my hand as I slowly tried to calm myself.

It was my second sleepless night in a row. Whatever had made the noise of the previous evening remained silent throughout the night. At first light I picked up camp and headed out with the horses. We rode steady for over five hours until finally I couldn't go any farther. Lack of sleep had taken its toll. We stopped at a spot where there was grass and water but not many trees. The horses drank and ate as I collapsed on the ground under one of the few trees that offered shade. When I awoke the sun was hanging low in the sky and a light breeze had blown in. I figured we had traveled maybe fifteen miles during the morning and decided to just stay put for the night. Food was on my mind and some more sleep wouldn't be a bad thing either.

After checking on the horses, I built a fire and put some beans and salt pork in the skillet, just when the coffee was about ready I grabbed my cup and poured. As I raised the coffee to my lips Hazel snorted. I looked to see her and Rusty pulling on their leads and trying to back as far away as the rope would allow. After throwing my coffee on the ground I grabbed the Winchester and went to the horses and waited. I stood there long enough for the fire to grow dim; night came calling as clouds slowly hid the moon. The darkness was overpowering. I sat down and leaned back against a tree. Both horses seemed glad that I was close and to be honest I was glad to be near the horses.

As the night progressed I fell asleep against the tree. I felt safe enough knowing Rusty would sense danger and hopefully he would wake me. At first light I rose and looked around. Both horses were cropping grass and seemed to not have a care in the world. I picked up the Winchester and decided to have a look around camp. I headed in the direction that the horses were looking when they were both spooked the night before.

Within in a hundred feet of my fire pit I found footprints, fresh footprints. How in the hell had this happened. In my year and a half of traveling the brush I had never had anyone sneak up on my camp. There had been a couple of times when someone had ridden up to camp and asked to enter. They had only wanted to share coffee and even then I had been ready for trouble with my Colt in hand the entire time. This though was a first, after what had happened the previous two days I was becoming a little more than spooked by the whole damn situation.

For the next hour I scouted the surrounding area trying to find where my unseen visitor might have had a horse tied up. I followed the footprints for more than a half mile until the ground grew hard and the sign vanished. No horse, just a man on foot that had made it to within a hundred feet of me while I slept against a tree. First an abandoned camp with no sign of whoever had been there, then the terrifying sounds of night before last. And now this. Here I was with two Winchester rifles, two Colt revolvers, and enough ammunition to start a small war, along with two very powerful horses, and I found myself with the fear of a small child that wanted to hide under the covers.

The beans and pork were still in the skillet from the previous night and sitting near the cold fire. A few ants had made it to the skillet after the fire had died away and were running around on my uneaten supper as if it was a barn dance. It didn't matter; I was starved and after ridding the skillet of the ants I ate like a wolf. A year earlier I would have found this disgusting but my time in the west had apparently hardened my outlook on things. It didn't take more than ten minutes to finish what was there and once that was gone I picked up the coffee pot and drank the cold brew straight from the pot. Never mind cleaning up anything I just broke up camp and put everything back on the two horses.

My only thought was to make it to a town as soon as possible and hole up a day or two until my nerves settled. Wouldn't my paw laugh if he knew his eldest son was running from the boogie man?

I rode Rusty fairly hard for five hours and then stopped. I switched to Hazel, who was a few years younger than Rusty and also hadn't had a rider in a few days. She was fresh and I was surprised at how strong she was. She handled like a race horse and I wondered if Rusty wasn't being pushed a little too hard. Without a rider he held up well, I think the two horses were trying to feel each other out. Hazel was trying to outdo Rusty but he was giving as good as he was getting. This little rivalry suited me just fine. I didn't exactly know where I was and hoped that before dark we came upon a small town, or even a ranch house. Anything but trying to spend another night in the woods with whatever, or whoever, it was out there. With the pace the two horses were going I felt it would be unlikely that anyone could keep up with us now though.

About an hour before dark the horses had slowed considerably. Neither had had water or rest the entire day and that went double for me. As the sky grew darker I felt sure another sleepless night lay ahead. I started looking for a place to stop for the night when a dim light could be seen ahead from over the next rise. I had slowed the horses to a trot but it still didn't take long before we topped a hill and there in the valley was as pretty a sight as I had ever seen, a town, and by the looks of it a substantial town.

It took half an hour to make it down the slope and reach the first of the outlying houses. I slid out of the saddle and started leading the two horses into town. Within minutes we were on Main Street and by the looks of things it must have been either a Friday or a Saturday night, I always lost track of the days while on the trail. People were everywhere; it looked like the saloons were doing a booming business. Suddenly the thought of traveling through a strange town leading a horse that didn't belong to me hit home like a hammer. I decided to head to the sheriff's office first. It might be wise to seek out the law before they had reason to seek out me.

The office was easy enough to find, it was in the middle of the street where all the saloons were located. I tied both horses to a hitch rail out front and then pushed the front door open. Inside were two men, both wearing the badges of deputies. They looked up at me and one of the men asked if I needed anything.

"Actually I don't know quite where to start but I do feel that I need to speak to the sheriff if he is nearby."

"Sheriff ain't here. He rode out of town about six days ago and hasn't made it back yet. Anything we can help you with?" One of the deputies asked.

I really didn't want to share my story with these two but with the sheriff gone I didn't have any other option. "I came across an abandoned campsite three days back. Horse tied up to a tree with a saddle and saddle bags lying close by. Looked like whoever was there just walked off and left everything just the way it was."

The other deputy asked, "What did the horse look like mister?"

"Well, I could describe her to you but she's tied up right outside if you would like to have a look."

Both men stood and headed for the door. "Let's just have that look," the taller of the two said.

When the three of us were outside I stood on the boardwalk while the two deputies did their job.

"This is Sheriff Coleman's horse. Where did you find her mister?"

Now if I hadn't stepped right in the middle of it. I come into town, a complete stranger, riding the horse of the town's missing sheriff. I'll be damn.

"Found her a good two days from here. I waited for a day and when no one showed up I loaded everything up and headed for the first town I could find." I said this hoping the two believed me; after all it was the truth.

Neither deputy spoke for a few minutes; they just looked over the horse and also the contents of the saddle bags and also the rifle. When one of them pulled the .45.75 from its rug he said, "Damn what a cannon. This ain't the sheriff's is it Cecil?"

The man named Cecil took the Winchester and examined it.

"Sure ain't. This is the first .45.75 I ever seen." He looked at me and asked.

"This yours?"

"No, it was lying under the blankets near the fire; the saddle was leaning against a big tree and the saddlebags were hanging over a limb."

Both men looked at the saddle.

"This ain't the sheriff's saddle either. His ain't half as nice as this one." Again they looked at me and asked.

"This your saddle?"

"Not mine. Like I said it was leaning against a tree. I did look in them two saddle bags and they must belong to whoever owned that gun, they got the ammunition inside that fits it."

The two took off the saddle bags and headed back inside. "Mister, until we figure out what is going on here how about you come inside with us and answer a few more questions," the taller of the two said.

Now who was I to deny such a request? "Sounds like the thing to do. I am as curious as the both of you, maybe even more so." With that the three of us went back inside.

It didn't take more than twenty minutes for the two deputies to determine that I had killed their boss and stolen all his belongings. It was an ambush on their part, as I was answering some of the stupid questions the two were throwing my way one of them pulled his gun and told me to sit still and shut up. The other deputy quickly came to his feet and relieved me of my Colt and gun belt. I was placed in a dirty cell in the back and told that the town's attorney would be in first thing in the morning to get the information he needed to charge me with murder. It looked like I had just found about the two dumbest deputies in the territory. I was mad as hell at the reception I had just gotten and my tone and choice of words reflected much of that little fact.

"Hey deputy, how in the hell do you plan on charging me with murder when you don't have a witness or for that matter a body? And one more little piece of advice, why would a man come into town and go straight to the sheriff's office if he had done what you say?"

The deputy that looked like his ladder might have been missing a few steps said, "It ain't our job to think about things like that, that is a task for the town lawyer and the judge, now you better shut the hell up before I unlock that door and teach you some city manners."

Now I was really hot. "Did you really just say that it isn't your job to think? If that's so then the sheriff has done hired the right man for the job. I tell you what , why don't you and that other dumbass standing behind you try to put them two horses that are tied up out front in a stable for the night and then come on back here. I'll be waiting for either, or both of you, to man up and come inside this cell. I figure if I'm going to be charged with murder then I just as well be guilty. You think either of you are smart enough to find the stable in your own town." I was mad and at the moment didn't care what I said. By the look on the two deputies' faces I think I might have convinced them that the inside of this jail was a pretty dangerous place for either of them at the moment.

"You just make yourself comfortable and we'll be right back," the taller of the two said. With that he slammed the big wooden door and they were gone. I decided that while they were taking care of the horses I would use my time to stretch out on the bunk and grab a little sleep just in case they came back and were really wanting to teach me that lesson they spoke of, if they did then it wouldn't hurt to be rested.

After the two deputies went out the front door they each grabbed the reins of a horse and headed down the street toward the stables. The man that ran the place was one Lester Fitch and he had been taking care of horses since he was five years old. He loved working with anything that had four legs but had a much lower opinion of critters that had less than that, namely people.

The two deputies, Cecil Spriggs and Bill Adkins led the two horses into the stable at the end of town and hollered for Lester.

"A Lester, you in here?" Cecil shouted.

Lester knew it was Cecil by the sound of his voice. Lester didn't think much of the man and thought even less of Bill. He felt both deputies took their jobs a little too seriously and more than once had asked the sheriff to get rid of them both.

"I'm back here Cecil; stop that damn hollering before you spook my guests." Lester always felt that the horses he stabled were just that, his guests.

"Come on up here Lester, we got a couple of horses that needs stabling for the night," Bill hollered just as loud as Cecil had.

Lester shook his head and made a mental note to speak to the sheriff again about hiring a couple of new deputies to replace these two fools. He hurried up front before the two started shouting again.

"Where did these two horses come from Cecil, you two haven't taken to horse thieving while the sheriff is out of town have you?" Lester asked.

"Naw Lester, it ain't nothin like that. We just arrested the man who murdered the sheriff. He's so stupid he came riding into town on the sheriff's horse. This other horse he claims is his, but I think he probably stole it too. Once they hang that bastard I'm going to see if the judge will see fit to give me and Bill here these two fine animals."

Lester looked at the horse Cecil claimed belonged to the sheriff. "You say you arrested the man that murdered the sheriff? I didn't even know the sheriff was dead. You'd think something like that would get around."

"Stop being a smartass Lester. Just put these two horses up for the night and the judge will determine the next move, you got that?" Bill said.

Lester didn't like being called a smartass. "Well I guess I would rather be a smartass than a dumbass Bill, now what do you think of that?"

"You better watch it Lester, what reason you got to be calling me a dumbass anyway," Bill asked.

"I'll tell you why Bill and I'm gonna talk real slow so the words can soak into that thick skull of yours. This ain't the sheriff's horse. I don't know about that other horse you got but I can damn well tell you right now that this one is not the sheriff's."

Bill and Cecil looked at each other. "This is the sheriff's horse Lester, why don't you take a closer look?" Cecil said.

"I don't need a closer look Cecil. This horse you say belongs to the sheriff has green eyes, the sheriff's horse has dark brown eyes and if you don't believe me then go to the clerk's office Monday morning and look up the paperwork. Hell, I sold the sheriff his horse and don't either one of you two stupid bastards question my knowledge of horses again. And one more thing, you said you arrested a man because he came riding in on this horse. I would imagine the judge is gonna want to know why a man was locked up for riding a horse with green eyes. Last I checked it ain't illegal to ride a green eyed horse."

Lester grabbed the reigns of the two horses and headed back through the barn leaving the two bumbling deputies to figure out what went wrong.

No sooner had Zeke dozed off than the door to the jail opened and then was slammed shut again. He waited for the door to the cell room to open. After a couple of minutes the two deputies came back but neither spoke at first. Finally the one named Cecil asked.

"What did you say your name was mister?"

Zeke wasn't expecting such a humble tone from either of the two.

"Zeke Conley from Kentucky. What happened at the stable?"

"What makes you think something happened at the stable Zeke?" Bill asked.

"Well, when you two left out of here a while ago you had just captured the most notorious killer this side of the Mississippi. Now you come in here as meek as mice asking my name, what happened?"

Cecil tried to save face by coming up with a little story. "Well we talked it over and decided you might be innocent after all. We were going to come back here and kick your ass for good measure but I guess now we will just let you go free and save the ass kicking for later if you don't behave yourself." Cecil chuckled and then unlocked the cell door.

As soon as the door was open Zeke hit Cecil in the jaw and he went down in a heap. Before Bill could respond Zeke shoved him against the wall and let him have two savage blows to the stomach knocking the wind out of the man. He also went down. He then stepped over each man and removed their guns. They were both sleeping soundly when he went out front and poured himself a cup of coffee. As he was pouring a little sugar into the cup he heard the two start to stir a little. Within a minute both came out of the cell area, both just stood and looked at Zeke.

"How did you two boys like your nap? I hope it was refreshing. Why don't you two come over here and get yourself a cup of this nice coffee, it will help with those cobwebs in your head," Zeke told the two.

Both men gave a discouraged grunt and did as Zeke asked. Each poured a cup of coffee and started sipping the strong brew without the aid of sugar. Zeke felt the need to get some information in order to find out what might have happened to the sheriff.

"As soon as you two feel like it, I would like to talk about your sheriff."

Both men cradled the coffee cups in their hands and slowly looked up.

"What do you want to know?" Bill asked.

"Well, let's start with everything both of you know. You accused me of killing the man and I would like to know why all the sudden you think he's dead."

"Well, there have been some pretty strange stories told about town for the last couple of months. People coming in from out in the territory talking of ghosts and demons. Men have told of being robbed of everything they own during the night as they slept. At other times there have been saddled horses riding into town without a rider. Even the homesteaders have been abandoning their spreads and staying in town until something is figured out. This is strange stuff Zeke, real strange stuff," Cecil said.

I thought of the abandoned campsite I had found and wondered what had become of the owner of the green eyed horse. Had he been taken away by spirits? Had some new demon arisen from the depths of the earth and started snatching men from their sleep without leaving so much as a note to tell anyone what was going on.

"Why did your sheriff leave town six days ago?" Zeke asked.

Bill took a long sip of coffee and then looked out the window.

"The sheriff has been keeping tabs on all these wild stories we been hearing about. It all started maybe six or eight weeks ago. Well, it finally became more than he could stand. Last Sunday morning he loaded up his horse and headed out of town. We tried to talk him out of it and even offered to tag along but he would have none of it. Said he was going to find out what was going on and damn the consequences."

"Sounds like your sheriff is no coward, it also sounds like he might be a fool for going out there alone. I just came from out there and let me tell you; by the time I got to this town I was nearly scared out of my wits. Now what do you two have to say to that?"

Cecil and Bill sat quietly and sipped their coffee. Neither had anything to add to what I just said. I walked over to the sheriff's desk and picked up my gun belt and Colt.

"Now wait a minute there, we didn't say you were released. As a matter of fact you are still under arrest until the judge says otherwise," Cecil said.

I strapped on the belt and looked at the two. "With all the monsters roaming around out there eating innocent men who are just trying to get a little shuteye you two might like it if I'm armed. Monster tries to eat you two then I might just be tempted to shoot it, but only after it has eaten off one of your legs first. Now how about the two of you giving me a break, or would you like another ass kicking like you got back there in the cell room."

Both men went to the stove and refilled their coffee cups. "Tell you what Mister Monster Killer, you got yourself a deal," Cecil said.

We all sat in silence and thought about what may or may not happen next. Finally fatigue reached out and grabbed me. "Are the two horses taken care of?"

"Both horses are down at Lester's. You can rest assured that they're in good hands," Bill said.

"Well, rest assured is a funny choice of words because right now my eyes are shutting down. Where is the closest place for me to catch some shuteye?"

"The closest place is back there in one of them jail cells," Cecil said.

"No thanks. That is the last place I want to be right now. You two might figure on getting even with me for kicking the hell out of you a little while ago." Both deputies laughed which was not what Zeke expected.

"Well, then the closest spot is across the street at the Lolli Pop," Bill said.

"Did you just say the Lolli Pop?" Zeke asked.

"Yea Lolli Pop, it's one of the best saloons in town and they got rooms upstairs. You go on over and tell them that Cecil and Bill sent you. You're sure to get a room," Cecil said.

Zeke laughed. "Tell you what, how bout I try to get a room without using your names. Something tells me you two wouldn't be above playing a practical joke on me."

"Say, what did you say your name was anyway Mister Monster Killer?" Cecil asked.

"I done told both of you that I am Zeke Conley from Kentucky."

"You got any monsters back in Kentucky, Zeke?" Cecil asked.

"Yea, we got scary stories about monsters back in Kentucky. I don't ever remember believing any of them though. Now if you two think you will be alright here by yourself tonight then I am going over to the Lolli Pop and see if they'll rent me a room for the night. It's been more than three days since I've had any good sleep."

"You get some sleep Zeke and first thing in the morning I think we need to come up with a plan. That sound about right Bill?" Cecil asked.

"I think that is a great idea Cecil. Tomorrow the three of us are going to go monster hunting and after that we can find the sheriff," Bill said.

Zeke just rolled his eyes and headed across the street. The Lolli Pop was doing a booming business. There was a band playing on a stage and the place actually had two bars. One on the back wall and another that faced the stage. The room was huge. Men were playing cards and pool in the back. Barmaids were hauling drinks by the tub.

Zeke went to the bar and asked one of the bartenders about where to inquire about a room for the night. The barkeep pointed toward the stairs and said there was a desk at the top where the rooms were rented. Zeke turned and looked to the top of the stairs and saw what he was pointing at. Within thirty minutes he had stripped off his trail clothes and slid under the sheets. He couldn't remember if he had any dreams during the night, but if he did he was sure they were great.

Next morning sunshine came through the window of the room and warmed Zeke's sleeping face. He opened his eyes and realized he might have just had the best sleep he could remember in years. After sliding back into his filthy clothes he made his way back to the sheriff's office. After this was all over he was going to take the longest bath in history and have his clothes cleaned. That was assuming he wasn't eaten by monsters first.

Cecil and Bill were both asleep in their chairs. The stove had grown cold and the coffee pot was bone dry. What kind of wet behind the ears deputies had the sheriff hired here anyway? Zeke slammed the big door and both deputies came to their feet with guns drawn.

"What the hell Zeke, you damn near gave us a heart attack," Cecil said as both men put their guns away.

"Sorry fellars, did I wake you?"

"Damn right you woke us you skinny bastard. Try to make a little less noise the next time you come in here," Bill said.

"I am truly sorry 'bout your sleep boys. Maybe next time I will just stay outside and throw pebbles at the window. Now wake your sorry asses up and let's go get some breakfast," Zeke told the two deputies.

"You know what Cecil? I think old Zeke there has a pretty damn good idea. We go get breakfast and while we are at it we can figure out a plan."

The three men went back across the street and entered the Lolli Pop. They found a table in the back and took their chairs. The place was nearly empty compared to the bedlam that was taking place the night before. Wasn't long before a lady came from the kitchen and took their orders. The three ate like starving wolves.

"Well deputies, what do you propose we do?" Zeke asked. "And by the way, I still don't know how I got in the middle of all this."

Bill said, "I tell you how you got in the middle of this Zeke, you came strolling into town with a horse that didn't belong to you. Until we figure out what happened to its owner then I would say you are still on the hook."

Cecil looked up from his biscuits and gravy and said, "I think the three of us ought to go out looking for the sheriff. When we find him he'll know what to do about all the mischief that's been going on around here. What do you think about that Bill?"

Bill kept eating and just shook his head.

"Does that mean you agree Bill, or are you just going to sit there with gravy on your chin looking stupid?" Cecil asked.

"Well Cecil, I think he agrees, and by the way, he can't help the looking stupid part," Zeke said.

All three men laughed.

The leading law firm in town was run by a man named Lloyd Shafer. Shafer had been in the town of Rapid City, South Dakota for nearly ten years. He arrived there from back east where he was raised and had also been educated. It didn't take long before he had made quite a name for himself. His speaking prowess in front of a jury had proved the downfall of many of the town's older and more experienced lawyers. It seemed he could cast a spell over any jury that was seated before him. This ability to win cases had proved profitable to the Shafer

Law Firm. As the years passed, Shafer had managed to acquire the general store, the slaughter house, and one of the three local banks, not to mention a number of other businesses in Rapid City and the surrounding area.

All this had not gone unnoticed by the circuit judge. Judge Thurman Preston had been on the bench for nearly twenty years, elected every six years by unanimous vote because no one had ever wanted to run against the popular judge. He was a widower, his wife of thirty-two years having passed away nearly two years prior. The judge had honored his wife by promising himself he would never remarry. He would spend his working days on the bench and his leisure time on his big front porch, which overlooked the courthouse and the town square. He might have been born in Virginia but he would die in Rapid City and this suited the judge just fine.

Judge Preston had kept a close watch on his town and also, in doing that, he had kept a closer watch on the Shafer Law Firm. It now employed four of the original six lawyers in town and this in itself bothered the judge. Three of the four had, at one time, been friends of Preston's. After their business dwindled, and finally died, each of the three had gone to Shafer, hat in hand, asking for a job. The two remaining independent lawyers were scrambling to pick up any work they could find, which sadly to say, was extremely meager.

It also dug deep into Preston that so much of the town's commerce was now controlled by the Schafer Law Firm. Shafer was from a large family, at least eight brothers and one sister. The sister was a striking lady by the name of Rachel Shafer. She was in her late twenties and had never been married, or at least that was the rumor. Another rumor had it that she had been married to a man back east that was still there waiting for her return. No one knew for sure.

Rachel was a beautiful woman and when she walked down any of the town's streets men would stop and stare. Not too obvious a stare, mind you, for fear of what one of her brothers might do if caught. Rachel had been educated back east; the same as her lawyer brother, and it was said she had graduated with honors from an all-girl school in New

York. With her beauty and education it was no wonder she never mingled socially in Rapid City with anyone of the opposite sex. Men this far west were usually only slightly educated or not at all and had no idea of what the word 'manners' meant.

Lloyd Shafer had sent for his sister when he got controlling interest in the city's largest bank. City Trust was the largest of the three banks, by number of customers, and also, volume of business. Another rumor was that Lloyd had taken over the bank for the sole purpose of giving his sister something to do; she was given the job of Vice President with Lloyd listed as the President. The bank had continued to grow under the leadership of Rachel, rumors were starting to circulate that one of the two other banks was on the brink of closing and this in itself hurt both competing banks reputation in town. No one wanted to deposit money in a bank that might fail. Judge Preston suspected Lloyd and some of his friends of starting the rumors about the rival banks but evidence was scarce.

Judge Preston had other doubts about the moral integrity of Lloyd Shafer. During more than one trial in which Shafer was council some less than trustworthy eyewitness accounts had been used to sway the jury. If Shafer couldn't win a case for his client honestly then he would win it dishonestly. Preston's doubts were not totally unfounded, at least not in the opinion of the judge. Preston had developed such a dislike for the lawyer that he had even stopped doing business at the general store which Shafer owned. Preston took a buckboard and traveled eight miles to another small town to purchase the items he couldn't find anywhere else. About the only place Preston still frequented in Rapid City was the Sage Grass, Liquor & Tobacco store.

The judge was not a heavy drinker by any means but he did like one stiff drink in the evenings after a long day on the bench. His favorite was a little known brand from Kentucky, the home state of his dear departed wife. The brand was called Old Grand-Dad and it was the only Bourbon the judge would drink. The judge drank so little that a bottle would last him an entire month, it had always been his habit to finish the last drink on the last day of the month and open a brand new bottle on the first of the following month. The Sage kept a case of twelve bottles in stock just for the needs of the judge. They also stocked another Kentucky brand that Preston had grown fond of, Kentucky Rolled Bourbon Cigars. These were made of Kentucky leaf rolled in paper that had been soaked in bourbon and aged until the paper was nearly dry. The taste was strong but had the sweet aroma that the judge admired. The smell was so fragrant that Preston called it courtin tobacco, what a man might smoke if he was trying to impress a lady.

Things around Rapid City had changed so much in the ten years that Lloyd Shafer had been in town that Judge Preston was considering moving away after retirement so he could live out his remaining years without ever having to see a piece of paper, or a building, with the name Shafer on it. Although he pondered these things he knew he could never leave the town where his beloved Lula was buried. He would stay put if for no other reason than that. He could just finish out his days sitting on his big front porch sipping Old Grand-Dad and smoking his Kentucky Rolled.

After finishing breakfast at the Lolli Pop, Zeke, along with the two deputies, headed back over to the Sheriff's Office. The plan they were supposed to formulate during breakfast never happened. Zeke was beginning to believe by the way the two deputies talked that they were almost afraid to leave town. After some of the things he had seen and heard in the last three days on the trail he was a little more than worried himself.

"Are you two going to tell me what you're going to do or should I just gather my horse and head back out of town the way I came?" Zeke asked.

Cecil, who seemed to be the more talkative of the two, finally spoke. "Tell you what Zeke, how about the three of us going over to Judge Preston's place and see what he thinks?"

"Now why would we want to go and talk to a judge Cecil?" Zeke asked.

"Judge Preston is the man who swore in the sheriff and he also swore in the both of us. I have known him for a long time and put a lot of faith in what he says. If anybody around here knows what should be done then it will be the judge," Cecil said.

For the life of himself Zeke couldn't figure out how a Circuit Judge could have any suggestions about what should be done in a situation like this. He thought judges were only needed after everything had pretty much been figured out and someone was charged and arrested. But for lack of a better idea he agreed with Cecil and that was that. The three headed out the front door and in the direction of the courthouse which, was also near the judge's house.

The judge's house sat on a small hill across from the town square and Zeke had to admit it was one of the most beautiful houses he had seen in these parts. It consisted of two full floors and also rooms in the loft that contained large dormer windows. There was a porch that wrapped around two sides in the front. Both floors of the house were covered with a brick veneer which made the entire structure look stout and masculine, no feminine touches had been incorporated into the design. The third floor dormers were covered in a painted lap siding of some sort and at each end of the house were two large brick chimneys. The roof looked to be covered in a dark slate tile. All in all, it was a very handsome house.

Cecil and Bill walked up the front steps and knocked on the front door. Within seconds a tall thin man of late middle age came to the door.

"Why hello Cecil, good morning Bill, what brings the two of you out on this fine Saturday morning?" The judge asked.

"Morning Judge, me and Bill brought along a friend and wondered if you were in the mood to help us out with a little problem we got?"

Upon hearing this, the judge looked at the end of the porch where Zeke stood. He was surprised to see a big smile come across the judge's face and as it did he came out the door and toward Zeke with a hand thrust out.

"Why good morning young fellar, I am Judge Preston but you can just call me Thurman."

Zeke shook the judge's hand and told him he was Zeke Conley from Kentucky. The smile never left the judge's face. He grabbed Zeke's shoulder with his other hand and said, "Kentucky, why my wife was from Kentucky. What part are you from?"

"Eastern Kentucky Thurman, about twenty miles from a little town called Martin. You ever hear of it?" Zeke asked.

"Martin, Kentucky, I sure have. I am from Virginia myself and I went across the Big Sandy River more than once when I was courting my Lula. She was from Lexington. Why don't you boys have a seat on the porch and I'll go in and get us some coffee." With that the judge was back inside before any of the three could reply.

The three men picked out a seat and sat down. Zeke leaned back in the cushioned wicker chair and admired the view the judge had of the town. You could see the entire front and left side of the courthouse and a good size portion of the town square. It was nearly ten o'clock now and people were starting to come into town to do their Saturday business. The square was filling up with children as their parents went about their town business.

Wasn't long before the screen door opened and the judge came out with a tray that held four white china cups and a coffee pot. He sat the tray on the small table in front of the chairs and said, "I don't know how you like your coffee so I just brought everything. You can help yourself while I bring over another chair."

The three filled a cup and each added sugar and cream. Zeke stirred his coffee and waited for the judge to get situated. Preston took a cup and then put in sugar and cream. His cup was nearly full before he added the first drop of the coffee. "As you three can see I like a little coffee in my cream and sugar." At this the judge let out a laugh. I had to admit, for a man I had only met ten minutes earlier, I was really starting to like the judge.

Once he had his cream and sugar slightly tinted with coffee he said, "Now, what is it we need to talk about Cecil?"

"Well Judge, I don't really know where to start so I will just start. The sheriff is missing."

That was it. Cecil spoke four words about our problem and then took a sip of his coffee. What the hell?

"What do you mean Cecil, I saw the sheriff in court Friday week and he wasn't missing then," the Judge said.

Cecil sat his coffee down on the small table and said, "Well he's missing now."

I looked at Cecil and thought, 'what a dumbass.'

The judge looked at me and said, "Zeke, you're from Kentucky, how about you tell me what's going on?"

I could tell the judge must have held people from Kentucky higher in his opinions than he did these two bumbling deputies.

"I'll try Judge. I arrived in town late last night and was immediately arrested and locked up by Cecil and Bill here for murdering the sheriff," Zeke said.

Bill broke in and said, "Ah Zeke, you weren't supposed to tell him about that."

The judge looked at Bill and asked for him to hush so Zeke could tell the story.

Zeke continued, "Well anyway Judge, when they figured out their mistake I was released. None of us knows what has happened to the sheriff. According to Cecil and Bill here he left town last Sunday morning looking for some clues to all the strange happenings that have been going on in the territory for the last few months."

The judge took a sip of his cream and sugar and then looked at Cecil and Bill. "I didn't know the sheriff had been out of town for the last week, if I had then I might have been inclined to lock my doors." Cecil and Bill took this to be a little barb at their abilities as deputies but decided it best to not respond.

"What kind of strange happenings are you referring to Zeke?" The Judge asked.

"Campsites without campers, saddled horses without riders, I don't know all the particulars but I am sure there is a lot more going on than just the two things I have mentioned," Zeke told the judge.

Preston sat his cup down on the small table and leaned back into his chair. None of us spoke as he stared across the town square at nothing in particular. Zeke couldn't tell if the judge had heard any of the rumors himself but something told him that a man in Preston's position would have heard at least one of the stories being told.

"You know, I was playing cards with some of the men from the courthouse a few nights back and they mentioned a couple of things that seemed quite out of the ordinary, something about men having their mules stolen in the middle of the night, no horses mind you, just mules. Said rumors were about that told of able bodied men disappearing in the middle of the night without a trace. I never put much stock into what they were talking about and I let them know it. Now though, I think I might have made a fool of myself by not taking them seriously. To tell you the truth, I laughed out loud at some of the stuff they were saying. Now though, I'm not so sure. No one has filed a missing person report and the man that lost the mules has never come to town to file a complaint. I need hard evidence before rumors become actual facts," the judge said.

"What do you intend to do about the sheriff Judge? Me and Bill here are just deputies and can't go off looking in the territory by ourselves."

The judge picked up his cup and again sipped the cream and sugar concoction. "I can't authorize the two of you to go out and look for the sheriff. My authority stops at the threshold of the courthouse. Let me think it over for an hour or two. How about the three of you meeting me at my office in say, two hours, which would be one o'clock. I am going to the telegraph office and see if I can get some advice from some higher ups." With that the judge stood and went inside the house. Zeke took it that the little meeting was over for the moment and they would pick it back up at the judge's office. The three men sat down their china cups and headed back toward the sheriff's office.

The streets were busy as could be; it was almost like a carnival had arrived in town. Women were walking around in flowery dresses with children by their sides; men were going about as if the day would end before they accomplished everything they needed to. When the three turned the corner and headed down the boardwalk toward the jail they noticed a crowd of people lined up outside the sheriff's office.

"Now what do you reckon that's all about Cecil?" Bill asked.

"Don't know but it can't be good," Cecil replied.

Bill took out his key and unlocked the front door to the office as people began asking where the sheriff was. Once the three made it inside the crowd followed. It would be safe to say that the little office was jamb packed by the time everyone squeezed in. There were even a few that couldn't make it inside and patiently waited outside on the boardwalk.

"Deputy, I need to see the sheriff, I don't even know who the sheriff is now but I need to see him just the same," a large woman said.

"Yea me too deputy, my brother has been missing for more than three weeks and it just ain't like him to be gone so long," another woman said.

That was when Zeke noticed that everyone here was either a woman or old man. There were no men of working age in the entire crowd.

Cecil looked over the crowd and said the first intelligent thing Zeke had ever heard him say.

"Does everyone here have a missing family member to report, is that a safe assumption?"

Most everyone in the crowd answered that they had.

For the next hour the two deputies and Zeke took down what information they could from the women and men in the crowd. Zeke was happy to know that both Cecil and Bill could read and write or else he would have had to take the statements from everyone by himself. When they were finished they had five missing persons, all men. There were also a few hogs, cattle and several mules. Cecil told everyone that he would be meeting with the judge shortly and asked everyone if they would come back to the jail at two o'clock that afternoon. Everyone indicated that they would.

After the crowd left the three men sat down and looked over the information they had gathered.

"At least now when we meet with the judge we will have the proof that something is really going on other than just rumors," Bill said.

After the way the deputies had handled the crowd Zeke was beginning to have a little respect for the two. They treated everyone kindly and when he looked over the information the two had written down he was impressed at the quality of the handwriting and the structure of the sentences they had written. It was apparent the two had schooled under a stern schoolmaster who took great interest in spelling and neatness.

Cecil produced a pocket watch, it was quarter of one. "We better gather this stuff up and head on over to the judge's office. There will be hell to pay if we keep him waiting."

All three jumped up and gathered the notes. As they headed out the front door Bill locked it from the outside.

"Say Bill, why is it that you keep the sheriff's office locked? Most other towns never lock the front door," Zeke asked.

"We used to do the same here until one day the sheriff came back and found someone had stolen a Colt out of the gun cabinet. Ever since then the door stays locked unless one of us is in there."

"Makes sense to me. Did they ever find the missing Colt?" Zeke asked.

"Yea we did. The sheriff spread word around town that he would let it go if whoever borrowed it would just drop it back off, and he gave them twenty-four hours to do it. The next morning sitting on the bench out front was the Colt, no bullets but at least we got the gun back," Cecil said.

"Does the town lock the courthouse on weekends Cecil?" Zeke asked.

"They do, but I reckon the judge will leave the front door open for us. If it ain't then we will just wait until he shows up. Can't have just anyone going inside the courthouse you know with all the legal papers they keep in there."

Bill shook his head, "What is the world coming to when they got to lock up the courthouse at night? 'Fore long every building in town will have locks on the doors."

"Naw Bill, it will never come to something like that. Sometimes I wonder where you get such crazy ideas."

"It will happen Cecil, and when it does then you just remember where you heard it first," Bill said.

The three men climbed the steps to the courthouse and pulled on one of the big double doors, it opened to everyone's surprise. They stepped into a large foyer.

"Now which way do we go Cecil?" Zeke asked.

"Ain't you ever been in a courthouse before Zeke? The judge's office in any courthouse is always behind the courtroom. Hell, I thought boys from Kentucky were smart until I met you," Cecil replied.

"Well pardon me all to hell Cecil. This is the first time I've been in your lovely little town," Zeke replied.

"Just follow me and don't use any foul language around the judge. He might swear a bit outside of court but you will never hear him utter a bad word while he is in this building. And he don't allow anyone else to use them kind of words in here either," Cecil told the other two.

The three went through the empty court room and headed for a door that was at the back and to the right of the bench. The courtroom was big, real big.

"This might be one of the largest courtrooms I have ever seen. You got that many lawbreakers around these parts?" Zeke asked.

"Not really. Back when this was just a little place not much wider than the road, the government thought it would be a good idea to build this big building to show people that this part of the west was going to grow. They were right. This town grew up it seemed all at once. One day it was nothing and now it's a city. The judge is proud of the fact that Rapid City is growing so fast and he is also proud that he maintains law and order with some of the harsh sentences he hands down. You break the law within a hundred miles of here and you will answer to Judge Preston," Bill said.

Behind the courtroom was a long wide hallway. All the offices were on the main back of the building. At the end of the hall was a tall door with two slender panes of glass. Cecil walked up and knocked.

"Come in," was all we heard from the other side.

Cecil turned the knob and pushed the door open. There was an office that had a desk and not much of anything else. At the back of that office was another door which was open and led to a much larger office. Inside, sitting at a large oak desk, was Judge Preston.

"Come on in and grab a seat gentleman, you are right on time. What is with all those papers you three are carrying?"

Cecil took the seat that was right in front of the large desk and sat down. Bill and Zeke took the two on either side.

"When we got back to the jail there was a crowd of people waiting on us Judge. The three of us talked to every one of them and took some statements. It appears there are five men missing," Cecil said as he reached the papers across the desk to the judge.

Judge Preston gathered all the papers and quickly scanned each. Although he looked at each paper quickly it was apparent he was a slow methodical reader. When he finished he laid the stack down neatly and looked up at the three men.

"Five missing men, all apparently middle aged. Not a one older than thirty-five. And the livestock seems to be either of working stock, such as the mules, or for food, such as hogs and cattle. I hope the three of you have an opinion and if you do then I would like to hear it."

The three looked at each other and then back at the judge. Cecil spoke first.

"I really don't know what to think Judge. One thing that puzzles me is the fact that the five men were apparently at the age where they should have been able to take care of themselves. Whatever it was must have been big and mean or at least one of the men should have been able to escape."

The judge thought this over and said, "So what do you think it was?"

"I think it's a bear Judge. I think it is a big mean bear with cubs' maybe. You know if you cross a momma bear with cubs then she will chase you down and kill you," Bill said.

"Then why didn't they find the bodies? Why didn't they find any blood? Why didn't they find any of the men's clothing, even if they were attacked and killed by a wild animal then I doubt that animal would have eaten their clothes," Judge Preston said.

"Maybe the bear took the bodies back to her den, took them to her den for the baby cubs to eat," Cecil said.

There was silence in the room for a while as each man played out a bear attack in his head. Judge Preston turned his attention to Zeke. "Conley, you haven't said a thing yet, what do you think happened to these missing men?"

Zeke thought about the question and also what he had experienced out on the trail before he made it to town. He had yet to explain the scary stuff he had been through during those three days.

"Judge, the three days I was on the trail just before I got to town and was arrested for murdering the sheriff," before Zeke could finish the judge started laughing as Cecil and Bill glared at Zeke. "Well there were some very strange things happening out there. It was so bad I tried to stay awake nearly all of those three days," Zeke said.

"What kind of strange things Conley?" The judge wanted to know.

"Well, I found an abandoned campsite. Everything was there just as if the occupant of that camp had just been spirited away. His horse was still tied to a tree and as best I can tell it had been there for a full day without water. I took her down to the stream to let her drink and then searched the surrounding area; I found nothing, not a sign. I searched again the next day as soon as it got light and again found nothing. The next couple of nights I heard some very strange noises, one was a crunching sound, kind of like you would hear a dog make if it had killed a big rabbit or maybe a raccoon and was crunching on its bones. That was when I decided to head into town and report what I had discovered and turn in the items, along with the horse, I had found at the camp site. The only thing I found, after hearing the strange crunching sounds, was what looked like something had been drug along, like maybe someone was trying to hide their tracks," Zeke said.

The judge looked at the big grandfather clock he kept in his office. It was just past two-o'clock.

"While you three were at the jail interviewing the families of those missing men I went to the telegraph office to send some wires. It appears some of the other towns around are missing a person or two, nothing like the five you got here but missing people just the same. How about we go and get some lunch and then I will check back at the telegraph office again. I'm expecting some judge stuff and after that I will decide what we should do. That sound alright with the three of you? To sweeten the deal a little I'll put the tab on the county for the food."

The words were barely out of the judge's mouth when both Cecil and Bill said that sounded fine to them. It sounded fine to Zeke too because his funds were starting to run a little low. As best he could tell, without actually pulling out his money and counting it right here in front of the other men, he had three dollars and twelve cents to his name. That would buy food for one day and one more night at the Lolli Pop. After that he would have to gather Rusty from the livery and hit the trail. He could live cheap out in the wilderness. Then he remembered that something might be out there eating people and decided he might need to stay in town a little longer, hungry or not.

"How about you Conley, you want to tag along and have some lunch with me and these trigger happy deputies our missing sheriff saw fit to hire?" Judge Preston asked. "And remember the town is paying."

"That sounds good to me Judge, we had us some breakfast over at the Lolli Pop about seven this morning and to tell you the truth I'm starting to feel a mite hungry," Zeke said.

The judge locked the door to his office and outside on the courthouse front porch he relocked the big double doors. You would think that a courthouse was the last place a criminal would look to rob. Times were definitely changing. As they walked up the main street Zeke asked where they were heading, the Lolli Pop.

"Oh no, if the county's paying then I always eat at the Rock Candy Café," the judge said.

"So the town has a saloon and restaurant called the Lolli Pop and another called the Rock Candy Café. Is there a reason why all the eating places are named after confections Judge?" Zeke asked.

"As a matter of fact, there is," the judge answered.

The four walked on for a while until Zeke said. "Well, are you going to tell us the reason?"

The judge laughed, "I said there is a reason, I didn't say I knew what it was."

That was good enough for the other three; they walked the rest of the way in silence. When the four men turned the corner where Main Street crossed Dakota Street there was a sign on the second building down that read 'Rock Candy Café'. It was a well thought out building and by the look of the place the food had to be good. There was a big covered sidewalk along the front where people were sitting. It became apparent that the restaurant was full and these people were just waiting their turn to get inside. If a restaurant had more business than it could handle, then that was another good sign.

"You three wait here and I'll see how long we have to wait," the judge said as he headed through the front door.

"It's a good thing that the judge is paying because I can tell you right now; I could never afford to eat at a place like this on the money I make as a deputy," Cecil said.

"You said it Cecil. I bet you a meal in here would cost a dollar and a half at least, maybe even two dollars," Zeke said.

"You two shut up before you embarrass me. They ain't no place where it costs a dollar and a half for just one meal," Bill added.

"Embarrass you, is that what I heard you say? With the table manners you got you'll be lucky if they even let you in the place," Cecil said as he laughed.

Just then the door opened and the judge stepped out. "I checked and they got a table in the back that will seat the four of us. We can wait here for a minute or two and they will send someone out to get us," the judge told the three. "Being a judge and all does have its perks. They put us in the front of the line."

Within a minute a pretty lady came out and told the judge that his table was ready if we wanted to follow her. By the look on Cecil and Bill's faces they would have followed her through the gates of hell. She was truly a looker. Judge Preston said for her to lead the way. If anyone out on the front porch was offended that the judge had just jumped line, they held their tongue. I guess you never know when you might find yourself in court and you really didn't want to offend the man who would be sitting behind the bench, just in case.

The four were led to a table in the main back that had six chairs. It was spread with a red and white checkered table cloth and in the center was a glass vase which contained fresh cut flowers. It was a good thing Rusty wasn't here or he might just eat the flowers Zeke thought.

The judge took the seat closest to the wall and sat down. As he did he scanned the rest of the room looking for anyone he knew, or more importantly, anyone he might have rendered a judgement against. In his years on the bench he had become quite a cautious man. On a couple of occasions in the past he had been confronted by men that felt he had been too harsh on them with his judgements. He really didn't care what anyone thought about him as long as they kept it to themselves. He had learned to always be aware of his surroundings and not be caught off guard.

His early years had been spent working riverboats out of Memphis, Tennessee. He had traveled up and down the Mississippi for eight years before deciding he wanted to get an education. During his years on the river he had been in his fair share of scrapes. Although the judge was getting a few years on him he still knew how to take care of himself.

Zeke, Cecil, and Bill, took a chair apiece and then looked around the room. As they suspected earlier, the place was crowded. It was the first time either Bill or Cecil had been inside the Rock Candy Café. With the meager wages the two earned as deputies it would probably be the last time as well. Zeke had been in places that were finer than this but it had been a few years.

"Afternoon Judge, what will the four of you be drinking?"

It was a lady named Charlotte who happened to be the daughter of the man who owned the café.

"I think I'll have sweet tea Charlotte, these other three might want something a little stronger. They have been telling ghost stories all day and need something to settle their nerves."

Charlotte looked at the two deputies and Zeke. "I love ghost stories, maybe you can share one."

Cecil took the lead and answered the question. "Oh, we only have the beginning of the story, we can't tell the whole story until we figure out the ending. That might take a few days. I think I will have the same as the judge is drinking."

Cecil had again surprised Zeke; he had answered the young lady's question, and done it in a gentlemanly fashion. Maybe Bill and Cecil only acted stupid when they were doing deputy business. Time would tell.

Zeke and Bill also ordered tea and Charlotte headed back toward the kitchen.

"What do they have good here judge, I can't afford much," Cecil said.

"Now I told you that the county was paying and I expect each of you to eat up. That is exactly what I intend to do, when the county buys I eat the best they have on the menu," the judge said.

"What is the best on the menu Judge?" Bill asked.

"Porterhouse, Black Angus Porterhouse. It is way more tender and not as gamey as that Texas Longhorn stuff and has a taste that will make your mouth water for days. When Charlotte comes back why don't the three of you order you one?"

The four men sat and talked and before long Charlotte came back to the table carrying a tray that had four tall glasses of tea and a bowl of sugar sitting on top. She picked up each glass and sat it in front of the men.

"I brought extra sugar just in case any of you like your sweet tea to be really sweet. How about it Judge, what will the four of you have?"

The judge looked at her and said, "I think I talked them into that big Porterhouse that this place is so famous for. And if the cook has any of them big sweet potatoes back there then I think that would be a good side. Oh and Charlotte, bring us out a basket of them cathead biscuits, I do love the cathead biscuits you serve here. Does that sound alright with you gentlemen?"

The three other men at the table all shook their heads in the affirmative.

"Sounds good Judge, it will be about twenty minutes. I will go ahead and bring out the biscuits but try not to eat too many, you wouldn't want to be filled up before the steaks get here now would you?" With that Charlotte turned and headed back toward the kitchen.

"What in the world is a cathead biscuit Judge?" Bill asked.

"It's just a regular biscuit but bigger. They put a little garlic in the batter. They also put just a little cheddar cheese in the mix and let me tell you something, you can make a meal out of the biscuits by themselves. I really don't know why they call them cathead biscuits though, go figure," the judge said.

"Well Judge, what do you propose we do about our missing people? The town folk are going to want some answers and they are also going to want their sheriff back, that is if he ain't dead already," Cecil said.

"I might be going over to Langley in a day or two. One of the wires I'm waiting on will confirm whether I go there or stay here. If I have to go then I am taking you two deputies with me and Conley can tag along if he likes. It seems there is a prisoner over there that they are afraid to transport to Rapid City. If he can't be brought here then I will need to go there. Langley has a courthouse and I have been there before but it's been a couple of years. The judge there has recused himself because he is the brother-in-law of the murdered man."

"What has that got to do with all the missing people Judge?" Bill asked.

"It doesn't have anything to do with it Bill, but the way I see it the area between here and Langley is where Zeke said he found the camp and heard that strange crunching noise. I figure we can kill two rabbits with one slingshot if we do a little looking around as we make our way to Langley. How does that sound boys?"

Zeke knew he wanted to figure out what had happened to all the missing people but he was broke and didn't even have the money to stake his way there. He needed to find work for a few weeks and then figure out what his next move was. Just then the judge spoke again and what he had to say pretty much solved Zeke's money problems, for the moment anyway.

"While we are gone the town's deputies can take care of the city. You two deputies are county employees and are required to travel with me between towns if there is a trial involved. Without a sheriff though, I will need to hire one more deputy and thought about offering the job to Zeke if he's interested. Pay is forty dollars a month and trail grub. I can put you on for a month or until we find the sheriff. How does that sound to you Zeke?"

Forty dollars a month and food sounded pretty good to Zeke. It would immediately solve his money problems and also allow him to help solve the mystery of the missing men. "You got yourself a deal Judge as long as it includes the livery charge for Rusty, my horse. When do I start?" Zeke asked.

"Day before yesterday Zeke, I figure you been on the payroll since before you came into town with that missing man's horse and rifle. Oh, and by the way, I like horses so I would say Rusty has been on the payroll as long as you have. Say, does your horse like judges, I wouldn't want to get kicked or bitten on this trip," the judge asked.

"Oh, Rusty loves Judges, roasted or raw, doesn't matter to Rusty," Zeke said. Everyone got a good laugh out of this, especially the judge.

"After we eat you three go back to the sheriff's office and start putting together what you will need from there for the trip. Figure on at least ten days, three to travel to Langley, four for the trial and three days back to Rapid City."

"That sounds like a plan Judge, but what about food for the journey? Should we go over to Shafer's general store and provision up?" Cecil asked.

"Hell no, I refuse to eat grub from that place. We will make our first stop at Wiley's over in Tyrone. He runs the General Store there and has nearly everything that Shafer's has." The judge said this with authority that wasn't really needed; he actually said it with gusto.

"Sorry Judge, I didn't know you had such a dislike for the General Store here in town," Cecil said.

"It's not that I dislike the store, it's the store's owner that I dislike. I refuse to allow him to make a profit off me or the county if I can do otherwise. We will provision at Wiley's."

Just then Charlotte brought out two big plates while another lady behind her carried the other two. Charlotte sat the first plate in front of the judge and the second in front of Zeke. She then took the two other plates from the lady behind her and sat them down in front of Bill and Cecil. We had been so busy talking to the judge that none of us had taken the first bite of the cathead biscuits that she had brought out earlier. By the looks on the three men's faces the judge knew he had made the right decision on what to have them order.

"How does everything look gentlemen?" Charlotte asked.

"Just fine my dear, can you bring out a bottle of that sauce I am so fond of for the steaks?" The judge asked.

Almost as soon as the words left the judge's mouth another lady came by and sat the bottle of sauce on the table. "I told them back in the kitchen how much you liked the steak sauce so they were already bringing it for you," Charlotte said.

"Everything looks perfect my dear, thank you," the judge said.

"Enjoy," Charlotte said as she turned and headed back toward the kitchen.

"Alright gentlemen dig in. I hate to rush such a fine meal as this but I need to get back to the telegraph office and check on my messages and the three of you need to start making preparations for our little journey," the judge said.

As each man began to carve his steak the judge opened the bottle of sauce and poured a generous portion on the side of his plate. He then carved his steak and before taking a bite he applied the sauce.

"What kind of a seasoning is that you poured out of that bottle Judge?" Cecil asked.

"It's steak sauce, and once you try a little of it then you will be hooked." The judge slid the bottle to Cecil.

Cecil never hesitated. He opened the bottle and poured some of the sauce directly on top of his Porterhouse. After he sampled it he was hooked. "You know what Judge; I think this would be good on beans."

"Slide that bottle over here and let me give it a try," Bill demanded.

After a few minutes it was unanimous, the sauce was delicious. Judge Preston ate heartily as did the other three men. "You boys enjoy this meal, for the next few days I would hazard to guess that we will be eating whatever we can put over a campfire. By the way what is it that you like to eat while you're out on the trail?"

Cecil felt compelled to answer since he had spent more time out under the stars than Bill.

"Beans Judge, lots and lots of beans."

The judge knew that Bill and Cecil had spent very little time away from town and wondered just how well they would hold up if they had to live for months with nothing but a horse and a rifle.

"What about you Zeke, you spend much time outside of a town?" The judge asked.

In nearly the last two years he had spent a grand total of seven nights in a house of any kind.

"Well Judge, I would say that the best food for traveling is bacon, skillet bread and good coffee, lots and lots of coffee. You eat first thing in the morning and last thing before turning in at night. If you get hungry during the day a little jerky seems to do the trick. It may seem a little unsettling at first only having two meals a day but you soon get used to it," Zeke told the three.

"Bacon huh, well let me ask you this. How on earth do you keep bacon out on the trail?" The judge asked.

"Trail bacon Judge, it is cured a little longer than regular house bacon and it has extra salt. It will keep for five or six weeks unless the weather is really hot and humid, then it might just last three weeks. And as for the beans, well they keep for months and months. If you keep your beans dry and your coffee sealed up then you will use it all up before it has a chance to go bad on you. If you are out there for very long then you might bag a rabbit or even a deer if you're lucky. You eat fresh anytime you can and after that you go back to the beans and bacon. Even out here, the way the west is growing up, you will come into a town every few weeks. If you plan your steps right then you will never go hungry."

The men continued to enjoy their food as each thought about what the next few days was going to be like. "You know Zeke, I think I am looking forward to a little rough grub for a change. Beans and bacon after a long day on the back of a horse sounds pretty good to me," Judge Preston said.

"By the way Judge, there is something I been meaning to ask you. That horse I brought in the night I got arrested by old Bill and Cecil here, what do you think is going to happen to it?"

"Well, if we find who it belongs to then he rightfully gets it back. If the man is dead and we can find out where his family is then we send word and they can come and claim what is rightfully theirs. Now let's say that the man is dead or we can't find him and we also can't find any of his family, then the horse and saddle belongs to the man who found them, along with everything else that was in that camp."

Zeke thought about this and then asked the judge, "Alright then, I have a suggestion. Since there will be four of us going on this little trip, I think we need a pack horse. We can take the hazel eyed horse I found and let her carry our stuff. Also I would like to take that .45.75 Winchester I found. There was plenty of ammunition in the saddle bags and I think the extra firepower might come in handy, especially since we don't know what we might be going up against."

Cecil looked at the judge and said, "I think that might be a wise decision. If each of us is trying to carry our own food on the horse we're riding then we are going to be riding some pretty tired mounts. I for one want my horse to be nice and fresh just in case some monster takes off after me."

The judge laughed. "You boys really think that some monster is the cause of all the missing men?"

Bill looked at Cecil and shook his head yes. The judge saw this and started laughing.

"Alright Judge, when some four eyed eight legged critter starts gnawing on you what are you going to do, hit it on the head with your gavel?" Bill asked.

"Well now that you brought it up, I think I can do a little better than a gavel. I still got my Navy Colts from a few years back. They are a matched set, one for my holster and another for my vest. I also got a little two shot derringer that packs a pretty good wallop. No one knows this but I carry it on me every day, especially while I'm on the bench. I have made a few enemies over the years with some of my decisions and the last thing I want is to need a gun and not have it. The better part of wisdom has taught me that it is better to have one and not need it. I believe in being prepared.

"You boys won't have to worry about me. I can handle myself out of doors and am looking forward to our little trip. Now don't get me wrong, I surely wouldn't want to be out there all by myself but with the three of you, I'm confident that we will do alright."

Cecil speared the last bite of his steak and just before popping it into his mouth said, "I sure hope so Judge. If we do get into trouble out there then it's just the four of us. There won't be any help if we run up against something we can't handle on our own." The four men enjoyed the last of their food as they thought about what Cecil had just said.

After the four finished their meals at the Rock Candy Café, Judge Preston put the entire bill on the County's account and also left a fifty cent tip on the table for Charlotte. As the men exited the restaurant the judge told them to head on over to the sheriff's office and start gathering the items they would need for the trip. He would meet them there as soon as he checked on his messages at the telegraph office.

As Zeke and the two deputies came around the corner and within view of the sheriff's office they could see that another crowd had gathered just outside the door.

"Looks like our list of missing persons might be getting a little longer," Bill said.

When they got to the front door of the jail it was obvious that the people there represented a single family. The oldest of the women standing in the group asked, "Is the sheriff in, I need to talk to him."

"No Ma'am, he's out of town at the moment on official sheriff business. Come on inside and maybe one of us can help you, we're deputies," Cecil said.

He unlocked the front door and everyone gathered inside.

"What is it we can do for you Ma'am?" Bill asked.

The woman looked like she had been crying and it seemed she could begin again at any moment.

"Well deputy, my name is Betty Spears, me and my family live about thirty miles from town on a small ranch, we raise cattle and horses. Four days ago my oldest son Johnny went out just before first light to tend to the milk cows and never came back. After about an hour I sent his brother Caleb to see why he had been gone so long and he never came back either. I took the rifle and went to see what might have happened and couldn't find a trace of either of them. I thought they might have went off into the woods hunting, although that wouldn't be like either of them to go off and not tell me first, that is what I hoped had happened anyway. By dark that night I feared the worst and the first thing next morning I loaded up the family and headed for town. We made it half way and something spooked the horses. It was late so I decided to make camp and continue on the next morning. During the night our pack mule must have got scared and somehow got loose and ran away. We came on in and came straight here."

Zeke asked the obvious question, "Ma'am, how old are your two boys?"

"Johnny is seventeen and Caleb is fifteen. Both are strong boys and they got good heads on their shoulders. Neither would have just wandered off and gotten lost," Mrs. Spears said.

"Where is your husband Mrs. Spears?" Bill asked.

"He abandoned us about a year ago. He went out one morning to spend the day checking fences and just never came back. I was so shocked, he never ever, let on that he was unhappy and I would have never suspected he was the type of man that would just walk away from his family."

Bill and Cecil exchanged suspicious looks.

"Where will you be staying while you're in town Ma'am?" Bill asked.

"At my sister's place, she's married to the man that runs the stable in town."

"Your sister is married to Lester Fitch?" Bill asked.

"That's right, they live just outside of town, we stopped by there on the way in and she said to stay as long as we liked."

"Well Ma'am, we have just come from a meeting with Judge Preston. He's at the telegraph office now and we are putting together a plan to go out and scour the territory for any sign of some missing men, your boys included. It might be a few days but once we find out anything then someone will find you and share what information we have," Cecil said.

Just before she went out the door she turned back and said with a shaky voice, "Please find my boys deputy, it just don't seem possible that two little sweet boys like that would be taken away without a trace." With that she and her family were out the door and gone.

Bill went over and closed the door.

"She said her husband ran off over a year ago, you know what I think? He was taken just like her two sons. That means that all this started that long ago, not just in the last couple of months like we first thought."

"I think you got a good point about that Bill. If her husband was taken a year ago, then it's possible that there are others in that amount of time that we don't know about. You take a man just passing through and gets taken then who is going to report it. Hell, it could be thirty or forty men. She said her pack mule was taken too. Sounds like a pattern to me. Men and boys of working age, none too young and none too old, and the mules, we can't forget about the mules," Cecil said. "What do you think Zeke? You heard everything that's been said."

Zeke pondered the question for a moment before answering. "I agree with what both of you have said."

"What do you think is gonna happen?" Cecil asked.

"Could be that unless the three of us aren't real careful then the judge might be the only one to make it back alive," Zeke said.

This brought a look of terror to both the men's faces.

"Do you really think the three of us could be next Zeke? What about Judge Preston, he's going to be riding along with us," Bill asked.

"Judge Preston is at least sixty years old; you heard what everyone has been saying. Only men and boys of a good size have been disappearing. No one very old or very young has been taken. That narrows it down to the three of us."

The room fell silent as the words sunk in. Cecil went over to the locked gun cabinet and opened it with a key he carried in his vest pocket. He pulled out a Winchester and two boxes of shells. "If I disappear then whatever takes me is going to have a few holes added to its hide."

As the three men gathered up the guns and ammunition they thought they might need on the journey over to Langley, Judge Preston came in carrying some messages in his hand. He looked more than a little put out.

"I was right, got to be in Langley three days from now. That is when the trial starts. That only gives us two full days and what's left of today to get there. If the weather holds up and we travel real hard tomorrow and Monday then we should make it just fine."

"If we travel real hard and don't watch out for ourselves then we may never make it there. I think caution is the only way to travel with all the mischief that's going on out there Judge," Cecil added.

"Well, we will be cautious Cecil, but we will also be in Langley by Monday night. I done been ordered by the Governor himself. He's afraid unless the trial takes place quick then there might be a lynching. And the man they want to lynch is none other than the governor's son-in-law."

"His son-in-law, what in tar-nation did he do?" Bill asked.

"Said he shot a man, said they also got a witness to the crime. And that ain't the best of it either. The man they say he shot is a Shafer, or at least has some Shafer blood. His name is, or was, Sonny Briscoe."

"A Shafer you say. Wouldn't be any relation to the Shafer we got here in Rapid City that runs that big law outfit would it Judge?" Cecil asked.

"You got it. He is a first cousin to Lloyd Shafer and as a matter of fact Lloyd left out of here Friday morning on the train heading for Langley. That is why we got to go by horse if we have any chance of making it to Langley by Tuesday when the trial starts. Shafer knew what he was doing when he left town on the sly."

"What happens if we don't make it in time for the trial Judge?" Bill asked.

"The governor's son-in-law hangs. The next man to run against the governor will probably use the fact that his son-in-law was a murderer to try to win the election. And guess who has already threw his hat in the ring, none other than Lloyd Shafer himself."

The two deputies and Zeke now knew that it was going to be a rushed trip to the town of Langley. It seemed that all the missing men were going to stay missing as long as the Governor was calling the shots.

"Time is growing thin gentlemen. You three get your horses and the gear you need from here and I will meet you at the livery stable. I need to go to my office and pick up a few things. After that, I'll stop by my house and then head on over to Lester's. If you get there before I do then have him to saddle my horse." With that the judge turned and headed toward the courthouse.

"Bill, what do you think we need to take in the way of weapons?" Cecil asked.

"Definitely a Winchester for the two of you and an extra Colt for each of us. I think I want that double-barrel Greener and three boxes of shells. If we get jumped then I want something that shoots far and wide, just in case. How about you Zeke?"

"Well, you two heard what the judge said about the horse and the gun I brought in from that abandoned campsite. Give me that .45.75 Winchester and all the ammunition that fits it. I'll just leave my old Winchester here. If you can spare another box of .45 cartridges for my Colt then I'll be set."

Cecil reached in and pulled out the big Winchester and reached it to Zeke along with the saddlebag that contained the ammunition that fit the big gun.

"You think you can hit anything with a gun that powerful Zeke? For that matter have you ever shot a .45.75 before?" Bill asked.

"Yea, I have. Back in Kentucky my paw had a couple of .45.75 rifles. I used to shoot them a little just to see how far I could hit a target the size of a water bucket."

"How far away did you put the bucket?" Cecil asked.

"The farthest I ever shot, with any degree of accuracy, was a mite over four hundred yards. At that range I could hit the bucket three out of four times. The problem is the breeze. On a calm day I could hit that bucket every time. The breeze though is the problem. A bullet that big traveling that far gets steered by the wind."

"You must have pretty good eyes Zeke. Four hundred yards is damn near a quarter of a mile. I could probably hit a wagon at that range but a bucket, no way," Bill said.

"My eyes are good Bill. The way I see it, if the monsters are far off then I will do the shooting. If they are close then you can do the shooting with that Greener. Does that sound like a plan?"

"Zeke, that sounds like a plan to me. By the time whatever it is gets close enough to any of us then it should be so full of lead it won't be able to do us no harm."

The good natured talk made the three men feel a bit better about what it was they were about to do. When it gets dark and the sounds of the night start to call your name then they would see. Right now each man kept his fears to himself as he gathered what they would need and then locked up the jail and headed for the livery.

Lester Fitch was busy doing what any good livery man would be doing at three o'clock in the afternoon, taking a nap. Any man who has ever worked a stable will tell you that the day starts very early and usually lasts until very late. Most will also tell you that it's hard, if not impossible, to get more than five hours sleep a night, so to make up the difference a midday nap is required.

Lester was sleeping soundly when Cecil and Bill stomped up on the front porch.

"Well Bill, it looks like me and you went into the wrong line of work," Cecil said.

"Well I'll be damned, sleeping in the middle of the day. Deputy work ain't bad but this livery stuff makes me wish I had taken a different path in life," Bill replied.

Lester opened his eyes and slid the hat back from his face. "Well I figure I didn't die and go to heaven in my sleep 'cause I don't think they would allow two river rats like you in."

"Well what do you know Bill, he ain't dead after all. One of us better go on over to the undertaker's office and tell him not to bother," Cecil said.

Lester got up from the swing he used for his daytime sleeping and stretched. "What is it you two wanted or do you even know?" Lester asked.

"We came for our horses, and by the way, Judge Preston said for you to saddle up his horse too. We are going for a little trip," Bill said.

Lester looked at the two deputies and then he noticed the third man. He stuck out a hand and said, "Lester Fitch, and you would be?"

Zeke shook Lester's hand and said, "Zeke Conley from Kentucky. I belong to that big horse back there, his name is Rusty."

"You know I wondered who the owner was. Bill and Cecil saw fit to bring your horse, and another one, in here late last night but never bothered to tell me the particulars. Is that other horse with the green eyes yours too?"

"Not exactly, Bill and Cecil arrested me for murdering that horse's owner when I came into town last night but I've served my time for that crime and am now officially a free man," Zeke said.

Bill slapped Zeke on the shoulder and said, "Do you have to tell that story every time your mouth flops open?"

Lester looked at the two deputies and said, "Well, don't you think much about that young Conley, it wouldn't be the first time these two buffoons slapped the cuffs on the wrong man. What is it I can do for you three?"

Bill said, "Lester, we done told you what we came for. We want our horses and the judge wants you to saddle his while you're at it. How long does it take you to wake your sleepy ass up anyway?"

"Not as long as you Bill because you're all ass," Lester shot back.

Just when it looked like the two deputies and the hostler were going to get into a fistfight the judge walked up.

"What in the world is all the shouting about? I could hear the three of you all the way down the street."

Lester jumped in before the two deputies could and said, "Oh nothing Judge, I was just explaining to our two fine deputies here why they're so stupid." With that Lester turned and went into the barn.

Judge Preston looked at Bill and Cecil. "Looks like the two of you just got your asses handed to you." He followed the hostler into the barn laughing.

Bill looked at Cecil and said, "You know Cecil, I believe the Judge is right."

"Shut the hell up Bill and let's get our horses, it's getting late."

As the men were putting everything together and preparing to leave Cecil noticed a cloth sack the judge was putting in one of his saddle bags. "What you got in the sack Judge?"

Preston walked over and opened it up so the three men could look inside. "Cathead biscuits from the Rock Candy Café, got us enough for supper tonight and breakfast in the morning, what do you think?"

Just as Bill was starting to reach his hand in and take a biscuit the judge closed the bag. "No way Bill, I told you this is for our supper and breakfast. We won't be at Wiley's until tomorrow morning. These here are the only provisions we got unless any of you brought anything."

Zeke knew the judge was right. In the rush to get out of town and put a few miles behind them before dark none of the three had thought of food. They had just finished that meal at the Café' and food just wasn't on their minds right now. The judge had the foresight to bring the biscuits and that would just have to make due.

Lester heard this and went to the back of the livery. He came back carrying a big slab of salt pork. "Here you go Judge, take this. At least the four of you will have a little meat to go with them biscuits until you make it to Wiley's store."

The judge took the pork and put it in the sack with the Biscuits. "Thanks Lester, I think for the next ten days we will be eating mostly trail food and this will get us started off real nice."

With that the four men mounted up and headed out with Zeke leading Hazel behind Rusty.

Lloyd Shafer was still a full day from Langley, South Dakota. He had received the telegram late Thursday and made preparations to leave on the eight o'clock train the following morning. He had booked passage on the lone Pullman sleeping car and had spent both Friday and early Saturday stewing about the fact that he wasn't allowed the best suite on the car. That particular room was occupied by a minor politician from Washington who was traveling out west on some sort of fact finding mission. Shafer was so steamed by this that he had made it one of his priorities to have the man's work discredited, and if possible to have him fired.

Shafer had managed to distract himself from this by working on the case he would be handling once he made it to Langley. He knew he had a two day head start on the Honorable Judge Thurman Preston. He also knew that if Preston didn't show then he would file the necessary paperwork to have the accused declared guilty and then hung. If he didn't manage to have the charges verified and the prisoner declared guilty then the only other outcome was a dismissal. If dismissed then he was sure the prisoner would be lynched upon his release. Either way Shafer stood to benefit. His old enemy, Doug Whitmore, was going to hang for the murder legally or lynched by a mob that wanted justice the old fashioned way.

It was a mystery that Shafer had been asked to prosecute Whitmore in the first place. The man who should be in charge of the prosecution had stepped aside due to some sort of conflict of interest and that was when word came to Rapid City for Lloyd Shafer to proceed to Langley with all possible speed.

Whitmore, with his family money and connections, could afford any attorney he wanted and was hopeful for a not guilty verdict. What he didn't know was that Shafer had laid the groundwork for this trial months before the murder had even taken place. With the friction that had developed between the two families over the years it wasn't a surprise that Shafer found joy in heading the prosecution. Once Whitmore was arrested for murder the accused had a telegram sent to the Governor asking for advice and help with his defense.

Lloyd Shafer had gladly taken the prosecution side of the case and hoped Whitmore would be found guilty and hung shortly after. The fact that Shafer had orchestrated the events that led to Whitmore's arrest in the first place practically guaranteed a guilty verdict.

Shafer's dislike for the judge in this trial, the Honorable Thurman Preston, was always hidden just under the surface. If Preston missed the trial Shafer would again attempt to have him removed from the bench. He had tried this once before and was unsuccessful. Anytime a trial was in the works that would be presided over by Judge Preston, Shafer would always request a jury. Not that Judge Preston would be unfair, but it was something Shafer wasn't going to chance. If a decision could go either way and it was up to the judge, and not a jury, then Shafer felt the judge would find against him.

At each stop along the way to Langley, Shafer had sent and received messages using an alias. He had not only the trial at hand to concern himself with but also plans to discredit the governor in any way possible. Shafer was looking to advance his station in life and a trip to the Governor's Mansion was just the beginning. He saw men such as the current governor and Judge Preston as minor nuisances to be brushed aside. This very trial held the promise to not only rid himself of Preston but also to discredit the governor. Shafer smiled as these thoughts played out in his head.

By two in the afternoon the train Shafer rode was nearing the town of Fort Clemens. It was the last town on the route which was of large enough size to have both a train coaling station and also a telegraph office. Not only did Shafer have messages to send but also he was to meet some men there that he had used in the past. They were the type that would take a job regardless of how messy it might be.

As the locomotive began to slow Shafer made his way to the exit in order to be first off the train. He knew the stop would last no more than forty-five minutes and in that short time he had quite a lot to do. Before the train came to a complete stop he stepped off and hurried toward the main street. Once there he went to the Dry Branch Saloon. The Dry Branch wasn't the nicest place in town but it was one of the busiest. It was a narrow two story adobe structure with a covered boardwalk across the entire front. On either side of the batwing doors were large plate glass windows. Men were entering and leaving which attested to the amount of traffic the establishment received. If men had business to transact, which might not be of the law and order type, then the Dry Branch was the place to go.

Shafer didn't like places like saloons but still made the rounds when necessary. As he was entering a couple of stout looking trail hands shoved through the batwings and nearly knocked Shafer to the ground. Now Shafer wasn't a coward, not by any means, but he knew when he was overmatched. These two were twice his size and both were armed, Shafer was not.

"Out of the way mister," the larger of the two said as he shoved Shafer again.

Shafer only smiled as he waited.

"I said out of the way mister and I don't intend to say it again." This time before the burly cowboy could shove Shafer again there was a gunshot.

Standing in the door of the saloon was a clean shaven man of about thirty. He was wearing a cross draw holster and in his hand was a smoking Colt. As the two cow hands stood there looking at the stranger the bigger of the two, the one who had been manhandling Shafer felt something wet running down his shirt. When he looked he saw blood. He grabbed his chest and felt around but there wasn't a hole anywhere to be found. He reached up where his left ear used to be and realized the ear was completely gone.

"Why you son-of-a-bitch, you done shot off my ear." The man went for his gun but before he made it there was another gunshot. This time blood ran down the other side of the burly cowboy's shirt. He reached up with his right hand and found that ear to now be missing too.

The stranger in the door spoke. He directed his words to the uninjured of the two cowboys. As he spoke he kept the Colt trained on the pair.

"I'm not sure if your friend there can hear what I have to say. I really don't think he has an ear for it but I'm going to say it anyway. If he pulls that gun from his holster then I'm going to fire a third shot and it will be aimed at a spot directly between where the first two shots struck. Just in case the two of you can't figure out where that is then I will tell you, right between the eyes. Now the best thing for you to do is get out of my sight."

The uninjured man grabbed his friend and headed down the boardwalk. Before they had gone far the one without any ears turned and shouted. "You're a dead man mister, you can count on it. A dead man you hear?"

Shafer watched them go before turning to the man in the door. "Hello Wes, your timing was perfect."

The man named Wes waited until the two cowboys were completely out of sight before answering.

"I thought I told you to start carrying a gun Lloyd. This far west of the Mississippi is no place for a man to go unarmed."

Wes Branham was a full time gunfighter and part time outlaw. He had held up the occasional train and even pulled two bank holdups while still in his twenties but now fancied himself a gun for hire. He had hired out to Lloyd Shafer three years back and in doing so had given up the trains and banks. Now he fancied himself a fixer of problems. His tool of choice was a Colt .45.

"Well, I do carry a gun at times but never during daylight hours. How would it look for the territory's next governor to be carrying a gun?" Shafer asked.

"Well, looks can be misleading. I think everyone would rather have a living, breathing, governor that carries a gun rather than an unarmed dead one."

Shafer laughed and slapped Wes on the shoulder. "That's why I have you around." With that the two turned and entered the saloon. Wes headed toward the back where he had been sitting before Shafer was troubled by the two cowboys. Both men sat down with Wes against the wall. Shafer always wondered why men who expected trouble always went out of their way to find it.

"What have you found out about the trial in Langley?" Shafer asked.

Wes refilled his shot glass from the bottle he had purchased earlier. "Trial is still on for Tuesday. I made sure the messages to Rapid City were delayed and that gives you a good two day head start like you said. What happens if the judge doesn't show?"

Shafer picked up the bottle and read the brand name on the label. He then poured a half shot into the other empty glass on the table and took a small sip. "What the hell? That tastes like horse piss."

Wes grabbed the bottle and said, "I happen to like this stuff and may I ask how you know what horse piss tastes like anyway?"

Shafer didn't answer; he just sat his glass down and pushed it away. "If the judge doesn't show then I believe the fine people of Langley will have themselves a lynching right there on the courthouse lawn."

"Now that is bad news, him being close kin of the governor and all," Wes said with a laugh.

"Don't you worry any about him and the governor. He was a no good banker and if he hangs I for one wish him a pleasant swing in the breeze."

Wes looked at his boss. "You mean you don't care?"

"That is exactly what I mean. It has been my intention for him to hang all along."

Wes thought about this for a minute. You mind telling me what you're talking about?"

"Well Wes, I don't think you need to know everything but I can tell you this. Doug Whitmore has been a problem for my family nearly his entire life and I don't think the family, or for that matter anyone else, will shed many tears when he's gone."

Wes fixed his boss with a cold stare. "But he didn't kill your cousin Boss."

"That's right Wes, and the less you mention about that the better off we will both be. I don't expect you to understand, and further more you don't get paid to understand. You get paid to do exactly as I say."

Wes could tell he had broached a subject that Shafer didn't want mentioned. "Sorry boss, what is it you want me to do?"

Lloyd thought a minute without looking at Wes. He was weighing his options and formulating a plan.

"Head out of Fort Clemens within the hour, I want you to slow down our judge from Rapid City. Make sure he doesn't make the trial on Tuesday morning," Shafer finally said.

Wes reached for the bottle again but Shafer grabbed it first.

"I want you sober Wes, no more whiskey today. This is important and time is growing thin. How many men do you have that you can count on?"

Wes frowned as he drew his hand back. "I got the same three that you know and a couple of others that I think are pretty damn dependable. It is just one old judge Lloyd; you act like we are going up against a regiment of mounted horse soldiers."

"The judge always travels with a couple of deputies and the sheriff when he holds court in other towns. At least this time it will only be the two county deputies."

"What happened to the sheriff?" Wes asked.

"Again you ask too many questions. I have eliminated the sheriff and that is all you need to know."

Wes knew what the lawyer meant when he said he had eliminated the sheriff. "Are you telling me you had him killed or has he gone missing?"

Shafer admired Wes, not only for his gun handling abilities but also for the fact that he was smart. He could not only put together a plan but he could also figure one out that he wasn't totally involved in.

"Let's just say he won't ever be going back to Rapid City," Shafer said. "You got any idea on how to slow down the judge and his two deputies?"

"By that I take it you don't want him to come upon any fatal accidents on the trail to Langley, just slowed down a bit," Wes asked.

"That's right Wes; the judge doesn't get a scratch, at least for now. The two deputies though might make a good addition to our missing sheriff," Shafer said as he stood to leave.

"No problem boss, I'm heading out now unless you think you might need a little help at the front door in case those two cowboys decide to return."

"If they return then I will deal with them with my fists. I doubt they would shoot an unarmed man," Shafer said.

Just then Wes realized something. "Shafer, I believe I just got you figured out. You go unarmed based on the fact that most men wouldn't shoot a man that wasn't packing. You lull your adversary into thinking you are harmless and then at the right moment you use your ability to box to get the job done. Tell me if I got it figured out or not."

"As I have always thought Wes, you are not only good with a gun but you have the ability to think. One more thing to remember Wes, you are the only witness to the killing of my cousin, don't allow yourself to be seen by the judge or the deputies until the trial." With that Shafer turned and left the saloon.

Wes picked up the bottle of cheap whiskey he had purchased earlier and headed for the back door to the saloon. No way in hell was he going out the front door after shooting the ears off a man not more than ten minutes earlier. As it turned out the back door plan was what the two rangy cowhands had suspected. They were both waiting in ambush.

Wes knew he would need to use a little caution until he gathered his belongings from the hotel he had stayed in the last two days and then went to the stable to saddle his horse. He stepped clear of the back door of the saloon and scanned the surrounding buildings and back alleys, there wasn't a soul to be seen. This in itself was all he needed to know. He suspected that the two were about and with all the blood on the one man's shirt he suspected that anyone who would normally use that alley and saw the two would find another way around.

He sat down the bottle of whiskey and drew his Colt. As silently as possible he eased out and checked the alley in both directions. It was cluttered with empty crates and other less than useful junk. As he eased down the alley as quiet as a mouse he heard two men talking from behind a stack of lumber. He took a position in the middle of the alley and then very deliberately pulled back the hammer on his gun. The noise was heard by the two men and they jumped from behind cover with guns in hand. Not a very well thought out plan on their part.

Wes crouched as he pulled the trigger. He made sure to shoot the uninjured man first and then with his second shot he took down the one without the ears. He deliberately hit both men in the right shoulder. Not wanting to kill the two he did want to make it difficult for them to return fire. Also, he felt the two trouble makers would need to learn some manners if they weren't able to threaten others due to the permanent injuries a .45 slug does to a man's shoulder.

After the two went down Wes approached and kicked away the two guns. Both of the bushwhackers were rolling around holding their left hands over their right shoulders and cussing Wes.

"Stand up both of you!" Wes shouted.

Both looked at the Colt Wes still held on them and then with a certain degree of difficulty managed to get to their feet.

"Why in hell did you shoot us like that mister?" The one that still had ears asked.

Before Wes could answer the town's sheriff and one of his deputies came running down the alley with guns drawn. Wes holstered his weapon and waited to see how things would play out. The sheriff looked at the two men and with no small amount of anger in his voice said.

"Well if it ain't Bart and Lee Sturgill, two of the sorriest excuses that ever walked around town." The sheriff holstered his gun as he said this. He looked at Wes and asked, "I suppose you got a pretty good reason for shooting these two?"

"I do," was all Wes said?

"Well that's good enough for me. Deputy, how about you take these two on over to the jail and when you get them both locked away nice and safe go over and find the doc. Take both of their guns to the general store and see what you can get for them. Give half to the doc and the other half goes into the jail fund for room and board," the sheriff said.

"Now wait a minute sheriff, ain't you going to hear us out. That bastard had done shot Bart three times today and me once. I demand justice," Lee said.

"Well Lee, I'm glad you brought that up. Justice is going to be thirty days in jail and then a one way trip out of town, that is assuming that neither of you develop any complications from them bullet holes you're both packing. Now if I was the two of you I would accept the sentence I just handed down. You two have been nothin but trouble ever since you blew into town a couple of months back. Take them on deputy."

With that the deputy led the two injured outlaws away.

The sheriff turned back to Wes and said, "Haven't seen you around town before. Mind telling me what happened here."

"Well Sheriff, my name is Wes Branham and I work for a bunch of lawyers out of Rapid City. Those two targeted my boss less than an hour ago and started pushing him around a bit. I intervened and put a stop to their mischief. They were both positioned back here to even the score. I made the mistake of using the back way in order to avoid the very thing I ran into. That is about the size of it."

The sheriff thought about this for a minute and finally said, "I reckon that sounds about right. How long do you intend on staying in town in case I need to ask a few more questions?"

"I was on my way to the hotel to grab my stuff when I was set upon by them two. I would be saddling my horse right now if that hadn't happened," Wes said.

"If you happen back through then stop by my office so I can close the file on what happened here today. If you never come back through then I will consider the matter closed anyway," the sheriff said.

Wes tipped his hat to the sheriff and headed toward the hotel. After gathering his saddlebags and then his horse at the stable he headed out of Fort Clemens a little after five-o'clock in the evening. His first stop would be about two miles out of town where the rest of his men had been camped out for the last couple of days. As he rode into camp he noticed the fire and coffee pot, along with horses and other trail gear, but there wasn't a soul in sight.

"Hello the camp," Wes spoke as he neared the clearing.

He slowed his horse and waited. Just when he was about to shout again he heard the distinct sound of several Winchester Rifles being cocked.

Wes sat his horse and waited. Just when he was about to turn and leave there was a raspy voice from the tree line. "Hello Wes, what took you so long?" It was Jed Muncy, leader of the five men that worked for Wes and Shafer.

Wes didn't answer, he just dismounted and headed for the coffee pot. "Jed, if you don't stop smoking and drinking so much that voice of yours is going to start sounding like an old Baldwin steam engine hauling a heavy load of logs up a steep grade."

The man named Jed walked out of the tree line and headed toward the fire. "Who are you anyway, my mother?"

Wes filled a tin cup and reached the pot to Jed. "From what I've been told you didn't have a mother, someone found you in a bobcat den."

Jed laughed, "My dear old momma could scream like a bobcat when I had done wrong. Did you manage to get us a job while you been living in town like city folk while the rest of us been up here shivering our asses off?"

"I did. Just met with Lloyd and he has us a three day job that starts as soon as you put out this fire and get loaded up. We got to head back toward Rapid City and set us up a little diversion. How long before the rest of these fellers can ride?"

"Bout ten minutes ought to do the trick. Say Wes, you didn't manage to get us a little advance did you, we ran out of beans this morning and you are enjoying the last of the coffee."

Wes reached into his saddle bag and retrieved the bottle of bad whiskey he brought from the Dry Branch Saloon. "Here you go Jed; see if this will tide you over until we get to the trading post."

Jed took the bottle and looked at the label. "Idaho Buck, why this happens to be my favorite Wes, but this bottle is nearly half empty. This all you brought?"

"It is, I couldn't just load up at the General Store with enough for six of us now could I? If we hurry along then we should be at Hound Dog's by dark. We can load up there and head on a ways before we make camp," Wes told the men.

With that thought in mind Jed hurried up the men and in no time at all the six were heading southeast at a fast trot. The Hound Dog Trading Post was owned by a man who, in his younger and more rowdy days, had held up two trains and spent nearly ten years in a sun baked prison down in Texas as his punishment. He still enjoyed telling that story to anyone who hadn't already heard it. Problem was he had told the story so many times that he rarely found a fresh set of ears to share it with.

The man who liked to tell that story went by the name of Bison, nothing else just Bison. No one really knew what his real name was. Some speculated that was because he was still wanted by the law in a few states for crimes yet to be mentioned. Others suspected it was because he had spent a good part of his youth as a guide for rich easterners who came west to hunt the wooly beasts. Wes and Jed had both agreed that the name was due to the man's colossal chest and his shaggy beard that protruded in all directions. In any case the Hound Dog was where Bison intended to spend his remaining days, selling goods to both whites and Indians alike. He liked to sit in his cushioned rocking chair and whittle dry cedar as he sipped homemade apple wine that he somehow managed to produce in a shed out back of the trading post. His recipe and ingredients were a well-kept secret; the result was a smooth yet tart taste that folks in the area had grown accustomed to. Bison sold it in quart jars with metal lids and as time went by he found he was selling more Apple Wine than anything else, more than even beans and bacon.

Wes and his band of misfits made it to the Hound Dog about an hour before dark and Jed went immediately to the counter and asked for a quart of Apple Wine.

Bison looked at Jed and said, "I told you before that there ain't no such thang. If you want any then you'll call it what I told you to call it."

Jed slammed his hand on the counter and said, "Alright Bison, just give me a quart of Apple Juice then. I just hope no one ever finds out that I drink something that sounds as tame as Apple Juice though. It sounds about as awful as ordering a glass of milk, yuck."

Bison reached under the counter and grabbed a glass jar and sat it on the counter. "That's a buck Jed and I want you to pay up first."

"Not so fast Bison, Wes is just outside and we will need some provisions this evening. He'll pay for everything including this Apple Juice before we leave."

Bison slid the jar to Jed. "If Wes is here then that's good enough for me."

Wes walked in and looked toward the bar. "Bison, is that Apple Juice to be put on my tab?"

"That's right Wes, he done said to put it on the tab you was about to run."

Wes looked at Jed. "Why do you drink so much? And for that matter why do you smoke so much. Hell, any half-blood Indian can track you not by the sign you leave in the dirt but by the smoke from your tobacco. That jar you got in your hand better last you for the next three days because I can tell you right now, I don't intend to buy any more until our little job is finished. You got that?"

Jed cradled the Apple Juice as if Wes was going to make him put it back. "I got it Wes, what kind of a life would a man be living if not for spirits and tobacco anyway?"

"Try more coffee and bacon." Wes turned to the man behind the counter. "You got time to fill a little order for us Bison?"

"Give me the list Wes. I'll fill it while you spend some more time educating old Jed here," Bison said as he looked over what the men would need.

Jed, who took himself as a tough outlaw, looked at Bison and said, "You better watch that smart mouth of yours Bison before I take a notion to shut it for you." Once Jed said this he wished he could take it back.

Bison looked up from the list. He slowly sat it down on his dirty little counter and reached a club like arm over and grabbed Jed by the shirt. "Did you mean what you just said to me Jed?"

Jed nervously looked at his opponent and had a quick change of heart. "You know I was just funning with you Bison. I would never say anything bad about a man who makes such good Apple Juice."

Bison released his grip on Jed's shirt and went back to reading the list. All the while this was going on Wes had been watching. "Jed, why don't you take that jar you got and go out and watch over the horses."

This was an exit Jed was glad to make. Wes looked over the place and noticed a shelf that had ammunition and a couple of worn out old single-action Colts. "Say Bison, how much for the two old Colts over there?"

"Twenty dollars each, both are worn slap out. So much ammunition has run down them barrels that now the shells just rattle around a little before they drop out the end. You can take both for thirty if you want."

"You got a deal, just add them to the tab and I'll pay you in full within the week, that alright with you?" Wes asked.

Bison quickly gathered up what the six men needed and tallied up the total. "You need some shells to go along with the guns Wes?"

Add me two boxes of Colt and two boxes of Winchester and that should do us just fine."

After the shells were added the bill came to a hundred and thirty five dollars. The men picked up the supplies and headed out the door. "I'll be back in a few days to settle up Bison and as before if anyone comes by asking any questions, you ain't seen any of us in at least a month."

It was the way Wes and Bison had done business for years. It suited both just fine. Bison suspected correctly that some of what Wes and his band of misfits done was a little shy of legal. He appreciated the business and was glad to go along with any tale Wes needed told. After all, Bison had been in trouble with the law before and was in no mind of giving anyone wearing a badge any information.

The six men rode away from the trading post and headed for a spot Wes knew of where he could intercept the judge and his two deputies. He hadn't quite figured out how he was going to slow down the three men without being seen but he had twenty four hours to think about that, he was sure he would come up with something.

Judge Preston, Cecil Spriggs, Bill Adkins and Zeke Conley, traveled late into the night on Saturday. The judge knew where he wanted to make camp and wouldn't settle for anywhere else. The only problem was that the judge had only traveled this trail during daylight hours and got the four lost a couple of times before he happened up on the spot he had in mind. It was a good two hours past dark when he finally raised his hand and said, "This is it, we will camp here for the night."

Zeke looked around and had to admit the judge did know how to pick his spot. With the help of a half-moon he could see good grass for the horses and a big deadfall to use for firewood. There was a small stream nearby where the water ran clear and cold.

"Well boys, what do you think? Can I pick 'em or can I pick 'em?" the judge asked?

Cecil looked over at Preston. "You can at that Judge. Next time though, try to find something before dark. I don't fancy setting up camp after the sun goes down."

Judge Preston gave his deputy a disappointed look. "Don't tell me you are afraid of disappearing in the night same as everyone else do you Cecil?"

"I ain't afraid of nothing when the sun is shining Judge. Darkness adds another element to the problem. Let's just say I don't like the dark when there is something unknown about that is snatching people," Cecil told the judge.

As Bill tended to the horses, the judge began to work on his fire. Cecil gathered the wood and the whole time he was doing this he carried his Winchester. He looked deep into the darkness and at each sound he heard he went dead still.

"Cecil, would you put that rifle down and bring some wood for the fire." The judge had managed to get a small fire going with what few sticks he could gather that were near the camp but he really wanted some bigger stuff that Cecil was bringing.

"Sorry Judge, I thought I heard something."

"Cecil, you been hearing something ever since we pulled out of Rapid City. Are you going to be like this the entire trip?"

"Damn right I am Judge. I got me a real bad feeling about this trip, a real bad feeling."

"Well, that real bad feeling you got is going to be in your stomach if you don't get me some wood so I can fry up this salt pork, now would you please hurry. Surely if the bogie man is going to get you he will wait until after you have eaten, he might like you better if you have bacon on your breath." Preston couldn't help but laugh at what he had just said.

After the five horses were settled for the night the men went about the task of a little coffee and food. Although the four had eaten a hearty meal at the Rock Candy Café earlier that day, it had now been more than ten hours since that feast. They ate like refugees. As a matter of fact, during the meal it was decided to finish off all the pork and cathead biscuits and then leave early the next morning without breakfast. They would make it to Wiley's General Store about a couple of hours after first light.

It was decided that one man would stay awake during the night and that could be rotated between the four men in two hour shifts. The three men that weren't on guard duty would sleep better knowing that someone was awake watching over them.

The night went off without a hitch. As soon as everyone was awake the judge looked at Cecil and asked for a headcount to make sure no one had been spirited away. All four men had been standing around the fire waiting on the coffee to brew when the judge said this. Bill laughed until his side hurt which made Cecil say a few words that won't be found in the Bible.

After Cecil calmed his tongue a bit he added, "Go right ahead Bill and laugh your silly head off. When I hear something tearing into you then maybe I won't come running, I'll just walk."

Zeke noticed the judge had a keen wit and never passed up the opportunity to get a laugh. Funny how a person in the position to either hang a man or set him free was the first to find humor in any situation. Possibly the pressure of deciding the fate of a man's life made judges look at things a little differently than everyone else. Zeke had been acquainted with a few during his life and it seemed they were all quick to joke.

The four riders made it to Wiley's by eight-thirty that morning and as they hitched the horses Zeke asked, "Did you bring money Judge, I know me and these two deputies are pretty much broke?"

Judge Preston turned from his horse and said, "Don't need any at Wiley's. I just sign the tab and he sends the bill to the Rapid City Courthouse. The state will be paying for this little trip, not the county. We load up good here and on the way back we can stop back if we need anything else. I always like to take a couple of bottles of Old Grand-Dad back home with me. I keep at least a full case in Rapid City but on these court trips I get a couple of extra bottles, courtesy of the state."

"What is Old Grand-Dad Judge?" Cecil asked.

"Bourbon Cecil, the best thing that ever came out of Kentucky, with the exception of my dear departed Lula of course, God rest her soul. Tell you what; I think I'll pick us up a bottle for the trip ahead. Might just calm your nerves a bit."

The thought of Bourbon brought a smile to Cecil and Bill's faces. Just then the door to the store opened and a man of advanced age stepped out onto the porch. "Judge Preston, I don't ever remember you being here at such an early hour. Must be a trial somewhere."

"Hello Wiley. You done got me figured out. Got a trial over in Langley and not a lot of time to get there. I picked up these three hobos' along the way and deputized them." Preston looked at the three men and then added, "Don't they look nice in their little deputy outfits."

Cecil just threw up his hands. The four men and Wiley went inside and began to gather the things they would need for the trip to Langley and also the trip back to Rapid City. Zeke looked around the place and admired the merchandise Wiley had on the shelves. One thing he saw that tickled his fancy was a Light Toss. He really didn't know what a Light Toss was but it seemed to be something that might come in handy if the name had anything to do with what it was made for.

"Say Wiley, what is this?"

Wiley looked over at Zeke and seen he was holding a Light Toss. The other two deputies were looking at the funny device too.

"Something new I just got in. Basically it's a two foot long piece of sawmill wood that is planed down thin and smooth on all four sides. They then soak it in Kerosene and cover the whole thing in wax. There is one end that lacks the wax and at that end is a touch of gunpowder. Just a small touch of gunpowder at that. If you need some fast light all you do is strike a match and touch it to the end with the gunpowder. That little bit will start the wood to burning and then it burns bright and slow. You can carry it around for maybe thirty minutes before the flame gets near the end you're carrying. Something else you can do with it is light it and throw it. It will illuminate a small area for a while."

Judge Preston, who had been looking at the shelf which held his beloved Old Grand-Dad, came over and looked at the device in Zeke's hand. "How much is something like that Wiley?"

"Fifteen cents each."

"Fifteen cents, you must be joking. It's just a piece of wood and some wax, how on earth do you figure anyone in his right mind would pay an outrageous price like that?" the judge said and then added, "I'll take six."

Wiley, who was used to the antics of the judge, started laughing. "I only got five Judge, you still want 'em?"

"I do. I think something like that is a pretty good idea, might come in handy."

Wiley had a big pone of cornbread on top of the stove cooling and potatoes stewing in a thick gravy in his big cast iron pot. "Is this the special of the day Wiley?" The judge asked.

"It is Judge. If you ain't ever had potatoes cooked in gravy before then you are in for a treat. You four want to try a sample?" Wiley asked.

"No Wiley we don't. We want plates full of the stuff. The four of us hit the trail early this morning without any breakfast. What food we had was ate up last night at supper and that's another reason we got here so early," the judge said.

"Well then each of you grab one of them plates over there and bring 'em over. You hungry looking bastards are in for a treat," Wiley said.

After the four had filled a tin plate they went out on the front porch and took a seat. Wiley was right about the potatoes and gravy, it was delicious. Cecil and Bill took the wedge of cornbread they were given and crumbled it on top of the potatoes. The two deputies had eaten this concoction before and even tried to make it back in Rapid City but with not much success.

After breakfast the four men thanked Wiley and then quickly packed the rations on Hazel, before long the judge and his military escort were back on the trail.

"You figure we will get how far today Judge?" Cecil asked.

"Well, it being Sunday and all I think the horse traffic will be pretty light, we should make good time." Preston again laughed.

"Horse traffic! This is a Billy-goat trail Judge. There won't be any traffic and if there was we could just ride around it," Cecil said.

"Slow down there Cecil, I was only joking. We should make it a little past half-way and then the rest on Monday, which is tomorrow," Preston said.

"What if we run into any trouble Judge, you done said the trial has got to start Tuesday?"

"What kind of trouble Cecil? We are in the middle of nowhere. We got five strong horses and enough guns and ammunition to invade Canada."

Cecil didn't answer but everyone knew what he was talking about. Every one to a man was a little edgy due to all the strange happenings and missing men in the territory. That was enough to remind the judge of another little matter.

"Say Zeke, where was it you found that abandoned camp?"

Zeke thought a minute and said, "I figure it's about a five or six hour ride from here, pretty much in the direction we're heading now."

Cecil took out his handkerchief and dabbed his forehead. He looked nervous all of the sudden. The four rode on in silence for a while. After about three hours they came to the first campsite Zeke had made after leaving the abandoned campsite.

"This is the spot I camped that first night Judge."

Preston looked around. "Is this where you heard those crunching sounds Zeke?"

"It is. My blood runs a little cold now just thinking about it."

Cecil had his handkerchief back out and looked a little pale himself.

"We best be moving on, can't afford to waste time. It looks like whatever happened here is over and done with," the judge said.

The four men turned their horses and headed back toward the trail.

"Crunch."

Cecil damn near fell off his horse. Bill had drawn his Colt and was looking around in every direction.

"What the hell was that Judge," Cecil asked.

Preston looked at Zeke. "Is that the sound you heard the other night?"

"It is, but this time it seems closer."

Cecil was white as a sheet. "Let's tap these horses into a run, I don't want to be here," he said.

"Wait just a minute Cecil; I want to have a look. It was night time before and I was all alone. Now it's broad daylight and there are four of us," Zeke told the nervous deputy.

Bill indicated that he wanted to leave too.

"Well Judge, it looks like the other two deputies vote to leave. What do you say?"

Without a moment's hesitation the judge said, "We investigate, this is the most excitement I've had in twenty years."

Cecil said with a sour expression on his face, "Let's just hope this excitement don't snatch and eat us all."

The four men dismounted and tied the four horses to a nearby tree. Zeke and Cecil carried their Winchesters. Preston had his Navy Colt and Bill carried the Greener Shotgun.

"Crunch."

Cecil raised his Winchester and was ready to fire into the brush where the noise seemed to be coming from. Zeke put a hand on the deputy's shoulder and told him to wait.

"We don't know what is out there. What if you kill something you don't want to?"

"Right now I want to kill whatever it is that's making that sound. Believe me I won't have any regrets," Cecil said.

"Listen, whatever it is can't be more than fifty yards away. You three spread out and let me go and investigate. If I get in trouble then you can blast away, that sound alright?" Zeke asked.

Bill and Cecil looked at the judge, "Go ahead Zeke, but I can tell you right now, I'm coming with you," the judge told him.

"Alright then, Bill and Cecil spread out and stay near the horses. Me and the Judge will investigate."

"Nice knowing you two," Cecil said with a shaky voice.

Zeke and the judge spread apart about ten feet and then started easing toward the spot where the sound had come from. About halfway there Preston stopped and whispered, "Can you hear that Zeke, sounds like something is crunching on bones."

Zeke had heard it the same time the judge had. Again the two men started easing toward the noise. As they started through the undergrowth the noise continued to get louder. When they had gone thirty feet the remains of a buffalo could be seen up ahead where it had either died or been killed, half of it was lying in a small stream. Something was on the other side of the carcass and that something sounded like it was eating.

"You stay here Judge and let me swing around and get a look at whatever it is."

The judge never took his eyes off the carcass but nodded his approval. Zeke eased around very slowly until he was able to see what was making the noise. When he got to where he could see clearly he was startled at the sight before him. Without thinking he lowered his Winchester and just stood there like a statue. Judge Preston never lowered his Colt though and decided to advance to where Zeke stood. When he got there he too lowered his weapon. Both men just stood there defenseless.

"What do you think we should do Zeke?" the judge asked.

Zeke didn't answer at first. After a minute he said, "Judge, how about you going back and see if one of the deputies has a pair of fencing pliers in one of their saddlebags?"

"You think it can be saved Zeke?"

"I don't know Judge. All we can do is try."

Wes and his five gun hounds had traveled hard Sunday in order to be at the spot where the ambush would occur. It wasn't as much an ambush as it was a warning. All Wes wanted to do was slow the judge down enough so that the trial never took place on Tuesday. He had yet to figure how he would do that but he knew exactly where it would happen.

"What you got in mind for the Judge Wes? You done said we can't kill him and the two deputies. What if gunplay shows up, we just supposed to holler that we don't want to shoot back?" asked Jimmy Conn.

"I haven't quite figured that out yet. What I do know is we can't kill them and we also can't run the risk of being seen."

"Well 'bout all we can do is maybe stampede their horses. I doubt the judge and his deputy escort can walk to Langley by Tuesday," Jimmy said.

Wes looked over at Jimmy. "You know for a dumbass outlaw type, I think you might be on to something."

Jimmy only heard the compliment in what Wes had just said, he had been called a dumbass before and had kind of gotten used to it. The six men rode on in silence as Wes contemplated his plan.

"That's exactly what we'll do. As soon as the judge and his men bed down for the night we'll ride in and stampede the horses. Fire a few shots in the air to keep their heads down and then ride away," Wes said. "We should be at the place I have in mind by four or five this afternoon. We shadow the judge and find out where they intend to camp. After that we wait."

Doug Whitmore, son in law to the governor of South Dakota, sat in his jail cell Sunday and wondered how he had gotten in such a mess. Sure, he had pulled the trigger and sure, a man had been shot but it was self-defense. The real problem was that there was only one other witness and that man happened to be a friend of the man he had killed.

It all started a week before when Doug had been asked to meet two men over at the livery. He had been told that the two men were interested in selling about a hundred horses to the army and before they could get the contract they needed the backing of Whitmore's bank. It had been Whitmore's assumption that he was to be shown one of the horses to determine the quality of the stock.

Once at the livery he was met by Wes Branham and Sonny Briscoe. The two men had three horses stabled there and led Whitmore to believe that this was a sample of the hundred head that were being corralled about fifteen miles outside of town. He looked over the three horses and then told the two men that he would need to see the remainder of the herd and also the paperwork where the horses had been bought. Once that was complete his bank would agree to be the intermediary for the deal. All the money would be handled by Langley Trust. Whitmore turned to leave the livery and go back to his office.

Just as he was about to leave the stable Sonny Briscoe told him to stop. Sonny then walked up to Whitmore and slapped him around a bit. He had been told by Wes to rough up the banker over a bad business deal he had put on one of Wes Branham's friends, which was a lie. There really wasn't a friend or a business deal. Wes had been told what to do by Lloyd Shafer and to make sure that Briscoe was killed in the stable and the blame put on Whitmore.

When it looked like Briscoe was going for his gun Whitmore clumsily pulled his own Colt and fired. Briscoe went down with a perfectly placed bullet right between his eyes. Whitmore didn't even look at Wes Branham he just turned and hurried back to his office. It was self-defense and when the sheriff came he was sure Branham would say as much. It wasn't to be.

Within the hour the sheriff came to the bank and arrested him on the charge of murder.

This had all happened on Sunday September 25th. Now one week later Whitmore was two days away from a trial where, if found guilty, he would be hung in the very town he called home. He had spent the remainder of that first Sunday in a jail cell consumed by confusion and despair. He was innocent which was the root cause of his confusion; and he was facing a death sentence which brought on the despair. The next day he was brought a telegram sent to him by a friend from Rapid City. The message said that Lloyd Shafer had agreed to prosecute Whitmore and practically guaranteed a quick guilty verdict and an even quicker hanging. The friend let Whitmore know that Shafer was a cousin of the deceased and had information that proved the killing was motivated by Whitmore's hate for the Shafer family.

Whitmore had heard of the Shafer Law Firm and knew of their trial successes. He harbored no hate for the Shafer's, even though they owned a bank that had been in competition at times with Whitmore's bank. If he had considered everything that had happened to him in those previous days then he might have taken a step back and considered the possibility that Shafer might be part of the problem instead of only being the newly appointed prosecutor. At any rate the trial was less than two days away and Whitmore's attorney had agreed to meet him on this Sunday before the trial. The train that was bringing Shafer to Langley was due to be at the depot at three that afternoon and Whitmore hoped beyond hope that Shafer wouldn't be on it. He was wrong.

Shafer's train arrived at the precise time of three o'clock that Sunday afternoon. He had no intention of coming to the town's jail to meet with the accused on Sunday even though that had always been his custom. He liked to talk to the man he was to prosecute without that man's attorney present. It wasn't exactly ethical but Lloyd Shafer never took ethics that seriously anyway. He doubted he would even go there on Monday, the last full day before the trial. He would use his time Sunday to check into the finest hotel in town and to have a pleasant meal before turning in for the night. Shafer had a lot to do and plan for and the trial wasn't in those plans. Sure he would benefit from the trial either way, acquittal or death penalty. As he figured it, why make preparations when either outcome suited his future plans just fine.

As it worked out one of the deputies did have a pair of fencing pliers, Cecil always kept them in a saddlebag to repair some of the corrals that were attached to Lester Fitch's stables. Although Cecil and Lester seemed to always be ready for a fight, the two had actually known each other since childhood. Not only that, but Lester was a distant cousin and neither really meant the bad things they said to each other. When Cecil had any spare time on his hands he helped out at the livery and the two actually enjoyed insulting each other. Lester needed the free help and Cecil enjoyed the free food that was always offered. After the fence mending was finished around the stables Lester always invited Cecil to supper. Dead broke deputies never turned down free food, especially the kind that Evelene Fitch could put on a table.

Judge Preston came back to the buffalo carcass and asked Zeke how the two should proceed. Cecil had tied out the horses and came over to see what it was the judge and Zeke were doing. When the two deputies seen what had been chewing the guts out of a dead buffalo, the two just stood there speechless.

"Judge, what do you think that is?" Bill asked.

Whatever it was slowly turned its head and looked at the four men.

"Best me and Zeke can tell from here is it might be a dog," the judge said.

"Are you sure Judge, as starved as that thing is I still never seen a dog that big before," Cecil told him.

Zeke took the fence pliers from the judge and said, "It's a dog. I think it's been caught in a snare of some sort."

All four men looked at the so called dog. It was big, that was for sure. It had long, darkish, brown hair, tinted with black in places. The coat was matted with dirt and gore. There were strands of barbed wire tangled in the coat and it appeared the animal had become trapped in the snare some time back. It looked like the animal had managed to pull the post the snare was attached to completely out of the ground and had been dragging the whole thing around while trying to find food and water. Apparently, when it found the dead buffalo, it had saved the animals life. By the fact that the buffalo had died and fell into the stream it had provided both food and water without the poor animal having to drag around that fence post. The sad thing was that the buffalo had been dead for quite some time. All it looked like was a hide draped over bones.

Zeke looked at the sight and felt a tremendous amount of sadness for the dog. There had always been dogs on the farm while he was growing up, but in all his life he had never seen one in such shape. The barbed wire of the snare had bit into the animals flesh and that was where some of the blood had come from on the coat. The rest was where the dog had chewed into the buffalo's remains and continued to naw its way inside as the days went by. Water was only a foot away so the dog must have just stayed in this spot for days. There really wasn't anything left of the buffalo except some scraps of hide here and there, and the bones. The dog had mainly been tearing away the bones and then chewing and crunching away trying to get some nourishment. It really hadn't been much.

"So that is what the crunching sound was I heard a few days back. It was this dog tearing the ribs out of that buffalo. Makes me feel pretty bad knowing I was this close and didn't come to help," Zeke said.

"Come to help, you can't be serious Zeke. If you go anywhere near that monster, then you're liable to be a side dish to that buffalo it's been gnawing on. I mean look at what it has done to the underside of that dead buffalo," Cecil said with no small amount of disgust.

The animal was partially inside the buffalo. It had been there for days and had eaten many of the smaller bones. That was part of the reason the dog was so hard to recognize, it was a gory mess. Apparently when it happened upon the buffalo carcass it was at the end of it strength. The fence post had wedged between two trees nearby and this was the end of the line for the big dog. Once the buffalo was gone that was it.

Judge Preston looked at Zeke and asked, "You think he's friendly? What I can see of his coat makes me think he's some sort of wolf. I say we feed him and then make a decision on whether we can cut him loose or not."

Cecil gave the judge a sour look. "That's real damn funny Judge."

Zeke looked at the judge and then back at the dog. "Tell you what Judge, how about I go over and try to cut him loose. If he seems unfriendly or dangerous in any way I'll stop."

Cecil said, "If you can't get him loose then what do you plan to do, we can't just leave him here snared like he is."

Zeke never answered Cecil's question, he didn't want to think that far ahead right now.

"Judge, how about you keep a Winchester handy in case I get into trouble," Zeke said.

"You're out of your mind Zeke, that thing might have rabies for all you know. And at the least he's a wild animal. You are about to get yourself chewed a new one. Hell, it's big enough to kill you," Bill told him.

Zeke told the three men to keep silent so as not to agitate the dog. He then slowly made his way toward the animal, all the while taking slow deliberate steps. The dog, which had gone back to crunching bones noticed Zeke coming toward him and slowly turned his head toward the man. Its face and neck was completely covered in gore and all you could see were the two dark eyes.

Zeke had made it to within ten feet and was starting to see the poor judgement he had used in attempting to rescue this animal. The closer he got the bigger the dog looked, it was enormous. Just when he was about to stop and re-evaluate his plan he noticed the dog open its mouth and start to pant. Then he noticed the tail start to slap the ground, although very slowly. It was as if the dog was glad to see him. Could he really be friendly or was he just baiting Zeke in for the kill.

Zeke continued to ease very slowly toward the dog all the time ready to jump away if needed. When he was an arm's length away he slowly made a fist and reached it toward the dog. Better to have a bitten hand than a lost finger. He thought this was a bad idea as he looked at the size of the dog's mouth; it could tear off his hand entirely. Just when he was ready to pull his fist back the dog reached over and licked it. He continued to lick as Zeke stood like a statue.

"He's friendly Zeke," Judge Preston said.

"You don't know that Judge; he might just be seeing what Zeke tastes like," Cecil added.

Zeke slowly pulled the pliers from his pocket and wondered if the dog would show aggression when he seen them. He didn't. Zeke eased a little closer and started snipping the strands of fifteen and a half gauge wire as easily as he could. The strands that stood out an inch or two from the big dog were what he went after first. As he snipped he threw the pieces to the side. Some that were left were tangled in the matted coat of the big dog. Zeke used his pocket knife, the one he also used to cut up his supper each night, to cut the bloody hair away from the snare. The strand that was around one of the back legs was the worst. It had cut into the upper thigh almost at the hip. The wound had started to get infected and it looked like the wire was actually inside the dogs flesh.

Zeke knew this was the part where he stood the most chance of being attacked when he tried to remove the wire. After snipping both sides of the wire he gently pulled the wire out of the injury. The dog howled and moaned but made no effort to bite Zeke. Once the wire was out, he worked on the part of the snare that was around the dog's powerful chest and neck. It took nearly ten minutes to completely free the dog. Zeke was covered in sweat from both the exertion and the fear of working on such a large predator. The smell had a lot to do with it to, it was truly enough to make a lesser man faint. Zeke hoped the smell of dead flesh was more to do with the buffalo than the dog's wounds.

After he snipped and removed the last of the wire he stood and took a couple of steps back. The big dog made an effort to stand but was too weak and eased back down into the muck and gore.

"Zeke, I think he must have some broken bones. It looks like you freed him but he still can't move," Cecil said.

The judge looked at Zeke; he was covered in sweat and blood. "Now what are we going to do?"

Zeke wondered where the judge got the word we from, nobody had done anything so far except himself.

"I'm probably going to carry him out," Zeke said.

The three men looked at Zeke and then at the big dog. Before anyone could speak Zeke went over and patted him on the head. When he felt he had regained his strength, and his nerve, he reached under the dog and with all his might he slowly picked him up. The dog, in his weakened condition, still had to weigh well over a hundred pounds. What was under the dog was now all over Zeke and he was afraid he was going to be sick. What kept him from being sick was the fear that the big dog would snatch him by the throat as he carried him toward the spot where the horses were tied out.

As Zeke carried the dog the fifty feet to where the horses stood, it moaned and cried out a time or two. He gently placed the dog on the ground and took a step back. His clothes were covered in blood and gore. The smell that had once been the domain of the dog and buffalo now included Zeke, and it was truly awful.

"Zeke, that dog can't even walk. You only cut him free so he can die up here. He'll never make it on his own," Cecil said.

Zeke looked over and only smiled. "Don't tell me you want to take him with us. He can't even walk," Bill added.

"No, I don't plan on taking him with us; I plan on staying here a couple or three days until he can travel."

Now the judge spoke, "I know what you're thinking Zeke and I will leave that decision up to you. I want to warn you though that whatever it is out here snatching men and mules will probably come after you if you are alone."

"I know that Judge but I was alone out here last week and made it all right. Maybe my luck will hold this week too."

"If I heard you correctly when you told us about last week you were terrified. You said you were grateful when you finally made it to town," Cecil added.

"That's right, but look at him. He will die for sure if someone don't stay here and doctor his wounds. If whatever is out there comes a calling then I plan to blow its damn head off." Zeke said this with anger in his voice. He truly meant what he said.

"The three of you take what supplies you need for tonight. You'll be in Langley late tomorrow and I will meet you there before the trial is over. Leave me Hazel and some extra bacon. I got some liniment in my saddle bags and I intend to patch this dog up, hot water to clean the wounds and liniment to dress them with. I can even make a poultice or two from some of the plants I've seen around here."

The judge hated to leave Zeke behind but felt the young man could handle himself, hell he had spent two nights out here just the previous week. "Cecil, how about you and Bill get what we need off Hazel. Leave that cooker so Zeke can heat the water for the dog's wounds."

Bill tried one more time to convince Zeke to abandon the dog. "Zeke don't do this. Out here ain't no place for a man by himself. That thing you are calling a dog has done been dead a week and just don't know it yet."

Zeke reached over and patted the big dog. "Done been dead a week. Done been dead a week. Been, I think that's what I'm going to call him. Ben."

When Cecil and Bill heard this they knew it was no use. Zeke would stay here and do what he could for the beast and there was no talking him out of it. Within thirty minutes the judge and the two deputies had what they needed out of the packs that Hazel carried. Before they left they helped Zeke set up a camp a couple hundred yards upstream from the remains of the buffalo carcass. At that distance the remains could neither be seen nor smelled. The last to be moved was Ben. The entire time the men had been preparing the camp the dog had just slept where Zeke had laid him when he brought him from the stream. Zeke, as gently as possible, picked up the big dog and carried him to the new camp. By the time he placed him about ten feet from where the fire would be he was exhausted and drenched in sweat.

Hazel and Rusty were tied out with long leads where they could approach the camp and also make it to water. There was good grass nearby so the two horses were as content as sheep.

"Zeke, we left enough to see you through for three or four days I figure. I left you three of them Light Toss sticks we got back at Wiley's. You still dead set on staying here to see to that big dog?" the judge asked.

Zeke stood up from where he had been inspecting the wounds on Ben." Judge, I might regret it but I just can't abandon this animal, especially with what he has been through." He looked over the items that were left to him and seen that the three men had left him nearly all the bacon they had, along with a small bucket he needed to carry water.

"Thanks for leaving the bacon. I plan on making up a thin stew for Ben. My paw helped mend an old dog back to health years ago. I plan on doing the same now," Zeke said.

"Well I wish you the best of luck. Don't you turn your back on this place or you might not make it, you know the peril that stirs in these parts Zeke," Cecil said.

With that the judge and the two deputies headed out for Langley. Zeke watched them go. His plan was to stay here for at least three days to let the dog get his strength and then find his way to Langley and the trial that the judge would be holding. With any luck he would be there before it was over. Suddenly he felt a chill, the realization of three days here alone had just hit hard, and it wasn't pleasant.

First thing was to gather wood and build a fire. With bucket in hand he went to the stream and brought back water and put it on the fire to heat using the cooker that had been left. He scrubbed his hands and arms in the stream and then with his pocket knife he cut up a small amount of bacon into very tiny pieces. He threw that in the pot and when it began to boil he stirred in some flour and a pinch of salt. He removed the pot and let the concoction thicken a little. When it cooled enough he poured a little onto a plate, one he was sure he would never eat out of again, and sat it in front of Ben.

The dog had been sleeping again but when Zeke put the food in front of him he opened his eyes and slowly raised his head. Zeke slid the tin plate a little closer. The dog took a sniff, sampled the food and then quickly licked the plate clean. Zeke put out some more and the dog did the same. After that Ben put his head down and lay there looking at Zeke. The friendship was sealed.

For the next hour Zeke carried water and warmed it slightly to wash as much of the dogs coat as he could. There was no telling what the side looked like where Ben lay on the ground and Zeke wasn't going to try to turn him over, that would happen when Ben wanted it to. Once finished he took the extra horse blanket he always carried and put it on the other side of the fire. He again gently picked Ben up and carried him over and placed him on the blanket.

Now that the dog was in a dry spot Zeke tended to the wounds that had been inflicted by the snare. A couple looked bad and to those he applied all he had, horse liniment. When he got time in a little while he would concoct a poultice and apply that to the worst of the wounds.

This had not only exhausted Zeke but also Ben; the dog had fallen asleep again while his injuries were being looked after. The big dog had some food in his stomach, his coat cleaned and his wounds treated as best as could be expected under the circumstances. Zeke still wondered if the dog had any broken bones but as far as he could tell there weren't any. The legs seemed alright other than thin from lack of food. There isn't much nourishment available from a buffalo's skeleton and hide.

Zeke spent the remainder of the afternoon gathering firewood and cleaning himself up. The shirt he had worn while rescuing Ben was thoroughly washed in the stream and hung out on the limb of a deadfall to dry. He walked around shirtless as he gathered the firewood and looked over what would be his home for the next three days. After completing this he stripped and washed himself in the same stream. He scrubbed his pants and then put them back on. The pants really needed to be hung near the fire to dry but he refused to walk around naked. He did convince himself to leave his gun belt off, no need to get the leather wet. Hazel and Rusty had used the time to crop grass and swat flies. While Zeke was naked in the stream trying to wash his pants he was sure Rusty was laughing at him, damn horse.

About an hour before dark Zeke decided to have a look around the campsite. He picked up his Winchester and went off into the brush. He wanted to know the lay of the land so he would be better prepared if trouble presented itself in the middle of the night. Darkness could actually be your friend if you knew the terrain. There were quite a few deadfalls around and they all seemed to be laying in the same direction. This would indicate some sort of strong wind, maybe a tornado. He noted the gullies, rises and depressions in the ground. The main thing he wanted to see was if the ground was soft enough to indicate footprints. In the spots where it was he saw one set of tracks that looked like a coyote, nothing else. The ground was either hard packed or rock, not good if he tried to follow anything that might pay him a visit in the night. Then he laughed at himself, do spooks leave tracks?

Zeke returned to the fire and began to make another thin bacon stew for Ben. The big dog was still sleeping soundly and this was good, what Zeke lacked in medicine could hopefully be compensated for with rest. He would feed him small portions every few hours and in a few days maybe he would have regained enough of his strength to follow the two horses on into the town of Langley. There he would find a good animal doctor and see that the big dog was brought back to health.

Ben awoke as soon as Zeke put the plate back in front of him. Again the big dog licked the pan clean. He was given fresh water from the stream and within minutes he was back asleep. The dog's coat was dry and now it looked a deep brown with black tips. This surely had to be some sort of wolf mix, yet Zeke had never seen a wolf this big before. He had seen some dogs that were half wolf and half Shepherd and they were big but still not as big as Ben. Also the dogs that were part wolf were not very friendly. Ben seemed to be friendlier than most people, probably smarter too.

Finally around ten that night Zeke decided to have some supper himself. He grabbed the skillet from his pack and started to fry up some bread and beans, along with strong hot coffee. He rarely drank his coffee this late at night but decided he needed it to stay awake, no sleeping after dark for Zeke now that his three companions had headed on toward Langley. He wouldn't have any of the bacon; that would be saved for his patient.

As he ate he wondered where Ben had originated from and how long he had been pulling around the snare and fence post. He noticed that Hazel had taken a keen interest in the big dog. She would come over as far as her lead would allow and look at Ben. This gave Zeke an idea. He got up and untied the end of the lead and gave it some slack. Hazel didn't hesitate; she walked over and put her head down near Ben.

Ben woke from his sleep and looked up at the big green-eyed horse. Hazel wasn't afraid of the dog; it was as if the two knew each other. What happened next answered that question. Ben raised his head and began to lick Hazel on the end of the nose. Hazel gently nudged the big dog as if to make him get up but he was in no shape. The horse turned and looked at me and then went back to where Rusty was standing. This was truly a mystery. A horse found tied up in an abandoned camp and a dog found hung up in a snare and it seemed the two knew each other.

Zeke sat back down and wondered how long he would be here. The place really gave him a bad case of the scares. Ben had now had two meals although they were really more like snacks. He had been cleaned up considerably and his wounds treated. Zeke intended to feed him the thin stew every three hours during the night. Hopefully by morning he would feel like trying to get up.

About three o'clock in the morning Zeke was feeling the strain of trying to stay awake. It had been more than twenty hours now that he had been awake and lack of sleep was starting to get painful. He needed something to wake himself up and, unknown to him at the time, that was what he was about to get.

Around three-thirty Zeke heard Hazel snort. The big horse had been quiet and still for the better part of an hour but now was alert with head held high. Rusty too was suddenly on edge. He stepped closer to Hazel and was looking off into the darkness wide eyed.

Zeke stood and ratcheted a shell into his Winchester. The sound woke Ben, the big dog raised his head and to Zeke's surprise his ears were up, the big dog was showing a little energy but so far hadn't done more than that. Zeke looked in the same direction that the horses were looking when he noticed Ben was looking in the opposite direction. Maybe the big dog was a little disoriented due to the effects of his injuries and also his meager diet while trapped by the snare. At any rate Zeke chanced a look in the same direction that had Ben's attention. There was movement in the darkness.

Suddenly Hazel snorted again and Zeke had no choice but to look in her direction, again he saw movement in the darkness just outside the reach of the firelight. Whatever was out there wasn't just one, there were two and maybe more, and they had him surrounded. The two horses were starting to pull against their leads.

Zeke suddenly remembered the Light Toss sticks that Wiley had sold the judge. He grabbed one from near his saddle but waited. Whatever it was had moved back into the darkness. The two horses had settled down a bit but were still nervous and alert.

All was quiet. Ben was still looking around but hadn't tried to get up, if he even could. Suddenly both horses bolted and ran the distance of their leads and then ran back. This time Ben raised up on his front paws and let out a tremendous growl, the big dog had a set of lungs on him. Whatever it was jumped from cover and ran into the night. Zeke quickly stuck the end of the Light Toss into the fire and after it caught he threw it with all his might toward the last spot where he had seen movement.

What he saw next sent a shiver down his spine. He raised the big Winchester and sent three shots in fast succession at that spot then turned and loosed three more in the opposite direction. He had drawn the Colt and held it in his right hand with the Winchester in his left, both ready to fire. He backed against a tree and waited for the end, as he waited he kept repeating to himself, 'Monsters.'

After Judge Preston and the two deputies left Zeke they headed toward the town of Langley at a fast pace. The three men never said much as the miles clicked by. All were thinking about the chances young Conley had out here all alone. Cecil and Bill were wondering what their chances were too. Everyone was on edge and the sooner they made it to town the better.

That night the three camped in a spot the judge had used before. He liked the spot for a number of reasons. Good water for his coffee and also for the horses. Good grass, but this was only for the horses he thought to himself with a chuckle, and a good view of the surrounding area. Cecil and Bill hated the site.

"Shouldn't we stake our claim to a more defensible position Judge? I don't like all this openness," Cecil said.

"I agree with Cecil on this one Judge, we are right out in the open here," Bill added.

"Now what are you two so worried about? There are three of us. How would you like to be in Zeke's shape tonight, all alone?" The judge said.

"Well that was Zeke's decision; he should have abandoned that big dog and came along with us, the shape the poor thing was in I doubt it will survive anyway. I liked our chances better when he was riding with us. Remember, he done spent three nights in these parts alone and survived," Bill said.

Cecil agreed with Bill, said four men were better than three. "Well, I do have to agree with your math Cecil, but if anything is out there then the three of us will just have to handle it, but if you two are so damn set on finding a better spot then I reckon we can move. I just thought it would be better here with the view and all, hard for anyone to sneak up on us."

Finally Cecil and Bill relented. Maybe the judge had a point. If trouble did come calling tonight it would have a hard time finding any cover other than the tall grass the horses were picketed in. The three men made their camp and enjoyed a supper of skillet bread and beans. The judge particularly liked trail food. Whether it was the food or the atmosphere he didn't know, it always seemed food tasted better out of doors. The three spread out their blankets and took turns during the night standing guard. Little did they know that by sun-up there would be only two left to make the journey on into Langley.

Monday at noon Lloyd Shafer was eating his lunch at a diner in Langley called the Longhorn Café. He had eaten there on previous occasions and found the food to be well prepared and the service was also to his liking. He particularly enjoyed the baked Trout that was caught in the cold streams coming off the mountains. As he sat and ate he scanned the streets for any sign of the judge. He doubted if Preston could have made it to town today at such an early hour, which is assuming he never met any unfortunate mishaps on his trip in. Shafer knew a mishap had been planned for the judge and wondered just how Wes and his crew of hard cases intended on slowing down the judge and his deputies. Wes was dependable but there was always the chance that something might have gone wrong. Shafer put these thoughts out of his head; Wes would know how to slow down the judge's party. This time tomorrow the case should be dismissed and the governor's son-in-law would most likely be lynched before dark.

Shafer should be spending the day before the trial working on the case against the accused. Why bother, Doug Whitmore had been set up from the beginning and now Shafer was just biding his time until the man was hung by an angry mob and the sterling reputation of the territory's governor was stained a bit by the event. Instead of thinking about a trial that in all likelihood would never take place he was considering the upcoming campaign he would wage against the governor, one in which he would use the lynching as proof of the governor's disreputable family.

As all these thoughts played out in his mind as Wes Branham, minus his gang, rode into town. Shafer placed two dollars on the table to cover his meal and went outside to hear how Wes had dealt with Judge Preston.

"Well Branham, I never expected to see you in town so early," Shafer said in a low voice.

Wes stepped down from his horse and looked at Shafer. "Didn't find the judge Lloyd, we waited at a spot in the trail and he never came through. This morning at a little after sunup I left the men to look for the judge and his deputies and then rode hard to get here to see how you wanted to handle things. They were told to find the judge's party and pen them down with long distance rifle fire. I stressed that neither he nor the deputies were to be harmed, just shaken up and prevented from making town in time for the trial." Wes also spoke in hushed tones as to not let anybody know what they were saying.

Shafer thought this over and then said, "Let's head over to the saloon and get a table. I need to consider this new development." With that the two men headed across the street to a saloon that had lots of room and plenty of tables where two men could talk without raising any suspicions.

Zeke spent the remainder of the night standing guard. He listened for any sounds and watched for any movement. The fire was allowed to slowly burn down to embers for two reasons. First, to allow Zeke's eyes to adjust to the darkness and second, he didn't want to be outlined by the firelight. Whatever was out there could see him but he couldn't see them in return. The Winchester was reloaded to replace the six rounds that were fired earlier. The Colt was loaded with six cartridges instead of the usual five. When things were a little less tense he never let the hammer rest on a round, that cylinder was always left empty. Now though the darkness of night and the shadows of day contained danger, every bullet was important.

When the sky began to brighten at around six-thirty the next morning Zeke was exhausted. His muscles were stiff and tired from both lack of sleep and tension. Ben had gone back to sleep almost as soon as whatever it was had ran back into the darkness. Both horses had calmed considerably shortly after the excitement had ended.

Zeke knew it was time for Ben to get his bacon and gravy. The big dog had eaten at three o'clock that morning shortly, before the visit by the creature, or creatures, that had tried to invade the camp. Zeke quickly stirred the ashes that remained of the fire and found some embers which he fed with some small dry twigs. Before long he had coffee going and doggie gruel in the pot. Ben never moved until Zeke slid the tin plate close to his nose. The big dog opened his eyes and raised his head. He made no attempt to get up but again managed to eat everything that was presented to him. Zeke checked his wounds and noticed they didn't look any worse than the day before. They actually had started to dry and some of the redness had gone away.

As Zeke made his own breakfast Ben watched. Once finished he took over a piece of skillet bread to see if the dog could handle anything solid. After it cooled a bit Ben scooped it up and then devoured the entire piece in one bite.

"I think you're going to be alright big fella, that is assuming we all don't get eaten ourselves." After he said this he stood and looked around the camp. Hazel and Rusty were both cropping grass and didn't seem to have a worry in the world. It was the two horses that had caught the scent of trouble the night before, especially Hazel. Ben hadn't stirred until after whatever was out there had already surrounded the camp. He was in such bad shape he couldn't spot trouble until it was already on him. That would change once he started to get his health back. It did seem that when he had let out that vicious growl the previous night that whatever was out there had made a hasty getaway. Maybe whatever it was didn't like the sound of a dog, especially one that could let out such a thunderous throaty growl.

"Three more days," Zeke said to himself as he stood and looked around. The thought was truly sobering. It would be bad enough for anybody what was well rested, he certainly wasn't. He was past tired and damn near falling asleep on his feet. He picked up the rifle and headed off into the brush and timber, a little movement on his part might just wake him up a bit. As he silently circled his camp he was keeping a close watch on the horses and Ben. No need to let them out of his sight. Zeke was a pretty good tracker and thought he could find evidence of what had been there the night before. He didn't, there wasn't even a broken twig to indicate the presence of what he had gotten a glimpse of in the darkness.

He returned to the fire and thought of his circumstance. He was at least a day and a half from the town of Langley, and that was at a fast pace. He was alone in a land that he barely knew and there was something here that was taking men and leaving no trace of what it was. And now it was hunting him.

Zeke walked over and patted Ben who for the moment had fallen back asleep. He was in a bad spot. Exhausted as he was he knew sleep would soon overtake him. Sleep meant death. This thought was terrifying. The best thing to do was to put some miles between himself and this place, he was sure that whatever had tried to invade camp the night before would be back as soon as daylight gave way to darkness. Would he really stay here and possibly lose his life trying to protect a dog he had just stumbled upon the day before.

A stubborn feeling began to grow inside him. At first he was hesitant to admit that he was afraid. Then he thought of the fact that he had not felt fear at this level since he was a small child. He stood up from Ben and looked around again. Zeke Conley was a man of action, always had been. He decided that he wasn't going to stay here and wait for whatever it was that was hunting him to return in the night when he was most vulnerable. He was going to load up and move on; hopefully the prey could stay one step ahead of the hunter.

Now the problem was to figure out a way to move Ben. Zeke had decided shortly after releasing the big dog from the snare that he would see him back to health. As he stood and considered the problem Hazel again walked over to the end of her lead and put her head down near the dog. She gently nudged him, not enough to cause pain but enough to wake him up. Again Ben raised his head and began to lick the big horse on the end of the nose. These two were not strangers. The two had known each other at some point in their past. She seemed at times curious as to why he wasn't up and moving around and at other times protective of the big dog.

As Zeke stood and watched the two he had an idea. Ben wasn't afraid of Hazel and she wasn't afraid of him. If he could somehow fix a flat spot on top of the pack that Hazel had been carrying and then put the big dog on top he might be able to travel. He could loosely tie the dog so he wouldn't fall off. Hazel wouldn't mind if Ben rode on top of the pack and Ben would probably be too weak to protest. He would saddle Rusty and lead Hazel with the big dog safely on top.

It was nearly nine in the morning when Zeke finally got the camp all loaded up and the pack positioned on the back of Hazel. He had arranged his supplies, meager as they were, so as to leave a flat spot on the very top. On this he put the horse blanket that Ben had used for his bed. When he had Rusty all saddled up and everything was ready to go he walked over and patted Ben. The dog had been watching the activities of the morning and it almost seemed as if he knew something was up.

Zeke gently picked up the big dog and carried him to where Hazel was tied. With a mighty heave he placed the dog on top of the pack. Ben looked around from his high perch and started panting. He wasn't nervous and seemed to be pleased by the fact that he was going to ride along on the back of a horse that he knew. Hazel even reached her head around and snorted at the big dog as if to say, 'Stay still and enjoy the trip.' Zeke took his rope and gently tied a few loops across the dog so he wouldn't move and fall off. When he finished he patted Hazel and then looked over his creation. He was quiet pleased, first at having the big dog mobile and second at being able to leave this valley and everything in it behind.

As Zeke climbed into the saddle on Rusty he had a strange feeling. He sat there for a second looking around. After a long pause it dawned on him as to what he felt; he was being watched. He pulled the Winchester from the gun boot and put it across the saddle. His fear of this place was now replaced by anger. He decided then and there that if his end was near then he would meet it with courage. Whatever was stalking him surely couldn't survive the power of a Winchester .45 .75, nothing could. As he pulled out of camp with the two horses and Ben tied on top of the pack Hazel carried, he scanned the area and decided that someday, if he survived, he would pay this place another visit and do a little hunting of his own.

Within minutes Ben had lowered his head and was sound asleep. Hazel seemed to take the utmost of care now that she carried an old friend. She never changed her pace or her gate, slow and steady was the rule now. At times she turned her head back to check on the dog. Zeke was extremely pleased with his idea. He knew he had to go extremely slow as not to shake Ben off the top of the pack and also to not irritate his injuries. The main thing now was that they were moving. He estimated they were covering about three or four miles an hour and should, with any luck, put twenty five miles between himself and his previous campsite by nightfall. Who was he kidding, it wasn't the previous campsite he was running from, it was from whatever had begun to hunt him. Zeke would settle that score someday but it would be on his own terms.

He stopped twice during the day to allow the horses to get water at small streams. While they drank he gave Ben small sips of water from his plate and also some small strips of tender bacon. A proper meal of doggie gruel would be prepared after they made camp at night fall. Zeke and the two horses took advantage of any hard packed areas they travelled as to not leave any sign. There were even some portions of the trail that were solid rock and this left no sign at all. Whatever it was back there would need to use a sense of smell to follow the horses.

As the day grew late Zeke began looking for a spot to camp. It had been more than thirty-six hours since he had last slept and he knew that unless he found a safe place in case he dozed off during the night he may never wake up again. It would be his second night of guard duty and he told himself he could do it, he must. If he did sleep it would be the nervous half sleep that came in five minute portions. Sleep is something that takes over and invades your awareness whether you like it or not.

About a half hour before dark they came across another of the small streams that were so abundant in this area. Zeke picked a spot that had some high grasses that the horses would like and fresh flowing water near a big deadfall. He sat his saddle and took in the terrain. It was good. He had a good view in any direction with only the occasional stand of trees here and there.

The first item to be unloaded was Ben. He never complained as Zeke lifted him from the top of the pack and placed him near the spot where the fire would be built. He seemed to be a little better than he had been that morning; no doubt he rested well as he was rocked back and forth by the big horse. He had been as content as a baby in a crib the entire day.

Ben didn't go back to sleep as he lay near the newly built fire and watched Zeke prepare his doggie gruel. He even managed to slap his tail up and down on the ground. As before, he ate his thin bacon gravy, except this time he seemed to want more. Zeke quickly made up another batch and sat it down in front of the big dog. He devoured every bite and then drank from the bucket that Zeke carried over.

As Zeke sat and ate his skillet bread and beans Ben watched him with begging eyes. Zeke finally gave up and took what was left of his supper and put it on Ben's plate. The big dog ate this and then lay his head down and within minutes was sound asleep. He was getting a little strength back and definitely a strong appetite. Zeke sat near the fire with his back to a big tree. The Winchester was always within reach, twenty five miles was a good distance from the events of the previous night but it wasn't a guarantee. Whatever was back there was hopefully still back there.

As darkness settled over the valley the sky took on an orangey glow. Clouds were thin and sparse and energized by the beams of a half moon. The coffee pot was refilled and set in the remains of the supper fire. As the flames died down, not to be fed for the remainder of the night, the smell of coffee drifted through camp. Zeke intended to sip on the contents of the pot until the next morning. If he did drift off to sleep then he hoped it would be the one or two minute catnaps that would refresh a man. It was a sort of one eye open, one eye closed kind of sleep that would warn him of danger if needed. No sleep at all was the safest but he knew two sleepless nights in a row was just too much to hope for.

Judge Preston woke up early on Monday morning hoping to put one more good day of riding under their belt, which would accomplish the goal of making it to Langley for the trial that was to start first thing Tuesday morning. It was still a good thirty minutes before sunrise and he wanted to hit the trail shortly after. He stood and stretched. Cecil was still sound asleep in his blankets. Preston took a stick and poked the fire which was about out. He had taken first watch the night before and Bill had agreed to take second with Cecil last. What the hell!

"Wake up Cecil, wake up," the judge shouted.

Cecil woke up with a start and threw back the blanket. He had his Colt in his hand and it was pointed at Preston. The judge jumped back.

"Put that damn gun away before you shoot me. Did Bill wake you for your watch last night?"

Cecil stood and tried to gather his bearings. "No Judge. I must have slept through the night. Nobody woke me."

Judge Preston grabbed his gun and tried to organize his thoughts. "When was the last time you seen him."

"Maybe right before I fell asleep. You had woke him up when your watch was over. I immediately went back to sleep because I knew my shift started in three hours. I never stirred again until you screamed at me," Cecil said.

"I didn't scream at you, and anyway if I was a bit loud it was to overcome your loud snoring," Preston said.

Cecil put his Colt away and grabbed his shotgun. After checking the loads of the Greener he hollered out, "Bill, you out there." He then looked over at the judge and added, "Maybe he's off in the trees taking care of business."

"Stop shouting Cecil until we figure out what's going on here."

"I think we know what's going on Judge, he's been taken just like everyone else that has traveled these parts," Cecil said as he scanned the surrounding area.

The two men made a quick search around the camp but never got out of sight of the horses. After determining that Bill was gone without a trace, the two came back to the fire. Judge Preston made a pot of coffee and then grabbed the skillet.

"Don't tell me Judge that you intend on eating at a time like this."

Preston stirred the ashes of the fire with a stick before turning to Cecil. "Yes, that is exactly what I am going to do. The worst thing to do now is to ride out of camp in the dark and hope to survive. We wait here and have some coffee and breakfast. When it is good and light we load up and head for Langley, that is after we have done a more thorough search of the area."

Cecil had started to calm down a bit. The judge didn't look nervous or afraid and this helped to calm the deputy. Judge Preston might not have looked out of sorts on the outside but he was both shocked and a bit scared at the thought of losing one of his deputies. He liked Bill and now he was gone.

The two drank their coffee and had some beans and bread as they watched the sun slowly rise into view. Once finished they loaded the two horses and then mounted up.

"On the way out let's look for any sign of what might have happened during the night," Preston said.

The two riders circled the camp in an ever widening loop but nothing could be found of the missing deputy and there was no evidence of what might have taken place. It was as if he had just been taken away by a winged beast. There were no footprints or signs of a struggle, no blood or torn shreds of clothing, nothing. The two men, once convinced that Bill was truly gone, turned their horses and headed for Langley. The quicker they made town the better. The judge was as frightened as Cecil but he managed to contain his fear on the inside. All his years of being a judge had allowed him to maintain a convincing poker face.

The two men traveled until dark and then talked over their options.

"I don't like traveling after dark Judge. We could be easily set upon before we knew what was going on," Cecil said.

The judge looked around at the ever darkening landscape. "Cecil, the trail runs on for maybe eight or ten more miles. The horses can see as well after dark as you or me can see in daylight."

"I don't like it Judge. We are traveling blind." Cecil was so concerned with the fear of the moment, which was being overtaken by another fear as the two rode, that he hadn't even considered the alternative, staying all-night out in the open again. The judge immediately pointed that out.

"Cecil, think about what you are saying. If we stop here then that means we camp here. Do you really want to stay out in this country another night?"

This new and more terrifying scenario certainly overtook the previous fear in Cecil's mind. "I had never really thought of it that way Judge. As much as I don't like traveling after dark the thought of making camp for another night is even worse. I reckon we push on but I'll tell you right now, I plan on pulling the trigger on this Greener the minute anything looks out of place."

As the two rode the judge said, "That is fine by me Cecil; you just make damn sure that I don't look out of place before you pull that trigger." With that the two rode on in silence, both listening for spooks.

Zeke fixed the first of Ben's night time gruel a little before midnight. The big dog had eaten at dark and then shortly after that fell sound asleep. Zeke had to stir up the fire a bit in order to make the bacon gravy that he was certain was bringing the animal back from the brink of death. Once finished he slid the plate close to his nose. Ben opened his eyes and looked around. Just as he was ready to lick the plate he straightened his head and looked past the two horses into the darkness. Zeke saw this and looked for himself. Nothing moved or for that matter seemed out of the ordinary. After a few seconds the big dog went after his meal and shortly after finishing was sound asleep again. Zeke was suspicious as to what had made Ben look into the distance, it must have been nothing or the two horses would have also become excited. Maybe the big dog was still trying to get his sense of direction and balance after his encounter with the snare.

Zeke had a look around and once he was satisfied that nothing was amiss he refilled his coffee cup and sat back down by the tree. As he sipped he leaned back and tried to relax. He might have tried a little too hard.

Zeke let himself fall sound asleep; he had been awake more than forty hours and the lack of sleep had finally won out. While he slept and began to drift off into the distance reaches of his mind there was silent movement at the edge of camp. Three pairs of eyes had seen the fire and were working their way toward the camp. Slow and silent, they stalked the sleeping man and his two horses. Horses were always suspicious of the dark and were extremely adept at recognizing danger before it got close enough to do harm. Both Rusty and Hazel were standing all three legged and content. Hazel, being the younger of the two horses, was also the most alert. She had already lost one rider to the darkness in the previous two weeks and she was more vigilant for that reason if no other.

What approached this night knew horses were about and also a human. They knew the abilities that horses possessed and were more concerned with the four legged animals at the camp than the two legged one that was now very still and seemingly asleep against a tree. As they approached they knew the horses could sound the alarm at any second. These three creatures were smart and had confidence in their stealthy abilities. As they approached they separated and looked for an opportunity to invade and overpower the unsuspecting occupants of the camp. After the horses and the man were dealt with it would be time for the three attackers to feed.

Ben happened to wake for no other reason than the fact that he had become accustomed to getting his tasty treat every few hours. That time had come and gone by at least an hour and his stomach told him he was hungry. He opened his eyes and without raising his head he scanned everything in front of him. He saw the man who had taken such good care of him after he released him from the vicious trap he had been caught in for days. As he lay resting and looking at the man against the tree his ears picked up a sound.

The thing about Ben was that he was extremely smart even though he was also extremely young, not quite a year old. He slowly raised his ears and listened hard, again he picked up the sound and it was getting closer. The sound was coming not only from in front but at least one spot behind the big dog. Ben knew he was in no condition to confront a predator. He waited for Hazel and the other horse to raise an alarm and awake the sleeping man. What happened next made the decision for Ben.

Behind the tree where the man slept something bolted from the darkness and advanced with astonishing speed. Ben hadn't had his legs under him in who knows how long and he wasn't sure they would work now. He never gave it a second thought as he sprang to his feet with all the energy his broken body could deliver. To his surprise he was up moving and the pain was minimal. Whatever it was hadn't seen him yet, it was totally focused on the sleeping man. Ben doubted he could intercept the creature before it got to Zeke. With that in mind he charged forward and at the same time released a ferocious roar.

Ben knew now that what he was attacking was not alone. His senses were on full go and even as he raced forward he knew more were behind him where the horses were. In his mind he would protect the man first and then turn his attentions to whatever it was behind him. He knew Hazel would have heard his roar and would now be all feet and hooves. A horse can be a very dangerous animal when spooked and he hoped his friend would be alright until he could come to her aid. Ben was going to attack all these strange looking creatures before they in turn could harm his friends. He bared his teeth and went into kill mode.

Zeke had been dreaming about a girl he had known back in Kentucky. He had never actually talked to her about his feelings but he always wanted to. She was his primary school teacher and she was also much older, and married, and he was only six, but what the heck, she was still the girl of his dreams.

He was startled from his sleep by a vicious roar from some sort of wild beast. When his eyes snapped open he was looking straight at Ben and the dog was running straight for him. Zeke put his hands up over his face to defend himself but to his relief the big dog ran right on by.

As Ben ran by Zeke, the dog could tell something didn't feel right with his legs. He wanted to go into the brush and grab whatever it was he had seen but suddenly he felt weak and things began to go dark. The big dog passed out while in full stride. As his body went limp he hit the ground and slid several feet.

After Ben had made his charge Zeke jumped to his feet and it was then that he noticed the two horses were bucking against their leads. Past the horses he saw movement. He reached over and grabbed the Winchester. After levering a shell into the breach he raised the gun and fired.

After two more shots he turned to see where Ben had gone. The big dog had collapsed not far on the other side of the tree. Zeke fired a couple of shots over the dog and into the darkness. He stood for a minute to see if the danger had passed. As he listened he eased over to where Ben had fallen, at first he thought the dog was dead.

He checked him out and although he was lying very still he was breathing hard and seemed to be either asleep or unconscious. The effort of saving Zeke's life had damn near killed the big dog. Zeke gently picked Ben up and carried him back to his spot by the fire, Ben came to as Zeke was putting him back on his horse blanket. Zeke grabbed his rifle and then checked on the two horses. Both had calmed considerably and this was a good sign.

Zeke went back to Ben and rubbed his head and ears. Ben had managed to catch his breath now and was starting to calm down and go back to sleep, exhausted from the exertion of his short run. Zeke couldn't believe he had fallen sound asleep himself and he also found it hard to believe that he had been saved by the very dog he had rescued two days before. It looked like the score was about even, Zeke one, Ben one.

If the same thing happened tonight as had happened the previous night then hopefully the danger was over, one attack per night. Zeke kept the Winchester by his side as he tried to calm himself by making the bacon gravy he knew Ben wanted. He slid the plate in front of the dog and Ben immediately went to work on his treat. As Zeke watched him eat he knew if it hadn't have been for the dog he would most likely be dead right now.

Why hadn't the horses alerted him, could it be that whatever was out there had learned how to sneak up on horses? If that were the case then they must not have known that Ben was around. That would mean this was a different set of creatures from the previous night. Ben had growled then and they had left in a hurry. Whatever it was must be afraid of dogs, no, they were afraid of big dogs.

Zeke refilled the coffee pot and set it back in the fire. As the coffee brewed Ben stretched out and went back to sleep. Both horses were busily cropping grass, both seemed relaxed now that the danger had passed. Hopefully this day would see him safely to the town of Langley.

As he sat and sipped his coffee, he wondered about the judge and the two deputies. There were three of them and surely they could fight off whatever it was that had attacked Zeke's camp the last two nights. Then he realized something, if whatever it was had learned how to invade a camp without alerting the keen senses of a horse then the judge's group might be in for some trouble. Ben had surely saved him on this night but Judge Preston and the two deputies never had the luxury of a dog in their group. Hopefully they posted one man during the night as a guard. He guessed he would find out once he made it to Langley.

As Lloyd Shafer and Wes Branham sat at their table in the back of the saloon the town's sheriff walked in, he was a tall man and extremely thin. He looked a little old to be a lawman but looks could be deceiving. Sheriff Jasel Farley was sixty-nine years old and looked every minute of it. He had been sheriff of Langley for more than twenty years which had to be some sort of record for a lawman in these parts. In all that time Jasel had managed to not get himself killed and he had also managed to not kill anyone in return. It seemed the closest the sheriff had come to dying was at the hands of his own wife.

Delores Farley, wife of the sheriff, had been a beautiful woman in her day. She had shoulder length brown hair and always kept herself presentable. So presentable that the town's previous mayor had took notice. Sheriff Farley, having first been elected to that office almost twenty years earlier, wanted to make a name for himself by keeping his town safe for the residents who had seen fit to elect him in the first place. He worked nearly all the time, even sleeping at the sheriff's office when needed.

As Sheriff Farley put in his long days keeping the town safe, his wife of ten years started putting in a few long hours of her own seeing to the needs of the mayor. This was unknown to the hardworking sheriff. It wasn't long before the infatuation of the two created a need, or desire, to do away with the sheriff altogether.

Sheriff Farley came home late one night after a long day in town and was surprised to find his supper had been kept warm and his wife was still up to serve it to her husband. This in itself should have been suspicious because Delores wasn't one to cook, or clean for that matter. Usually when Jasel got home he had a wedge of leftover cornbread and a piece of cold ham for supper, this night though the table was spread with his favorite, baked chicken and rice along with garden peas and green beans.

Delores filled the sheriff's plate and slid it in front of him. Jasel sat down and dug right in. "Honey, not to be one to complain, but this chicken and rice tastes a little bitter, you sure you used the right ingredients?"

Delores quickly turned away from her husband to hide the look on her face. She hoped what she had really added to her husband's favorite dish was strong enough to do what she wanted it to do but not strong enough to be noticed. Once she got her composure she turned back to Jasel and said, "It's the same dear. Maybe you should eat more; the first bite might have just seemed different."

Jasel was extremely hungry and went on eating as his wife suggested. After a few more bites he accepted the strange taste if for no other reason than it had been such a long time since he had experienced a home cooked meal. Before he finished what was on his plate, Delores put more of the funny tasting chicken and rice on top of what was already there.

Jasel looked up at his wife and asked, "Why don't you fix yourself a plate and join me?"

"Oh Jasel, I have already eaten, I really didn't know what time you would be home so I fixed myself a plate earlier."

By the time Jasel had finished his second plate he thought of something that didn't make sense. "You say you fixed yourself a plate earlier Delores?"

"That's right dear. I ate almost an hour ago," she said with a nervous shake in her voice.

The sheriff prided himself on the fact that he could usually tell if someone was lying to him. Dealing with lawbreakers on a daily basis will do that to a man.

As he pondered his wife's answer he noticed that he didn't feel quite right, he suddenly felt tired and his thoughts were muddled. Without noticing it he asked nearly the same question again, "You say you already fixed yourself a plate before I got home?" He asked as he sat his fork down and looked at the pan which contained the baked chicken and rice.

Delores quickly turned and went into the kitchen, not bothering to answer her husband.

Now Jasel knew something was up. "If you say you already had your supper then why was the pan full when you filled my plate?" He asked his wife.

She didn't answer; she just kept busy in the kitchen. Jasel looked at the pan again and then thought of the way his wife had taken care of him during his supper. She had filled his plate twice and he had eaten nearly all of what had been placed on it. He looked at the two pots that contained the two different vegetables and then realized that neither had been put before him; he had only been offered the chicken and rice.

As he tried to focus on what this all meant he began to feel light headed. Whatever was happening to him was taking place very fast. He looked up and noticed his wife peeking around the door that separated the kitchen from the dining room. She was looking straight at him and this time she didn't bother to hide that fact.

Jasel pushed back from the table and noticed the effort was difficult. When he tried to stand his legs wouldn't support his weight. He headed forward and fell on the floor, striking his head on the edge of the table as he went down. He, for some reason, thought of how rough the rug felt against the side of his face as he lay there looking at the wall. The last thing he remembered was his wife's shoes only inches from his face, she was standing over him but not offering to help. As his eyes slowly closed he wondered if they would ever open again. Darkness soon claimed him as his thoughts gave way to nothingness.

Delores Farley stood over her husband and made no effort to check on him. She listened to him breathe and knew these were most likely his last breaths. She held a skillet that she was supposed to use to hit him after he had passed out. The plan was for her to say that he had come home and gotten in an argument with his wife and started beating her. She and her mayor lover had devised this scheme and so far everything had gone exactly as planned. Actually it had gone better than planned. The fact that Jasel had hit his head on the table meant she wouldn't have to use the skillet now after all.

Once she hit him with the skillet she was to summon the town's deputies and tell them that she had killed her husband in self-defense, after all he was trying to kill her. The poison she had put in the chicken and rice casserole would be what had actually killed the sheriff but that would remain a secret. The death could be blamed on the trauma to the head. He would be just as dead either way.

Delores put the skillet back in the kitchen and ran out the front door in search of one of the towns three deputies. She found Carl Nolen in the sheriff's office half asleep. It was his night to walk the streets of Langley once every two hours. Other than that he could sip coffee and try to stay awake, a job he was now failing miserably.

"Deputy, wake up, something terrible has happened," Delores said as she shook the drowsy deputy.

Nolen nearly fell out of his chair as he went for his gun. "What the hell," he said as he scrambled to his feet.

"It's Jasel, I think he's dead," she said and hoped it sounded the way she wanted it to with enough terror and fear to seem real.

"Dead, has he been shot?"

"No deputy, nothing like that. He came home a little while ago and I don't know what was wrong with him. He started cussing everything in sight and then attacked me. He beat me with his fists. I finally got away from him and then, and then," she said between sobs. "I hit him with the supper skillet. I hit him and I think he's dead. I had to or else he was going to kill me," Delores said as she cried fake tears and hoped her little act was convincing.

Deputy Nolen was now fully awake but found it hard to believe Delores was talking about somebody he had known for at least ten years. "Dead you say, and he beat you. I can't believe it. Jasel Farley is one of the most respectable men I have ever known." Nolen remembered the part about Jasel beating his wife, there wasn't a mark on her. "If he beat you then where are you hurt?" he asked.

Delores, in all her haste to tell her story, had forgotten to smudge a little ash from the fireplace in her home onto one of her cheeks and also her forehead in order to make it look like she had really been beaten by her husband. Presented with the deputy's question she at first didn't know what to do. She recovered quickly though. "Hurry deputy, you must get over there now and see what you can do. I fear it is too late and he is already dead."

Deputy Nolen listened to Delores and her ridiculous story. The way she said it and the words she used seemed more than made up but he was also worried that something really had happened to his boss. After he grabbed his hat the two headed for the door.

Deputy Fred Slone had just made the last of his rounds for the night and was checking in with Deputy Nolen before heading home when he met the two coming out of the sheriff's office. Delores Farley looked like she was extremely upset. "Howdy Carl, Howdy Missus Farley, anything wrong?" he asked as the two came out of the sheriff's office.

Nolen looked at Slone and said, "Fred, you're just in time. It seems there is a problem over at the sheriff's house. How 'bout you coming along?" just then Nolen thought of something else. "Fred, go by and get the doc. See if he can hurry over to the sheriff's house and you come over with him."

Fred knew something was bad wrong and didn't ask any more questions, he just turned and ran down the boardwalk toward the doctor's house. He was there in only minutes and knew he might have a little trouble getting the doctor up. It seemed that the town's doctor was a sober professional during the day and a raging drunk at night. Fred beat on the front door until it eased open and the business end of a shotgun slid out.

"Who's there?" the voice at the other end of the shotgun asked.

"It's me Doc; put that shotgun down before you hurt somebody."

"Who's me?" the voice asked.

"It's Fred Doc, Fred Slone. I need you to come with me over to the sheriff's house."

The shotgun slid back inside and the door opened. Dr. James Hatler Collette stood just on the other side on legs that wobbled a bit as his bloodshot eyes tried to focus. Fred knew he had his hands full now trying to get the doctor over to the sheriff's house.

"Howdy deputy, would you like to come in for a drink?"

"Naw Doc, we got to get over to the sheriff's house. I think he might be hurt."

Dr. Collette weaved around and tried to absorb what he had just heard. "The sheriff is hurt you say, what happened, did he get shot?"

"Now Doc, which one of them three questions you want answered first?"

The doctor thought about this and looked back at the deputy. "If you're trying to be a smartass deputy then you're doing a pretty good job. Let me get my coat and we'll head on over." Instead of a coat the doctor put a hat on his head and said, "Alright, now I'm ready."

Fred stepped inside and grabbed a coat off the coat tree and helped the doctor put it on. "Doc, could you please hurry, Jasel might be in a bad way and really need your help."

Doc Collette stumbled out his front door and headed down the street. Before he made it ten steps he turned back to Fred and said, "You better go back and get my bag. I think it's on the kitchen table."

Fred turned in frustration and ran back to the doctor's house. The bag that contained Collette's stuff was right where he said it was, on the kitchen table. There were two empty bottles of whiskey sitting there too. Fred grabbed the bag and ran back to where he had left the doctor. To his surprise Dr. Collette was nowhere to be seen.

"Come on Fred, if the sheriff is hurt then we need to hurry." Fred looked to where the voice had come from and saw Collette heading down an alley. It appeared the doctor was sobering up fast and was going in the right direction.

Once at the house Jasel and his wife lived in they found the front door open. Fred went in ahead of the doctor and found Carl kneeling beside the sheriff. There was blood on the floor and a slight cut on the sheriff's forehead.

"Here he is Doc, come on in and see if he's dead," Carl said.

To everyone's surprise the sheriff opened his eyes and said in a weak voice, "Is that you Carl?"

"It sure is sheriff, what happened to you?"

Sheriff Farley slowly looked around the room until he saw his wife. He managed to say, "She fixed supper, don't any of you touch it. I think she done something to it."

Just as Carl stood Delores grabbed the pan of chicken and rice and headed for the back door. Carl looked at Fred and said, "Stop her, don't let her get rid of that until we have a look."

Delores heard this and ran toward the door even faster. Fred caught her and took the pan away. The sheriff's wife just went over and sat at the kitchen table. She didn't bother to look at the two deputies or the doctor anymore.

Fred looked at the food in the pan and then held it close to his nose. "Whew, that is not right."

Carl walked over and took the pan. He looked over the chicken and then he held the pan close. "I don't reckon I ever had a dish that smelled like this Mrs. Farley. What would you call it anyway?"

Delores looked at the two deputies and thought she might still be able to get away with what she had done. "It's Jasel's favorite, chicken and rice." She then added, "He likes to put some special herb in it. I never add the stuff, he always does that himself. He keeps it in the cupboard if you want to take a look."

The two deputies looked at each other and then at the sheriff. Jasel was being tended to by the doc and had heard what his wife had just said. "Is that true sheriff? Did you add something to your food?" Both deputies knew the answer. The sheriff slowly shook his head no.

Delores knew she was caught and started to cry. "He is out of his head. He attacked me and then hit his head on the table."

Fred knew this was not the story she told when she came to the sheriff's office. "I thought you said you hit him with a skillet to defend yourself?"

Delores turned away, "That's right, it was a skillet." She wasn't convincing at all.

Just then Mayor Leonard Webb walked in. He looked over the room and his eyes fell upon the sheriff who was lying in the floor by the dining room table. "I heard the sheriff just tried to kill his wife," he stated to no one in particular.

Carl stood up and stretched his shoulders. Once this was finished he swung without warning and hit the mayor hard on the jaw. Mayor Webb wobbled back on his feet and then his eyes rolled back in his head. He collapsed in a heap on the floor. Delores, upon seeing this, screamed and ran to the mayor's side.

"Look at that Carl, she runs to the mayor and not once has she attempted to show any concern for her husband. I told you I thought something was going on between them two and you never believed me," Fred said.

Carl walked over and looked at the mayor and Delores. "I just didn't want to believe someone could be so low Fred. I didn't want it to be true for Jasel's sake. Now what do we do?"

"I say we lock 'em both up until morning, in different cells of course, and let the judge decide."

As it worked out Delores turned out to be bad at the murder business, and the sheriff recovered fully. Where she had gone wrong with her and the mayor's plan was baking the poison with the chicken and rice. If she had baked the dish first and then applied the rat killer afterwards then the sheriff would have gotten the full dose. As it was when the poison was baked it reduced the effect it had on the sheriff. Luckily for Jasel, he survived and shortly after his wife and the mayor left town. The judge at that time was a friend of the mayor and decided he didn't have the evidence to convict. He let them go without even having a trial to the dismay of the sheriff and his deputies. Needless to say that judge was defeated the very next year and he too soon left town.

When Jasel Farley walked into the saloon he noticed Lloyd Shafer and Wes Branham sitting off to the back and in deep conversation. The sheriff knew both men and was aware that each had a part to play in the trial that was to start the next morning. He walked over to say hello.

"Evening Mr. Shafer, evening Wes," the sheriff said as he approached the two.

Shafer looked toward the voice he just heard and when he saw who it was he replied, "Evening Sheriff. Care to join us for a little drink?"

"I would, but I'm on duty. I wanted to ask if you think the trial will start tomorrow."

"Well, I sure hope so Sheriff. All we need is a judge, can't have a trial without a judge," Shafer said.

The sheriff thought this was strange. Judge Preston would be the presiding judge at the trial and as far as the sheriff knew he had never missed a trial yet. "Judge Preston will be here Mr. Shafer; he always arrives the evening before when he is to hold court in Langley."

"Well it's nearly eight o'clock Sheriff. He had plenty of notice about this trial and should have been here before now," Wes chimed in. "In the past when he was to hold court has he ever shown up this late?"

The sheriff thought about the question. "Well, come to think of it, I don't ever recall him ever being this late." Sheriff Farley looked out one of the big front windows at the fading light. "Maybe I'll go down to the livery and see if he has left his horse there."

As the sheriff turned to leave Wes said, "What happens if the judge don't show Sheriff? The folks in this town want Whitmore hung and I don't think they will wait until another trial is scheduled."

Sheriff Farley stopped dead in his tracks and turned back to the two men. "If Judge Preston doesn't show up, and I can't imagine that he wouldn't, then another trial will need to be scheduled. As far as the town wanting a hanging, they will just have to wait on two things."

Wes looked at Shafer and then at the sheriff. "What two things are you talking about?"

Sheriff Farley didn't like Wes and he had yet to form an opinion about Shafer, but he was leaning toward dislike also. "Number one is another judge, and number two is a guilty verdict. As of right now he has only been accused."

"Well Sheriff, you're not the judge and if you were you could figure out the simple fact that there is an eyewitness to that murder and as far as I'm concerned that makes him ready to hang tomorrow if the trial doesn't take place," Wes said.

Sheriff Farley took a step closer to the table where Shafer and Wes sat. "Yeah, I got all that Wes. The only thing that troubles me about the case against Whitmore is the witness." Farley knew that Wes Branham was the third man who was in the barn and also the only witness to the shooting.

Wes got to his feet and faced the sheriff. "What are you trying to say Sheriff, and if I was you I'd be real careful with my choice of words."

Farley wasn't a gunfighter and he knew in a draw and shoot situation that Wes Branham would probably win. This didn't matter to the sheriff. He had been told a month earlier, by the town's doctor, that when his wife and the former mayor had tried to poison him he had consumed enough of the rat killer to damage his organs, probably his liver. The doctor had told him in no uncertain terms that he was dying.

"Thanks for that friendly piece of advice Mr. Branham. I will choose my words very carefully, and here they are. I think you led Doug Whitmore into that barn to set him up for a murder he didn't commit. I also think you are an outlaw and a thief. Now how do you like them words Branham?" the sheriff said as he prepared to draw on Wes if he needed to. What the sheriff lacked in gun skill he made up for in raw courage.

Just as Wes reached for his gun Shafer stood between the two. The last thing he needed was for the man who worked for him to kill the town's sheriff. "Hold on a minute here. What do you say the three of us just forget what has been said here this evening? No harm done."

Wes looked at Farley and sneered. The sheriff looked at the two and just before he turned to leave he tipped his hat. "You two enjoy what's left of your evening." Just before he exited through the batwing doors he turned back and added, "If you ever want to finish our little conversation Branham I'll be around." After he said this he turned and headed for the livery to check on the judge.

Wes glared at Shafer. "Why did you do that Lloyd? I've killed men for far less than what that two bit sheriff just said."

Shafer took a long pull on his beer. "Because you are the main witness against Whitmore, now how would it look if you had killed the sheriff? Pretty damn bad that's how."

Wes sat back down and pushed his beer away. "I guess you're right, but once this trial is over I can't guarantee I won't kill that old bastard."

"Once this trial is over you are more than welcome to deal with the sheriff in any way you see fit as long as no one knows it was you," Shafer said.

"You don't need to put any worry into that little problem; no one will know how Sheriff Farley met his fate. I can promise you that," Wes said.

It was after midnight when Judge Preston and Cecil Spriggs rode into the town of Langley. As the two rode down Main Street they each wondered what had happened to Bill Adkins the night before. Had he been killed by whatever it was that had been taking men in the middle of the night. Had he lost his mind due to fear, fear of the unknown and ran off into the darkness. That was doubtful but without any hard evidence it was anybody's guess as to what had happened to the deputy.

As the two approached the livery Cecil said, "Maybe Bill got here before we did Judge. He might be in the hotel sound asleep for all we know."

"I wish that were true Cecil but we are leading his horse. I doubt he could have walked here faster than we rode and anyway, why would he do such a thing?" the judge asked.

"I don't know Judge; I guess it was just wishful thinking. I believe we both know what happened to him. Ain't any way for a deputy to meet his end though? Hell, everybody deserves a funeral and a grave," Cecil said.

The two men were silent as they rode up in front of the livery stable. After tying the three horses to the hitching post out front Judge Preston walked up and knocked on one of the big doors at the front of the barn.

"Who the hell is it?" a gruff voice asked from inside the barn.

"It's Judge Preston, open up; I got horses for you to tend to."

There was a clinging sound from the other side of the door and shortly thereafter one of the big doors swung out. A short fat man stepped out carrying an old single shot shotgun. He squinted in the darkness and finally said, "Why hello Judge, I was starting to get worried about you. Why are you traveling so late?"

"We had a little trouble on the trail. Has there been anybody here from Rapid City in the last few days?"

The hostler rubbed his stubbly chin and then looked off into nowhere. "Just that Shafer fellar Judge, he got here a couple of days ago. I reckon he's going to try that man that committed the murder. Say Judge what's your opinion about that?"

Judge Preston laughed, "Now you know I don't have an opinion. It's my job to remain impartial."

The hostler accepted this and asked, "Well Judge, you and the deputy don't need to worry about these three horses, I'll see they get put away just fine." Just then the old hostler noticed that all three horses were saddled. "Say Judge, did you run off and leave somebody on the trail. You got one more saddled horse than you need."

"Well that's the trouble I mentioned earlier. I would stay and fill you in but I got to get to the hotel and see if they got a couple of rooms for me and Cecil here." With that Preston and Cecil grabbed their saddle bags and headed up the street.

Zeke managed to stay awake the rest of the night. As the sun came up he thought about the problem at hand. He was still a good day's ride from Langley. He had been attacked both nights since the judge and the two deputies had ridden out after finding Ben trapped in the snare. If he loaded up now and headed out within the hour he could possibly make town an hour or two after nightfall. This was not such a bad course of action except for one thing; he was dead on his feet. If anything happened during the day he doubted he could function at a hundred percent, hell the way he felt now he doubted if he was even fifty percent. As the sky brightened and sunshine washed over his face he felt even more tired. Warm sunshine will do that to a man.

Zeke knew he wouldn't make it to Langley today, it was just too far and he was too tired. If today held true to past events he would most likely be safe until nightfall. He would get a couple of hours sleep right here and then go as far as he could and camp one more night, it was the only plan he could formulate. Sleep was just too hard to keep at bay for a man who had been awake for the better part of three days. First on the list was to see to his horses and Ben.

Hazel and Rusty watched as Zeke stiffly got to his feet. The two horses only needed to be moved and they were set for another few hours. After untying the two he moved them to another tree about twenty feet upstream where fresh grass waited. The two immediately went to pulling grass and swatting flies with their tails, they were happy not to be on the trail first thing in the morning.

Ben had stayed in his spot by the remnants of the fire watching and waiting for his breakfast. He was getting used to being fed without having to hunt down his food. This wouldn't last long though because as soon as he got back a little strength he intended to find himself a big juicy rabbit, Ben loved rabbit.

Zeke fixed up a little flour and diced up bacon and heated it over the fire. When finished he slid the plate over to Ben's nose. The big dog didn't dig right in this time, which was unusual. As Zeke watched the dog slowly got up on his front paws and then slowly he stood on his back legs. He stood there for a few minutes as he looked at Zeke and wagged his tail. When he felt he had stood long enough he sat back down and began to eat his treat. Zeke was impressed. He knew the dog was still in a bad way but he had made remarkable progress in the last few days. As soon as Ben was finished with his breakfast he put his head back down and within seconds he was sound asleep.

Zeke hurriedly made himself a quick breakfast of skillet bread and coffee. After he finished this he checked both his Winchester and Colt and once satisfied he leaned back against the tree and fell sound asleep. He hoped Ben and his two horses would warn him if another attack was imminent. As tired as he was he would just have to take his chances.

The first time Ben woke up after his breakfast he looked around and noticed that the man had fallen asleep again. He remembered what had happened the night before when the creatures had attacked, the man was asleep then too. Ben felt stronger than he had in weeks so he decided to just lay by the fire and keep watch on things. When he looked over at Hazel the big horse was near the stream picking on some tall grass. Ben always wondered why horses ate such nasty stuff. The only thing he had ever found useful about grass was when his stomach hurt. He could nibble on a little of the stuff and it always made him throw up, after that his tummy always felt better. Maybe that was it, horses always had a stomach ache and that was why they liked to nibble on grass all day, go figure.

When Hazel noticed that Ben was awake she trotted over to the end of her lead but it wasn't quite long enough to allow her to make it all the way to where the dog lay. She patted the ground with one of her front hooves and Ben slapped his tail on the ground. Both were glad to see each other. Zeke snored away as he dreamed far off stories of his youth. At the moment everything in the world was as it should be, at least as far as these four were concerned, Rusty included. Rusty looked at Zeke, and then at Hazel and the dog. At the moment he didn't have a saddle on his back and he was enjoying this immensely.

After Ben figured Zeke had slept long enough he let out a howl. Zeke, startled from his sleep jumped to his feet with Winchester in hand. After a quick look around he realized there was no danger. When he looked at Ben he was laying by the fire slapping his tail on the ground. Hazel and Rusty were both standing by the stream, mouths full of green grass and looking straight at him.

By the look of the sun it was well past noon. He decided to quickly make Ben another snack and then load up and pull out of camp. Langley wasn't getting any closer and it never would if he didn't start moving. It took Ben exactly one minute to gobble down his lunch and then it took Zeke forty-five more to load up and clear out of camp. It was probably after one-o'clock, maybe even two in the afternoon, when the four started moving. This time Ben stayed awake a little more as he rode on top of the pack Hazel carried. The big horse again turned her head from time to time to check on her friend. Zeke noticed this and wondered what story these two shared. He was sure it was a good one.

The four traveled at least four hours and covered maybe fifteen or sixteen miles by Zeke's best guess when a slight noise could be heard off to the right of the trail they traveled on. Zeke reined in Rusty and sat his saddle and listened. It was then that Ben jerked his head in the direction of the sound and his ears were immediately up as the big dog listened. Off in the distance was a sound that sounded like crying. Ben raised his head even higher and after listening a minute he looked at Zeke and then started barking. This in itself startled Zeke. He figured Ben was pretty smart and wondered what the barking meant.

Zeke tapped Rusty and headed off in the direction of the noise. As soon as the four started moving Ben stopped barking and got very quiet. The dog could hear much better than Zeke, he wondered what they were heading into. The good thing was that Ben and the horses didn't seem nervous in the least. The three could smell and hear trouble and this didn't seem to be the case at all. Zeke even noticed that Rusty was actually moving a little faster than normal as if he wanted to get to where the sound was coming from.

Zeke trusted the senses of the three animals but he still held the Winchester at the ready, just in case. As the four got closer the noise was definitely the sound of a child and that child was crying. Once Zeke realized this he was alarmed at the fact that a child was near and that child was in distress. As much as he wanted to ride toward the noise at a full gallop he knew he had to use caution. The crying seemed to be of sadness and not the kind that accompanies immediate danger; this at least told him he could continue ahead with caution. If it had been a child screaming in fear he would have charged in with guns blazing.

When Zeke came to a clearing he was still a few hundred feet from the crying but now he could see the source. He stopped his horse and had a good look around. What he saw was a wagon and a cold camp. There was a little boy sitting up front in the wagon and a woman trying to tend to two horses. She apparently hadn't noticed Zeke. When she turned from the horses to try and comfort the little boy she saw a man and two horses. On top of one of the horses was what looked like a body?

The woman immediately sprang into action; she picked up an old shotgun and pointed it in Zeke's direction. Now the last thing Zeke wanted was to get shot by a complete stranger so he quickly put his hands in the air. His Winchester was balanced across his saddle and he hoped it didn't fall to the ground.

Zeke spoke in a smooth calm voice, "Ma'am, I didn't mean to startle you; I heard crying and came to see if a child was in need of assistance. If you like I can turn and ride out."

The woman considered this before speaking. "Who are you?" she asked.

Zeke thought if he told her who he was and where he was heading then it might just keep him from getting shot.

"My name is Zeke Conley and I'm heading into a town called Langley. I was traveling with a judge and two other deputies but we had to split up a few days back." He hoped this reassured the woman.

She thought about this for a minute and then she held the shotgun a little higher. "What about the body you got tied to that other horse?"

This puzzled Zeke, couldn't this woman see it was a dog. Then he noticed that at the angle she was standing she couldn't really see Ben. Before Zeke had time to answer Ben raised his head up a little higher.

"My goodness is that a live bear you got tied on top of that horse?" she asked.

"No Ma'am, that's Ben. We found him caught in a snare a few days back and managed to set him free. He was in such bad shape that I decided to stay behind and tend to him. He's the reason me and the rest of my group split up. The judge had a trial to oversee this morning and couldn't be held up. I stayed behind. I'm on my way to Langley now."

The woman looked puzzled. "If you stayed behind then you must not know of the trouble that's been happening in these parts."

Zeke suspected she was talking about the missing men. "I only know that there are some things going on that I can't explain. What trouble are you talking about?"

The woman looked over at the little boy; he had stopped crying and was looking at Ben. "There were four of us. Two nights back both my brothers went missing. We stopped here and made camp Sunday night. Everything seemed fine, the next morning they were gone along with both of the mules we were using to pull the wagon." The woman wiped a tear from her eye as she went over and picked up the little boy. "This is Keene. He's only three years old and has been terrified since his uncles went missing, they were very close."

Zeke looked at the little boy. He was still looking at Ben and seemed truly fascinated by the big dog. "How do you know your brothers were taken Ma'am?"

She pointed toward the stream that ran by the camp. "Over there, you can see where they were dragged away."

Zeke was both startled and fascinated. He had looked for evidence of the intruders ever since he stumbled upon the abandoned campsite where he had found Hazel. Now was it possible that he could see some evidence?

The woman still held the shotgun in one hand even though she held the child in the other. "Why are you still here, do you think your brothers might be coming back?" Zeke asked.

"No, I don't think they will. The reason me and Keene are still here is that I can't hitch the horses to the wagon. Everything was made for the mules and now they're gone. I've been trying since yesterday to make the hitch work for the horses but can't. The mules were small and I don't know how to make the rigging work for horses."

Zeke looked at the rigging she had been working on and knew she would never be able to hitch the horses to the wagon with what she had. "Ma'am, I don't know if you trust me and I wouldn't be surprised if you didn't after what has happened here. But I can tell you this; you can't stay out here all alone. There are things happening in these parts that just can't be explained, at least not yet.

"I planned on making it to Langley by tomorrow and would be glad to help you get there but I can't do it if you're going to hold a shotgun on me the entire time."

The woman thought about this and asked, "You said you are a deputy, where is your badge?"

Zeke realized he wasn't wearing his badge. He had taken it off when he had washed his shirt in the stream two days back after rescuing Ben.

He reached into his pants pocket and pulled out the badge and pinned it on his shirt. "Sorry Ma'am, when I got that dog loose from the snare and carried him to safety he was a mess. What was on him was pretty much on me so I had to wash my stuff in the stream. I guess I just forgot to put my badge back on."

She thought about this and then put the shotgun in the seat of the wagon. "My name is Martha Ellen McCoy. And as I told you this is Keene. If you can help us get to Langley then I would be grateful." She looked around the camp and then added. "I really don't want to stay here another minute."

Zeke looked at the little boy and said, "Hi Keene, my name is Zeke Conley and that big dog over there is named Ben."

The little boy smiled at the dog and then said, "Ben, I like that name."

Zeke tied his two horses to the back of the wagon and then looked over the rigging that the mules had used. There wasn't enough to work with because the entire thing had been made for small mules. He thought about what he had and what was here. With any luck he could make something work but it wouldn't be very strong. If hard pulling was needed, or a fast run, then what he made probably would fail.

"I think I can make something work but we're going to need to go real easy on everything. Maybe it will get us into Langley, maybe it won't. I can promise you one thing; you won't be left here on the trail alone," he said.

The woman smiled and said, "Trying is better than nothing. After you get the rig made would you see if you can find my brothers?" She looked off into the trees. "Maybe they are near and maybe even hurt."

Zeke knew the two men were probably long gone but couldn't leave without at least giving it a try. "Yes Ma'am, before I get your two horses hitched up I'll go and have a look. I wanted to check out those tracks you say are near the stream anyway."

Zeke headed off to where Martha Ellen had said she saw the tracks. She was right, near the stream on the other side it looked like a struggle had taken place. It wasn't much of a struggle but the signs were there. It looked as if someone had been overpowered and then pulled into the brush. Zeke followed until the ground became hard packed and the sign disappeared. The tracks of whatever had attacked the men were not anything Zeke had seen before. There were claw marks at the front of each track, big claw marks. The one thing Zeke couldn't figure out was the lack of blood. Anytime he had ever tracked an animal that had taken prey there had always been blood. This time there wasn't even a single drop.

After the sign stopped Zeke returned to camp and began to work on the harness for the two horses. Within a couple of hours he had something rigged up that looked like it had been built by a total drunk but when he backed the two horses into the rig it fit pretty well. He snapped and tied until he felt the contraption would hold together. As he worked on the horses Martha Ellen had been busy getting everything packed up. Little Keene had spent his time playing with some small wooden figurines that looked like cowboys and Indians. He stopped at times to look at Ben and also call the dog's name. Ben was happy to just stay on the pack Hazel carried and sleep.

By the time everything was loaded and ready to move it must have been after six-o'clock in the evening. Just before pulling out of camp Martha walked to the edge of the forest and shouted the two names of her brothers. No reply came from the tree line, only the chirping of birds. She looked back at Zeke and he could tell she was crying. He quickly turned away and checked on Ben. Zeke could never remember when he wasn't affected by the tears of a woman.

"We better get moving Ma'am. I want to put a few miles between us and this place before nightfall. As late as it is now I doubt we'll be able to travel more than an hour and a half. At least you will be away from the spot where all the trouble happened," Zeke said.

Martha Ellen quickly climbed into the seat of the wagon. Little Keene was already in the back sitting on some blankets and playing with his wooden toys. She released the big lever that kept one of the front wagon wheels locked and then took the reins. Zeke held his breath as the two horses started to pull. The wagon began to move and after a few feet he began to breathe easier.

The group travelled until nearly dark when they came to a spot that looked suitable to build camp. There was water nearby and grass for the four horses. Zeke untied Ben from the top of the pack and carried the big dog to a spot near where the fire would be built. It was the first time that Martha Ellen and Keene had actually got a good look at the dog. Keene especially took an interest in Ben. As the little boy looked he continued to ease over to where Ben lay. Zeke stayed close, not knowing how Ben might react to such a small boy. When Keene eased close enough he slowly held out his hand. Ben slapped his tail on the ground and then started licking Keene's fingers. Zeke let the two become acquainted and then he picked Keene up and carried him back to his mother who had been watching the entire time.

"Better not let him near the big dog unless I'm around. I only met Ben a couple of days ago and don't know how he might act around children, for that matter I probably don't know how he'll act around grownups either," Zeke told her. She said that was a good idea, the dog really frightened her, although she was glad he was near.

Zeke tied Rusty and Hazel near the water and allowed the two to drink. He usually liked to let the two cool down a bit before leading them to water but the wagon had travelled at such a slow pace he felt both horses were fine as it was. The two that pulled the wagon were a different story. Although they hadn't travelled very fast or hard it was still a chore for the two to pull the wagon over the rough trail.

Zeke put the wagon where he wanted it and then took the two horses out of the crude rigging he had built earlier in the day. He rubbed the two down and then led them to a spot near the other two horses. Hazel immediately walked over and nipped the flank of one of the two and Zeke knew he would have to separate both pairs. Rusty wouldn't have caused any trouble but Hazel liked to let everyone know that she was boss. He really liked the big green eyed horse but found out she could be a bitch when she wanted to.

The two horses were led downstream fifty feet or so and then allowed to drink. There was good grass for all the horses and they immediately went after it. While all this was going on Martha Ellen had been busy building a fire and seeing to young Keene. Wasn't long before the smell of coffee travelled through camp and the sound of a young child playing could be heard. Zeke noticed that Keene hadn't cried any more that day; the last had been when he rode up on them earlier. Funny how children can sense danger and when they feel it's gone they go back to what they do best, playing.

As darkness fell upon the camp Zeke gathered enough firewood to last the entire night. When this was finished he made the doggie gruel that Ben had become so used to. Martha Ellen looked on curiously and finally asked, "Surely you don't intend to eat that disgusting creation, I will fix supper for the three of us as soon as you get out of the way."

Zeke laughed, "I surely would like something other than my own cooking for a change. This mess I got in the skillet is for Ben. I've been feeding him this doggie gruel ever since we got him free of the snare. I do believe it has helped him."

"Well you just put that skillet of yours to the side once you've fed that dog. I'll use my pots for the cooking if you don't mind," she said.

Zeke put Ben's food in the pan and then sat it in front of the big dog. Ben looked up at Zeke and slapped his tail on the ground. After Ben was fed Zeke went to the stream and washed out his skillet and also the pan that he had been using for a doggie dish. As he checked on the four horses Martha Ellen prepared supper, although he didn't know what it was.

Zeke carried his saddle over to a tree near the edge of camp. It was a good spot where he could observe his surroundings and also keep an eye on the horses. After he spread out his bed roll and had the saddle just where he wanted it he went back to the fire and grabbed his tin coffee cup. Martha Ellen had stirred up a pretty good looking supper for herself and little Keene. She had made biscuits and ham, along with thick gravy. It looked and smelled better than anything he had eaten since leaving Rapid City.

"Grab yourself a plate off the back of the wagon," she said as she fixed a plate for Keene. The young boy had spent his time sneaking up on Ben. He was still a little afraid of the big dog and that was probably a good thing. Zeke hadn't been around Ben long enough to really know what kind of personality he had. As Keene slowly eased closer to the dog Ben had kept a close watch on the child. He didn't look threatening at all and even seemed to enjoy the attention. Each time when his mother felt he had gotten close enough she would tell him to come back to where she was fixing supper. He would obey but within seconds it would all start again as he began to ease back toward the dog.

Finally she walked over and picked him up and sat him on the back of the wagon which was facing the fire. She scrubbed his hands and face with water from a bucket and then sat his plate beside him. "Now you eat your supper young man and stop worrying about that dog. I think Ben will be fine lying over there by the fire." The little boy grinned at his mother and then picked up his biscuit.

"Mr. Conley, you are more than welcome to sit by the fire with us." She had sat two ladder back chairs between the fire and the wagon. She pointed to one and said, "Keene will be just fine on the back of the wagon, he likes to sit up high while he eats."

Zeke sat down in one of the two chairs and said, "You can call me Zeke if you like. The only person that ever called me Mister Conley was the preacher back home."

Martha Ellen filled the plate Zeke had gotten from the back of the wagon and reached it to him. "Alright then, Zeke it is. I hope you enjoy what I fixed for supper. My brothers always like biscuits and ham at night. I always make enough for breakfast the next morning; they like to hit the trail early."

Zeke looked at the plate and what it contained. "This certainly looks mighty good Ma'am. I usually have a little skillet bread and jerky. If you don't mind me asking, where were the four of you heading?"

Martha Ellen took a plate and sat down in the other chair.

"Well, it is a long story; I don't know really where to start," she said.

"Well I plan on staying awake to stand guard so you can talk as long as you like, it will help keep me awake," Zeke told her.

Martha Ellen got up and refilled both her and Zeke's coffee cups and then sat back down. As she done this Zeke noticed that she refilled both cups out of habit. She must have been raised this way and never thought twice about not doing something for someone else.

"Well, Keene and Keene's dad and I were living on a big farm in Virginia that his family owned. It was a good life and everything couldn't have been better. The farm had always been prosperous. We had been married a little over two years when the flu came through the area. Stan's mother and father fell ill first and for a while it looked like they were going to pull through but it wasn't to be. One day both took a turn for the worse. Both died within hours of each other. Stan's older brothers and some of the farm hands dug the graves and the funeral was held the next day. This was a year ago and little Keene had just turned two years old.

"It was bitterly cold and there was a snow on the ground. I think digging those graves in the frozen ground and being out in that weather must have weakened Stan. The next day after the funeral he took sick and within three days he died too. The family had another funeral."

Zeke noticed Martha Ellen wipe back a tear as she told the story. "So Keene isn't your son?" he asked.

"No, he is my stepson, but no mother ever loved a child more." Martha got up from her chair and went over to where Keene was nibbling on his supper and still looking at Ben. She checked his plate and then as she ran a hand through his shaggy hair said, "If you eat all the food on your plate I will see if Zeke will let you pet Ben again." Keene smiled and then took a big bite. It was evident the boy always needed coaxing in order for him to eat his meals. Martha Ellen returned to her chair by the fire.

"Anyway, after Stan died the oldest son took possession of the farm. It seems there was a law of some sort in Virginia that anytime a mother and father died then everything went to the oldest son. Nothing was given to any of the other children unless there was a will. When Stan took sick and it was apparent he wouldn't recover he told me not to worry. There was a will his parents prepared years back and it gave title of the farm to both sons. He said both Keene and I would be taken care of. That will, if it existed and I don't doubt that it did, never turned up. Stan's older brother Willis went to the county seat and had the title changed to reflect that he was the sole owner of the farm."

Martha Ellen again got up and went back to check on Keene. He had nearly finished his plate and was anxious to pet the big dog, although by now Ben was sound asleep after having his own supper. After telling him that his plate had to be completely empty before he could get down she again returned to her chair by the fire. Her plate was sitting by the fire and she never made an attempt to pick it up. It was apparent she had lost her appetite.

After some time she again picked up the story where she left off, "Willis and his wife never liked me very much. Stan's first wife, which was Keene's mother, died during childbirth. I guess Stan felt he needed a wife, he came to my father's farm not more than a month after they buried Keene's mother. We had known each other from church and he always seemed nice enough, anyway he sat down with my father and myself and in a very business-like way said his baby boy needed a mother and proposed right there on the spot. My father told him to come back the next day, allowing me twenty-four hours to think it over.

"I was eighteen years old at the time and really hadn't been courted by anyone. Eligible men, where I came from, are few in number. There were plenty of prospects but my father made sure they stayed away if they didn't meet his standards. Anyway, after Stan left that evening my father gave me his blessing if I thought I wanted to get married. He said he knew Stan's father and mother and had always held them in high esteem. I don't think I slept more than thirty-minutes that night. By morning I had made up my mind. My answer would be no."

Zeke had listened to the story and hadn't said a word until now. "You said no?" he asked.

"That's right, I didn't want to get married just yet and I also didn't want to leave my mother and father."

"But you did eventually marry him though?" Zeke asked.

"The next day I told my parents what I had decided and they accepted my decision. Later that day Stan came back and he brought his one month old son with him. When I saw that little baby, and knowing he didn't have a mother, something in me told me I wanted to raise the child as my own. In less than a minute that little boy changed my mind, and also my life." Martha Ellen was looking at Keene as she told this part and she was smiling the whole time.

"We were married the very next Saturday and I couldn't have been happier. If there was a sad part to the marriage it was Willis and his wife Sue. I believe they thought Stan should have waited longer before remarrying. If it hadn't have been for Keene I do believe Stan would have waited a lot longer to get married and maybe not even remarry at all. Even if a man has a child he has still got to work. You do see what I am talking about don't you Zeke?"

Zeke looked up from the fire and said, "I see fully. We had a few men back home that lost their wives. It always seemed that if they had kids then it wasn't long before they found another wife. That's just the way things are I reckon," Zeke said.

Martha Ellen smiled as if she had to prove something to herself. It was as if she were getting something off her conscious. Zeke may have been the first person other than her family that she had told this story to. He wasn't one to judge the actions of someone else unless the actions were of a violent nature.

Martha Ellen continued, "Anyway, after a few weeks it became apparent that I wasn't welcome. I was part of that family only because of Stan and now he was dead and gone. My two younger brothers made the trip from my parent's farm, which was about twenty miles away, with the news that the flu had taken both my parents as well. It seemed that most of the older people fell ill and just couldn't recover. Stan was probably the youngest to die and it was probably due to him digging his parent's graves in a blizzard, I think it weakened him.

"When my brothers were preparing to leave Willis and his wife asked me to go with them. They said my ties to the family ended when

Stan died. I was allowed to gather what few things I could put in one trunk and that was it." Again the story made her eyes water.

"Did their abandonment also include Stan's only son?" Zeke asked.

Martha Ellen looked over at Keene who was now climbing down from the wagon. "Not at first. They wanted him to stay with them but I was the only mother he had ever known. When Willis and Sue tried to explain to Keene that I was going away and he would be staying with them he wouldn't have it. He was barely past two years old but he was smart enough to know who he loved and wanted to be with. He made fists with both of his little hands and looked at Willis and Sue. He told them he wasn't staying and they couldn't make him. He kept saying that they weren't the boss of him. No way was he going to let his mother go without him."

It was such a sad story but also a little funny thinking of Keene with his little fists saying they weren't the boss of him. Zeke couldn't imagine what kind of people this Willis and Sue were. He had never met them but he had formed an opinion just by what he had heard, and it wasn't a good one.

"Anyway that was a year ago. Keene and I went back to my parent's farm. Without my mom and dad there it just wasn't the same. My brothers and I decided to sell the place and head west to make a fresh start. It didn't take long for the sale to take place, it was a good farm and a lot of people wanted it. There was an auction and we got a very good price. My brothers and I, Keene included, decided to head out here with no true destination in mind. The first town we came to that we liked would be our new home. We would find some land and start over. Now though I guess it's just Keene and myself." She hung her head and added, "My poor brothers."

Zeke realized she must have thought her brothers were dead, and that could be the case, but he felt he had to say otherwise. "Your brothers might still turn up. There have been some pretty strange things going on in these parts for several months now. Men have been going missing from all over. What I can't for the life of me figure out is why hasn't a body shown up. From what I gather there are at least fifty men missing and for that many to have been killed there would be a body somewhere." Zeke told her this hoping she would take some comfort in the fact that they might still be alive. He also knew that whatever had stalked him the previous night or two probably wasn't taking any prisoners. What he had glimpsed in the shadows on those nights surely would have killed him and then feasted on his bones. The thought sent a shiver down his spine.

Martha Ellen smiled and looked as if her thoughts were far away. Finally she said, "I can only hope, but if they are alive how will I ever know?"

Now Zeke felt that stubborn part of him rising up again. "Well you may never know. I made myself a promise a few nights back when I was nearly abducted, after I make it to Langley and check on the judge and his friends then I can give up my badge. I made the judge a promise I would see him through to the end of the trial. After that I plan on coming back to this area and do a little scouting around." Zeke reached over and patted the big .45.75 Winchester. "I might even do a little hunting myself." He said this and he truly meant it. Whatever was out there taking men couldn't possibly stand up to the power of a Winchester.

Just then Keene handed his empty plate to Martha Ellen and said, "Now I can pet Ben again, please mommy." She took the plate and patted him on the shoulder. Well it looks like you ate everything on your plate. A promise is a promise; you can pet Ben as long as Zeke says it's okay. And if it is okay then I think you had better let Zeke hold your hand while you are around that big dog. Remember we are strangers to Ben and we don't really know if he likes us yet."

Zeke stood from his chair and held out a hand, "Come on Keene, let's see if Ben enjoyed his supper." As the two walked toward the big dog Keene looked back and grinned at his mom. Martha Ellen took the opportunity to clean the plates and put everything away. Ben looked up as Zeke and the little boy approached. He held his head high and his tail began to slap the ground. Zeke reached down and patted Ben on the head and again Keene slowly reached out his hand. It was apparent Keene wanted to play with the big dog but he was still a little afraid.

Ben reached over and licked Keene's fingers and the little boy laughed. Zeke figured this wasn't the first child Ben had seen. When Keene stepped a little closer Ben rubbed his head and neck on the child's pants. It was settled, Ben and Keene were now fast friends.

Suddenly Ben's ears perked up and he looked off into the darkness. Almost at the same time the big dog stood, which startled the little boy. Keene turned and ran back to his mother ready to cry. Martha Ellen had seen this and at first thought Ben was being aggressive toward the child. After watching Ben for a minute it was apparent now though that he was looking off into the shadows. Zeke had drawn his Colt and was also looking and listening hard.

To Zeke's surprise Ben advanced toward the darkness slowly as if he was stalking prey. His ears were up and his teeth were bared as he crept forward in silence. The hair from between his ears and continuing past his shoulder blades was standing nearly straight up. Zeke admired how ferocious Ben looked even though he knew the big dog didn't have much fight in him in his current condition. As Ben advanced Zeke eased over and got his Winchester.

Martha Ellen and Keene were standing near the fire and the little boy looked terrified. He asked, "What is wrong mommy? Why is Ben being so unfriendly?"

"He is protecting us Keene. Something is out there and he doesn't like it," Martha Ellen told the little boy. Keene now smiled at the thought of his new friend protecting him.

Ben continued to advance until something behind him must have gotten his attention. He stopped and looked back in the direction of the horses. Zeke also looked that way and noticed Hazel and Rusty were on edge. The two horses that belonged to Martha Ellen were also nervous and all four were pulling at their leads. Now Zeke had a problem. He had tied the two pairs of horses several yards apart and this in itself created a situation. It was harder to protect everything when everything was so spread out.

Zeke didn't figure he had to worry about anything out there with a weapon. All the troubles so far had been from creatures that were yet to be identified. He didn't figure he had to worry about men with guns, although he probably would have preferred it. Whatever was out there, for some reason, was more terrifying than lookin down the business end of a Colt.

He made a decision that he hoped he didn't regret. "Martha, throw some more wood on the fire, keep it bright and hot."

Zeke grabbed the last Light Toss and waited. Ben had given up on whatever he had first sensed in the darkness and was now approaching Hazel and Rusty. The big dog decided that if the camp was surrounded he would defend the horses first. He knew Zeke had the big rifle so he wasn't too concerned about the people. As he advanced he saw movement in the distance. It was on the other side of the horses by no more than ten steps, steps he could cover in seconds.

Ben crouched low and prepared to go into the brush. He felt good but he remembered he had also felt good the night he had attacked whatever it was that was trying to get Zeke while he slept against the tree. That made no difference now, he would attack again and this time he would kill whatever it was. As the horses began to buck and were ready to tear loose from their restraints Ben made his move. He picked out a target in the darkness, although he knew there was more than one.

When it looked like something was coming after Hazel and Rusty Ben took off with a burst of speed that even surprised himself. He was smart enough to know that he was still in pretty bad shape but it was now or never. The big dog leapt past both horses and went toward the brush and trees. He couldn't recognize the smell of what it was but knew it was the same as he had tried to attack the night he passed out. He waited for the fatigue and strange feeling to return as it had on that night but so far, nothing.

As he rounded the area where Hazel and Rusty were tied he saw his prey. In the darkness Ben could see much better than a man. What he saw was tall and strange looking, it also looked powerful. It didn't matter, Ben charged in anyway. At the last second he leapt into the air and at the same time let out a savage growl. Whatever it was tried to sidestep Ben's charge and then kill the big dog from the side or from behind. Ben had expected this and adjusted his leap at the last second. He had it.

Ben grabbed whatever it was by the neck and also pushed away with his powerful front legs. This was a sure way to kill. Whatever it was though was tough and also very strong. It jerked away and batted at Ben with strong legs. Ben sprang at the beast again but this time it was more than ready. As Ben was ready to clamp down again on the creature's neck it reared back and swatted at him with powerful front limbs. Ben was struck twice and both blows had an impact on the weakened dog.

Ben knew he was up against something that knew how to fight back. He adjusted his next attack and went low, he was after the legs and this time he succeeded. He found flesh and with his powerful jaws he bit hard. He tasted warm blood in his mouth but the taste was strange. It was a taste he had never experienced before. It didn't matter, he wasn't here to eat, he was here to kill.

Ben twisted and tore at the flesh. Just then he was hit hard on the back of his right shoulder and he had to release his grip. It only took him a second to recover but that was all the creature needed to hobble off into the darkness. As he prepared to give chase he saw more of the creatures and they were between him and the one he had injured.

There were three besides the injured one that had now made it to the safety of the forest. Two were to the left and another was several steps to the right. Ben knew to attack the one that was isolated first and once he had dealt with it then he would try to separate the last two and kill them one at a time. As he charged right his prey turned to run. Ben launched himself again and grabbed the beast by one of its shoulders, both Ben and the creature went down and as the two rolled the other two ran in to assist and also kill this animal that was extremely fast and vicious.

Even in a fight like the one Ben was in now he could still identify threats other than the one he battled. He knew the other two were on their way and would be on him in seconds. He tore and bit at the one he had tackled but before he could kill it the other two were on him. He was struck hard on his right hip and that entire leg immediately went numb. There was no feeling at all and with that he found himself barely able to move, he was still in the fight but now he was facing three and he was injured. As badly as Ben wanted to kill his prey he knew he couldn't take on that many and survive. He would probably die here and now. With that something happened in Ben's mind that had never happened before. He went mad with rage and bloodlust.

The big dog was now injured and extremely dangerous. There was little spacing between himself and the strange beasts he battled. In his fury he changed tactics, he would go low and instead of grabbing to hold and tear his prey he would just bite fast and release. If he could bite all three of the creatures he might possibly be able to retreat and then look for another opportunity. As he charged in again he noticed the strength coming back to his injured leg. Ben went in hard and fast. The three were in a group and this actually made it easier, he quickly moved around the three with ferocious swipes of his sharp teeth, he brought blood from all three.

As he looked over the situation again in order to make another attack, the two that were the least injured moved away into the darkness followed by the third as it trotted after them. If Ben had all his strength he would have given chase but for some reason now he felt the exhaustion coming back. He watched until the three were out of sight and then turned and headed back to check on the horses and Zeke. He didn't know what had become of the first one he had attacked, if it did survive he knew it would never be the same again, he had done too much damage.

Zeke had heard the vicious fight in the darkness and hoped Ben could handle himself. He doubted the big dog could do much in the shape he was in. When it grew quiet he knew the fight was over and wondered if the big dog was alright. After several long seconds Ben came out of the brush and headed back toward the camp, he walked with a slight limp. When he got close Zeke noticed all the blood around Ben's mouth and on the front of his legs. Had he gotten himself injured?

Just as Zeke was ready to check out the big dog he seen its eyes. Ben still had a vicious look on his face and his bloody teeth were still bared. He was breathing heavy and his rasping breaths actually sounded menacing.

Martha Ellen saw the look on the dog and asked, "He looks like he might still attack; it looks like he still wants to kill?"

"Better stay up on the wagon, after a fight like that it might take a few minutes for him to calm down. In the state he's in he might not recognize any of us right now," Zeke said. He had seen this before. Back home he had seen dogs that had been in a bad fight attack their own masters without knowing what they were doing. A dog like Ben could still kill until he calmed a bit.

As Ben made his way back to the fire Zeke continued to look around the camp site, everything seemed quiet now. The four horses had calmed considerably. Martha Ellen and Keene were both looking at Ben as he hobbled over to near where they sat in the wagon. When he made it to his spot by the fire he flopped down completely out of breath. When Zeke saw this he knew the fight was now out of the big dog.

"Martha, keep a lookout while I check on Ben," Zeke said as he headed over to the fire.

Zeke gently patted Ben on the head and then looked him over. There didn't seem to be any injuries anywhere on the dog. His legs looked fine and this was a bit puzzling, Ben had limped back from his fight. The only explanation for this would be that he had been hit or bitten but whatever it was hadn't broken the skin. Zeke gently opened Ben's mouth and peered inside. All the teeth seemed fine, none loose and none missing.

Other than breathing hard Ben looked to be alright. It was apparent all the blood had come from whatever it was he had been fighting with. Come first light Zeke would track the wounded animal and see what he could find out.

"Is Ben alright Zeke, he has an awful lot of blood on him," Martha Ellen asked.

Zeke stood and looked down at the dog. "I think so. I believe all the blood is from whatever it was he was fighting. Come first light I think I'll have a look around. How is Keene, is he scared?"

Martha Ellen patted the boy on the head. He was smiling as he looked at Ben. "He was a little scared at first but when I told him Ben was protecting him he was all smiles."

"Well, whatever it was is gone, at least for the time being. Why don't the two of you get some sleep while I keep watch? I haven't had much rest myself in the last few days and I might need you to spell me in a few hours if you feel up to it," Zeke said.

"I would be glad to. I don't think it would be wise to not be on guard. What do you think it was?" She asked.

Zeke had seen something the previous two nights, mostly in the shadows and what he saw still made a shiver run down his spine. He had replayed that event in his mind over and over and still didn't have a good explanation. "I don't really know, but I can safely say that Ben isn't afraid of whatever it is. As bad a shape as he's in he still charged. If that dog was in good health then I for one would feel a lot better about things." Zeke meant what he said but what he felt was that the chances of the three of them making it to town were about fifty-fifty. He couldn't fend off whatever it was if they came in numbers and Ben couldn't take on as many as it appeared there were.

Martha Ellen picked up little Keene from the front seat and put him in the back of the wagon. She climbed up also and they both covered up. Zeke checked both his Colt and Winchester. They were both fully loaded and the action was good. He felt if he could stand watch long enough for Martha Ellen to get some sleep then he just might be able to grab one hour himself, the way he felt he could probably sleep standing straight up if he had to. The next morning the three of them would head for Langley and come anything short of hell itself they would make it. It was times like this he wished his father was with him. In his mind he could hear Haskell telling him, "There ain't anything out there that you and I can't handle. Whatever it is would be damn wise to steer clear of the two of us."

Tuesday morning dawned bright and sunny without a cloud in the sky. Judge Thurman Preston was up before the sun rose and had already made use of the hotel's bathhouse. It was the first time in three days he was clean shaven and wearing clean clothes. Cecil was still snoring away when the judge kicked at the door and demanded to be let in.

Cecil, after the third kick, managed to stumble over and open the door. "You better have a damn good reason for waking me up like that. If not then I'm going to kick somebody's ass," he said before he realized he had just threatened his boss.

Judge Preston just laughed as he pushed his way in. "Cecil, I didn't realize you liked to sleep 'till the crack of noon every day."

Cecil looked out the window at the bright sky and said. "I'm sorry about what I said Judge, I didn't know it was you. I must have been really tired; I don't ever remember sleeping till noon before."

"You didn't sleep till noon Cecil, I was just joshing you. Get your sleepy ass over to the bathhouse. I can't have one of my deputies showing up for a trial looking like he just came off the trail."

"What do you mean one of your deputy's Judge; as of two days ago I'm your only deputy." Cecil felt a little sad now that he had mentioned Bill.

"Listen Cecil, I've been giving that little matter a lot of thought. As soon as this trial is over and as soon as Zeke makes it to town then the three of us are going back into that wilderness and see what we can find out. Bill might still be alive and if he is then it's up to the three of us to rescue him," Judge Preston said.

"What if Zeke don't show up Judge? Whatever got Bill might have gotten him too."

"Well it ain't anything we can figure out now, we got us a trial. Now you hurry up and make yourself look presentable. You and I represent law and order, and we also represent Rapid City. When you get finished at the bathhouse then come to the lobby. I plan on having me a decent breakfast for a change and you can too if you hurry."

At the mention of food Cecil forgot all about Bill. "Sure thing Judge, don't go off and order without me."

Just before the judge headed for the stairs he turned back and said, "And I want to see them whiskers of yours shaved clean Cecil. Nothing makes me madder than a bailiff or a deputy in my courtroom with a three day growth of beard."

Cecil hadn't expected to shave for at least two more days but there was a good breakfast waiting if he done as the judge asked, "Sure thing Judge, that was the first thing I was going to do this morning, anyway." He lied.

Thirty minutes later Cecil walked into the dining room, which was at the back of the hotel's lobby. He spotted Judge Preston sitting off to the side at a table, he was reading a newspaper. "Howdy Judge, what kind of food has this place got this time of day?"

Judge Preston looked up from his paper. "Morning Cecil, you look a lot more presentable, and a lot less ornery, than you did earlier."

"I feel a lot better too Judge. That is the first good sleep I've had since we pulled out of Rapid City Saturday night. You know Judge, I like trail food as much as anybody but it does feel nice to sit down at a table that is covered with a cloth, don't you agree?"

"I do at that Cecil. I checked around to see if anybody has heard of a man with a crippled up dog coming into town and the answer was no."

"Well Judge, I doubt Zeke could have beaten us here, if he ain't been eaten by whatever it was that got Bill then he should be here in a day or two." Again Cecil was saddened by the thought of Bill being taken in the middle of the night.

There were several other men and women seated at other tables. Cecil looked over what they were eating and the sights and smells only increased his appetite, everything looked great. "What are we having Judge?" Cecil asked.

"Do I look like a waitress to you deputy, I wear a robe not a damn apron."

"Naw Judge, come to think of it you surely don't, but if you were I would have to say you'd be a butt ugly one at that." Cecil laughed.

The judge just shook his head. He knew Cecil was only having a little fun. If an attorney ever made such a remark he would hold him in contempt. Cecil was so silly he probably held himself in contempt. Judge Preston sniggered to himself at the thought. Cecil thought the judge had found his remark humorous.

"Glad to see you in a good mood this morning Judge, I was afraid you might be a little mad at me for threatening you when you nearly kicked my door down."

The judge looked up from his paper again. "Naw, I ain't mad Cecil. I just hope you are as full of fight when we go hunting monsters after this trial is over."

Cecil's good humor left him as he considered what the judge said. He was a brave enough deputy but the fear of the unknown was something he would still need to conquer. He was snapped out of this dreadful thought when a lady walked up to the table holding a coffee pot.

"Are you boys here for breakfast or just some coffee?" She asked.

"Oh yes Ma'am, the two of us are here for breakfast and coffee. What do you recommend?" the judge asked.

"Oh, I think the cook can whip up about anything the two of you are hungry for. On weekday mornings he makes French Toast along with the usual, ham and eggs," she said.

Cecil rubbed his chin. "French Toast you say. I don't reckon I ever ate any foreign food before. What do you say Judge, should we give it a try," Cecil asked.

Judge Preston looked at the waitress and said, "You will have to forgive Deputy Spriggs here, he don't get out much. I think the both of us will have the French Toast and also eggs, scrambled is my preference with lots of coffee."

The waitress looked at Cecil and asked, "How would you like your eggs deputy?"

"Definitely not scrambled, sunny side up if you don't mind, and some jelly and biscuits on the side. Me and the Judge here been on the trail a few days, trail food has left us a mite hungry."

The young woman smiled and headed back toward the kitchen.

Judge Preston looked at Cecil. "By what you said I take it you never heard of French Toast before?"

"Never have Judge, what is it anyway?"

"All you do is take bread and put it in a skillet along with a little butter and a beat up egg. Then when it's done you pour a little maple syrup over it. I think you will like it."

"Sounds nasty to me," Cecil said.

"Well when it gets here you just take a nibble. If you don't like it then just slide your plate over to me," the judge said.

That suited Cecil just fine; he doubted he would like anything from France. "Well Judge, it sounds like you can have mine anyway, how fresh can anything be after traveling that far?"

Judge Preston just gave up. "Fine by me Cecil, you can just sit and watch me enjoy my breakfast."

Wasn't long before the table was filled with plates of food and the judge dug right in. Cecil looked at his and decided that something that smelled so good had to have a little taste to it. He took his fork and cut a small piece of the funny lookin toast and then tasted it expecting to be disappointed. He wasn't, there was the definite taste of egg and the bread was as fresh as he ever had. He noticed the judge had completely covered his with maple syrup and was shoving huge bites into his mouth. Cecil grabbed the glass jar that contained the syrup and noticed it had been warmed. He covered the funny looking bread and again took a bite. It tasted as good as anything he had ever eaten in his life.

The judge had been watching and thought he would have a little fun. "Well Cecil, slide that plate over here. I hate to see good food go to waste."

"No way Judge, this is the first foreign food I ever had and I think I kind a like it," he said with his mouth full.

"Cecil, for the last time it ain't foreign, it's made right here with good old American flour, and eggs from an American chicken."

"So why is it called French then Judge?"

"Just shut the hell up and eat Cecil, we got to be getting over to the courthouse."

Once the two men were finished the judge asked how much for the two meals and the waitress said it was a dollar eighty. The judge laid two dollars on the table and got up. "That was mighty fine Ma'am. We'll probably be in all week for breakfast and most likely supper too. What is the supper special during the week if I might ask?"

The young lady smiled and said, "Oh supper is our busiest time. The special changes each night but if you liked the breakfast then I'm sure you'll like our supper."

"That sounds fine Ma'am. We'll be back here later today to try out the evening food." With that the judge and Cecil headed for the door. The street was coming to life. Most of the storefronts had been unlocked and people were already conducting business. Judge Preston and Cecil headed toward the town square and the courthouse.

"Say Judge, why are we heading to the courthouse at such an early hour? The trial isn't set to start until ten-o'clock," Cecil asked.

"I wanted to see if anything has changed since we got that telegram last Saturday. A lot of stuff can happen in three days Cecil. Plus, I need to get acquainted with any updates to the charges that were filed last week against the accused. You and I have been out of touch with society ever since we pulled out of Rapid City."

"That makes sense to me judge. What part am I supposed to play in this trial?"

"You will be in the courtroom during the entire trial. I never like to run a trial with bailiffs I don't know. I heard once that a judge came to a town and ran a trial that was pretty unpopular with the townsfolk. It seems that when a little trouble broke out in the courtroom the three bailiffs that were assigned to the trial were a little slow in responding.

By the time they decided to get involved the judge had a black eye and a busted jaw," the judge said.

Cecil thought about this for a while and then said. "That is about as awful a thing as I ever heard. Tell you what Judge, if anyone tries to start beating on you then I hope you're the judge that presides over my trial because I will damn sure shoot someone."

Judge Preston always liked Cecil and Bill; they seemed to be hardworking deputies and honest, two traits that were a must for a lawman. He believed Cecil would shoot someone if they headed toward the bench with mischief on their minds. That was one of the reasons he always brought his own deputies when he held court anywhere other than Rapid City.

"Glad you feel that way Cecil. I would still feel better if there were one more of you though."

"Well, maybe Zeke and that God-awful dog will show up before long. I doubt if Bill is gonna be able to make it," Cecil said.

"Now Cecil, I intend to find out what happened to him and I am counting on your help. The more I think about it the madder it makes me. When whatever it was took Bill it was an assault on my court. I might just take a month or two leave of absence after we get this trial over with. I plan on spending some time out there in the wild and if something mean as hell is waiting on me then so be it. I ain't so old that I can't put up a fight." Judge Preston had made fists with his hands as he said this and Cecil truly believed the judge was ready to go right now if not for the trial.

The courthouse for the city of Langley wasn't as large, or as nice, as the one in Rapid City but Judge Preston had always found it pleasant enough when he had been forced to hold court there. The building actually had two courtrooms, a small one downstairs, which shared that floor with the rest of the city's offices. The larger of the two courtrooms was on the second floor, along with three more offices which were used by the judge and his clerks.

Judge Preston and Cecil made it to the courthouse at a little before eight o'clock and found the front door locked.

"Well Judge, looks like they don't want me and you in their pretty little courthouse," Cecil said.

Judge Preston grunted and headed toward the sheriff's office. Sheriff Jasel Farley was already at the jail; as a matter of fact he had been there all night. The previous evening, after he had the little conversation at the saloon with Wes Branham and Lloyd Shafer, he had made his rounds of the town and by the time he made it back to his office he was exhausted. He knew the doctor told him to not get overly stressed and also not exert himself too much but he was sheriff and he would do his job until he dropped dead from his illness. No one in town knew he was dying except the doctor and the undertaker. Jasel felt he had to make his arrangements in advance; he didn't like the thoughts of being laid to rest in a pauper's grave. His funeral was paid for in full and he had warned the undertaker to not utter a word to anyone.

Jasel had made a will when he found out he was dying and his time was growing short. He owned his house and the one acre of land that it occupied. There were no debts to settle and he even had a little money in the bank. Everything he owned was to be given to the church, his church. He had been a member there for years and had even been married in the building. His small estate would make a nice gift. He had no children and no family left that he knew of so he felt the church was his family.

When Judge Preston and Cecil walked through the front door Jasel was busy at the stove making a big pot of coffee. "Why Judge Preston, you finally made it, and hello to you Cecil. What on earth kept you two so long? I figured the two of you would have been here on the train yesterday or the day before."

"Hello Sheriff, good to see you. It seems the message for me to be here was delayed. You know, I think it was the intent of someone for me to miss this trial altogether."

"You know, I was afraid of something like that. This town wants a hanging and they want it in the form of a lynching. You two want some coffee, I make about the best there is in these parts," the sheriff said.

"I believe I do Sheriff," Cecil said as he headed for the pot. "Say Jasel, how is it you're looking so thin? The last time I was here you must have been at least twenty pounds heavier."

"Oh I don't really know deputy. I guess I've just been working too hard is all I can figure," Sheriff Farley said.

Cecil accepted this but the judge thought something else was at play. Not only did the sheriff look thinner but he was gaunt in the eyes and his skin had a grayish look to it.

"Since the prosecuting attorney had to step aside for reasons of conflict do you know if his replacement for the trial has shown up?" The judge asked.

"He has Judge; he's been here for a few days. As a matter of fact I had a little talk with him last night at the saloon. He was sitting at a table talking to a gunfighter that I believe you are about to get acquainted with."

"A gunfighter you say." Judge Preston looked at Cecil. "What is the rest of the story Sheriff?"

"Well Judge, Wes Branham is the only witness to the murder of Sonny Briscoe. I am not a lawyer Judge, but something tells me that there was some dealing under the table between them two. And something else you might want to know is that I believe some men were sent out on the trail between here and Rapid City with the intent of slowing you down. I don't know this for sure but there was some talk at the saloon a few nights ago and one of the men that overheard the conversation likes to share his information with me. I go a little easy on him when he's drunk and in exchange he gives me information."

Judge Preston went to the coffee pot and filled himself a cup. "You think they were going to try and kill me Jasel?"

"I don't think so judge. The word I got was that they were told to stand off and fire a few shots over your head, you know, slow you down but not harm you. A man that is getting shot at tends to travel real slow and in the shadows if you know what I mean," the sheriff said.

"Well we weren't shot at sheriff but we did lose a man out there," Cecil said.

"You lost a man. How did he die?"

"We don't know for sure he's dead. We just got up yesterday morning and he wasn't there. His horse was still tied where he left it the night before and all his gear was still in camp. He just vanished. And from what I gather he ain't the first. People been coming into Rapid City reporting missing family members for the last month or so."

Sheriff Farley considered what he had just heard. "How many people are missing judge?"

"Don't know for sure maybe twenty maybe fifty. All we do know is that families say their menfolk are being taken. No women or children, just the men," the judge said.

The three men were quiet as each thought about the possibilities that might explain what was happening.

Judge Preston snapped everyone back to life when he asked, "Sheriff, is there a reason why the courthouse would be locked at this hour?"

"Locked, have you already been to the courthouse this morning?" Farley asked.

"Yes I have Sheriff, that's how I know it's locked," the judge shot back.

"Well Judge, if that don't beat all. It should have been opened an hour ago. What do you say the three of us head on over and see what on earth is going on?" the sheriff said.

By the time the three men made it to the courthouse there was a crowd standing at the front door.

"Look there Judge, I believe that door is locked," Sheriff Farley said.

"Jasel, I'm a judge, don't you think I can tell if a door is locked or not?"

The sheriff looked at Judge Preston and realized he might have made him mad. "No disrespect Judge, I was just talking out loud. I ain't never seen that door locked at this time of day unless it's Sunday."

The crowd at the front door separated as the sheriff walked up. "Sheriff, I thought there was going to be a trial here today. That damn

Doug Whitmore was supposed to stand trial and then answer for what he has done," one of the bystanders said.

Someone else in the crowd said, "They were supposed to send us a judge from Rapid City. I say we go ahead and hang Whitmore since that slow ass judge never showed up." No one in the crowd recognized Judge Preston, he only made it to Langley when he was needed and that usually meant every other year.

Cecil looked at the judge and wondered what was going to happen next.

Judge Preston thought he would check out the sentiment of the crowd to see what kind of problem it was going to be to seat an impartial jury. "Who is this judge you speak of friend?"

"I never met the man, but if his decisions are as messed up as his calendar then we might as well go home. A judge like that shows up now, I might just be tempted to kick his ass myself."

Another one of the crowd added, "I met him once, he is short and fat. The man is so fat his black robe won't even fit around his belly."

The first man added, "And since he decided that he ain't gonna show up then I say we go over to the jail and hang that Whitmore right now." The crowd started off the front porch of the courthouse. Just as they made it to the street Judge Preston decided he had heard and seen enough.

"Gentlemen, if I might have a moment of your time."

The man who had done the most talking decided to have the final word. "I don't know who you are and don't really care. Me and these other men got us a hanging to see to and if you try to get in the way then we might just hang you too."

This was more than Cecil could stand. He liked the judge and he hated loudmouth troublemakers. He ran off the steps of the courthouse and grabbed the man who had threatened his boss. The man drew back his right fist to strike the deputy but Cecil was ready. He grabbed and twisted the other arm until he had it behind the troublemaker's back. He held it up high, nearly to the point of breaking the man's shoulder. He then shoved him along and up the stairs to where the judge stood.

"Now you listen to me and you listen good. This man in front of you is Judge Thurman Preston. You are going to apologize to him and then I am placing you under arrest. If you don't do exactly as I just said then I might shoot you right here in front of this courthouse."

There wasn't a sound from the group of men. Judge Preston looked into the crowd and asked, "Sheriff Farley, would you bring that man wearing the red checkered shirt up here please." The judge was talking about the man who had said he was short and fat.

"Be my pleasure Judge." Jasel walked over and grabbed the man the judge had described by the arm and said, "Me and you ain't going to have any trouble now are we Claude?" The man named Claude looked up the stairs at the judge and said, "Naw Sheriff, I reckon we ain't."

Jasel and the man named Claude walked up the steps right in front of the judge. "Here he is Judge," the sheriff said.

"What is your name mister?" the judge asked the man that had threatened him that was being held by Cecil.

"Boley sir, Sam Boley," the man said.

"Well Sam Boley, if I heard right you are going to be arrested right after you apologize to me, do I have it figured out so far?" the judge asked.

"I reckon so," Boley said.

The judge stood and waited, finally he asked, "You do know how to apologize don't you Boley?"

Before anyone knew what was happening Boley yanked his arm free from Cecil and threw a punch at the judge. To everyone's surprise Judge Preston ducked under the punch and came up with his right fist and struck Sam Boley squarely under the jaw. Boley weaved a time or two and then fell forward onto the floor of the courthouse porch.

Judge Preston stepped over in front of Claude and asked the same thing. "If I heard right your name is Claude. I believe you need to apologize also and you know the consequences if you try what that man lying on the floor tried."

Claude didn't hesitate, "Yes sir Judge, I am truly sorry if I said anything that might have seemed out of the way."

"Well then Sheriff Farley, I believe if Claude here will help Sam Boley to his feet then they need to be getting on over to the jail. Make sure there is at least one empty cell between them and Whitmore. Don't want to think these boys would reach through the bars and try to do something bad to the accused."

"It would truly be my pleasure Judge. Alright Claude get Boley up off the floor and let's be getting to the jail."

After Sheriff Farley left, along with his two newest prisoners, Cecil said, "Well Judge, so much for getting inside the courthouse."

There were still several people standing around. "Does anyone here know where Judge Simon Lester lives?" Preston asked.

"I reckon I do Judge. If you like I can lead you that way," a man in the crowd said.

"Come on Cecil, let's follow this man to Lester's house and see if we can figure out what's going on," Judge Preston said.

The man's name was William Sloane. He introduced himself as they walked through town. "I was on my way over to the general store to get a sack of mule feed when I saw the big crowd at the courthouse. I got there in time to see that man throw a punch at you Judge. Where did you learn to fight like that if you don't mind me asking?"

Judge Preston was pleased that someone had seen him handle the trouble at the courthouse. "I was a Riverboat Captain back in my younger days. Being Captain didn't really carry any weight with the crew though. It was a pretty rough bunch and they would just as soon whip a Captain as anybody else. I got my jaw cracked a few times until I finally learned how to fight. It's amazing how fast a man can learn when his nose gets busted enough, wasn't long before I started getting a little respect. You know that is the first punch I've thrown in at least thirty years and I'll tell you something else, it felt good to dish it out like I did back in the old days."

"I'll say Judge. You put old Boley down pretty quick. I've seen him in a fight or two and he's pretty good. I believe a few days in jail might just be what old Boley needs Judge, if you don't mind me saying," Sloane said.

The judge listened to Sloane as they walked. "Say Sloane, what do you do here in Langley?"

"I raise horses to sell and a few mules along too. People will come from all over to buy a good horse. Been doing it my whole life," Sloane said.

Cecil thought he would have a little fun, "What do you mean your whole life, you ain't lived your whole life yet."

Sloane laughed, "I reckon you got a good point there deputy."

Just as the three rounded a corner in the street Sloane said, "That would be Judge Lester's house there on the far corner, the one with the two big evergreen trees in the front yard."

Preston and Cecil both looked at the oversized house and were impressed. The house was of stone on the first floor with wood lap siding above that. There were large dormers above the second floor indicating another floor. As the three men approached they noticed a man sitting on the front porch. When the man saw the three he got up and hurried down the steps.

"Thurman Preston, of all people." When they were close enough the man thrust out a hand and said, "My goodness Judge, how long has it been, two years?"

Preston grabbed the man's hand and as they shook he said, "That would be my guess Simon. I believe it was that Adkins trial. Seems anytime you get anything you can't handle they send for me."

Judge Lester laughed and then shook Cecil's hand along with Sloan's. "Not at all Preston, they like me to handle all the tough trials and just let you in town for the small stuff. Come up and have a seat on the porch."

"Maybe later Judge, I came over to see if you would know why the courthouse is all locked up this morning?" Judge Preston asked.

"Locked up, why you must be joking," Sloane said.

"Not at all, I've been trying to get in that building for the better part of an hour now."

Judge Lester looked in the direction of the courthouse, although it wasn't in view from here. "Let me grab my coat Thurman. This requires some looking into."

As the four men headed back to the courthouse Sloane felt like he was now a man of importance. He was walking along with a deputy and not just one judge but two. Suddenly it dawned on him that he might not look all that important after all, he might look like a criminal being escorted to jail. "Tell you what men, I better be getting over to the general store, I'll probably see you in town from time to time," he told Cecil and Judge Preston.

"Thanks for showing us around Mr. Sloane," Judge Preston said.

As the deputy and two judges got within view of the courthouse the crowd had grown considerably. It seemed a little louder than earlier also. One man seemed to be giving a speech from the top of the steps. "If they don't intend to have trial today then I say we go over to the jail and have a trial of our own. We yank that bastard Whitmore out of there and string him up from the nearest tree."

Several people in the crowd seemed to agree with this. They all had their backs to the two judges and Cecil.

"Crowd looks pretty mean Judge; you think walking right back up there is the wisest thing to do?" Cecil asked.

Judge Lester answered the question, "That is exactly what I intend to do deputy."

As Lester pushed his way up the steps some of the men turned to protest but once they saw who it was they wisely held their tongues. When he got to the top he looked the speaker dead in the eye and asked. "I don't believe I recognize you friend and I know pretty much everybody, now what's your name?"

It was evident that the man was not from the town of Langley because he didn't know the judge. "I don't recognize you either," he said. Then he added, "Oh, now I remember you, you're the bastard I'm getting ready to whip right here and now."

Again when Judge Preston heard this he ran to the other judge's defense. As before, Preston punched this man in the jaw and, as before, this man went down in a heap. The crowd got louder and started for the steps until Cecil pulled his Colt and fired a shot into the air.

It was now Cecil's turn to speak, "Anyone who attempts to climb those steps will be shot, no one approach until I can figure out what's going on here. These two men are Judge Preston and Judge Lester and as an officer of the court it is my duty to protect them. I want everyone here to go about their business." No one moved. Cecil raised his gun and fired again, he then pointed it toward the crowd. "I mean now," he said. With that the men started to move off but there was a considerable amount of grumbling.

Judge Lester pulled a key from his pocket and unlocked the big front door to the courthouse. As he did Sheriff Farley came running down the street and he had his gun drawn. "What happened here Judge, I heard two gunshots."

"You did at that Jasel. Why don't you arrest that fellar laying there on the floor?" Lester said.

Sheriff Farley looked down at the man and then at Judge Preston. As he smiled he asked, "Preston, I would say you must have been a damn good boxer in your day."

"Hell, he's a damn good boxer now," Cecil said as he laughed.

"Tell you what Judge Lester, I'll take this man to jail and then get one of my deputies to stand guard over there. Place is starting to fill up. Say do you recognize this fellar?" Farley asked as they got the man up off the floor of the porch.

Lester looked at the man, "Can't say as I've ever laid eyes on him before."

Farley looked at Judge Preston. "As soon as I can get somebody to watch over the jail I need to talk to you Judge, it might be important."

Preston figured it had something to do with the man he had just hit. "Sure thing Sheriff. Cecil and I will be right here with Judge Lester trying to figure out what's going on."

"Shouldn't take more than thirty minutes," the sheriff said as he hustled his new prisoner down the steps.

"Come on in Preston. Cecil, how about you relocking that door? I really don't want anyone in here until I can figure out what has happened to all the bailiffs. There is sure something strange going on this morning and until I can figure it out, I don't want anyone else in this building," Judge Lester said.

Once Cecil had the door locked the three men climbed the stairs and headed for the clerk's office. "I want to have me a look at the docket. When I left here yesterday it was my intention to steer clear of this place until the Whitmore trial was over. I didn't want to taint any decisions a jury might come to if they see me here and felt I had a preference one way or the other, which I don't."

Cecil and Judge Preston followed Lester into a rather large office that contained four desks and lots of book shelves. After looking at a paper on one of the desks Judge Lester went to one of the shelves and took down a large long ledger. There was a long counter at the front of the room where people could place any number of books as they scanned for whatever it was they might be looking for.

Lester put the ledger he selected on top of the counter and scanned the pages until he found what he was looking for. "Why this states that the trial has been dismissed due to the absence of the presiding judge."

Preston stepped forward and scanned the spot where Lester held his finger. After viewing the page he stepped back and looked out the window and down at the street. The crowd was back and even larger this time.

Now who could have changed the court docket in your courthouse Judge Lester without your knowledge?" Preston asked.

Again Lester looked at the ledger. "It appears that whoever changed the docket never signed it. But it looks like they did manage to say that the order was given by me, which is a damn lie. This was entered first thing yesterday morning and whoever is behind it managed to spread the word to the entire courthouse staff. That's why no one is here, everyone took the day off and it would seem that I am to blame."

As Preston scanned the town square he saw Sheriff Farley coming back down the street toward the courthouse. There was another man walking with the sheriff and he was also wearing a badge, Preston assumed he was another of the town's deputies.

"Say Lester, how many deputies does the town of Langley employ?"

Lester turned away from the ledger and looked out the window, "Three deputies along with Sheriff Farley, why do you ask?"

"That man walking with the sheriff, is he one of the towns deputies? The badge he is wearing appears to be of a different type than the one Farley is wearing," Preston said.

Lester squinted hard but couldn't make out what Preston was talking about. "You must have pretty good eyes Judge, I can't make out the badge and to tell you the truth I don't believe I have ever seen the man wearing it before either."

Lester turned to Cecil who was sitting at one of the desks taking it easy, "Deputy, could I ask a favor of you by letting the sheriff and that man with him in the building."

Cecil said he would be glad to and headed for the stairs. Within minutes Cecil was back along with Sheriff Farley and the stranger. The man was of average build but had the look of someone who had seen many days on the trail. He wore a cross draw holster and his badge was that of a marshal. His hair was well past his ears and un-kept. He had at least a week old growth of whiskers on his face. The eyes were cold gray in color and he had the look of a hunter, only this man hunted other men.

Lester stuck out a hand and said, "I don't believe we have ever met. My name is Simon Lester and I am the judge here in Langley."

The stranger stuck out a hand and shook. "Actually we did meet once before Judge. My name is Pete Savage."

Marshal Pete Savage was nearly forty years old when he first met Judge Lester. He had been in Langley on that occasion disguised as a prisoner in order to obtain information. Savage was a stout man at the time and had lost little even though he was now heading toward fifty, not quite there yet but pushing it just the same. He was a man who could bed down under the stars for months at a time or clean himself up and pass as a congressman, whatever the job required.

He was in town now to observe the trial of the governor's son-in-law and report everything that was happening. Savage was good with a gun and even better in a bar fight. He was tough and honest, two traits that were rarely found together this far west. He could out drink anyone at the table or not touch the stuff for months depending on the job at hand. When the Marshal's Service had a tough assignment then it was Savage who usually got the job.

Judge Lester looked over the stranger and still couldn't place the man, or the name. "With a name like Savage I'm sure I would remember you."

"When we met before Judge I was wearing cuffs and was a guest of Sheriff Farley's over at the jail. At the time I was going by the name of Willie Stiles."

You could tell by the look on the judge's face that he suddenly remembered the man who now stood before him. "That was six or seven years ago, maybe even ten. I do remember you now. You were clean shaven and wearing city clothes. If I remember correctly you were charged with bank robbery and not just one but three. I also remember that you managed to escape the day before your trial, do I have everything about right so far?" It was evident that Judge Lester was curious now that he was face to face with a man who had escaped from his jail and never stood trial for the crimes he had been accused of.

"You have everything correct Judge. The reason I never stood trial was that I never committed the crimes I was accused of. The territorial governor at that time sent me into this area undercover in hopes of obtaining information on who was actually committing the bank heists. While in jail here I did manage to get some information on the actual robbers but it never brought anyone to justice, at least not yet. Sheriff Farley here was in on the plan and was not allowed to speak of it by order of the governor himself. When my job here was finished the sheriff unlocked my cell door and I rode out of town in the middle of the night. It was written up as a jail break and that was the end of it," Savage said.

Lester looked a bit put out at being used by the governor. "And what is it that brings you to Langley now Mr. Savage, or is that name and that marshal's badge just another story you and the governor have cooked up?"

Savage looked at Lester and decided the judge might be a bit mad at being misled all those years ago. "I can assure you that my name is really Pete Savage and I really am a Deputy United States Marshal. I am here again on orders from the governor. It seems his son-in-law has been charged with murder and I was told to be here the day of the trial which is today."

Lester looked over at Judge Preston. "Well Judge, I think with all that has gone on here today we need to sit down and try to figure out a plan."

Preston looked at the marshal. "Why did the governor feel you were needed here today Savage?"

"The governor never mentioned it in his telegram to me Judge. The message said to be here by nine o'clock Tuesday morning and nothing else. I suppose he felt a little extra law might be a good thing given the sentiments of the townsfolk."

Lester looked at Preston and said, "Well Preston, what do you intend to do?"

Judge Preston turned to face the men in the room. "Cecil, how about you and Sheriff Farley gather up the attorneys and the bailiffs, get them here fast if that is at all possible. Have the bailiffs get the rest of the clerks and court officers here. Once we have the courthouse staff here then I intend to have the trial that I was sent here for. We will open the doors and pick us a jury out of that group out there on the courthouse lawn."

"Do you think there are twelve individuals out there that haven't already formed an opinion of guilt? You heard what they said earlier. We were threatened ourselves," Lester said.

This was what Judge Preston was counting on. "We will pick us a jury Judge Lester, but after questioning them if I find they are not one hundred percent impartial then I will preside over the trial and render a verdict myself."

Lester smiled. He liked Preston and found him to be a fair man. He also knew that finding twelve people in the town of Langley that didn't want to take Whitmore out back of the courthouse and hang him this very minute would be damn near impossible.

"I think that would be the route to take Preston. If you do eliminate the jury then I might sit in the courtroom and watch. How do you feel about that?" Lester asked.

Without hesitation Preston said that was an excellent idea. "Well Cecil, everything is settled. If you and the sheriff could hurry along then we might be able to get this trial started by noon."

With Cecil and Farley gone it just left the two judges and the marshal in the courthouse, Lester stationed Savage at the front door with instructions to not let anyone inside the building until the bailiffs were found and sent over. By ten-thirty most of the clerks and the three bailiffs were present, another hour should see everyone there. Lester still had the issue of who had altered the court docket and why the entire courthouse staff had been given the day off but decided he would deal with that after the trial. Right now the most important thing was to conclude the trial and hope things in town cooled down a bit.

After a little time passed Lester said, "Alright Preston, the courthouse is staffed and the three bailiffs are here." Lester said this as he took out his pocket watch and observed the time. "Twelve fifteen, a little late to start a trial don't you think?"

Preston was still looking out the window at the crowd that was now bigger than it had been at any given time during the morning.

"By the looks of things out there I believe we need to at least set things up for the trial. If that can be done quick enough then I will call everyone to order and at least begin. Maybe that will calm a few of the hotheads in town that are dead set on a hanging."

"Well Preston, I think that might be the best plan of action given the hour." Lester looked at his bailiffs, "You three are now taking orders from Judge Preston here. He will also be using my chambers at the courthouse for the duration of the trial. I expect at least one of you has worked for Preston before; he was here about two years ago and oversaw that Bartley trial. If a jury is seated then I will make myself scarce, but if twelve impartial jurors can't be found Judge Preston will be hearing the evidence and making a ruling himself. If so then I intend to hang around just in case I might be needed." Lester looked at his friend, "As of now Preston, the courthouse is yours."

Preston thought about his options. He had a trial to conduct but he also had a town that, from all appearances, was ready to erupt. Violence was a real possibility if the trial didn't take place soon. It was also a possibility if he rendered a verdict that didn't meet the town's expectations. That didn't play into his thoughts, he was a judge and he would do what was expected of him, the hell with whatever anyone else thought.

"Marshal Savage, if the governor sent you here to help out then might I assume you will be taking orders from me?" Judge Preston asked.

Savage smiled at the judge, "That is exactly what I'm expected to do Judge."

"As of now, I want you to oversee the bailiffs during the proceedings. The four of you unlock the courthouse door and see that everyone out there understands that if they enter this buildings I expect them to be orderly at all times. I will have anyone who acts otherwise jailed immediately and you can tell them that.

"Sheriff Farley, I need you and one of your deputies to bring over the accused and put him in the adjoining office and keep him there until I send for him. Bring him through the side streets and enter the building by way of the back door while the bailiffs are getting everyone in the courtroom, maybe you won't be noticed."

That left Cecil as the only lawman available. "Cecil, go over to the hotel and see if you can find the Honorable Lloyd Shafer. Have him come to the courthouse immediately and when he gets here to find me. Lester, do you know who Doug Whitmore has for an attorney?"

Judge Lester looked at Preston and said, "I thought you knew judge, no one in town will represent him. All the other attorneys are afraid it will be the ruin of their practices. Unless he hired someone this morning then I would hazard to guess that the accused is not represented."

This little piece of information made a bad day even worse for Preston. "I can't try this man unless he has an attorney that is unless he has chosen to represent himself."

"No, he hasn't decided to be his own attorney. He just can't find anyone that is dumb enough, or maybe hard up enough, to take the case," Lester replied.

Judge Preston thought a minute and asked, "If he isn't represented Lester, then what do you propose I do, after all this is your town and these are your people?"

Lester smiled and Preston immediately knew he had a plan, "Judge Preston do you intend to call a jury?"

"Yes I do. After a few questions are asked then I plan on dismissing the jury and preside over the trial and render a verdict myself. As of now I have serious doubts about finding an impartial jury. Unless I am thoroughly impressed by the twelve jurors then they will be dismissed. Why do you ask?"

"Well, I was just thinking, and you have every right to turn me down. Since I won't be presiding over these proceedings how would you feel if I took on the job as defense council? Before I was appointed judge that was how I made my living, defending those who were accused. I from time to time look back on those days and reminisce."

"You know Lester, I figured as much. Don't you feel there might be a conflict if I allow you to defend Whitmore?"

"Not at all judge. I've never heard of this before but I also have never heard of anything against it. It's been a few years but I think I remember the basics. And just between me and you I don't like that Lloyd Shafer, not one bit. I would hate to lose to him but on the upside if

I win then it might just bring him down a notch or two." Lester said this with a smile on his face.

"All I can do is consider it for now Judge Lester. Let's see how the jury selection goes and also if Doug Whitmore is open to the idea of you representing him," Preston said.

"Oh, I think if it comes right down to it Whitmore will be glad to have me representing him. Better me than no one."

"Just between you and me, I kind of like the idea, but we will have to wait and see. Let's not let this be known for the time being. Don't want to make it look like we planned the whole thing. It might also be better if Whitmore asks for you to be his attorney," Preston said.

After a little consideration Lester said, "If he asked for me then it would look like it was his idea, I like it."

It took nearly an hour for the bailiffs and Marshal Savage to get everyone seated in the big courtroom. The walls around the back and both sides were lined with others that couldn't find a seat. Some of those standing were doing so on purpose. If you were seated on one of the benches then you might not get to see everything that went on in the courtroom. Those standing wouldn't miss a thing.

Once Savage had warned everyone what would happen if they made any noise or acted up in any way he went back to the judge's chambers and notified Judge Preston that all was ready.

"Go back out there Savage and let everyone know that it will be a few more minutes. Sheriff Farley, bring in Whitmore so I can meet the accused, also bring in Lloyd Shafer," Preston said.

Within minutes Doug Whitmore was led in by the sheriff. Seconds later Shafer walked in.

"Close the door Sheriff so we can have a little talk," Preston said.

Shafer looked at Preston and said, "Well Judge, it looks like you made it to Langley safe and sound, any excitement on the trip in?"

Preston found it odd that Shafer would ask about any mishaps on the journey to Langley and wondered if he knew more than he was letting on. "Just a little Lloyd, I have asked you and the accused to be here in order to get acquainted with who is charged and also to know who his council is. Mr. Whitmore, is your attorney around so I may have a word with him."

Doug Whitmore looked around the room and then at the judge. "I haven't been able to hire an attorney your honor. I have sent word to several and only gotten a few responses."

"And what have the responses been?"

"All have been the same, no. It seems everyone is afraid to represent me."

Shafer was looking at Preston, and he was smiling. "Well Preston, how do you intend to proceed, you can't have a trial unless this murderer has an attorney."

Preston looked at Shafer and said, "You will refer to the accused as Mr. Whitmore or the accused. Until there is a trial and he is found guilty I expect professionalism from you."

"I am truly sorry Judge Preston. Not sorry for calling the accused a murderer but for filing another petition to have you removed from the bench as soon as I make my way back to Rapid City. As far as I am concerned there isn't going to be a trial, Whitmore doesn't have representation. Have the sheriff take him back to his cozy little jail cell."

Judge Preston stood up from the desk and pointed an angry finger at Shafer. "One more remark like that and I will have the sheriff escort you to a cozy little jail cell. There will be a trial and it will start today."

"There will be no trial Preston as long as Whitmore fails to acquire council," Shafer said.

Preston sat back down and smiled at the man he would rather beat the hell out of than be nice to. "His council is standing before you Shafer," Preston said as he pointed to Judge Lester.

Shafer looked at Lester and said, "You can't be serious, a judge can't defend a man in his own courtroom."

"It isn't his courtroom Shafer, it is my courtroom. Lester is the only man within a hundred miles who is willing to defend Doug Whitmore," Preston said.

"The two of you can't be serious, a judge is a judge. Lester gave up the right to practice law the minute he agreed to be appointed judge of this territory."

"You make a good point Shafer. I would like you to quote any laws that say a man who is appointed judge loses the ability to practice law anytime in the future. If you can do that then I won't allow Lester to represent Whitmore," Preston said.

Shafer shifted on his feet. This had caught him totally off guard. He knew of no other time when he had heard of anything like this, either for or against a judge acting as an attorney in a murder case. "Nothing comes to mind at the moment but I am sure there is a statute against what you are proposing. I will need more time to do a little research if that would be possible."

Preston smiled. "Time is something neither I nor this town can justify. You saw those people out there, they want a trial today. If I grant a postponement then who knows what will happen."

Now Shafer was smiling. He knew he had Preston in a predicament. If the judge went ahead with his plans to allow Judge Simon Lester to act as defense council then he could probably have any decision Preston granted reversed on appeal, if it ever got that far. A guilty verdict would not need to be appealed though, the accused would be hung right here in the town of Langley. A not guilty verdict would probably never make it to appeal either. The accused would be broken out of jail and lynched right here in the town of Langley also. Either way Shafer would get the results he wanted. The governor's ability to get re-elected would be severely handicapped by the fact that his very own son-in-law was hung for murder. Then Shafer thought of something else.

"I see your point Judge Preston. I would request though that you preside over the decision rather than allowing a jury to hear the evidence. As you mentioned, the sentiments of the townsfolk would make it nearly impossible to impanel and impartial jury, do you agree?"

The sudden change in manner and tone by Shafer didn't go unnoticed by either Preston or Lester. Shafer had even referred to Preston as Judge Preston. Shafer was smart and also devious, two traits that by themselves meant little. Combined it could only mean trouble for whoever stood in his way.

"Then it's agreed, Lester will represent Doug Whitmore. The only thing that needs to be addressed is whether Mr. Whitmore will accept said representation." Preston looked at Whitmore and asked, "How do you feel about what has been agreed upon here this afternoon Mr. Whitmore?"

Doug Whitmore, who had yet to speak concerning his new attorney, looked at Judge Lester. He had known the judge for many years and had a high degree of respect for the man. He was still caught off guard as to why a judge would want to represent him in a murder trial though. He also wondered if the judge was capable of putting on a defense that was adequate against an opponent as capable as Lloyd Shafer. In any event, this appeared to be his only option at the moment, no other attorney would represent him and he had tried them all.

"I will gladly agree for Judge Lester to represent me. I do wonder though how a trial can take place if my new attorney has yet to hear the facts of the case and, for that matter, hasn't even heard my side of the story."

Lester looked out the window and spoke now with his back to everyone in the room. "I realize that you and I are at a disadvantage at the moment. Events have transpired very quickly and I agreed to step in at the last moment to defend you. I will promise you this," Before Lester finished his statement he looked over at Lloyd Shafer and realized he was about to divulge some information that he really didn't want the opposing attorney to know about at this time. "Maybe we will talk in private later and I will let you know what I intend on doing."

Shafer was a bit surprised; he doubted Lester could know much about the case at hand. If he did have some facts that were not apparent to the prosecutor then he would deal with them when they were presented. Right now all he was concerned with was to get the trial underway. Not only did he want to get back to Rapid City and out of this dusty little town but he was also worried about his star witness, Wes Branham. The man was a menace and Shafer was still trying to figure out how he had come to rely on such a man. Wes was ruthless and spent too much time with the bottle. If he ever got drunk and started spouting off about what really happened in the barn when Sonny Briscoe was killed then there would be some explaining to do by both Wes Branham and the prosecutor for the case, Lloyd Shafer.

At that moment Shafer made a decision, after the trial here in Langley was concluded he would see about silencing Wes Branham permanently. He couldn't have his plans destroyed because someone liked to get drunk and then mouth off about how tough he was. Branham would be eliminated soon after the trial was concluded.

Shafer looked at the judge, "Well Preston, how do we proceed?"

"First let me take a vote on something that needs to be resolved. Do you Mr. Whitmore, request a jury trial or would you rather your fate be decided by the judge which as you know by now is me?"

Doug Whitmore knew the sentiments of the town and wanted nothing to do with a jury. "I prefer that you preside over the trial and then render the verdict Judge."

This was what everyone in the room wanted. "Well if no one has any objections then I agree. The trial can begin immediately and at the end I will make my decision."

Just then one of the bailiffs knocked on the door, once admitted he informed the judge that the courtroom was filled and nearly overflowing. More of the townsfolk were standing outside, unable to enter for lack of space.

"Well then, I would advise you Judge Lester and you Mr. Shafer to proceed out front and get ready for a trial. Cecil, how about you and Sheriff Farley taking Mr. Whitmore back to the adjoining office and wait until I send one of the bailiffs for you." Just as Cecil and the sheriff were ready to exit the judge's chambers Preston added, "And when I send for Whitmore I want both of you to bring him in and stay near him the entire time. Keep a close eye on the crowd, if you see anything out of the ordinary then I want you to take care of it." The two lawmen didn't speak but they did acknowledge that they both understood.

Once everyone was outside and going about the tasks at hand Judge Preston got back up and went to the window. He stood there observing the men in the street. Preston didn't know the particulars of the case he was about to hold court over but he found it odd that so many people held such a violent opinion of a man who was a simple small town banker who, as far as he could tell, had never broken the law in his life. Preston also wondered how many of the men in the street owed money to Whitmore.

Preston put on his robe and headed for the courtroom, at the door that led to the bench stood a bailiff. "Head on in and call the courtroom to order bailiff," Preston said.

The man turned and went in before the judge. "All rise for the Honorable Judge Thurman Preston," he said with a loud booming voice. Preston realized this was probably the bailiff that announced for Judge Lester if for no other reason than his loud deep voice.

Preston entered and took his seat at the bench. As he did he said, "You may be seated."

He looked over the courtroom, it had been nearly two years since he had presided over this same room and he remembered it well. He also remembered that case and how hard it was to keep the spectators quiet and under control, and that wasn't nearly as serious a trial as the one he was about to begin.

"Will the two attorneys approach the bench?" Preston asked.

As both Shafer and Lester came forward someone in the room shouted. "Why that one ain't no attorney, that's Judge Lester. If he was any kind of judge he would have ran this trial himself. Instead he had to send off for a no good judge from Rapid City."

Judge Preston looked over at Savage and nodded. Marshal Savage walked over along with one of the town's deputies and grabbed the smart mouthed spectator. "Come along mister, you are under arrest."

The man protested and started to resist. "You ain't arresting nobody mister, Hell I don't even know who you are." As he was about to get free of the marshal, Savage took out his Colt and hit the man on top of the head. He fell to the floor and went still. Savage and the deputy grabbed the man by the arms and slid him from the courtroom.

Judge Preston waited until the three were outside the courtroom and then warned the audience. "That is just a sample of what will happen if anyone else tries to disturb these proceedings. Does everyone understand me?" No one said a word and for that matter no one even moved.

When Lester and Shafer turned back toward Preston the room was completely silent. "Gentlemen, it is nearly three o'clock and we haven't even had lunch yet. I propose that we adjourn and reconvene at nine o'clock in the morning. This will also give Lester here time to familiarize himself with the case that has been dumped in his lap. Do you agree?"

Shafer was indignant. "I don't agree judge. We are all here so let's get this trial started. We can work into the night if need be. I promise you it won't take that long for me to present my case and then we can hang Whitmore first thing in the morning."

Preston looked at Shafer. "Keep your voice down. What makes you so sure you got enough evidence to convict? And as far as a hanging you are forgetting one thing, that's my decision to make, not yours."

"I've got enough evidence Judge; you're forgetting that I have a witness."

"Oh, I am forgetting nothing. We will get to talk to your witness. As far as today goes, I believe it would be best to start the trial tomorrow. Lester how do you feel about the trial taking place first thing tomorrow morning? If you think that would be best then that is what we will do."

Lester knew what he was about to say would make Shafer mad and he actually hoped it did. "I agree with you Judge, at such a late hour I think the trial should take place tomorrow. It will give me time to get acquainted with the facts of the case."

Preston looked at Shafer. "Then tomorrow it is. Everyone be here and ready to proceed at nine o'clock." Preston tapped his gavel and said loud enough for the entire courtroom to hear, "Court is adjourned until nine o'clock Wednesday morning."

Zeke stood guard for the remainder of Tuesday night. Martha Ellen and Keene slept comfortably in the back of the wagon. Zeke knew the woman had spent the time prior to his arrival worried about what had happened to her two brothers and also the predicament they were both in, stranded in the wilderness without help will do that to anyone, especially a mother with a young child to care for. As tired as he was he decided to let the two sleep. Once it became daylight he hoped the danger would be over. The creatures had yet to cause trouble during daylight hours.

The night became chilly and what little cloud cover there was couldn't hide the moon and all the stars. It seemed anytime the moon was out it would make the night colder. Zeke kept a good fire going and was well into his second pot of coffee when the sky grew light gray as morning approached. When it was completely light he decided to make Ben his breakfast, he was too tired to even think about food for himself. Ben had slept the entire night, Zeke decided to not wake the big dog for his three o'clock snack. He had been in a vicious fight the evening before and sleep was probably the best thing for him right now.

Zeke took his knife and began slicing small pieces of bacon from the ever dwindling slab the judge and the two deputies had left him ever so long ago. Ben came to as the bacon sizzled and the flour and water thickened. When the thin stew was finished the plate was slid over. Ben stood and stretched. He then did something that both surprised and pleased Zeke. Before he ate he walked over and butted Zeke's shoulder with his head. He then proceeded to eat his breakfast.

Now what did that mean? He had seen dogs show appreciation by licking a hand before but never had he been head-butted. This was truly a strange animal, smart but strange. After finishing his breakfast Ben done something else that was new, he walked down to the stream and stood right in the middle of the clear cool water as he drank. After he finished he waded out into the middle of a small pool and swam across. He then investigated the other side and after a few minutes he reentered the water and swam back. Once out he stood and violently shook, when he came back to the fire and laid down on his rug he was a different looking animal, he was clean. He even looked cleaner than he had when Zeke had tried to wash him up after rescuing him from the snare.

Zeke grabbed the coffee pot and went down to the small stream to get a refill. He made sure to go above the small pool that Ben had used as a bathtub. A large tree had fallen at least a year back and this was what had blocked the little stream and made the pool. Zeke hadn't gotten a good look the night before and hadn't noticed anything. Now though looking at the deadfall and the pool of water he spotted something at the bottom of the clear pool. It was a boot, a leather boot.

Zeke walked closer and tried to see if anything else might be at the bottom of the pool. His fear was that the boot might be attached to a body, it wasn't. He looked around and found a long branch which he stripped of limbs except for one at the end which he cut off except for about two inches. He now had a long pole with a hook on the end. With this he fished out the boot and then with the boot in one hand and the coffee pot in the other he headed back to the fire.

As he sat and waited for his coffee to brew he looked over the boot. It was not of the usual store bought variety. It looked to be made by someone who took pride in his work. The stitching along the sides was very intricate. The patterns made a picture that looked to be of a large deer or maybe an elk. It was hard to tell with the leather so swollen from being submerged in the water for so long. The sole was worn down but not thin. Whoever owned this boot had paid good money to have the stitching applied in such a pattern. Zeke stood the boot by the fire to let the leather dry.

He filled his coffee cup and wondered if he should wake Martha Ellen and Keene. After a minute he decided against it, he would let them sleep. For a man who had slept little in the last three days he felt pretty good. He was tired but not sleepy, which he felt was odd. Maybe he was learning to live without sleep. At this thought he laughed at himself. He might have laughed a bit too loud because he heard stirring in the wagon. Seconds later Martha Ellen climbed down from the back of the wagon and looked at Ben and Zeke.

It was the first time Zeke had noticed her that she wasn't really consumed by sadness or grief at the loss of her two brothers. Now she looked rested and ready for the day. As she walked the short distance to the fire she was smiling. "Good morning, I suspect by the look of you that sleep never paid you a visit last night."

Zeke supposed he looked a mess. The more a man goes without sleep the more haggard his appearance will become. "Not a wink. Guard duty is something me and Ben here take very seriously. He slept like a baby and I watched him," Zeke said with a chuckle.

Martha Ellen laughed too. "That's the first real sleep I have had in a couple of days. Keene slept well himself knowing Ben was looking out for him. Let me make you some breakfast and then you can catch a little nap before we head for Langley. I don't think the three of us need to be out here after what happened last night."

As she went through the motions of getting what she needed from the back of the wagon Zeke thought about what she had said. The woman was smart and also the kind who took charge. She knew what needed to be done and in what order it needed to be in. It was the first time he had looked at her when she wasn't talking to him. It was then that he noticed she was a very attractive woman and not only that, she was a hard worker. He wondered what would happen to her and the little boy once they made it to Langley. He would see them there safely, along with the help of Ben.

As she went about getting breakfast on the fire Zeke thought he would have a little look around. As he walked toward the area where Ben had battled the unknown creatures he wondered what he would find. As he approached the spot he held the Winchester at the ready, not that he expected to find anything but the gun did make him feel better.

Martha Ellen seen him heading toward the tree line and told him to be careful, she then looked at Ben, who was laying by the fire, and said, "Ben, go with him." She was pointing at Zeke as she said this and Ben immediately jumped up and went along. Zeke was both impressed and surprised. Impressed that Martha Ellen cared and surprised that Ben understood the command she had given him.

As he approached he could see the broken underbrush and on some of the grasses he saw blood. He bent and inspected what he had found. There was more than it first appeared. The ground was trampled in places and it was apparent a scuffle had taken place.

Ben sniffed the ground and let out a low growl. Zeke straightened and looked into the tree line. There was movement. Ben advanced slowly and by the look of the big dog he was ready for another fight. His ears were up and the hair from his head down past his shoulder blades was standing up.

Zeke raised the Winchester but didn't pull the trigger. Until he was sure what was out there he held his fire. As he slowly moved forward he kept looking back at times to check on Martha Ellen and Keene. The child was still asleep and his mother was still busy with breakfast. She was unaware of what was happening. Zeke knew he couldn't advance into the brush, what if others were on the other side of camp and this was just a trick to leave the boy and woman unprotected. As much as he wanted to charge into the brush and confront this unknown danger he knew he had to return to camp.

Zeke started backing up and at the same time he held the gun at the ready. When he was out of the low brush he called Ben. The big dog didn't come at first but after a second call he came bouncing out of the brush. It was apparent by the look on the dog's face that he wanted to have another go with whatever it was out there. As the two came back into camp Zeke noticed Martha Even was looking off in the direction of where the horses were tied.

"Zeke, while you were scouting I thought I saw something on the other side of the horses."

"What was it, could you tell?"

As she continued to look into the distance Rusty and Hazel began backing away from the stream they had been picketed near and this lead the other two horses to take notice. Zeke started toward the four and as he did he told Martha to keep a close eye on Keene and stay near the wagon. Ben was now on the scent of this new threat and was advancing along with Zeke.

All four horses had now backed as far away from the stream as their leads would allow. Zeke patted Rusty on the forehead and this seemed to calm the big horse. Hazel saw this and bit Rusty on the left flank. With a threat this close Hazel was still mad because she never got her head rubbed, go figure.

Zeke made it to the edge of the stream and went to a knee. Ben jumped in and swam the pool of water for the second time this morning. Once on the other side he never bothered to shake the water off. He was much too interested in whatever it was in the tree line. Zeke watched as Ben crouched and advanced not unlike that of a panther. The dog was stealthy as he continued to stalk his prey. All at once the big dog sprang to his feet and pounced into the brush. The howl he let out as he did this was vicious beyond reason, but short lived. Whatever it was had either killed the big dog or was something Ben decided he didn't want to attack after all. His howl went quiet in an instant.

As Ben sprang into the brush there was the scream of a child. Zeke jumped to his feet and ran through the stream above the pool of water, all the while shouting for Ben. Everything was quiet as Zeke made his way into the brush. Once he made it to where Ben was he found the big dog standing over a small boy as he continued to look into the brush. When the child saw Zeke he stood and dusted himself off.

Zeke quickly looked around but saw nothing else, just this boy who must have been five years old, no more than six.

"Are you hurt?" Was all Zeke could think to ask in his astonishment.

"No sir. Is this your dog?" he asked as he looked at Ben.

"We travel together. Who are you and are you alone?"

The boy looked at Zeke and said, "My name is Jarrett Bayliss and I wasn't alone until about three days ago."

Zeke asked, "Is there anyone else around here or is it just you?"

"Just me! I've been lost ever since my family got taken." With that the boy sat down and began to cry. It was evident that whatever had happened to his family had just erupted into full realization and his emotions were fragile.

Zeke knew the best thing to do was get the child back to camp and out of these trees. He still wasn't sure of what was out there but was certain that whatever he and Ben had sensed on the other side of camp fifteen minutes ago wasn't this child. The way Ben had acted it had to be the creatures from the previous night.

Zeke reached down and with his left arm picked the child up and began carrying him toward camp. As he came out of the trees Martha Ellen and Keene were standing by the wagon. When she saw what Zeke was carrying she ran down to the water's edge and took him from Zeke. She hugged the child and told him it was alright. As she walked toward the wagon and Keene she was talking to the child and trying to calm him. It was working. Jarrett grew quiet as he looked around the camp. Zeke was glad Martha was there; his attempts to soothe a troubled child were almost comical. His voice was gruff and his tone was one of distress due to the danger that lurked in the shadows of the trees. Martha's voice and words were kind and pleasant, the thing a little boy needed at such a time.

Keene walked over and met his mom half way, "Who is that mommy? Why is he crying?"

At the sound of Keene's voice Jarrett stopped crying and looked. Martha sat him down and he looked at Keene. "My Name is Jarrett, who are you."

"My name is Keene and this is my Mommy."

Keene looked up at his mom and said, "His name is Jarrett, I like that name mommy. Can we keep him?"

When Keene said this both boys looked up at Martha and waited for an answer.

Zeke found this hilarious but didn't dare laugh. Martha bent down beside both boys and said, "We need to find out his story and see if we can help. Right now I think he needs something to eat." At this Jarrett's eyes widened. It was evident the boy hadn't had food in a day or two, maybe more.

Ben had gone back to his horse blanket by the fire but instead of sleeping he sat and watched this new member of the group. As Martha quickly prepared breakfast she asked Zeke if he felt the danger had passed. Zeke looked around camp again and said, "I feel as though we are being watched." He said this in a low tone so as not to startle the two boys.

"Keene, why don't you take Jarrett to the wagon and show him your wooden cowboy," Martha told her son.

Keene smiled and said, "Come on Jarrett, let's go play." It was apparent Keene was excited to have someone near his own age to play with. Jarrett went reluctantly from the fire all the while looking at the pot and skillet Martha was working with, the boy was extremely hungry. Martha uncovered a basket and got out a biscuit that had been left over from the previous evening. "Jarrett take this, it will be a little while before I have our breakfast ready." Jarrett immediately grabbed the biscuit and took a big bite. He chewed furiously as his eyes gave the look of thanks. He followed Keene to the wagon and both boys climbed up.

Martha turned back to Zeke. "How long has he been alone out here?"

"A few days I think, he indicated as much when I found him. His memories are painful though. He broke down at the mention of his family."

Martha looked toward the wagon. "I saw Ben lunge into the brush and let out that awful growl right before Jarrett screamed." She looked at Zeke for an explanation.

"I believe Ben knew the boy was there, his senses are strong. I think that whatever it was that had the horses spooked a little while ago was also stalking Jarrett. After Ben pounced I found him standing over the boy and he was looking into the trees. I think Ben might have saved the boy's life," Zeke told her.

"Do you think he was in the woods the entire night and afraid to come into our camp?"

Zeke thought over the question, "I don't think so. With the battle Ben had last night he wouldn't have stayed silent if he was close enough to hear. I think he has been running ever since his family disappeared. He probably started at daylight and made it this far when Ben found him. I also think the creatures were stalking him and if he hadn't made it to our camp then they would have had him. He also led them to us, although he didn't know it."

Martha quickly finished preparing the breakfast and was getting four plates when she said, "Let's get everyone fed and break camp. I think with all that is going on out here our luck might be running out. We need to make it to Langley before nightfall. You haven't slept yet; do you think you can make it?"

Zeke looked at the two little boys as they climbed down from the wagon and ran toward the smell of breakfast. For some reason he thought of his father back in Kentucky and wondered how he would answer the question. "We will make it Martha, don't you think otherwise." She smiled as he said this.

The two boys ate big breakfasts, especially Jarrett. When he was finished he looked at Martha Ellen and asked if he could lie down, he was tired. Zeke suspected he had spent the last few days, and nights, on the run and had only slept when the fatigue was more than he could handle. Martha took him to the wagon and covered him up in the back where she and Keene had slept the night before. When he was all tucked in she came back to the fire. Keene wanted to know why Jarrett didn't want to play. "He is tired; I think he might sleep the entire day if we let him. Now I want you to help mommy."

"Sure thing, what do you want me to do?"

"I want you to play real quiet and not disturb your new friend. He needs some rest and I promise when he wakes up he will feel more like playing. Can you do that for mommy?"

Keene smiled and said, "I sure can, I will be so quiet no one will know I'm around." He said this loud enough to be heard a mile away and it made Zeke chuckle.

As Martha Ellen put away everything from breakfast she put one last pan of biscuits on the fire. "We won't be stopping for lunch Zeke; I plan on putting a little ham in these biscuits as we make our way to Langley. The hour it would take to stop and cook something to eat would mean three or four more miles we would need to travel after dark."

Zeke had been busy gathering the two horses and hitching them up to the wagon. Both horses knew the feel of the wagon harness from the previous day and neither wanted anything to do with that four wheeled mess. Both protested as he backed each into the harness. It took some coaxing but Zeke finally got the two hitched up.

By eight-thirty everything was ready except Ben. Zeke waited to see if the big dog wanted to ride on the pack Hazel carried or walk. Ben knew Zeke was ready to move out of camp and at the last minute he stood up and looked at Hazel. Zeke took this to mean he wanted to ride. When he walked over to pick him up Ben moved away.

"Alright Ben, I guess you feel a little like walking this morning, might be good for you at that."

Martha looked at Ben and thought it was cruel to make the poor thing walk in the shape he was in. "Zeke Conley, surely you are not going to make that skinny dog walk all the way to Langley?"

It was now apparent to Zeke that Ben probably had a way with the ladies. "No Ma'am, he feels a little like walking this morning, after a while if he gets tired then I can put him back on the pack Hazel is carrying."

This seemed to satisfy Martha. She looked at Ben as he stood there ready to move on down the trail. Zeke realized that Martha wasn't one to hold her tongue if she thought a man was about to do something that didn't suit the way she thought something ought to be. She grabbed the handle to the brake and before releasing it she turned to look at Jarrett. He was sound asleep. She slowly released the brake and jiggled the reigns. The two horses slowly moved forward with the wagon close behind.

Zeke followed on Rusty with Hazel bringing up the rear. Ben bounded about as if he had just been set free, and in a way he was. This was the first traveling he had done under his own power in who knows how long. He would go to the front and led the wagon and horses a while and then he would return to the rear and walk beside Hazel, this went on for more than an hour at the pace set by the wagon and the two horses. Finally his eagerness to travel seemed to wane, his walk slowed and he just stayed beside Hazel. Zeke had kept a close watch on the dog and wondered how long he could keep this up in his weakened condition. Finally Ben stopped in his tracks and just stood there looking at Zeke.

"Martha, I think Ben is all tuckered out. You keep going while I load him on top of Hazel's pack." Zeke hurried and lifted the tired dog on top of the pack horse. He loosely tied the ropes around the dog to keep him from falling off and then remounted Rusty and hurried to catch up with the wagon. They never got more than a couple hundred feet ahead and still that was more than Zeke was comfortable with. The wagon was making good time and he would have had Martha to stop if he thought she could get that far ahead while he situated Ben. He still worried about a daytime attack from the creatures that had seemed to call every night since he had freed Ben from the snare.

The little wagon train made good time and by two in the afternoon Zeke decided to stop at the next stream and allow the four horses to get a drink. No more than ten minutes went by when a small creek presented itself. As the horses drank Zeke retrieved the boot he had found at the bottom of the pond. He had tied it on Hazel's pack that morning and hadn't looked at it again. He hoped he could tell more about it after the leather dried and the stitching on the side shrunk back to normal.

As he scanned the boot Martha Ellen looked over and when she did she let out a gasp, "Where did you find that Zeke?" She asked.

"At the bottom of the pond this morning, I was letting it dry out to see if I could tell anything about it."

She reached for the boot and Zeke handed it to her. "Why this belongs to my oldest brother," she said.

Martha looked at Zeke and said, "We have got to go back and search for them."

Zeke knew if they went back it would most likely be the end of all of them. "Martha, we have traveled a good fifteen miles and if we turn back now then we won't make it to our previous campsite until well past dark. We can't search after dark, and if we do go back and camp there again do you really think we will survive the night?"

The look on Martha's face was one of despair. She wanted to find her brothers but she couldn't risk what might happen if they did go back. "You're right Zeke. We will go on to Langley tonight. I will find someone to watch over Keene and Jarrett and I will come back tomorrow."

Zeke knew she was talking nonsense. Apparently she thought she could just ride back, find her brothers and be back in Langley the same day. She had been through a lot and wasn't making good decisions at the moment. Keene made the decision for her.

"Tomorrow morning we will come back and find them mommy, you and me."

Martha looked at the boy and realized how foolish she had sounded. She was talking like a three year old. She patted Keene and said, "Maybe we will wait in town a day or two and let them catch up with us."

Keene accepted this, "That is a good idea; I don't want to come back out here unless Ben comes along with us."

Martha looked at Zeke and said, "I guess I sounded foolish didn't I?"

Zeke knew she was only worried about her family, "Not at all, you sounded brave." With that they moved off in the direction of town.

It was nearly three in the afternoon when they left the stream and continued their journey toward Langley. While at the stream Zeke had untied Ben and lifted the big dog off the pack on Hazel's back. The dog drank and when Zeke tried to lift him back to the pack he stepped away. He patted him on top of the head and then went to his saddlebags to find some deer jerky. Ben gobbled up the snack and then walked to the wagon. It was apparent he felt strong enough to walk a bit farther as he had done that morning. Zeke climbed back in the saddle and they moved out.

It was shortly after they left the stream that Jarrett stirred from his bed in the back of the wagon and stretched. Keene pulled on his mother's shoulder and told her Jarrett was awake. The little boy came forward in the wagon and climbed in the seat beside Keene and Martha Ellen.

"Well look who's up, are you hungry?"

Jarrett shook his head yes. Martha reached behind into the basket that contained the biscuits. She reached one to both boys and then looked at Zeke who was riding about twenty feet behind the wagon.

"Are you hungry?"

This was music to Zeke's ears. "Yes Ma'am."

He rode up along beside the wagon and Martha reached him one of the biscuits. Zeke thanked her and then allowed Rusty to lag while the wagon got ahead again. The biscuit was good and he finished it in minutes. He chewed slowly enjoying food that had been made by someone who really knew how to cook. When Zeke made his own food he really never took pains and ate it regardless of taste. It wasn't that he didn't like good food, it was just that after so much time in the wilds he was happy with just about anything he made.

As the wagon rolled and bounced along at a steady pace Martha started asking Jarrett a few question. She was very careful about how she worded what she asked the child, not wanting to cause him to cry.

What is your last name Jarrett?"

"Stiles Ma'am, my name is Jarrett Stiles. Me and my family are from Kentucky."

"Kentucky! That is such a wonderful place. Keene and me came through there a few months back and I never saw a more beautiful place." She noticed he never seemed upset about what he had just said. He had answered her just matter-of-factly.

"What caused you and your family to head west?"

Jarrett thought for a minute before answering. "My maw and paw had a big farm there, lots of tobacco, lots of horses and cattle. My maw told me a blight took the tobacco crop two or three years in a row. I saw it on the leaves, it looked like mold, you know the kind that grows in places. Anyway, my paw sold the farm and headed us this way."

Again Martha noticed the boy wasn't upset at the memories he had just described. He told the story as if he never had a part in it, as if he was a spectator rather than a participant.

"How old are you Jarrett?"

Again the boy thought about his answer. "I am almost five years old," he told her.

"Well you are a big boy for five years old. Keene there is three." Jarrett looked at Keene and the younger boy smiled back.

Now she had to ask a question that she was sure would upset the child. "How long have you been out here all alone Jarrett?"

He looked into the distance. "I don't know for sure, I lost track of how many days and nights it's been. We woke up one morning and my paw was missing. It was just me and my maw and paw anyway, just the three of us. After paw went missing we looked around for a while and then just waited, after so long our food ran out."

"Didn't you and your mother try to ride to a town and get help?"

"We would have but when paw went missing the horse got took. We had two big mules that were used to pull the wagon but they were gone to. Seems what ever happened to paw happened to our horse and mules too."

Martha knew she had to ask the next question and hoped it didn't cause the boy to cry. "Where is your mother Jarrett?"

At this he burst into tears, "After so many days and the food ran out she went off looking for paw. She told me maybe she could at least find one of the horses or mules. I was to stay in camp with what little food was left and she would be back for me. I waited and waited. She never came back," he said between sobs.

Martha reached over and patted the child. She looked back at Zeke who was close enough to have heard. He could only shake his head.

Zeke heard the entire story and was now listening to the heartbreaking sobs of a boy too young to understand. He knew he needed to get the child's mind off his worries, if that were possible.

"Howdy Ben, ain't you getting tired yet with all that walking." Zeke asked this just to get the attention of the two boys in the wagon.

Ben, who had been leading the wagon waited until they passed and stood looking at Zeke. Both boys turned in their seats to see what the big dog was going to do.

"Martha, it might be good if Ben sat in the wagon a while if you would allow it. He is starting to look a little tired again."

At the sound of this Keene giggled and then Jarrett asked, "Oh boy, can he?"

It had worked. Jarrett was now so focused on having this enormous dog sitting behind him and Keene in the wagon that he had forgotten all about the loss of his family. He was young enough to be easily distracted. Martha stopped and Zeke quickly dismounted and lifted Ben into the wagon. He went straight to the front and laid down directly behind the two boys. Both immediately went to petting the big dog and Ben went to slapping his tail on the floor of the wagon. All three were now happy as could be.

Martha Ellen was quiet as they rode on, no doubt wondering where the boy's father and mother were. It no doubt brought back questions of what might have happened to her two brothers. When she thought of the creatures that had attacked the camp the previous night she shuddered.

By six that evening Zeke estimated they were still thirty miles from Langley. He wondered how Martha felt about traveling four or five hours after dark but when he looked at her he knew the answer. She was looking into the distance and her expression was one of concern. She was afraid of the darkness that would soon overtake them. Zeke wasn't too fond of the prospect either.

An hour before dark he asked her, "Do you feel alright about traveling after dark?"

She looked around again and then at Zeke. "What choice do we have? We can't stop and make camp, the danger is just too great." She twisted in the seat and looked straight at Zeke. "Do you have an extra gun?"

"Zeke looked at her in surprise. "Do you know how to use one?"

"I most certainly do. I can handle most any gun. I am not fond of a shotgun or a black powder rifle though. Both tend to kick too hard for my shoulder."

Zeke reached into his left hand saddle bag and retrieved a .36 caliber Whitley. "This is all I have other than my Colt and Winchester. This old gun has been in my saddle bag for the better part of a year. I got just enough ammunition to load it fully once. After that you can just throw it at whatever you were shooting at." He reached the gun over to her as he said this.

Martha took the pistol and looked it over. It was well worn and even had a little rust on one side of the barrel.

"Is it ready to fire, it looks like it needs to be cleaned?"

"The outside looks a little rough but I promise I keep it clean and in working order. I actually won it in a poker game nearly a year ago. The man I was playing cards against was six dollars and fifty cents short on his bet and he threw that gun in the pot to cover his shortfall. I won the hand so you could say I got exactly six dollars and fifty cents in that gun, not counting the bullets."

Martha put the Whitley down beside her, on the side opposite from the two boys. "I intend to use it to protect these two children. You, Mr. Conley with your Colt and Winchester, and me, with this Whitley should stand a better chance now. And that don't even count Ben." She turned to look at the sleeping dog. "I would put more weight in Ben than in all these guns."

Zeke wondered why she would put so much more faith in a dog than a man carrying a Winchester. The way Ben fought the night before she was probably right. If the big dog could be nursed back to full health he would truly be a deadly adversary, as bad a shape as he was in now he could still hold his own it seemed.

As darkness gathered around the lone wagon and rider Zeke could tell Martha was getting nervous. He pulled the big Winchester from the boot beside his right leg and placed it across the saddle. He checked his Colt and then put it back in the holster. If anything caused any trouble tonight he intended to let both guns do a little talking. As they rode he kept a close look out on their surroundings. The two boys had climbed in the back of the wagon and seemed to be asleep, one on each side of Ben. Jarrett had even thrown one of his arms on the big dog. Ben didn't care, he was sound asleep too.

The sky was mostly clear and the moon lent what light it could spare on the travelers. The horses were allowed to pick their way knowing they could see much better than a man or a woman.

"How far do you figure we are away from Langley Zeke?" Martha asked as she looked into the distance.

"Nearly twenty miles as best as I can tell. I haven't travelled this trail often, maybe twice at most. But the judge and the two deputies said they could make it in one hard day of riding Monday. I figure with what little ground I covered while I was tending to Ben and what we have covered today we are about twenty miles out." He said this but he knew he could be off by ten or fifteen miles. If that were the case then they would be traveling all night.

"As bad is it is out here Zeke I am wondering if we are doing the right thing, you know, traveling in the darkness like this."

Zeke knew she was saying something she probably didn't really mean. If they did stop and make camp then she would just as surely wonder if they had done the right thing by stopping. It is just human nature to second guess every decision.

"I can't really say which the best is at the moment. We were lucky last night. I believe Ben is a match for whatever is out there but he is still not healthy. He would charge right into the middle of a fight again but what if he was just lucky last night. What if he was killed and then we had to fend off whatever it is without him. He has mixed it up each of the last three nights he has traveled with me. The first night he could only growl but it worked. The second night he charged at one of the beasts but fell flat on his face before he made it half way. Last night he done the best so far. He fought with at least one, maybe more, and survived. He is getting stronger but his luck can only hold out for so long. If he were completely healed then I would say stay here for the night. As it is I don't like his odds. And if they manage to kill Ben then I don't like our odds."

Martha considered what Zeke said as the wagon bounced along. "I trust your judgement. We need to make it to safety for the two boy's sake. We will travel until we make town. What if we are attacked on the trail after dark though?"

Zeke thought of what his father would do at a time like this. It gave him the answer he wanted. "We will fight." That was all he said. The answer wasn't just in what he said but the way he said it. There was no doubt about his determination. Martha felt a little better about their chances now. That wouldn't last long.

Two hours after dark Zeke began to think they had outrun whatever it was that had been stalking him for the last three nights. The moon was bright enough to allow the trail they traveled to be seen pretty well. Where previous wagons and horses had travelled the earth was bare. It made to parallel ribbons in the darkness bordered by greenery. The path could be seen running into the distance. Without the moon Zeke knew it would be almost impossible for a man to see where he was going. The two horses pulling the wagon trotted along seemingly without a care in the world. It was times like this that Zeke thought horses actually half slept as they walked. Their ears were down and they held their heads low.

Ben hadn't stirred since Zeke had lifted him into the back of the wagon. He was laying right behind the seat that Martha and the two boys now sat in. Both boys had rested and were now with Martha on the front seat of the buckboard. Zeke had lagged back about fifty feet in order to keep a better watch on both sides of the wagon and to also make sure nothing got close to the wagon from behind. By the position of the moon he figured it must be around eleven o'clock. He couldn't be sure but he thought Langley was still a good fifteen miles in the distance.

They hadn't met a single traveler on the road the entire day. Zeke knew the road was well traveled by the barren track they traveled on. At any other time he figured they would have met a rider and horse at least once an hour, people traveling between towns or the occasional rancher and his family heading either into town to conduct some business or out of town on their way home. On this day though there was nothing, no horses, no wagons, not a soul.

As he rode he thought the lack of travelers could only mean one thing, people were afraid of whatever it was out here that had been abducting men. Since the trouble had made itself evident on that first day when he found the abandoned campsite and Hazel tied to a tree he had hoped abduction was the correct word to use for the missing men. He just couldn't let himself think that something was actually taking full grown men for food. What he had glimpsed in the darkness over the last few nights though still sent a shiver down his spine. Men were being taken and what he saw in the darkness looked like it could very easily kill grown men and devour their flesh.

As they rode and he pondered the events of the last few weeks he could feel the fatigue start to take over. It felt like weeks since he had actually had any solid sleep. His head hurt and his muscles ached from lack of rest. He knew he wasn't nearly as alert as he should be at a time like this. It was due to this extreme fatigue that he never noticed the movement over to his left. They rode on not knowing that an ambush had been set for this very spot.

When Rusty raised his head and looked off into the foliage Zeke still never took notice. Hazel had sensed something at the same time as Rusty. Both horses were looking left with heads held high and ears up. Both horses sniffed the air for any sign of danger. Rusty picked up his pace in order to close the distance between him and the wagon. This was enough to slowly register to Zeke that he needed to snap out of the half sleep he had allowed himself to fall into.

As one of the few clouds hid the moon for the briefest of moments the trap was set. Whatever it was that had been tracking the slow moving wagon and rider for the last few hours now advanced. Zeke, now wide awake because of Rusty's quicker pace, picked up the Winchester and chambered a round. Just as he noticed movement near the wagon he was knocked from his horse by something that had lunged from at least ten feet away and taken him completely out of the saddle. Rusty bucked and sidestepped the spot where Zeke and the creature had fallen.

When Zeke hit the ground the air was knocked from his lungs and he felt and heard a rib snap. He had lost the grip on the rifle and didn't know where it had landed. Whatever had knocked him to the ground was now on its feet and standing over him ready to finish him off. In the darkness he could tell that it was big, really big. He clawed for his Colt with his right hand and that was when he knew he had broken at least one rib. The pain was truly overwhelming; it was so bad he feared he would lose consciousness. When his hand wrapped around the familiar handle of the Colt he could tell that whatever it was now had him. If he couldn't draw and fire then he was dead.

The terror now represented by this creature completely overtook the pain of his broken ribs. With a speed that even surprised Zeke he had the gun out and just as he was ready to pull the trigger he was stepped on hard just below his stomach by the creature as it came at him to get to his exposed throat. This slowed his shot and destroyed his aim. Now all he wanted was to hear the noise that only a Colt .45 can make.

Zeke gave up on aiming and just pulled the trigger. The noise was tremendous, but reassuring. He didn't know if he hit the creature but suddenly whatever had been there wasn't on top of him anymore. The smell of the spent cartridge burned his nostrils but this helped to sharpen his senses. The discomfort in his chest was now being shared by a pain in his lower gut. Zeke fought through both and looked in the direction of the wagon.

Just as Zeke was knocked from the back of Rusty two of the unseen creatures were advancing, with speed, on the wagon. The one that got there first jumped completely into the back on its way to grab the occupants of the seat from behind. Ben had been sleeping soundly and was startled awake when he felt the wagon bounce. He raised his head and saw something moving over him on its way toward the woman and the two boys in the front seat.

When a dog is down, and penned on its side, it is at its most vulnerable, Ben knew this and knew he was about to be killed. If he died then he knew the little boys and the woman would be next.

In the situation he was in he couldn't use his legs and claws, only his teeth. He snapped for the throat as best as he could but missed. What he did clamp his jaws around though was even better. He had the creatures face in his mouth. Ben clamped down hard and twisted. He felt hot blood spew into his mouth as he tore flesh and bone. As he did this he knew he had to get on his feet. With a desperation that only comes from a wild animal that knows it's about to be killed Ben muscled his way up not letting go of his grip on the creatures face. Finally on his feet Ben knew now that his attacker had become his prey.

Ben pushed hard toward the back of the wagon with his powerful legs. He released his grip at the back of the wagon and whatever it was hit the ground and only thrashed about due to its injuries. It was then he noticed another one at the front of the wagon. As he ran the short distance of the wagons bed it gave him the speed to launch into the air and land directly on top of the second attacker.

When the first one had landed in the back of the wagon Martha had snapped the reigns against the horses, putting the two into a fast trot. She knew if she pushed the two very hard then the haphazard rigging that had been originally made for two short mules would most likely break. She heard the commotion in the back and turned to see something large on top of Ben and heading her way. She instinctively reached her arm around the two boys and pulled them toward her. She held the reigns in her left hand. Just as she was ready to jump from the wagon and pull Keene and Jarrett off with her she saw Ben spring up and it looked like he had the head of whatever it was in his mouth. She saw the two moving toward the back and it looked like Ben was actually pushing it out of the wagon.

Martha noticed movement to her right and looked in that direction. What she saw nearly took her breath away. Something horrible was running at the wagon and it was only feet from the two boys she had her arm around. Just as she thought it would jump on the wagon and grab Jarett, who was sitting farthest away, she saw Ben launch himself over the side and tackle the monster.

This was her only chance. Martha tapped the reigns and the two horses broke into a furious run, more so from the attack than her urging. If the rigging failed then it would just fail. She had to get the two boys away from whatever it was that had attacked them. As Martha and the two boys rode away as fast as she dared go, she wondered if Zeke was already dead. She prayed for his safety, and as an afterthought that of Ben too.

The second creature Ben attacked was far stronger than any he had fought before. When they both hit the ground Ben was clubbed and bitten. He retreated a few feet, not from fear, but to get a perspective on just how big this thing was. Compared to the others it was enormous. His senses told him that there were others but they were moving off in the direction of the fleeing wagon. It was just this one and Ben now.

Ben tasted the strange blood in his mouth of the one he had tried to tear the face off of. It was nasty, same as the ones he had injured the previous night but he just couldn't recognize the taste. Didn't matter, he had one right in front of him and this one wasn't leaving. Ben circled and looked for an opening. Enough playing around, it was time to kill one of these beasts.

When he found an opening he charged in fast. He grabbed a hind leg just above the knee and bit hard. Again the hot strange blood filled his mouth. He released his grip and continued to circle. He had to be careful; this one was big enough, and strong enough, to kill him if he wasn't careful.

Just as Ben was ready to attack again he heard a gun go off. He saw flesh near the creatures head erupt in a spray of blood. It wasn't a fatal shot because whatever it was turned and ran into the darkness. Ben never gave chase. He instead looked into the distance and listened to the rattle of the fast moving wagon. He wanted to go after it and make sure the two boys were okay but he also wanted to see if Zeke was going to be alright without him. He knew the man wasn't on his horse, and for that matter, the two horses weren't anywhere to be seen.

Zeke was on the ground bent in a fetal position as he tried to overcome the pain. Ben walked over and looked the situation over. The two were all alone. Ben could sense the two horses were in the tree line hiding. Hazel was actually watching from the cover of darkness and when she sensed the creatures were gone she stepped out. Ben saw her and yelped. Both Hazel and Rusty walked over to where the big dog and Zeke were. Zeke had finally managed to holster his gun and roll onto his knees. He had thrown up and this in itself had helped. His ribs hurt like hell, he suddenly felt like he might throw up again.

He looked down the trail and wondered if Martha and the two boys had made it away safely. Once the two horses made it to where Ben and Zeke were the big dog sat and began trying to clean himself up. Zeke continued to scan the immediate area to see if he was still in danger. He saw nothing. His Winchester was actually standing straight up, its barrel stuck in the ground. He pulled himself to it and yanked it free, which brought another wave of pain from his ribs. Once he caught his breath he looked at the gun. Everything seemed alright except the end of the barrel was jammed solid with dirt. He couldn't fire the big gun and he was in no shape to clean it. His Colt would have to do. Before standing he replaced the bullet he had fired and then re-holstered the gun.

With great effort, and no small amount of pain, Zeke finally made it to his feet. He took a couple of steps and then fell straight forward. As soon as he hit the dirt he blacked out. Ben looked at the two horses and then back at Zeke. As he looked at the fallen man both Hazel and Rusty raised their heads high, they were consumed with fear again. Ben caught the scent at the same time as the horses. He scanned the surrounding area and knew the creatures were back and in numbers he hadn't seen before, there were at least five. Ben might not have been able to count but he did know how many of the terrible creatures were out there.

The two horses picked a spot that presented an escape route and went for it at a full gallop. When both hit the tree line they didn't stop. Ben stood and circled Zeke, as he scanned the surrounding area the creatures started to move in. Ben was unafraid; he would separate and kill them one at a time. As he prepared to isolate one that he knew he had tangled with earlier, and had injured, all five sprang up and ran in his direction. Separate and kill now turned into stand your ground and die. This he would gladly do.

The wagon with Martha and the two boys was still moving at a good pace. The creatures had tried to follow and for a small while they had actually been able to keep up. Martha, as scared as she was, had let the horses run at a fast pace but soon slowed them down not knowing they were being followed. She kept looking back to see if Zeke and Ben were coming but the only movement she could see in the moonlit darkness was dust and pebbles flying up from her own wagon wheels. She wanted to stop and go back but knew that would put the two boys at risk. No, she would slow the horses a little but she would not go back. As she kept her two horses at a fast trot she said another prayer for Zeke, and before ending it she added Ben too.

After less than a mile the creatures realized the wagon wasn't going to stop and they didn't want to continue to give chase. They still had a victim on the ground along with the wolf and two horses. Horse flesh was good and they also knew what a wolf tasted like, having killed one that had been abandoned by its pack after it had somehow been injured. When they had happened upon the injured predator he was asleep, but alone. It wasn't easy but they surrounded it and managed to kill the beast. They ate everything, even the bones. Wolf meat was good and they knew if they ever found one isolated again without the rest of the pack they would feast once more. They turned back with anticipation of an easy kill.

Martha didn't know where they were or how far the town was. The horses continued to move with purpose. They actually wanted to run at a full gallop but Martha kept them at a good trot, not wanting to crash the wagon into a tree or run it into a ravine. She knew if she could make out the outline of the road they traveled the horses could too. After an hour of steady travel she thought she saw a twinkle of light, the kind that may come from a candle in a window or maybe even a lantern. It was there for only a second as the wagon entered another stand of trees. After a few minutes she saw it again, this time there were two points of light in the distance. As she got closer the two became three and then there were more than she could count.

What Martha had seen wasn't the light from a ranch or farmhouse, nor was it the twinkling of someone's campfire. It was the outlying houses of the town of Langley, South Dakota. As the wagon got closer she could see several houses and in the distance the town itself. It wasn't long before she was approaching the outer most street of the town. In spots there were kerosene street lights and she could even see some of the townsfolk out on the boardwalks although at such a late hour she didn't know why. Martha hadn't been around many towns of any size in the west and wasn't aware that Saloons stayed open until the small hours of the night to serve to men that either traveled late or just didn't want to go home.

As the wagon made its way onto the main street of the town Keene pulled on his mother's arm. "Mommy, is it time to eat yet? I'm hungry."

Keene was sitting between his mom and Jarrett, the older boy stationed on the outside. Jarrett looked at Martha and realized he was hungry too. "I'm hungry too," he said.

The two boys had gotten over the scare of a couple hours back and were now concerned more with their stomachs than with anything else.

Martha was glad to see the two boys talking. They had been very quiet after the attack but now seemed fine.

We need to find the sheriff's office first and report what happened, then we will find somewhere to eat, is that okay?" she asked. Both boys smiled.

Martha was still extremely worried about Zeke and Ben. As she had ridden into town she kept looking back to see if they were back there, they weren't. Now she had to find the sheriff and tell him what had happened. About halfway down the main street past any number of Saloons and other businesses she spotted what she was looking for. A small sign hung from a pole which had the words, Sheriff's Office written in faded black letters.

Martha had gotten several looks from the men who were walking the streets undoubtedly heading from one Saloon to another. She stopped the wagon in front of the building and set the brake. When she climbed down she told the two boys to stay in the seat until she could check the door.

She grabbed the door knob and twisted, it wasn't locked. She hurried back and helped each boy down from the wagon seat. As she started back toward the door it swung open, Deputy Carl Nolen looked out. He had heard the wagon pull up and then when the door knob rattled but no one came in he decided to investigate. He was surprised to see a young woman and two small boys headed in his direction.

"Evening Ma'am, are you in need of the sheriff?" He had noticed the worried look on her face.

"Yes, I am, something awful has happened on the trail into town and someone needs to go back and help."

Carl knew the sheriff had gone home for the night and Fred Slone was doing his rounds of town to check on things. The only other town deputy was also at his home asleep. "Well come on in here and bring them two boys," Carl said.

Martha guided the two very hungry boys into the Sheriff's Office. There were a few chairs against one wall and a bench on another. She put the two boys in the chairs and then turned to the deputy. "We must hurry deputy, I am afraid something awful has happened and it might be too late."

"Can you tell me what has happened?"

"We were attacked and the man who was bringing us to town is still out there. I am afraid he is hurt. He is traveling with a big dog and I'm afraid that both of them might get killed."

Carl had heard what Cecil and Judge Preston had said about finding the big dog hung up in a snare and nearly dead. He had also been hearing the stories of men disappearing in the dead of night. "Ma'am, you just make yourself at home, there is coffee on the stove over there. I'm going to go and get Judge Preston and Cecil, they're the two who were traveling with that fellar you just spoke of when they found that big dog. I won't be gone no more than ten minutes." With that Carl slammed the door and was gone.

"Mommy, are Ben and Zeke alright? I heard what you said to that deputy," Keene asked.

"I don't know, I really don't,. I'm sure Ben is protecting Zeke. And remember, Zeke has his gun," Martha told the two boys. This seemed to satisfy the two but she knew it wasn't true. Deep down she suspected that both Zeke and Ben were dead. The thought made her start to cry.

Carl looked at his pocket watch and saw that it was almost midnight. He knew the judge and the deputy were staying at the boardinghouse that Ancil and Mabel Lafferty ran. It wasn't more than a ten minute walk from the sheriff's office but Carl wasn't walking, he was running. Carl was young and in pretty good shape so he was there in less than five minutes. He tried the door but found it to be locked. He pounded on the door jamb and shouted that he needed to see the judge.

Ancil Lafferty answered the door in his nightshirt and he had a Smith & Wesson revolver in his right hand. When Carl began to pound on the door the second time Ancil recognized the voice and immediately unlocked the heavy front door, "Carl, come on in out of the cold. What is the matter?" Ancil asked.

"I need to see Judge Preston real quick Ancil, it's important."

As Ancil turned to go up the stairs he was met by both the judge and the deputy. They had heard the commotion and were coming down to investigate. When Carl saw the judge he took off his hat and said, "Judge, I got a woman over at the jail who just rode into town with two little boys. She said the man she was traveling with knows you and you need to come there at once."

Judge Preston thought about this and said, "Deputy, I don't know anybody around here, what makes you think she knows me?"

"I don't think she knows you, she said she was traveling with a man and he was traveling with a big dog that he rescued from a snare a few days back."

Preston turned to look at Cecil. "Zeke, it's Zeke and Ben!"

"Let's get our coats deputy, won't take a minute." With that Judge Preston and Cecil raced back up the stairs and were back in no time.

"Lead the way," was all Preston said to the deputy.

It took longer to make it back to the jail due to the judge's age, he just couldn't run that fast anymore. Once there they found the woman sitting in a chair and the two boys asleep on the long bench. Carl told Martha who the two men were.

"So you are the two men who were with Zeke when he found Ben?"

Preston was now convinced that the woman had really been traveling with Zeke. "Yes we were Ma'am. Can you tell us what has happened?"

Martha reached over and patted Keene as she talked. "It is a long story and I fear that by the time I tell it then it will be too late for you to help."

Preston knew he needed facts if he was going to help Zeke. "Just tell me the important stuff; you can fill me in on everything else after we have found Zeke."

"Zeke came upon Keene and me a few days back. We were stranded and he agreed to help. I didn't trust him at first, that dog he was traveling with didn't look trustworthy either. He agreed to see us safely to Langley and I really had no other alternative. That night we were attacked by something and Ben, that's the dog's name, well he went into the brush and fought off whatever it was. It seemed we were being hunted down. We were trying to make it to town tonight when whatever is was attacked us again. Ben was sleeping in the back of the wagon and when one jumped in to snatch the boys and me Ben went after it, the last I seen was him fighting in the back of the wagon and then jumping off the side to attack another one that was trying to grab the boys from the ground. The horses spooked and the last thing I saw was Zeke being knocked from his horse by more of the monsters." At this Martha burst into tears.

The judge looked at the two sleeping boys, "Did you say Zeke came upon you and one of the boys named Keene, what about the other boy?"

Martha looked at both boys and added, "The other boy is named Jarrett, and we came upon him earlier today. He was alone." Martha lowered her voice. "His family is missing."

Just then the door to the office opened and Marshal Savage walked in. "He wasn't expecting to find the judge and Cecil there. "Hello Judge, I just came over for some free coffee."

"Savage, do you feel like a trip tonight?" Cecil asked.

"A trip, what's happened?"

Judge Preston spoke up. "The man we told you about who stayed behind to tend to an injured dog. Well he's in trouble and maybe even dead."

Savage was a man of action and never turned away from trouble. "You don't say? Damn right I'm ready for a trip. You just point the way and tell me what I need to know."

Judge Preston turned back to Martha and asked, "Where did this happen Ma'am."

"On the trail to town, maybe a couple of hours ago. You need to hurry."

Savage looked at Cecil, "You going with me deputy?"

"I'm going. Whatever it is out there killed my friend Bill. He was traveling with us, went missing Sunday night."

Savage done a quick calculation. He pointed out the obvious, "Me and you ain't enough."

Judge Preston stepped forward. "I make three and time is wasting."

Just then the other night deputy walked in. "Fred this is Martha and these two boys are hers. They need someplace to stay and I would suspect some food. You take real good care of her; maybe take them over to Ancil and Mabel's place," Carl said.

Fred looked at all the people in the office and said, "Sure thing Carl, but you mind telling me where you are going?"

"Me and these three are heading back up the trail, might be some trouble waiting on us there," Carl said.

The judge and Cecil headed to the livery and quickly brought back their horses. Savage grabbed a shotgun from the cabinet behind the sheriff's desk and then went after his horse as well, Carl had his tied up out front. The four men, not knowing exactly what to expect, each took a shotgun and twenty rounds of ammunition. They were also armed with Colts which had become standard for all lawmen west of the Mississippi.

"What about rifles?" Judge Preston asked. "I would feel much better with a Winchester than a Greener."

Savage answered with what the two deputies already knew. "Winchester is no good at night. Shotgun is a sight more messy at close range and from what I have heard about what is out there waiting on us a Greener is what we want."

The judge was satisfied. As the four men headed out the door Carl turned back to Fred and told him that after he got Martha and the two boys situated to see if the hostler could look after the wagon and horses that the three had rode in on. He agreed and wished the four men good luck. Carl hoped they wouldn't need it.

The four men quickly mounted up and rode out of town at a full gallop. Carl knew the road well and was in the lead from the start. He told the three men that after a hard ride of thirty minutes or so they would slow a bit and start looking for any sign of Zeke and Ben. He knew if the wagon had traveled at a slightly fast speed for an hour and a half then he could be there in less than half that time on horseback. As the four horsemen rode each thought about what they might be riding into. Cecil, who had been the really spooked after Bill had gone missing was now anxious to confront whatever it was that waited for them in the darkness. He patted the holstered Colt at his side and hoped he got to put a few holes in whatever it was that had gotten his friend, time would tell.

After thirty minutes of hard riding the four men slowed a bit but still made good time. Carl turned in the saddle and said to the other three, "After another ten minutes at this pace I think we should slow to a trot. I figure if what the lady said is accurate then we should be getting real close by then. I probably don't need to remind any of you but I will say it just the same, stay sharp." The other three riders shook their heads in agreement.

Hazel and Rusty had been gone for a while as Ben waited for the creatures to attack. He circled Zeke's body every few minutes not knowing if he was dead or alive. As he did this he was also focused on the creatures in the darkness. After their initial advance they had stopped and even backed off a bit. Ben waited by Zeke and wondered why they had stopped. The five were still there and he knew exactly where each crouched in the darkness. As time went by Ben sat down beside Zeke and listened, he could hear him breathing, he was alive after all. Ben knew that when the creatures attacked again he couldn't keep them away from Zeke, there were just too many.

After the longest time Ben finally got a clue as to why they hadn't attacked yet, there were more on the way. He perked up his ears and listened, he also sniffed the air. By the sounds he could detect there were several more out there and they were not that far off from the ones that were crouched nearby. Unless Zeke woke up and used his gun then both he and his friend would die. As the sounds grew closer Ben stood and looked around, what he sensed was not good.

Suddenly the noise stopped. The creatures were well hidden and completely surrounding Ben's position by Zeke's side. He reached down and licked the injured man on the face in an attempt to wake him up.

The man never stirred. Ben turned away from Zeke and thought out his options. There were just too many for him to handle alone. The plan he would use was to just kill as many as possible before he was killed himself, along with Zeke.

Ben would wait for them to advance and then he would attack one of the two he had injured on the previous nights. The injured beasts would be slow and an easy kill. After he took care of the two injured ones he would then return to Zeke's side and tangle with any that made it to him. If they all charged in at once then he would do as he had done the previous night. Go low and snap at their bare unprotected front legs, bite hard and then move before he was injured himself. He would cripple as many as he could, not going for the throat or a kill unless the opportunity was too good to resist. Ben was smart enough to know that even if he grabbed one by the throat it would still take more time than he could spare to finish it off. In the time it took to bring down an animal and tear out its throat the others would be on him. If they managed to pen him to the ground then he would die early in the fight and so would Zeke. That was no good; if he was going to be killed tonight he hoped to take as many of the strange creatures as he could with him.

Ben didn't really understand what death was but he knew it was bad. He only killed for food or in self-defense. To be killed was a sensation that he might just get to experience tonight.

Finally, they made their move and so did Ben. He charged the one he knew was the most injured. In three or four quick steps he made it to his startled victim. Ben took it down with a leap that knocked it off its feet and then one quick bite to the throat. It wasn't dead when he left it but with the amount of blood spraying from its neck he knew it wouldn't last long.

The other injured one was farther to the right but there was an uninjured beast in the way. Ben acted as if he were going to jump but instead went for the legs. He bit and slashed hard with his teeth but never stopped as this previously uninjured one went down. He then made his way to the other injured creature which had turned to run away. No matter, Ben leapt onto the creatures back and latched onto the neck. Another quick bite and tear and he let this one roll to the ground as he had done with the previous two.

Several more were within feet of Zeke now and Ben sprinted to get into the fray before they could kill his friend. As he charged he used another of his vicious ploys on the remainder of the creatures. He let out an earsplitting howl and then went into a vicious growl. Several of the creatures turned just in time to see an enormous wolf flying through the air. Ben had launched himself airborne in an attempt to bowl over as many as possible. It worked, dog and creatures went down in a pile and that was when Ben knew he was near the end of his fight. They were on him.

He was clubbed by powerful legs and bitten by strong jaws. He was slashed and struck multiple times. While this was happening he was dishing out some punishment of his own. He bit and tore anything that presented itself. He also tore flesh with his feet. In such a fight it is amazing what a cornered and desperate dog can do, and what it can sense. Ben knew Zeke had been grabbed and was being dragged toward the tree line. Ben couldn't go and help, he was taking too much of a beating himself. As he was being pinned by the creatures and unable to help Zeke he felt the shadows of hate overtake his mind again and he quickly went mad with rage. As the big dog slashed with both teeth and paw he dropped again into the bloodlust that had consumed him the previous night. His eyes glazed over and frothy foam ran from his mouth. His last seconds alive would be his greatest.

As the big dog was being bitten and chewed to death Zeke came to and felt the odd sensation of being dragged. Whatever was happening was bringing immense pain to his broken ribs. He still held the Colt in his right hand. When he finally managed to raise his head a little he saw Ben a few feet away in a vicious fight with several of the monsters. In the dim light he got a glimpse of the big dog's eyes just before he was completely covered by the beasts, the eyes looked red as if the devil himself had just occupied Ben's body. The noise of the fight was truly terrifying.

Zeke raised the gun and, although unable to aim at anything in particular, he fired a shot anyway. He pulled the trigger again in hopes of either hitting whatever it was that was dragging him or at least scaring it off. He was still being pulled toward the tree line after the second shot. He raised the gun again and pulled the trigger, again and again until the Colt finally clicked empty. Just before Zeke was himself torn to shreds he heard what he thought were hoof beats. The pain soon put him under; as he slipped away he thought he could hear the faint voice of his father.

"Did you hear that, was that a gunshot?" Cecil shouted.

"It sure the hell was," Savage shouted as he spurred his horse into action.

All four men sent their mounts toward the sound of the gunshots at a full gallop. As they rounded a steep curve in the trail the tree line parted and they could see what looked like two different fights taking place with about twenty feet separating each.

Savage quickly looked over the sight and made a quick decision. "Don't shoot into the fray, shoot high, one round each with your Colts."

All four men drew and shot high. The sound of four .45 caliber Colts fired at once and four mounted horses at speed got the attention of whatever it was in the trail. In the moonlight the four riders saw creatures breaking off from the fight and heading into the brush and trees at seemingly supernatural speed.

"What are those things?" Savage shouted.

No one answered him, no one knew.

All four riders pulled up and stopped next to Zeke's body. There was another body in the road a little farther away but this one was not a man, it was a big dog. Judge Preston and Cecil jumped down and went to Zeke. Savage and Carl stayed on their horses and continued to scan the area. Preston gently rolled Zeke over.

"Is he dead?" Carl asked.

"He's breathing. Looks like we got here before they had a chance to kill him," Preston said.

As everyone was focused on Zeke, Ben managed to get on his feet and instinctively he headed toward Zeke. He was still in the fog of battle, the only thing he noticed was that his friend was still surrounded.

Savage saw movement and looked in that direction. "Is that the dog you were talking about Judge?"

Cecil turned and saw a monster of a dog heading in his direction. The dog was injured and was wobbling as he walked. The animal's face was covered in blood and frothy red foam ran from its mouth. It was the eyes that were the scariest of all though, they were black as coal and at the same time seemed to glow red. As injured as he was Ben still managed to advance, as he did he growled and slowly opened his mouth to reveal long bloody teeth. Ben was still dishing out death if only in his mind.

Judge Preston stood and faced the dog and then began to talk to him. "Ben, do you remember me. Ben! Ben!" He said over and over as the big dog advanced.

"Better step back Judge, you and Cecil both." Savage knew the dog was hurt bad and didn't know if he recognized the judge and Cecil.

"Ben saw Zeke stretched out on the ground and thought he was dead. As he walked toward these men he felt he could trust them, he knew the monsters were gone and these men had something to do with it. When the judge started talking Ben actually recognized the voice as one of the men who had rescued him from the snare. He stopped and shook his head and coat. It was painful.

"Ben, come over here, come on boy," Judge Preston said.

Ben was coming out of his fog now, but he was in great pain. He slowly walked as best as he could over to where Zeke lay and as he did he stopped growling and took on the face and demeanor of a dog that liked to be around people. Preston and Cecil backed away as Ben approached, not knowing if he was going to attack them or not. When Ben got to Zeke's side he looked at the two men standing in front of him and then he lay down right beside his fallen friend.

Savage and Carl had continued to look into the tree line. Whatever was out there had moved away in the face of four men mounted on powerful horses. Both men held their shotguns at the ready. Now that they knew where Zeke and Ben were the next shots fired would be to kill.

"Cecil, get me the canteen from my horse," Preston said.

Within seconds Cecil had it and then slowly took his bandanna and dampened it with the cool water. Preston took it and slowly wiped away the dirt and blood from Zeke's face. As he did this Zeke came to. He tried to fight at first thinking he was still being attacked by the creatures.

"Whoa there Zeke, it's me, Judge Preston."

Zeke looked toward the sound of the voice he had just heard and tried to focus his eyes.

"Judge, is it really you?" Then he thought of the dog. "Ben Judge, you have got to go and help Ben."

Ben had caught his breath now and at the sound of Zeke's voice he reached over and licked him right in the face. Zeke smiled and tried to laugh but the effort brought on a round of intense pain. He lay his head back down and thanked the Lord for bringing both himself and Ben through.

"Judge, I really don't think we should stay here very long. I still don't know what it was we ran off but it looked like there were six or eight and I for one don't want to be here if they take a notion to come back," Savage said.

Cecil stood and looked into the brush and then did something that was totally unexpected. He leveled his twelve-gage Greener and pulled the trigger. He then turned and fired another shot in the opposite direction. As he quickly reloaded the two empty chambers he shouted. "Come on back and lets you and me have us a little ruckus." After he had his gun reloaded he done the same thing again, he fired a shot in each direction.

Preston stood and put his hand on Cecil's shoulder. "I know how you feel deputy. When this trial is over I think me and you need to come back out here and find us some answers."

Cecil lowered his shotgun and then wiped his forehead with the back of his shirtsleeve. "You can count me in on that little trip Judge."

Preston knelt back beside Zeke and asked, "How bad are you hurt, do you think you can ride."

"Mostly my ribs Judge, if you can get me in the saddle, I think I can ride. Do you have my horses?"

The judge looked around. "Savage do you see any horses tied up around here?"

All four men were now scanning the surrounding area. No horses could be seen. As Ben lay and watched he also wondered where the two horses were. He knew he was in no shape to help them if they were in trouble. He raised his head and howled a long low note that, to the four men, sounded both poetic and haunting. Within seconds the sound of hoof beats could be heard. All four men leveled their guns in the direction of the sound. Coming down the trail from the opposite direction that Preston and his men had come in on, trotted Rusty and Hazel.

Hazel marched right up to the men and put her head down to inspect Ben. The big dog raised his head and began licking the horse on the muzzle. Rusty just stood back and looked over these new horses and riders. He recognized the judge and Cecil and the two horses they rode but he was a little cautious of the two new horses and riders. Rusty never gave Zeke a second look, he would be okay, he always was.

Preston and Cecil slowly helped Zeke to his feet. It seemed his most serious injury was his ribs; everything else looked like minor cuts and scrapes. Cecil grabbed the reins of Rusty and held him while both Carl and Preston helped Zeke into the saddle, which brought on a whole new round of pain. When they felt Zeke could stay in the saddle on his own both Cecil and Carl mounted up. The judge held the reins of Hazel and looked at the other men. He knew what was coming next.

"Mount up Judge; you want me to lead the extra horse?" Savage asked.

Zeke raised his head and looked at Savage. "We ain't going nowhere without Ben."

Savage knew the boy was hurt, probably badly and thought the pain might have been clouding his judgement. "Yes we are young fellar. We rode out here at breakneck speed in the dark to save you and now we are leaving."

Zeke tapped Rusty and lead him up to where Savage sat his horse. "Mister, I really appreciate what you done and all but if Ben doesn't go back with us then neither do I."

Savage was starting to get a little irritated at this. "Then I will just arrest you right now and lead you off to jail until your head starts working again."

Zeke might have had a few broken ribs and a few more injuries of a lesser nature but he wasn't leaving Ben out here alone, the two had nearly died together. A rush of anger and adrenalin seemed to ease the pain as Zeke drew his Colt with amazing speed. Savage was startled by the sight of a .45 aimed at his face.

"Now mister, as I said, I really do appreciate what you done riding out here in the middle of the night and all but I don't think I'm gonna let you arrest me tonight. Now why don't you turn that little horse you're riding and head on back to town," Zeke said.

Savage looked at the other men and wondered if they were gonna do anything.

"Marshal, I think Zeke there might have a point. Me and the judge done left him out here in the middle of nowhere and couldn't for the life of us talk him out of it. I don't think he will shoot you but if I was you I would forget that part about arresting him," Cecil said.

Judge Preston knew Zeke would stay here if Ben wasn't taken back to town. He really didn't want to leave the big dog behind either but didn't know how they were going to take him with them. "Marshal, I don't think I want to leave Ben out here either. Zeke, how do you intend to take him with us, he looks about as bad after his fight with whatever it was out there as he did the day we found him tangled up in that snare."

Zeke pointed to Hazel. "Just pick him up and put him on top of that pack Hazel is carrying and then tie him on with some rope so he don't fall off."

All three men looked at the big horse with the hazel green eyes and noticed the pack she carried was flat on top. "Is that how you got Ben this far Zeke, on top of that horse?" The judge asked. Zeke only smiled.

"Well I'll be damned Judge, that was some pretty smart thinking. Ben was in too bad a shape to walk when we found him so old Zeke here done made him a dog saddle on top of that horse," Cecil said.

The judge and Cecil went over to Ben, who had calmed down considerably after his vicious fight, and patted him on the head. Ben accepted this and even managed to slap the ground with his tail a time or two. Both men then gently picked the big dog up and put him on top of the pack Hazel carried. With some rope Cecil and the judge loosely tied him so he couldn't fall off.

Judge Preston looked at Zeke and asked, "Does that look about right?"

"That looks just fine Judge, and thanks," Zeke said through gritted teeth.

"Don't mention it; I think I would have stayed out here with you and Ben before I would have left. That big dog must be one hell of a scrapper, any other animal couldn't have survived half what he's been through?" the judge said.

Savage, up until now, had been quiet after having a Colt pointed in his face. "Well, if everyone is satisfied I think now would be a good time to head back to town before whatever is out there decides to have another go at us, and one more thing young man. When we get to town I might just still arrest you for pointing that gun in my face."

Zeke just gave the marshal a grin as he tapped Rusty into a trot.

Judge Preston thought he needed to cut the marshal down a notch or two. "You go ahead and arrest him Savage. I'll just drop the charges anyway for lack of evidence."

Cecil looked at Savage and immediately burst out laughing. With that the tension was broken because even Savage started to laugh. As the five man party, plus one badly beat up dog, trotted down the trail toward Langley eight pairs of eyes peered from the timber and watched them go. This wasn't over.

As the men slowly made their way Zeke held onto the saddle horn with his left hand and just let Rusty follow the other horses. His chest hurt with every breath he took. Ben, once placed back on top of the pack Hazel carried, had immediately fallen asleep. His injuries now included bruises, cuts and even a few vicious bite marks not to mention his previous wounds from the snare. He was beat up really bad but at least he was alive.

As he slept he dreamed of younger days not that far in the past when he had played and romped along with the other dogs from his litter. Happy dreams always help with the healing. Hazel turned her head from time to time to check on him, as before she walked steady and sure footed knowing the big dog was hurt.

As the men rode they all kept their shotguns at the ready. They made it to Langley a little after four in the morning. Once they had the town lights in sight Carl rode ahead to get Doctor Collette roused and over to the clinic he ran. He suspected the doctor might be a little drunk at this hour of the morning. When he arrived it took a few minutes of hard knocking to get him to the door. When the door finally opened Carl was looking at one sorry mess. The doctor was standing in his night shirt and he didn't look to steady on his feet. His gray hair stood in all directions and he was unshaven.

"Doc, we got to get to the clinic. We got a man coming in that needs your attention."

Collette tried to focus as he looked around Carl. "A man you say, well where is he? I don't see anybody."

"Naw Doc, he is still on his way."

"Well when he gets here then you come and get me; I'm going back to bed."

As Collette turned to go back into the house Carl grabbed him by the shoulder. "That won't work Doc; he's hurt bad and needs you to come to the clinic."

"Well why didn't you say so deputy? That makes all the difference in the world. The clinic opens at eight o'clock; I usually get there about fifteen till." Again Collette turned and headed back inside.

This really didn't surprise Carl, he had gotten the doctor out on numerous occasions before and this was pretty standard stuff. "Doc, I need you to get yourself over to the clinic right now. You grab your coat and let's go."

The doctor had finally managed to part the cobwebs in his head enough to realize this might be serious. "Alright Carl, but when we get there I need you to help with a few things, like coffee and the fire."

Carl always started a fire in the big stove and put on a pot of coffee when he roused the doctor in the middle of the night. "You got yourself a deal Doc." Carl also liked the fact that doc Collette only drank Arbuckle brand coffee and this was the deputy's favorite. He couldn't afford it on his meager salary so he always drank lots when it was free. After Collette got his coat on and tugged a hat over his mop of hair the two men headed down the street toward the clinic.

The weather had deteriorated during the night. The moon had decided to hide at this early hour as clouds now filled the sky. A cold breeze had picked up and it felt like it might snow. This far north and this late in the season meant snow was not uncommon for early October although unlikely. By the time the deputy managed to get the doctor to the clinic it was nearly five in the morning. The building was cold and dark and Carl immediately went about the task of building a fire. A new fire in a cold stove meant that coffee was at least thirty minutes away. Carl needed it after the night he had but the doc needed it much more to help him sober up.

Ten minutes after they got the clinic unlocked the other four men rode up outside. Zeke was gently helped down and led inside. Doc Collette had by now nearly gotten his wits back and quickly headed his patient toward a room he used for examinations. As this was going on Savage looked at the judge and asked, "What do we do about that dog Judge?"

Preston looked at Carl and asked the obvious, "Do you have anyone in town that works on animals deputy?"

"Sure do, old Amil Boggs does. He is about the best horse doctor around."

"Well that is good news. Does he work on dogs too," The judge asked.

"Don't think so, just horses."

Savage thought that wouldn't be a problem. "As big as he is just throw a damn saddle on the dog and Boggs won't know the difference."

"Is that the only animal doctor there is deputy, surely in a town the size of Langley you got somebody that works on dogs and such," the judge asked.

"Well, Boggs is pretty good with horses; maybe a dog and a horse ain't that much different on the inside," Carl said.

"All we can do is try. Cecil, how about you and Carl leading Hazel over to this Amil Boggs place and see if he can help. Ben needs attention and maybe a horse doctor can help. It'll take the both of you to get him off the back of that horse anyway."

Just then Doc Collette came out of his examination room and headed for the coffee pot. It wasn't quite done but in the doc's shape it really didn't matter. He filled a white porcelain cup about half way full and then finished it off with cream that was sitting in a big ice box by the door. In the ice box were what looked like bottles of medicine that must have required cool temperatures?

"How is Zeke Doc?" Preston asked.

"Got some bruised ribs. Got a bunch of other stuff to, what in the world happened to him anyway?."

Preston and Savage were the only two in the room besides the doctor, Cecil and Carl had headed off leading Hazel and Ben on their way to find help for the injured dog.

"We don't really know Doc," the judge said. "He was attacked by something is all we know for sure."

Collette took a long pull on the slightly warm coffee and didn't seem to mind the taste at all. "What do you mean attacked? What attacked him?"

"Again Doc, we don't really know. When we rode up he was being dragged away and the dog was in the battle of his life. I think if we had been a minute or two later then both would have been killed," Preston said.

The doctor looked at Savage hoping the lawman could shed more light on what happened. "Marshal I need to know what attacked him. If it was a man or an animal I need to know which it was. You said he was being dragged away, what was dragging him?"

"Well, we couldn't really tell but there were a lot of them, maybe six or eight. I do know that it wasn't men they were fighting with; he was being taken by some sort of wild animal I have never in my life seen before. When we got there we fired a few shots and whatever it was ran into the trees. The dog was taking the worst of it, they were piled on top of him and it looked like he was near the end of his rope. They would have surely killed him if we hadn't got there when we did. It looked like they were dragging the boy into the trees to kill him too."

The doctor took another sip of his cold coffee and thought about what he had just heard. "That man back there has some bite marks on him. It doesn't look like the marks are from any animal I have ever seen before though. Funny looking marks if you ask me, sharp teeth, but from what, I can't say." With that Collette got a couple of bottles of medicine out of the icebox and headed back into the examination room.

Judge Preston walked over to the stove and felt of the coffee pot, another minute or two should do the trick. "Marshal Savage, what do you think it was out there this morning?"

Savage walked to the coffee pot and poured himself a cup. He really didn't care if it was hot or not, he had surely drunk worse on the trail before. "I can't say for sure judge, it was just too dark. Whatever it was could move fast, especially after you fire a couple of shots over its head. I've seen some stuff in my time, can't say I ever seen something like that though. I think I will put away the horses Judge, and then catch a few minutes sleep. You still intend on starting that trial this morning?"

Finally Preston felt he had waited long enough for his coffee so he poured his cup full to the top edge and took a sip. "Got no choice Marshal, the trial has got to get underway. I know I can count on you and Cecil to help keep the peace in the courtroom. We three may be dead on our feet but it ain't anything we ain't seen before. If I get too tired then I plan on taking a little nap during the lunch recess."

"I thought that would be your answer Judge and that sounds fine with me. The way I see it the sooner we get this trial over with the sooner I can head back out there and hunt down whatever it was we saw attacking Zeke and Ben."

Preston smiled. "I hoped that would be your plan after the trial is over. I lost a deputy to whatever we saw out there and I for one take something like that personal. When you ride out of here in a few days then I'm going with you."

Savage gave the judge a funny look. He wondered how a judge figured to hunt down dangerous animals. "Alright then it's settled. After the trial we take us a little hunting trip. I plan on spending my spare time between now and then getting the supplies we'll need."

Preston looked at Savage and asked, "What kind of supplies are you talking about? If it's grub I like to pick out my own trail food."

"Guns Judge, I for one want something with a little more kick than a twelve-gauge shotgun. Now don't get me wrong, a twelve-gauge can do a lot of damage at close range but past fifty or sixty feet I want something that can bring down big game. When I hit something with a big Winchester then it will go down and it will stay down. I don't believe in ghosts, spirits, or monsters. When I kill us one of whatever it was out there then we can get us a good look-see."

Judge Preston sat down his cup of the wretched coffee Collette seemed to like, maybe if it was heated a little more it would be better but he didn't want to hang around the doctor's office any longer. "Savage, you head on out and get a little sleep. I think I can get me in an hour myself. Make sure you are cleaned up for court though. I run a tight ship and my officers and bailiffs are expected to look professional."

Savage tipped his hat to the judge and as he went out the door he said, "I for one like court Judge, gives me a chance to show off this shiny Marshal's Badge." With that he was gone.

As Savage walked out, the doctor walked back in. "Collette, if there is any change in your patient back there then you make sure you find me. Most of my time will be spent at the courthouse for the next few days. And don't you worry about your bill either. Rapid City will take care of it, Zeke in there is a deputy and we take care of our injured lawmen."

Preston turned and headed for his room at the hotel. He couldn't remember when he had been this tired before but he was sure it had happened.

Carl and Cecil made it to the stables where Amil Boggs done his horse doctoring. It was on the edge of town on the lower end away from most of the other businesses. The building was a large affair with the usual double doors in the front. On the side of the barn and attached was a room with a flue pipe coming out the top and a porch with a swing hanging from the rafters. There was a regular size walk door and on the right side of that was a large double hung window.

Carl walked over and knocked on the door and as he did he said, "Amil, this is Carl, I need to talk to you." After that Carl knocked on the door again. Within seconds a lantern was lit inside and the light shone through the window. After some fumbling with the lock the door swung open and a man who must have been in his late sixties or maybe even early seventies stepped out onto the covered porch.

"Carl, is that you?" The man asked with a rough gravelly voice as he held the lantern high.

"Yea Amil it's me, how you feeling this morning?" Carl asked.

The old man looked around. "I feel alright deputy but I don't really think its morning yet."

"I have to agree with you about that. Say Amil, the reason I woke you up so early is I need your help. We got this dog and he's in a bad way, you think you can take a look at him?" Carl asked.

"Be glad to Carl, but I don't know much about dogs. Where is he?"

"We got him tied on the back of that horse over there," Carl said.

Amil held the lantern higher and looked in the direction the deputy pointed. "Well let me get the barn opened up and then you can bring him in."

Amil walked over and slid open one of the big double doors. He disappeared inside and began lighting three big lanterns. Cecil led Hazel inside and then Carl closed the door. Cecil looked around; it was a typical barn with a wide center hallway and stalls on each side. The front side room they stood in though had a cast iron stove and wooden floor. As Amil went about lighting his stove Cecil and Carl went about untying Ben.

Amil pointed to a table that was near the stove and said, "Just put him on that table."

Ben roused a little as he was being untied. Cecil was a little afraid of the big dog and it looked like Carl was scared to death. When they had him untied Cecil reached up and patted Ben on the head and with a gentle voice he said; "Now you be a good dog so we can put you on that table over there." Ben licked Cecil's hand. That was all it took for man and dog to bond. Cecil lost all fear of the big dog at that moment.

"Alright now Carl, lets me and you gently lift him off this pack and try not to hurt him, he's hurt enough as it is," Cecil said.

Ben whimpered a little as the two men struggled to get him off the pack and onto the table. With that done Ben immediately lay his head back down and closed his eyes. He was in pain and not only that he was hungry and thirsty. He knew these men were going to help him though. As he lay on the table he thought of Zeke and wondered where he was. Ben had taken a liking to the man ever since he had cut him loose from the snare.

Amil looked at the dog for a minute and finally said, "I have never in my life seen a dog that big before. Not even half that big. He favors a wolf but much larger. Is he going to protest when I start poking and prodding on him?"

Cecil said, "Well, I really don't know. He has never offered to attack any of us but we haven't been around him that much."

"The both of you stand on each side of him and be ready to help if he tries to get mean; I'm going to look him over and see how bad he's hurt," Amil said. Both Cecil and Carl got on each side of Ben and stood there as the old horse doctor looked him over.

Amil felt each leg to check for any broken bones. He looked over the head and even inside Ben's mouth. He checked over the injuries to the shoulders and hips, some old from the snare and some new from his battle with his enemies. After he finished he walked over and put a coffee pot full of water on the stove.

"Well Doc, what do you think?" Cecil asked.

"Nothing is broken as far as I can tell. He has some pretty bad cuts and it looks like he has been hit pretty hard on his right hip and his left shoulder. A few of his teeth are pretty loose but they will tighten back up in few days. It looks like he has been beat half to death and starved the other half. What happened to him?"

"We found him caught in a snare a few days back. We cut him free but he was in no shape to travel so one of the men that was traveling with us agreed to stay behind to see to the dog. They were set upon a few hours ago and by the time we got there both Zeke and Ben were nearly killed," Cecil said.

Amil looked at the two men with suspicion in his eyes. "What were they fighting with?"

Cecil and Carl looked at each other and finally Carl said, "We don't know. It was dark and we only got a glimpse."

This explanation seemed to satisfy the doctor. "Well, I think I will be alright with Ben now. He didn't protest when I was examining him so you two go and get yourselves some sleep. You both look like shit."

"You think he is going to be alright Doc?" Carl asked.

"If I can keep his wounds from getting infected and there isn't anything busted up inside I think he will be alright. What he needs more than anything is some food to give him strength and some rest. I plan on cleaning him up and doctoring his injuries. I got me a good recipe that will put some strength back in him too. Rest and food is the best medicine right now. Give him four days maybe five and he'll be well on his way to a complete recovery."

"That's good news Doc. I'll be back about midday to check on him," Cecil said. Ben didn't care what any of the men were saying, he was sound asleep.

Before the two men left they placed Ben down on the floor near the stove. Amil had taken a couple of horse blankets and made a soft bed for the dog to lie on. Ben was warm and for the first time in a long time the big dog felt safe.

"Now you boys head on along and leave me to my work. This dog needs something to eat and a little water. After that I plan on stirring up a poultice to put on a few of these injuries. Come on back anytime you want, I'm always here."

Carl and Cecil both headed out with hopes of catching a little sleep before they had to be at the courthouse. By the time Carl made it to the room he rented over the general store he was dead on his feet. When Cecil made it to his hotel room he collapsed on his bed not even bothering to close his door or take his boots off.

Judge Preston managed to sleep an hour and twenty minutes before waking. He felt surprisingly good for a man who had been out most of the night. Once awake he went to the wash room that was attached to the hotel and cleaned himself up. If he felt good when he first woke up he now felt even better. As he shaved, he wondered how much trouble he was going to have out of Cecil. That was one deputy who could stay up late but never wake up early.

Preston threw his towel in a basket by the washroom door and gathered his comb and razor. As he walked to the end of the hall past his own room he noticed Cecil's door wide open. At this, he assumed the deputy was already up, he was not. There, sprawled across the bed was Deputy Cecil Spriggs. He was so still the judge first thought he might have passed on during the night.

"Cecil wake up, you got just enough time to clean your badge packing ass up and get some breakfast before court today." The deputy never moved.

Preston reached down and shook the heel of Cecil's boot. "Cecil, if you want some breakfast you better wake up and I mean right now." Cecil never moved, he did fart loudly and that was enough to back the judge up.

"Cecil, damn you, if you do that again I'm going to charge you for assault with a deadly weapon."

With that Cecil laughed loudly. "Ah Judge, don't be mean. I'm awake."

"I'll be downstairs at the same table I was at yesterday. Hurry up and shave, and clean the rest of yourself up too. Get on downstairs for some food. Time is a wasting," the judge said.

"Sure thing boss, just give me a few minutes alone with my razor and I'll be right on down."

"You better spend a few minutes alone in that tub in the wash room, it has running water and I expect you to try some of it out." With that Preston turned and left the room.

Downstairs he was surprised to find the dining room nearly filled. He wasn't able to get the same table he had the day before but was still able to find one near the back wall. As he sat he looked over the other patrons. He doubted anyone would know who he was since the trial hadn't started yet but he was sure he would be well known by the next morning. As he sat he noticed a familiar face across the room and that face was looking at him, it was Lloyd Shafer. Shafer didn't try to hide the fact that he had spotted the judge and Preston didn't remove his gaze either. What started out as a staring contest was short lived. Shafer got up and with coffee cup in hand headed toward the judge's table.

"Judge Preston, I am surprised to see you so well rested this morning."

"And why is that Mr. Shafer?"

"I heard you and a bunch of deputies were out all night chasing monsters. Did you find any?" Shafer said this with a laugh.

"Not exactly Lloyd. What I consider a monster is anything that is more revolting than what I have seen in my courtroom. I doubt if that is possible."

Shafer took what the judge said to be directed at him and wasn't going to let it go unanswered. "Well now Thurman, since we are on a first name basis here I would like to say that I also hold that same opinion but mine would pertain to those seated behind the bench and not in front of it."

Preston liked nothing better than a verbal jousting match especially if it involved someone he disliked as much as Shafer. "First names are fine with me Lloyd. In this case my first name is Judge and that should quickly be followed by Preston. Do you follow me?"

"Oh yes Thurman I do. But out here on the street I will call you anything I like, do you follow me?"

Both men only smiled at each other. As Shafer turned and headed back to his table he got in one last barb. "What do you plan to do with your life after you are removed from the bench Thurman?"

"That's an easy one Lloyd. I plan on using all my waking hours investigating how it is that you came to land in Rapid City. I want to look at a few deeds and research a few of the business dealings you've been involved in over the last ten years, should be a lot of fun."

It was evident that Preston had struck a nerve with his remarks. Shafer stopped dead in his tracks and glared back at the judge. He didn't say anything but by the expression on his face Shafer looked like he was ready to have a fit. Wisely, the tall attorney let it pass and returned to his table. He would settle the score with Preston at some date in the near future. There were a few things in Shafer's past that would look very bad if they ever came to light. He knew now that he would need to eliminate the judge instead of merely having him removed from the bench. This idea actually brought a smile to the lawyer's face.

Just as the judge got his food Cecil wandered into the room looking all clean shaven and refreshed. He glanced in the judge's direction but not before looking over the other patrons. He spotted Shafer and was spotted himself. He tipped his hat but the kind act was not reciprocated.

Shafer didn't like the sheriff of Rapid City and this dislike also extended to the deputies.

"Howdy Judge, I hope you left me a little something or did you order everything in the kitchen for yourself?" Cecil said this as he continued looking in the direction of Shafer.

"Now Cecil, you know I left you a bite. If there is one thing I hate it is your stomach growling while I'm trying to hold court."

"Thank ye kindly Judge. Did you happen to notice Shafer sitting over there near the opposite wall?"

"I did deputy, as a matter of fact he walked over here and he and I traded a few words, not very kind ones but we traded just the same."

"I'll tell you something, I don't like the man, never have. And one more thing just between you and me, I don't trust him neither. I can spot me a low down crook from a mile away and when it comes to Shafer maybe even two miles."

The judge took a biscuit and reached it to Cecil. "I done ordered for you deputy and told them to bring it out in ten more minutes. I thought you would take a little longer to skin them whiskers of yours but here you are. Take this biscuit and try some of that butter on it, might just keep you busy until your plate shows up."

After Cecil got his plate he and the judge ate in silence. Preston was contemplating the trial and Cecil was still stewing over Shafer being in the same room. Halfway through the meal Preston reached over and took a biscuit from Cecil's plate. Cecil stopped chewing and looked at the judge.

"Now why did you take that biscuit Judge, if you don't mind me asking?"

"I took it to replace the one I reached you earlier. I never gave you my biscuit, I just loaned it to you until your food showed up. Now we're even."

"Never knew we were keeping score judge. You ain't going to charge me interest on the loan of that biscuit are you?"

"I just might, it depends on whether I'm still hungry when my plate is empty."

Cecil took the judge at his word and quickly finished his food before Preston reached across and swiped something else. Once finished the judge paid the tab and then stood. He paid particular attention to Shafer and who he might be sitting with, it just happened to be Wes Branham, the state's main witness against Doug Whitmore.

When Judge Preston and Cecil Spriggs made it to the courthouse it was a few minutes before eight-o'clock. There were several people standing in front of the building and even more on the steps and porch. The crowd might not have recognized the judge but they had no trouble seeing the badge Cecil wore on his chest. It was almost biblical as the crowd parted and allowed the deputy and the man with him to climb the stairs.

Once inside Preston went up the stairs and into the main courtroom. It was empty, which was a relief. Apparently after the excitement of the previous day everyone outside was using a little more caution about barging in. The two men proceeded to the back of the courtroom and went directly to the judge's chambers. Inside, sitting at his desk, was Simon Lester.

"Well good morning Simon, didn't expect to find you here this early," Preston said.

"Been here more than an hour Thurman. I figured I better familiarize myself with the evidence if I'm going to represent the accused."

"Well I hope you have found something good because the odds of your client winning are looking pretty thin. The state has a witness and Whitmore only has his good name. Those people outside want a hanging and nothing short of a miracle is needed to prevent it," Preston said.

Lester looked up and only smiled. "Now Judge Preston, you haven't already formed an opinion before you have seen all the evidence have you?"

"Not at all, but this is starting to look like you need to pull a rabbit out of a hat in order to win."

"Don't have a rabbit Judge. I will do the best I can to save that man. I truly believe he has been framed and intend to fight Shafer tooth and nail until I have an acquittal."

"That's the spirit. I also believe something is amiss here but my beliefs are not what I base my decision on, it is the facts," Preston said.

"I know Preston. If I lose it won't be for a lack of effort. I might be a little rusty as a lawyer but my years on the bench have taught me a thing or two. I plan on giving that man a vigorous defense," Lester said.

"I would expect nothing less. Maybe you should prepare out in the courtroom. Neither of us would want anything to look like I was helping you."

"I was about to say the same thing." With that Lester gathered his work and proceeded to the defense table in the courtroom.

"Cecil, go out and see if the bailiffs have made it yet."

Once the three court bailiffs were gathered up Preston instructed them on where each would be stationed. Savage made it in at eight-thirty and was told to stay in the courtroom at all times during the trial. Jasel Farley, the sheriff of Langley, got there at fifteen minutes before nine.

"Sheriff, how do you feel about the sentiments of that crowd outside?" Preston asked.

Jasel thought a second before answering. "I've been out since before daylight Judge. Seen a bunch of people this morning and talked to several. Most won't be any trouble but a few will. A few don't think much of you for the way you had people locked up yesterday, said you are a ruffian and a bully."

Preston laughed. "That's the first time I've ever been called a ruffian, probably been called a bully before but that was a long time ago. Don't know many men in their sixties who could be a bully. Is Carl anywhere nearby? I need the accused brought over from the jail and I don't want you to try it on your own. Be a sight if Doug Whitmore was lynched before he got to the courthouse."

"Carl is at the jail now trying to wake up. It must have been one hell of a night you fellars had out rescuing that fellar over at the doctor's place, and that big dog."

"It was a close call for both of them. The boy and that monster of a dog were seconds from being killed when the four of us rode up. As soon as I can get this trial squared away me and Savage are heading back out there to try and get us some answers."

Farley looked at the judge in astonishment. "You can't be serious. The two of you wouldn't last a day out there. I've been hearing stories and what I hear is all bad."

"Well Sheriff, we plan on going and you brought up a good point. I was hoping on a little help from some of the townsfolk. When we go we need more men, the more people we got the better our chances are. But if it comes right down to it then it will be just me and Savage."

Farley never hesitated. "You can count me in on that little trip Judge. That will make three of us. How about that deputy of yours named Cecil?"

"You know, I forgot about Cecil. After the way he acted last night I would say he's itching for a fight. He lost a friend to those monsters and has got up some backbone in the last few days, he'll go."

"Then your little two man search party just grew to four. I'll talk to Carl and see if he might want to come along. You think five men is enough?" Farley asked.

Preston looked out the window as he answered. "Not by a long shot. We need six or eight to succeed. It will take at least two men at a time on guard duty for any of us to get some rest at night. One man doesn't stand a chance, that's how we lost the other deputy on the way to town."

"You worry about your trial Judge and let me see what I can do about finding a few more men." With that Farley went out the door.

At nine o'clock Judge Preston entered the courtroom. The three bailiffs were stationed at each exit and all were armed. Cecil stayed near the bench and to the judge's happy surprise he carried a Greener shotgun. As Preston seated himself behind the bench he looked over the crowd, which was substantial. By the looks of things when the courthouse had been unlocked fifteen minutes earlier there must have been a mad rush as people swarmed toward the available seats, all were full and those in the crowd unlucky enough or slow enough were forced to stand around the back and on each side of the spectator seating. The substantial courtroom was filled to capacity. One sight that was especially worrying was that several of the men were armed; gun belts and Colts were worn by several of the men and even one woman. If trouble erupted Cecil and the three Bailiffs would be hard pressed to stop it.

Preston felt he needed to set a few rules before he got down to the court's business, "Ladies and gentlemen, if I may have your attention." The room grew quiet. "I see that some of you in the crowd are armed. Let me make this as clear as possible. I am going to instruct the three bailiffs to go around the room and gather all the guns you are carrying. You are more that welcome to stay and watch the trial but you will do it unarmed. Now anyone who wishes to keep their weapons are more than welcome to do so but you will do it outside the courthouse. Anyone who refuses this order will be arrested and after this trial I will deal with you then. In the meantime you will be housed in the Langley jail. Bailiffs, please gather the guns and lock them in the office beside my chambers."

As the three bailiffs went about their task Preston and Cecil looked about the room. Most of those who were armed simply turned and left the courtroom and in doing so there was a fair amount of grumbling. This task was made easier by the appearance of Pete Savage who also carried a Greener shotgun. If anyone thought Cecil looked tough with his shotgun then they were probably terrified by the appearance of Savage. The judge had to admit that the cross draw holster wearing marshal was a menacing sight even without a shotgun; he had the distinct look of a predator. As Savage peered about the room, Judge Preston noticed most of the grumblers had quieted down considerably.

Once the courtroom had been cleared of guns Sheriff Farley and Carl entered, along with Doug Whitmore. The accused was wearing a suit and looked very much the banker he was. This had been suggested by his council Simon Lester the previous evening. Lloyd Shafer had protested to Judge Preston. His argument was that Whitmore was a criminal and should look the part. Preston had reminded Shafer that Preston wasn't a criminal, only a man who had been accused of a crime. Again Shafer vowed under his breath to deal with Preston at a later time.

Once everyone was seated Preston advised Shafer to call his first witness.

"I have only one witness Your Honor." To use the term 'Your Honor' went against Shafer but he knew he had to show respect in the courtroom. "I call Wes Branham to the witness chair."

Wes Branham, who had been sitting silently in the back of the courtroom slowly stood and as he made his way forward Cecil and Savage noticed he still wore a gun. It was in a holster and was partially covered by his coat. Undoubtable while he was sitting the bailiffs who had been disarming the crowd had missed it and Wes had failed to turn it over. Both Cecil and Savage leveled their shotguns at Wes and then Savage spoke. "Surrender that weapon mister!" It was a demand, not a request. If either of the lawmen had discharged their shotguns it would have hit more than just Wes Branham, it would have been a bloodbath.

Wes smiled and held up both hands. "You two can take it yourself if you like."

Both Savage and Cecil had known for years that a man who attempted to take a Colt out of another man's holster would soon be a dead man. It was a trick outlaws had used for years. When you reached for the man's gun you would be leaning toward that man and unable to bring your weapon to bear. As you reached for his gun, he could draw and either shoot you or at least force you to surrender your own weapon.

Savage would have none of this. He marched forward and pressed the twin barrels of his Greener against Wes Brenham's throat. The barrel was aimed upward at a slight angle so the slug would continue toward the ceiling after blowing Branham's head completely off. Wes noticed the angle of the gun and realized Savage was smart, real smart.

"I told you to surrender your weapon. Do it now," Savage whispered.

Wes slowly unbuckled his gun belt with his left hand and reached it to Cecil. None of this was missed by the other men in the room. It went far in thwarting any further attempts at rowdiness in the courtroom for the remainder of the day.

Once Cecil had Wes's gun and belt, Savage roughly searched Wes, all the while holding the Greener against the man's throat. Once satisfied Wes wasn't carrying a hideaway he removed the Greener. There was a distinct mark on Wes's neck where the barrel had been pressed.

As Wes walked toward the witness chair he said loud enough for everyone in the courtroom to hear, "This is how a man who is a witness to a murder is treated while the murderer is allowed to wear his Sunday best and is treated like a savior." Several men in the crowd grumbled, but not very loud. The memories of Savage and his shotgun were just too fresh.

Once Wes was seated a clerk asked him to raise his right hand and then swore him to tell the truth. Wes agreed.

"Mr. Shafer, you may approach the witness," Judge Preston said.

Shafer ran Branham through the events that led up to the killing of Sonny Briscoe. Once Shafer was finished Judge Preston allowed Lester a chance to ask a few questions of the witness.

Next Shafer called the sheriff to the stand. Jasel Farley was sworn in and again Shafer began asking questions. By the time he finished and it would have been Lester's turn Preston called for a lunch recess. It was nearly twelve-thirty and everyone in the courtroom was ready for a break.

"Cecil, how about you and Savage joining me for a little lunch," Judge Preston asked. Both men agreed because they knew Preston always picked up the tab and also because they didn't want to allow him to walk about town without some protection. They feared some of the men who had been in the courtroom that day would like nothing better than to rough up the judge, maybe even kill him in cold blood.

The three men headed back to the hotel and went straight for the dining room. It was filling up fast, no doubt with some of the people who had been in the courtroom that morning. Again the judge went straight toward the back of the room and sat at his favorite table.

"I thought you said you were going to take a little nap during lunch Judge. After that rescue we done in the middle of the night I figured a man of your age might be tired," Cecil said with a grin.

"My age, did you really just say that Cecil?"

"Well Judge, I just figured you ain't as young as you used to be, that's all I'm saying."

Preston knew Cecil was just having a little fun. "Well, I guess I am a year or two older than you deputy. Now show a little respect to your elders if you want me to pick up the tab for your meal."

Cecil smiled as he anticipated his lunch, "Meant no harm Judge, just having a little fun."

Savage and Cecil kept a close watch on the crowd that had now filled the dining room of the restaurant. Both men were holding their forks in their left hands, always keeping their gun hands free. Normally neither would have needed to be on guard to this extent but something just didn't feel right about the people in the room. Preston never worried, he had two good men at the table and he was also packing a small gun in his pocket. It was a two shot derringer and it would kill a man just as quickly as a shotgun. The only shortfall of a derringer was that after two shots you had to reload. Preston didn't care, if it took more than two shots he was probably dead anyway.

As the three men ate Lloyd Shafer walked in. He spotted the judge and immediately headed in that direction. "Well Preston, I think my case is iron clad. I have an eye witness and Lester has nothing. Do you think we can have a ruling this afternoon and then a hanging immediately afterwards?"

Preston was appalled that one of the attorneys for a case that hadn't been decided yet would approach him and ask such a question.

"The accused hasn't been found guilty. I suggest you ask no more questions at this time Shafer."

"The remainder of the trial is only a formality Judge. I have proven my case beyond a reasonable doubt and expect a guilty verdict as soon as court resumes."

"Have you forgotten Shafer, Lester has yet to cross examine the sheriff?"

"I don't know why he would even bother. The sheriff has already testified as to what he knows. There is nothing he can possibly add."

Preston was getting angry that an attorney would try to sway him during recess. "Shafer, if you say one more word while I am in recess then I will hold you in contempt and have one of these two lawmen take you away to jail, is that understood?"

Rather than answer Shafer only shook his head and then turned to leave.

"That guy is an ass Judge. I never liked him in Rapid City and I like him even less here in Langley," Cecil said.

The judge cut up one of the two pork chops on his plate and never responded to Cecil's remark. He was too mad over the fact that Shafer would come in and try to dictate terms to him. Preston was trying hard to not allow Shafer to influence his decision. Then something dawned on the judge. Shafer might be trying to get him to rule against him and find Whitmore innocent. The reason was obvious. The town wouldn't like a not guilty verdict and would probably mob the courthouse and hang Whitmore and the judge himself. It made sense. This was on the judge's mind as he finished his meal and was escorted back to the courthouse by Savage and Cecil.

At two-o'clock on the dot the judge tapped his gavel and brought the courtroom to order.

"Mr. Lester, would you like to question the sheriff?"

Lester stood and indicated he would.

"Sheriff, let me remind you that you are still under oath," Judge Preston told him.

Lester slowly walked from his table where Doug Whitmore sat and approached the sheriff. He cleared his throat and looked at the sheriff.

"Sheriff Farley, how much time elapsed between the time Sonny Briscoe was shot and when you arrived on the scene?"

"Not more than a minute, I was on the boardwalk around the corner and heard the gunshot. I immediately went around the corner and was notified by Wes Branham that a man had been shot in the barn behind him."

Lester looked over some notes he held in his right hand. "And what did you do after you were notified by Mr. Branham that a shooting had occurred?"

"I asked him to show me so he turned and went inside the barn."

Lester continued to look at his notes. "And what did you find inside that barn sheriff?"

"Once inside the barn I found Sonny Briscoe face down on the floor. His gun was still holstered. Lying on the floor about fifteen feet from the body was another gun."

Lester, still looking at his notes suggested for the sheriff to continue.

"Well, I asked Branham who shot Briscoe and he said Doug Whitmore had been there to look over some horses he and Briscoe were dealing on. The conversation between the two got heated and that was when Whitmore pulled his gun and fired. Briscoe never had a chance."

Lester finally looked up from his notes and asked. "Was there anyone else in the barn?"

"No, it was just Wes Branham and me, along with the body of Sonny Briscoe."

"Now Sheriff, what did you do with the gun you found on the floor?"

"I picked it up and put it in the safe in my office," the sheriff said.

"Has anyone else had access to that gun in the time it has been in your safe?"

"No, that particular safe is only opened by me. No one else has the combination. There is another larger safe in the sheriff's office that the deputies use," Farley said.

"What did you do after you took the gun to the safe you mentioned?"

"I went to the bank and arrested Doug Whitmore and charged him with murder. He admitted to shooting Sonny Briscoe but said it was in self-defense. He said Briscoe was beating him with his fists and when Sonny picked up an axe he knew he would either have to shoot him or be killed himself."

Lester looked around the court room, first at Lloyd Shafer who was smiling and then at Wes Branham who was looking at him with a sneer. "Sheriff Farley, was there an axe anywhere near the body when you first walked into the barn?"

"No, there wasn't. I went back to the barn after I locked up Whitmore and had another look around and there wasn't an axe in sight."

"Sheriff Farley, did you happen to bring that gun from your safe to court today?"

"Yes I did. I brought it and gave it to the clerk first thing this morning. It has been in her possession all day."

Lester walked over to the clerk and she reached the gun to him. It was wrapped in brown burlap. Lester carried the package back to the sheriff."

"Now Sheriff, did you examine this gun after you found it on the floor of the barn where Sonny Briscoe was found?"

"No I didn't. I just picked it up and took it to my safe."

"Sheriff, can you examine the gun and tell me how many bullets it contains."

At this point Shafer leapt to his feet and said, "Your Honor, this is a waste of time. Lester is occupying the courts time without any idea as to what he is looking for."

Judge Preston looked harshly at Shafer and said, "Sit down. Lester will be allowed his questioning of the sheriff just as you were allowed your questioning."

Shafer glanced back at Wes Branham and this fact was not missed by either Lester or Judge Preston.

Lester went on with his questioning. "Now Sheriff, I would like you to examine the gun and tell me how many bullets it contains."

Sheriff Farley unwrapped the burlap and then opened the cylinder that held the bullets, he looked at the gun and then at Lester. "Why, there are six bullets in here, all six are in their chambers."

Lester knew where he was going with this but no one else did. "Sheriff, if you see lead in all six chambers then I would suggest you look at the brass end of each bullet and tell me what you see."

Farley looked at the other end of the cylinder and said, "Well I'll be, five of the brass cartridges are like new. The sixth one though has an indention where the hammer struck the brass but the bullet didn't fire."

"Sheriff, can you explain how something like that could happen."

"I certainly can. When a bullet is struck by the hammer it fires, plain and simple. Now that is if the bullet is not defective in anyway. About one in five hundred cartridges are defective," the sheriff said.

Lester looked at his notes again although he knew exactly what he was going to say. "What would make a bullet defective sheriff?"

"Several things can go wrong. The most common is that during manufacturing the powder isn't put in the cartridge. This can happen if it is very humid on a particular day. The nozzle might get gummed up. There are always men inspecting for this but it can still get missed. Another answer would be that the lead wasn't properly sealed against the brass cartridge. This allows moisture to get inside and make the powder useless."

Lester looked at Judge Preston before continuing. With the slightest of winks he got the judge's attention and then cut his eyes toward Cecil who was standing to his right. Cecil also saw this and knew something was about to happen.

Lester then continued, "So Sheriff, if I understand what you're saying, there were only three men in the barn when Sonny Briscoe was shot. Mr. Branham has already testified to that, am I correct so far?"

"Yes, that is right," Farley said.

"And Branham testified that each of the three men were armed, do you agree with this?" Lester asked.

"Yes I do."

"Well, if Briscoe's gun hadn't been fired, and if Whitmore's gun malfunctioned and didn't fire then the only other man in the barn must have committed the murder."

Everyone in the courtroom looked at Wes Branham and realized that Doug Whitmore hadn't committed the murder after all.

Lester turned to the judge and said, "Judge, I request that the charges against my client be dropped and a charge of murder be issued against Wes Branham."

As Lester was saying this Branham stood and bolted toward the rear door of the courtroom. He was too late. Cecil and Savage had heard where the trial was going and each had made their way to the back near the big double doors. As Branham made his hasty exit from the rows of seats and entered the center isle of the courtroom he was met with the shotgun Savage held, the same shotgun that had been pressed against his throat earlier that day.

"Stop right there Wes!" Savage said.

By this time, Sheriff Farley had made his way from the witness stand and produced a pair of wrist irons. "Stick out both arms Branham and don't say a damn word." Farley was mad as hell that an innocent man had nearly been sent to the gallows by this no good bastard. Branham knew he was as good as dead so he did what any cornered animal would do, he fought. He first pushed Savage into Cecil and both men hit the floor. He then turned on Sheriff Farley who held the cuffs in both hands. Just as it looked as if Wes might get his hands on Farley's gun there was a gunshot. Wes stood still for a second until a small trickle of blood ran from his right eye, the eye was gone. A second later his knees buckled and he fell to the floor, dead.

Everyone looked to the front of the courtroom where the shot had originated. There, beside the prosecutions table stood Lloyd Shafer and he was holding a revolver, there was a trail of smoke coming from the end of the barrel. He slowly put the gun back inside a leather shoulder rig which was well hidden by his coat. As Shafer holstered his gun he was relieved things had worked out the way they did, a moment earlier

Wes was being arrested for the murder of Sonny Briscoe. Shafer was sure he would have been implicated by Branham. If the trial had worked out the way he wanted then Whitmore would have been hung and he could have dealt with Branham in his own good time. Not the best of outcomes, but at least what Wes Branham knew would now go with him to his grave.

As Farley stood and tried to absorb what had just happened, both Savage and Cecil got back on their feet. Savage was trying to figure out how Branham had managed to knock both himself and Cecil to the floor. He was a man who took pride in his work and this added to his frustration at being knocked off his feet by an unarmed man. He marked it up to the fact that both he and Cecil thought they had Branham and this belief led them to be overconfident. It was a mistake that he would never make again.

The courtroom had gotten loud, either from the fact that Whitmore was innocent or Branham had managed to get himself implicated and then shot. Judge Preston tapped his gavel loudly and ordered everyone to return to their seats and be quiet. He then asked one of the bailiffs to go and notify the undertaker.

"Mr. Lester and Mr. Shafer, would both of you approach the bench?" Preston asked.

When the two men were in front of Judge Preston he asked, "Shafer, I need to know how you intend to proceed." The judge already knew what was expected but had to hear it from the prosecutor first before he could make a ruling.

Shafer glanced back at the body lying in the center isle of the courtroom. He looked back at the judge and said, "I ask that the charges against Doug Whitmore be dropped."

Simon Lester was smiling and enjoying the moment. Judge Preston savored the moment also. He was sorry that Shafer had shot Wes Branham, that would have been a trial that Preston would have enjoyed. He tapped his gavel and announced in a loud voice that the charges against Doug Whitmore were dismissed.

Preston felt he needed to warn the crowd of something else. "The evidence proves beyond a doubt that Doug Whitmore could not have killed Sonny Briscoe, his gun is still fully loaded. I know the town and also a few of the newcomers would have liked to have seen a hanging today and there could still possibly be one." Both attorneys and the spectators got very quiet wondering what the judge meant by the last statement.

Preston knew he had everyone's attention now. He went on, "If anyone approaches Mr. Whitmore, Lloyd Shafer, Simon Lester or me with the intent of causing any mischief I intend to have that person arrested and tried five minutes after he is presented in front of this bench. Whitmore is an innocent man; the man who shot and killed Sonny Briscoe was Wes Branham. This case is closed and let me tell you now; I mean what I say about not causing any more trouble in this town. Anyone who thinks otherwise will be sorry he did. Now I want everyone here to leave and go about their business."

Cecil and the three bailiffs headed everyone toward the double doors in the back of the courtroom. The grumbling the judge expected never occurred. Apparently the townsfolk felt the murder of Sonny Briscoe had been avenged. Once everyone was out Preston ordered the doors to be locked until the undertaker could take away the body.

Lester felt it was time he took back his courtroom. "Preston, how about me and you heading back to what, up until five minutes ago, was your chambers and get us a little drink?"

Preston looked at his pocket watch and noticed the time, Five-thirty. The day had seemed to pass in a hurry. "Well Lester, I think that is a pretty good idea, and might I add, that was some fine lawyering even if you are just a judge." Both men headed to Lester's office. Both Cecil and Savage tagged along too when they heard the word 'Drink.'

Once in the back office Lester took a key from his front vest pocket and pulled out a bottle of Old Grand-Dad. He sat four glasses on his desk and began to pour.

"Say Lester, how is it you and me drink the same brand of Bourbon. I thought everyone west of the Mississippi only drank that horse-piss the Mexicans haul up here," Preston asked.

"You must be losing your memory Preston. You brought a bottle of this stuff with you from Rapid City a few years back. I liked it, so now I get two bottles shipped to the general store each month. After the trial we just had maybe I will need four bottles shipped in every month," Lester said.

Again Preston asked, "That was some fancy lawyering you done out there. What tipped you off to the fact that Whitmore's gun misfired?" Preston said as he took one of the glasses.

"Couple of things really. I know for a fact that the only way Doug Whitmore could hit a barn was if he was standing in it, Briscoe was shot dead center in the chest. Now that is a pretty good shot if you ask me. Whitmore is probably the worst shot in town, hell he's the worst shot in the entire territory. He and I used to target shoot a little.

Another thing I know about Whitmore, he doesn't know how to take care of his gun. The damn fool told me that he washed his bullets in soapy water once a month. Said he was afraid a dirty bullet wouldn't shoot straight. When we would target shoot half his ammunition failed to fire, wet powder."

That explained how Lester knew about the gun Whitmore carried. As the four men sipped the powerful Bourbon, Cecil asked a question that neither Lester nor Preston wanted to deal with at the moment.

"Say, what is the law pertaining to a lawyer shooting a man in a courtroom?"

Lester looked at Preston and Preston looked at Lester. Neither really had an answer.

Finally Lester answered. "Well any shooting needs to be heard by a jury. But in this case where two judges saw the entire thing and would be witnesses at trial I would say the matter is closed. How do you feel about that answer Judge Preston.?"

"A trial would be a waste of time. Branham was going for Sheriff Farley's gun and if he had gotten it then I'm sure he would have killed several people before he could have been stopped. As much as I hate to admit it and as much as I would have liked to try Lloyd Shafer I would say the matter is closed also."

This seemed to satisfy both Cecil and Savage. The four men finished their drinks and stood.

"Well Lester, I better be getting along. I want to check on Zeke. You know that trial was so distracting I haven't given that boy much thought today," Preston said.

"Well I'm sure if he had taken a turn for the worst old Doc Collette would have sent word. My guess is he's been sleeping all day. Bad as he was tore up that would be the best thing for him right now," Lester said as the three men left his office.

When Preston and the two lawmen made it to the street they were pleasantly surprised to see that the crowd that had been in the courthouse was now gone. Only a few people here and there could be seen going about their business.

"How would you two like to accompany me to check on Zeke and Ben? If both are doing all right then I say we go find us some supper, my treat again," Preston said.

Cecil really liked the sound of that; he was never one to turn down free food. Savage, who was still smarting at being knocked to the floor by Wes Branham, mumbled that it sounded good to him as well. As the three men walked they talked about their next move. All three knew monsters lurked in the territory.

"You think Bill is still alive Judge?" Cecil asked.

Preston never answered at first, in his heart he felt that all the missing men had probably been killed. "I would like to think there is a logical explanation for what has happened. We all saw what was going after Zeke and Ben last night, or at least we think we saw. Anyway, it would be a longshot for any of the missing men to turn up. I think they're all dead."

Savage agreed with the judge. "By the looks of what we saw last night I doubt if any man could have survived. I've put a lot of thought into what we were up against and what we need to do. No doubt about it, we have got to hunt one down and kill it. We load it up on a horse and bring it back to town so people can get a good look."

"How many men you figure on taking for a job like that Savage?" Cecil asked.

"I say the more we can get to help us the better chance we have of bagging one of the critters. That also gives each of us a better chance of survival, two or three men would probably get themselves killed. You saw how many they were last night."

Before the three could finish their thoughts on the problem at hand they had made it to Doc Collette's. The three men went inside and were surprised to find Zeke sitting at the kitchen table playing cards with Collette.

Preston looked at the two men and then said, "After all the trouble we went to last night to save you the least you could do is act injured. You look about good enough to put in a full day's work."

Zeke threw down his five cards and grinned at the three men. "I feel fine."

Cecil looked at the judge and said, "Ain't much for words is he?"

Collette threw down his cards and stood. After he stretched he headed for the coffee pot. "He has some beat up ribs is all. Nothing broken mind you but he is going to be pretty sore for the next few days. I treated all his scrapes and scratches and he was lucky, none were very deep. I just can't figure it out. Animal attacks a man; it bites and tears him up pretty good even if it don't kill him. It looks like whatever it was never had enough time to do a lot of damage. That big dog over at the stable probably got the worst of it. I got word though that he is going to be alright too. Take a few days to heal, just like Zeke here."

"When will he be able to travel Doc?" Savage asked.

Collette took a sip of his coffee and grimaced. "What do you mean travel?"

"We got to be getting back to Rapid City. The three of us are planning a hunting trip and thought since old Zeke here is healing up so fast he might want to go along with us."

Preston and Cecil didn't want to go back to Rapid City; they wanted to leave from Langley. "Why Rapid City Savage, why can't we leave from here?" Cecil asked.

"No guns and no ammunition here. It seems that all the people coming into town to escape whatever it is out there have bought up everything that will shoot. There ain't three bullets anywhere in town to be bought, I checked earlier today."

"You know, that might work to our advantage. We head on back to Rapid City and put together our kit for the trip. That will give Zeke here enough time to heal and maybe even that monster of a dog he calls Ben. I for one would like to have that critter along, he's big and he's mean, might come in real handy. We head out on the train first thing in the morning. We'll take our horses on the train to. The railroad can put them in a cattle car and they will make the trip in style. Zeke and Ben can catch the same train in a few days after they feel a little better."

"Are you sure Judge, ain't ever heard of no dog riding a train before, horses but not a dog," Cecil said.

"When we get to Grand Rapids I'll send a telegram to the railroad. I'll get it all cleared for Ben to have a seat on the train," Preston told him.

"I don't know if that dog can fit in a seat Judge," Cecil grumbled.

"Then I'll arrange for him to have two seats." Preston said with a laugh, "Zeke, how does all that sound to you?"

"Sounds fine to me Judge, I want another crack at whatever it was out there that damn near killed me and Ben. I would say Ben wants a second go around too."

"Then it's settled. You need anything Zeke before we go?" Preston asked.

"Just go and check on Ben, make sure he's being taken care of."

"You got it. Doc, send the bill to me in Rapid City. I'll see to it you get paid right away," Preston told Collette. With that the three were out the door and heading toward the stables.

Another surprise waited for the three men there. If they thought Zeke was healing fast then Ben looked like he was ready for another rumble with the creatures at any time. Sitting on the porch was Amil Boggs and there on a rug in front of the porch swing sat Ben. He had some patches of hair missing and what looked like bandages here and there but the big dog was alert and sitting up warming himself in the weak afternoon sun. When he saw Preston and Cecil he stood and ambled off the porch and met them halfway. He walked straight and only had a slight limp. Ben recognized two of the men who had helped him at the snare and also rescued both himself and Zeke the night before.

Cecil and Preston patted the big dog and looked him over as Ben stood and inspected Savage, who he didn't recognize.

"Well Ben, ain't you a sight better than you were when we brought you in here last night," Preston said.

Amil Boggs stood and stretched. "Seems that big dog has taken quite a liking to a potato and buffalo stew I made day before yesterday. Every time I try to have me a bite he just looks at me with them big brown eyes of his trying to make me feel guilty. After a bite or two I just give up and reach it to him. I believe two things are going to happen here while I treat that big dog, he is going to get better and I am going to lose weight." Amil thought this was funny by the way he laughed. Ben decided he had paid enough respect to the three men who had rescued him as he yawned and went back to his rug.

"How is he doing Mr. Boggs, other than the obvious? I thought he looked about dead when we dropped him off here last night," Cecil said.

"I thought the same thing. After I got him cleaned up and looked over his wounds he wasn't that bad after all. He was mostly tired. Whatever it was he was fighting with probably had him beat and Ben knew it. All I can figure is when an animal like that knows he's in a fight for his life he don't hold nothing back. If he is going to die then what the hell, just go for broke. He uses every ounce of energy he's got, maybe it's enough and he gets away, maybe it ain't and he dies. No wild animal I ever seen before goes down easy, if it's a mountain lion or a raccoon, either way, they go down fighting as if they had supernatural strength.

After Ben rested up indoors all night he woke up this morning and has spent the better part of the day polishing off that big stew I had."

"It seems horses ain't the only thing you know how to work on after all Boggs," Cecil said.

"I like horses but in my life so far I might have picked up a thing or two about other animals as well. Take that dog there. He's more wolf than dog and that might be another reason he's healing so fast. Few years back, well maybe it was thirty years ago, I was a trapper. There was a pack of wolves in the valley I was trappin' in and I was afraid if they got good and hungry they might lay into me some night. Well the trappin' was good and as it worked out them wolves liked beaver meat. I was getting at least one or two pelts a day and after skinning the varmints out I quartered the meat and placed it about a hundred yards from my camp. After a week or so those animals figured out where their meals were coming from and never acted aggressive toward me again, as long as I stayed at least a hundred feet away. They would eat and then go off scrounging around for something else to torment and kill.

"This one wolf I noticed had some strange markings on his coat. It looked like he maybe had been in a fight with a mountain lion or something. He had a scar on the right side of his face where the fur wouldn't grow back. Now he wasn't the biggest in the pack but he wasn't the smallest either. Anyway, I saw him every day for weeks. One day he showed up and something had either torn off, or bitten off, the paw to his left hind leg. I figured it would be the end of him. Didn't happen. It never even slowed him down that much. He went on living and within a couple of days he was acting pretty much as the other wolves. All I can figure is in the wild a wolf has got to heal fast if it's going to survive. Ben here is more wolf than dog and I would reckon to say that he will be as good as new in another day. He still needs to eat better in order to hide those ribs he's so proud of showing off but other than that he's in pretty good shape. I started another stew about three this afternoon and he gets most of it." Ben seemed to understand this because he reached over and licked Boggs hand.

"I better go and check the stew; Ben might have just tested me to see how I taste." Boggs laughed as he got up from the swing and headed inside to check on his stew.

"Boggs, me and these two are heading over to the hotel to get us a bite to eat ourselves. Probably see you bright and early in the morning." Just as the three turned to leave Preston thought he would have a little fun, "Oh, and if by some chance you aren't here in the morning we'll just assume Ben liked the taste of you after all."

As the three men entered the restaurant attached to the hotel they looked the place over. It was jamb packed. "Looks like everyone headed over here after the trial. Just when they were ready to turn and leave Simon Lester stood from a table in the back, he was waving for Preston's group to come over. Once they got there they found Simon Lester and Doug Whitmore.

"Judge Preston, why don't you and your two companions join us for a little supper, I'm buying," Whitmore said. Whitmore caught the eye of one of the women serving and asked if another couple of chairs could be rounded up. Wasn't long before three empty chairs presented themselves to Preston, Savage, and Cecil.

Once everyone was seated the same lady who had gathered the extra chairs asked what the three would have. Lester and Whitmore had just started carving on two large Prime-Rib steaks and this looked fine to the three newcomers.

Whitmore looked at the lady and said, "Why don't you bring the same thing Judge Lester and myself are having if that is alright with you gentlemen." They indicated it would be fine. Cecil was like a child at Christmas, he couldn't remember the last time he had enjoyed a big Prime-Rib steak.

"Well Mister Whitmore, I do believe you are in a chipper mood this evening," Preston said.

Whitmore politely chewed and swallowed before he answered. "Yes, you are correct. This morning I was sure I would be hung at dusk. Now, thanks to the fine work of Judge Lester here, I have been completely exonerated."

Even though the trial was over Preston still had a question and it had been nagging at him the entire day. "Mr. Whitmore, I do have a question and if you don't want to answer I completely understand."

Whitmore's mood couldn't be bothered no matter what kind of question Preston asked. "By all means Judge, ask away."

"Well, when Sheriff Farley arrested you I think your story was that you had shot Sonny Briscoe in self-defense. If that were the case then how do you explain the fact that your gun didn't fire the fatal bullet? Actually it didn't fire at all."

Simon Lester spoke before Whitmore had a chance to respond. "Preston, you must be a mind reader, we were just talking about that when I spotted you at the door. I had a little talk with Sheriff Farley right after the trial and asked him the same thing. He told me the murder was a set up in order to get Sonny Briscoe shot and to lay the blame on Whitmore. Said a bartender heard some men talking in his saloon a few nights back. As it turned out they were a little drunk and didn't care what they said or who heard it. The men doing the talking were part of a gang and Wes Branham was the leader of that gang. The men were a little put out at the fact that Wes was getting paid quite a bit more than they were."

Again Preston asked the obvious. "Then why did Whitmore say he had shot Briscoe?"

Now Whitmore spoke, "When Briscoe came at me with the axe I pulled my gun out and pulled the trigger. All I know is I heard a gunshot and Briscoe dropped the axe and fell to the ground."

"Where was Wes Branham during all this?" Preston asked.

"He was standing behind me and to my right. When I turned to flee the barn I brushed beside him. He never made a move to stop me. It all made sense after what I learned at the trial. My gun didn't fire but Wes's did. I think he had plans to shoot Briscoe at the same time I did. Everyone knows how bad I am with a gun. Either way, if both guns had fired then Briscoe would have been just a dead and I would have still been hung."

"But how could they have explained the two bullet holes and only one bullet being fired from your gun?" Preston asked.

Lester had the answer to this last question. "After the shooting Briscoe's body was taken to the undertaker's office. After twenty four hours when no one came to claim it he was buried at the town's expense. When a man is killed and it is a cut and dried case no one really looks over the body to see if he was shot once or ten times. I doubt anyone would have noticed or cared if he had one hole in him or two."

Preston seemed satisfied. "Well, I think you got it straightened out. From now on though if a man is shot I think the undertaker needs to file a report with the sheriff in case something like this happens again."

Judge Lester thought this was a good idea too. As the men were talking two women from the kitchen brought the food for the three newcomers. Once everything was in place Cecil said a quick, "God bless this meal we are about to enjoy." Even as he was asking the blessing he was reaching for a biscuit.

Again Preston asked a question. "Well, if it was a set up then who done the setting up?"

Now Cecil thought he would say something. "Judge Preston, if you don't mind me saying, the trial is over and Whitmore is innocent."

Lester looked at Doug Whitmore and asked, "Now who do you know that would want Briscoe dead and you hung for his murder?

This got the full attention of Judge Preston. "Now that is a good question Lester."

Everyone at the table was looking at Doug Whitmore. He chewed his food slowly as he pondered the question. "Well, the man who would have benefited from my death the most was none other than Lloyd Shafer. His bank in Rapid City had been in competition with my bank for years. He has even approached me a couple of times and told me to name my price. I told him I wasn't now, or for that matter never would be in the mood to sell my bank to him."

"That would explain why he would want you dead but not Briscoe. Surely Shafer wouldn't want his own cousin murdered," Preston said.

Now Cecil chimed in, "Shafer didn't like Briscoe even if they are cousins. Briscoe had been a black eye on that family for years. He drinks too much and gambles too much. More than once old Shafer has had to bail him out of jail. He fights and drinks and runs around with the wrong sort of women if you know what I mean. I heard Shafer is going to run for governor and with Briscoe out creating the wrong kind of headlines in the newspaper it would be in his best interest to eliminate the man, cousin or not."

The other four men at the table looked at Cecil in near astonishment. "Cecil, for a deputy I think you got a pretty good brain lurking around in that skull of yours somewhere," Preston said.

Cecil just grinned and took a big bite of his steak. As he chewed and drippings from his steak ran down his chin he said, "While you were beating your gums I done figured it all out."

Preston said, "Yea Cecil, you figured it out, now take that napkin and see if you can figure out how to wipe your chin."

As they ate Preston was in deep thought about Lloyd Shafer. He knew his opinion was biased and with good reason. Shafer had landed in Rapid City and within ten short years managed to buy up nearly the entire town. It had always nagged at Preston that there just wasn't enough business in the town for a lawyer to make that much money in such a short time. He had known men who had worked their entire lives and never made that kind of money, and these weren't just anybody, they were extremely smart hardworking men.

After the five men finished their meals Savage headed off to the train station to secure tickets for the three that were leaving on the seven o'clock the next morning. Cecil and Preston headed back over to Doc Collette's to check on Zeke again and have a little talk. It was getting near seven-thirty and dusk was attacking the town from the east with a vengeance, it was winning. It would be completely dark in minutes. A man was out with a ladder lighting the few lamps along Langley's main street.

Collette was sitting under the covered front porch to the clinic. "Well boys, did you check on that monster of a dog over at Amil Boggs. Hope he's doing alright. I hate it when a man loses his dog."

Not the question the two expected from the doctor. "How is it you know so much about that big dog Doc?" Cecil asked. "

"Oh I was over at the saloon a little while ago; I take my suppers there when I got a patient to tend to. Seems everybody in town knows about that dog and his battle last night. Lots of people around here are terrified by the strange things happening out in the territory and are glad to know that Ben gave them a good thrashin' for a change. If I was a little younger then I might want to go out there myself. I hate all this about women and families losing their menfolk, it just ain't right," Collette said.

"I doubt you want to go out there Doc, grown men taken in their prime and most of the time without a clue. We lost a deputy on the trip over from Rapid City. Don't know what happened, he just disappeared in the middle of the night without a trace," Preston told the doctor. "We came back to talk to Zeke some more if he's up to it. We got a plan and need to let him in on it."

"Zeke went inside about thirty minutes ago. Said he was tired and felt like sleeping," Collette said.

Cecil rubbed his stubbly chin and said, "We just going to head out of town in the morning without telling Zeke we left Judge?"

"No, I don't think so. If we are going on the seven o'clock and taking the horses with us I think he needs to know. Say Doc, how would it be if we wake him, that shouldn't cause him any problems should it?" Preston asked.

Just then the screen door squeaked open and Zeke hobbled out. "I thought I heard you two out here. Did you check on Ben, is he alright?"

"Just came back from there but we did have a little supper first. You won't believe it, that big dog is ready to go out on another adventure and he can't leave until you get all healed up," Cecil said.

"Zeke, we need to be getting back to Rapid City on the seven-o'clock in the morning. Savage said we need to go there in order to provision our little hunting expedition. We were planning on leaving from Langley but this town don't have much left in the way of ammunition or guns. Savage said we'll go back to Rapid City and prepare. How does that sound to you?" Preston asked.

"I suppose that sounds fine as long as I go with you. I'll be ready and at the train station in the morning."

"No you won't. You stay here a couple of days and heal. When Doc Collette thinks you are fit to travel he'll let you know," Preston said.

Zeke accepted this but wasn't all that happy. "What about the two horses and Ben, Judge?"

"That is the second thing I came here to talk to you about. Marshal Savage is at the depot now acquiring tickets for us on the seven o'clock train in the morning. With your permission, I would like to take your two horses along with ours on the train as well. Savage is checking on getting them placed in a cattle car or even a box car if possible. The railroad takes real good care of horses is what I hear. When you and Ben leave in a few days then your horses will be there waiting on you. I'll have the train tickets waiting on you and Ben when you're ready to leave. Probably charge me full price as big as that dog is though," Preston said.

"That sounds pretty good Judge. Just promise me you won't take off chasing monsters without me."

"You got my word on it. We ain't waiting so much on you as we are on Ben. I would feel a lot better knowing that big wolf is along in case we get in over our heads."

Zeke laughed, "Thanks for the vote of confidence Judge."

"Don't mention it!" The judge and Cecil wished Zeke good luck and then headed toward the hotel to get some rest. Savage was there waiting with the news that the three men, and their horses, were booked on the seven-o'clock. Both of Zeke's horses were also included if that was still the plan.

"Then we're all set. I for one am anxious to make it back to Rapid City and see what other mischief has happened in our absence," Judge Preston said.

Savage wasn't finished. "Well, I think that some mischief is going on the train with us in the morning Judge. Lloyd Shafer was in line in front of me at the ticket office. He booked passage on the seven-o'clock as well."

Preston made a sour face. "I surely hope he takes a seat on another car. If I disliked the man before the trial then I dislike him even more now. Maybe it won't be so bad though, after all I will be traveling with a deputy and a marshal."

"You just say the word and I will gladly arrest him for you Judge. After I get him all squared away in the Rapid City Jail then we can figure out what to charge him with," Cecil said with a humorous tone.

Preston looked at the deputy. "I'll keep that in mind deputy. Maybe if he insults me again I'll take you up on it."

The three men parted company and headed for their rooms. As tired as Preston was he still had a hard time falling asleep. There were just too many things rolling around in his head. For one, the outcome of the trial had really startled him. If it hadn't have been for the efforts of Judge Lester he was sure Doug Whitmore would have been hung. The talk during dinner had also got him thinking about what kind of a man Lloyd Shafer really was. Could he really have had a hand in the murder of Sonny Briscoe and the set-up of Doug Whitmore? Finally at three in the morning, or there abouts, Preston fell asleep. He was back awake by five-thirty and at a few minutes before six both he and Cecil walked into the restaurant. Within minutes Savage joined them.

The three men ate biscuits and gravy and finished quickly, they were anxious to get to the depot. All three men watched as the five horses were loaded into a cattle car. Once Savage was satisfied with the arrangements for the horses, and was also satisfied with their safety, the three men boarded the only passenger car that was allotted for the trip to Rapid City. Halfway down on the depot side of the car sat Lloyd Shafer. Preston tipped his hat as they walked by, Savage and Cecil only glared at the attorney. Shafer returned Preston's nod and then smiled at the two lawmen. They had both just earned a place on Shafer's get even list.

The train pulled out at six minutes after seven and made steam for the town of Fort Clemens. This was the first coal and water stop for the engine between Langley and Rapid City. Once there, Shafer decided to grab his lunch at the café in the depot. It was also the idea of Preston and the two lawmen but once they saw Shafer sitting there they walked right on through the depot and headed for the nearest saloon that served food. The meal went quietly as the three contemplated the journey at hand. Within a few days they would be heading out into the wilderness hunting something that could very easily kill them to the last man. Once Zeke and Ben arrived in a few days their little army would consist of exactly four men and one big dog, not very good odds. As it worked out Sheriff Farley and Deputy Carl couldn't come along. If the trip had started from Langley then the two would have gladly gone along.

The rest of that Thursday was spent bouncing along in a passenger car. Shafer sat as far away from Preston and the two lawmen as possible and this suited the judge just fine. They would be in Rapid City late in the afternoon on Friday. Cecil knew the train took three days from Rapid City to Langley and only two days to get back and he wondered why that was. None of the three men had an answer. In truth Langley sat at a higher elevation and the train pulled harder and slower in that direction.

"Judge, I don't think we'll be in town early enough tomorrow to acquire the supplies we need. First thing Saturday morning maybe the three of us could go together and purchase the guns and ammunition for the trip," Savage said.

Preston had just realized something, the only general store in Rapid City with guns was the one owned by Lloyd Shafer. Savage didn't hail from Rapid City and wasn't aware that the general store was owned by the lawyer Shafer. Cecil knew the judge wouldn't go there if it was the last store on the face of the earth.

"Cecil, when we were at Wiley's Trading Post a few days ago did you happen to notice if he had much in the way of guns and ammunition?" Preston asked.

"You know me Judge I always look at the guns when they're on display. Wiley has a pretty good selection. He keeps a lot of ammunition too. Some of the trappers and prospectors come in there so they don't have to ride all the way to Rapid City. I think Wiley does a good business in ammunition. Some of them older mountain men and trappers still carry black powder guns and he has a fair amount of that too."

This caught the attention of Savage, "What kind of guns has this fellar Wiley got on hand."

"In the way of handguns I saw a few Colts and some smaller caliber Smith and Wesson models, the type you might use as a hideaway. Had several Winchesters, one was even a .45 .75 like the one Zeke found in that abandoned campsite. Maybe there were two or three Sharps; I would have paid more attention if I knew we might be needing that stuff. Oh, he had a few of them new Parker 10-gauge shotguns too. I always wanted to fire a 10-gauge just to check out the kick," Cecil said.

"By the sound of it you paid pretty good attention Cecil," The judge said.

"Well, if it's all the same to you, I would like to take a look at the stuff this Shafer has in stock at his General Store anyway," Savage said.

"Look all you want but if the town is paying then it will have to be at Wiley's," Preston said.

"Must be some sort of grudge you hold against Shafer. I just hope this place you call Wiley's hasn't been cleaned out like the store in Langley. We might be too late already," Savage added.

Zeke felt well enough Thursday morning to go and pay a visit on Ben. He walked slowly and was accompanied by Doctor Collette. The morning was cool and a heavy breeze was working its way down from the north. The feel of snow was in the air. Zeke and the doc found Ben laying on the front porch sound asleep. Amil Boggs was swinging and looked ready to nod off himself.

Ben heard footsteps and lifted his head to have a look around. There, coming down the boardwalk was Zeke and some other man he had never seen before. Ben had thought a lot about Zeke since the big fight the other night and wondered if the man had been killed in the fight or maybe died later. This was a wonderful sight for the big dog. Ben lunged upright and bolted off the porch. Zeke saw what was about to happen and tried to turn sideways to protect his sore ribs. It didn't help; Ben raced up and nearly knocked Zeke to the ground. He was all over the man. If ever a dog was glad to see someone then this was it. After Ben calmed a little Zeke reached over and patted his head. This set the big dog off again and he bounced up and down as Zeke and Collette made their way to the porch.

By the time Zeke got to the swing and sat down he was completely exhausted. He was fortunate Ben hadn't bowled him over and further injured his bruised ribs. As Zeke sat and tried to catch his breath from the exertion of walking over Ben came and lay down at his feet. The dog was so big that the swing wouldn't move; Zeke's feet were lodged under the big dog. Collette couldn't get over the size and look of the animal. He had heard some talk around town but this was the first time he had actually gotten to see the critter.

"It was the first time Zeke had met Amil Boggs. Although both men were sitting side by side in the swing Zeke stuck out a hand anyway and said, "Zeke Conley from Kentucky. Looks like you got Ben in pretty good shape in the short time he's been here."

Amil shook Zeke's hand and said, "It's a pleasure to meet you. Ben there was quite excited to see you."

"Yeah, me and that dog have only known each other a few days, but it feels like a lifetime. Me and a couple of other men found him all tangled up in a snare and cut him free. Since then I believe he has saved my life at least twice. I figure that big dog and myself are now trail partners if he'll have me," Zeke said.

Amil looked at the dog, which was lying on Zeke's boots and said. "I think by the looks of it he has done adopted you. I'll tell you right now, I'd rather have that dog as a friend than an enemy. I truly believe he could handle about anything around these parts 'cept maybe a grizzly or a really big mountain lion." Amil thought a second and then added.

"Average size grizzly would take off for higher ground once he got a good look at that furry critter."

"You ever saw a dog that big before?" Zeke asked.

"Never in my life, seen some big dogs and even some big wolves but this one here takes the prize. I done me some checking in my animal books while you were over there laid up in Collette's people clinic. Dog this big happens once in ten thousand. Book said dogs this size are rare, real rare. I tell you something else about old Ben; he's about as smart a dog as I've ever been around. Sometimes it almost seems he understands what I'm saying. Now you watch and let me show how smart he is."

Amil looked into the distance and never made a move. "Stew." That was it, he just said stew. Ben stood and looked at Amil and started drooling. "See what I mean," Boggs said.

Collette looked at the horse doctor and said, "How would you like to trade patients, I done beat this youngster at least fifty times playing cards. Ben sounds smart enough to at least make the game a challenge." Ben heard his name but never took his eyes off Amil. He had heard the word stew and was wondering what was taking so long.

"How would you two like to have some lunch with me and Ben? I just made a fresh stew and would like some different company to help me with it for a change. Ben talks to much while I'm trying to eat." Amil stood and walked inside, chuckling as he went.

Collette looked and Zeke and said, "Lunch sounds mighty fine to me. You want to try some, Amil makes a mighty fine stew." Zeke agreed and the two along with Ben went inside.

Amil sat three plates on the table and one in the floor. Ben knew the drill; he immediately sat down and went after his lunch. Zeke and Collette sat down just as Amil sat a cast-iron skillet on the table which contained a fresh pone of cornbread. The smell of stew and cornbread quickly filled the room. Ben let out a small yelp and then Amil said, "Oh yea, I almost forgot." He quickly cut the corn bread into wedges and put one on the edge of Ben's plate. Collette saw what just happened and doubted if he could actually beat the dog at cards, or checkers either for that matter.

The three men ate heartily. The stew was as good as Zeke ever had and the cornbread reminded him of how his paw made it back in Kentucky. Ben finished first and moved over beside the big warm cook stove. He stretched out in front and in minutes was sound asleep.

"Collette, you are more than welcome to borrow that dog for a few games of checkers but don't come back here whining when he wins all the time." Amil burst out laughing and within seconds Zeke and Collette joined in.

After the three men finished Amil gathered the three plates from the table and the one in the floor and stacked all four in his wash basin. Zeke wondered how well the dishes got washed knowing Ben had used the same dishes as the men, too late to worry about that now. He heard it said once that a dog was cleaner than humans. How could something like that be true when a dog had the unpleasant habit of occasionally licking its own butt? The thought had the effect of causing a strong gag reflex. Luckily Zeke managed to hold it back.

The three men left the kitchen and headed back to the front porch. Boggs and Collette both rolled a cigarette and shared the swing. Zeke sat on the edge of the porch and enjoyed the moment. His stomach was full and he was safe for a change. Ben was now seemingly coming back to health and that was good. The judge and Cecil were on their way back to Rapid City where he would be joining them in a few days. The best part was the hunt they were going to take. Whatever was out there was going to pay for what had been happening. Either that or they would all die.

Zeke and Ben spent Friday and Saturday healing up and enjoying stew and cornbread with Amil Boggs. The train didn't run on Sunday so Zeke planned on leaving first thing Monday morning. He and Ben would be in Rapid City by late Tuesday evening. He was anxious to find out what his three companions had done in preparation for the trip. Zeke really missed his big horse Rusty and wondered how he had handled the train ride; Rusty had never ridden on a train before. Hazel would be with him and something told Zeke that big green eyed horse would probably like to see Ben again. The two had a history, he was sure of it.

By Monday morning Zeke could tell his ribs were on the mend. It didn't hurt as much now to breathe. Ben was as good as new. He looked like he had put on a few pounds and his coat was beginning to get a shine to it. Must be a stew shine Zeke thought.

Amil Boggs and Doc Collette came to the station to see the two off. Zeke thanked the two and said he was going to come back for a visit soon. Ben licked Amil on the hand and then rubbed his head and neck on his pants. As they boarded the train it looked like Amil was losing his best friend. The old man was about as sad a sight as Zeke had ever seen.

"If you come back to visit bring Ben with you and let him spend some time here. I'll fix him a big buffalo and potato stew," Amil said.

At the word stew Ben stopped and turned around. He looked at Amil and barked twice. He then turned and followed Zeke into the passenger car. Zeke took an aisle seat and let Ben have the window. Shortly there were two toots on the train's whistle and then a jerk as the engineer put steam to the drive wheels. Ben hung his head out the window and barked at Amil. The old man took off his hat and waved at the big dog. Zeke wondered how it was that Ben had such an effect on people.

The two day trip to Rapid City was uneventful. Zeke found it strange how Ben kept his head out the window the majority of the trip. At times it looked like the dog was licking at the wind. On some of the downhill grades where the train picked up speed his ears actually flew back from his face in the wind. This dog really liked to ride the rails.

Zeke and Ben made it to Rapid City at seven-thirty Tuesday evening. The first stop would be at Lester Fitch's livery to check on his two horses. As they walked Ben kept a keen eye out on the activity of the town. He especially perked up as they walked by the Lolli Pop Restaurant. The aroma coming from the eating establishment caught Zeke's attention too. He and Ben had just eaten rough grub during the two day train ride. A forty-five minute coal and water stop didn't allow a man to a sit down meal. The best the two could do was grab a few biscuits and maybe some cold ham. At the prices they charged Zeke couldn't afford much. By the time the two made it to town Zeke was flat broke other than thirteen cents rattling around in his pocket and was wondering where his evening meal was coming from. He knew Ben was hungry too. After checking on the horses he intended to head over to the Sheriff's Office. Maybe they had a little food there or possibly he could get an advance on his thirty day deputy wages.

It was already dark by the time the two made it to the livery. Fitch was carrying water to the horses he had stabled and saw a tall man walking down the street accompanied by a pony. The pony wasn't wearing a bridle or being led by the man which was strange. When they got closer he saw that it wasn't a pony at all, it was a dog. Ben looked at the big barn and by the scent he could tell that Rusty and Hazel were nearby, probably in the barn eating that nasty hay they seemed to like so well.

"Well if it ain't Zeke Conley from Kentucky. When I saw you last you were being hounded by them two stupid deputies," Fitch said.

"Howdy Mr. Fitch, you wouldn't happen to have a couple of horses here would you by the name of Rusty and Hazel."

"I sure do, got 'em both in the back eating a scoop of oats and swatting flies. I got to keep that big green eyed brute away from the other horses, she's a bit bossy."

"I've only known that horse for right at two weeks and I got the same impression. She tried to get the better of Rusty; the thing about him though is he just doesn't care. One horse or a hundred Rusty don't care unless the grass gets picked down too low."

"Say, what is it you got standing beside you there?"

Zeke reached over and patted Ben on the head. "This here is Ben. We found him all tangled up in a snare Sunday last. He kind of adopted me."

"Is he friendly?" Fitch asked.

"He is as long as he's treated friendly," Zeke told the livery man.

"I got a big stew bone back in the side room over there. I done finished the stew for supper this evening and wonder if it would be all right to give the bone to him," Fitch said. Ben heard the word stew and took a step forward.

"Fitch, if you give Ben a stew bone then I would say he's your friend for life."

Fitch hustled back and got the bone with Ben following his every step. Within a minute Ben came out of the side room where Fitch took his meals and in his mouth he was carrying his supper. Ben walked outside the barn and sat down on the boardwalk. He was hungry and had in mind to make short work of the big bone. Zeke hoped he was as lucky in getting his own supper.

"I think he'll be alright out there by himself if you want to come on back and check on your two horses," Fitch said. Ben would be alright, there wasn't another animal in town big enough to mess with him or his stew bone.

Rusty and Hazel were in side by side stalls and both hung their heads over the gates when they heard Fitch coming down the center aisle.

"Hello Rusty, you big ornery galoot," Zeke said.

Rusty nickered when he saw Zeke. Hazel too recognized him. "You two enjoy your train ride the other day?" Zeke said as he patted both horses on the nose.

"Judge Preston had them sent over as soon as they got off the train, said you would be here in a few days."

"Did the judge say anything else?" Zeke asked.

"Said to feed these two up and make sure they were ready for a hunting expedition. Said a few of you fellars were going out into the territory and get some answers. The town is missing a sheriff and a deputy, not to mention a bunch of the folks that were living out on farms around here."

Zeke thought about this and knew the trip was still on. "That's right, we plan on finding evidence of what's been taking people."

"Sounds like a bad idea if you ask me. Whatever's out there must be mean and it must be smart. Just too many able bodied men missing. You'd think at least one of those missing fellars could have shot and killed one of the monsters. People make it to town and they don't leave, afraid to," Fitch said.

All this talk had Zeke wanting to get to the sheriff's office and find out the latest news. "You happen to know if somebody is at the sheriff's office this late Fitch?"

"Should be, I was by there about an hour ago and Cecil was there talking to a marshal. I think his name was Savage. That man was sure named right 'cause he has the look of a hunter, maybe even a predator."

Zeke patted the two horses one last time as he turned to exit the barn. "I better be heading that way Fitch. Thanks for taking such good care of my horses. I'll draw some pay soon and come back and settle up."

"No need for that, Preston said the town was paying for both horses keep."

This was indeed good news for Zeke. He was a man who always paid his bills and at the moment he was broke, except for the thirteen cents he carried. "Thanks Mr. Fitch. I'll be back tomorrow to check on the horses again."

Zeke thought he might have to sleep in the barn unless other accommodations presented themselves. Then he remembered the spare bunks at the jail. At least he would have a place to lay his head even if he didn't get any supper. As Zeke walked outside Ben was just finishing that big bone Fitch had given him. There was pork grease all over the dog's mouth. As the two walked up the street Ben continued to lick his lips. Even if Zeke went hungry he was glad Ben got food. He thought back to the shape the dog was in when they found him tangled in the snare and eating what remained of the carcass.

The window to the sheriff's office shone some light as the two came up the street. The town was still busy but you could tell it wouldn't be long before everything was shut down. Zeke stepped up to the door and pushed it open. The smell of fresh coffee overwhelmed his senses. Cecil was asleep with his feet up on the sheriff's desk and didn't hear Zeke or Ben come in. Zeke patted Ben on the head and then pointed his finger at the sleeping deputy. Ben knew the drill; he slowly walked over and gave

Cecil a big lick on the face. The deputy was so startled he pushed back in the chair he was sitting in and fell over backwards cursing the entire time. This didn't bother Ben; he walked over and licked the deputy again.

Cecil got to his feet and although he had dog slobbers on his chin he was still extremely glad to see Zeke and the big dog. "Ben you old rascal, it is sure good to see you boy. I got a little something left of my supper in the back." Cecil went into the small room that had the bunks and came out with a brown paper sack. He reached in and got out a fried chicken leg and a biscuit. "Here you go boy. I got this for free at the restaurant a while ago." He put the food down on top of the empty sack and Ben immediately went to eating. Ben and Zeke had been in town for less than an hour and the big cur was already eating his second meal and Zeke hadn't had a morsel.

Cecil rose up and looked at Zeke, "How's the ribs doing?"

"Good I guess, still a little sore though."

"Well that's understandable, why don't you get yourself a cup of coffee, I made it fresh about four hours ago," Cecil said.

"Don't mind if I do." Zeke knew if it was four hours old it would be pretty bad but he really didn't care.

"You been over to check on your horses yet?" Cecil asked.

"Just came from there. Say, you wouldn't have another chicken leg around here would you?"

"No I don't. You hungry?"

"Starved, me and Ben been living on biscuits and a piece or two of pork chop for the last two days. I would have gone to one of the restaurants but I'm a little short of funds right now."

"You broke Zeke? Don't tell me you done spent all that money you made being a deputy." Cecil knew Zeke hadn't drawn any pay from the few days he had been packing a badge but couldn't resist getting in a plug on the boy.

"Not drawn any pay yet, you already know that Cecil. Preston promised me a month's pay and grub and I ain't even worked the month yet. I was lucky the man at the train depot in Langley remembered the three of you when you bought your tickets. I showed him my badge Monday morning and he said he would just send the bill for mine and Ben's tickets to Judge Preston. I couldn't believe the three of you would pull out of town and not leave me a stake to get back here. I thought I was promised tickets for me and Ben."

"You know Zeke; I asked the judge about that when we were on the train. He said he wanted to see how you could survive on your wits. He thought about getting you and Ben a ticket like he promised and leaving five dollars for food but thought it would be a good test to see how you handled yourself. Looks like the judge will be mighty happy to know you got here and without a penny to your name to boot."

Zeke was a little bit mad to know the three men had abandoned him in Langley. After a second he realized the judge was probably right. He wanted to see if Zeke could manage to make it to Rapid City on his own.

Zeke reached into his pocket and pulled out the thirteen cents and held it out for Cecil to see.

"Better hide that, wouldn't want Preston to know you made it to town with money to spare," Cecil said as he burst out laughing.

"You think Ben will be okay here if we lock the door and head over to Preston's house. He said as soon as you got to town to bring you over. I 'spect he's waiting now. He probably heard the train whistle when it pulled into town," Cecil said.

"Ben will be just fine. I think he probably needs a nap anyway after all he's had to eat since we blew into town a little while ago. Locking that door is probably a good idea though, wouldn't want anyone walking in here and Ben mistaking them for a trespasser," Zeke said.

"All right then it's settled. Preston's place ain't that far and if you're lucky he might even have some supper left."

"Lock the door and let's get on over there. Ben you catch you a few winks and we will be right back." Ben looked at Zeke and Cecil and then yawned real big. He was happy to stay right where he was.

The night was pitch black and the wind blew with the feel of snow. Late October usually brought a storm or two but they usually didn't last very long. As soon as a little snow fell then a day or two later the sun would show it a little attention and run it away. November was a totally different story. This far north meant short days and cold temperatures. Once snow fell by the middle of the month it might hang around until spring, especially in places that were shaded. Both Zeke and Cecil pulled their collars high and their hats low.

"Boy, I tell you what Zeke; I'm tempted to dig out my old winter coat. First cool spell of the season tends to freeze my ass off," Cecil said.

Zeke was a little cold himself and wondered what he was going to do for a coat. Every spring he would discard whatever he had worn the previous winter. He just wasn't in the habit of hauling around his winter wardrobe during the summer months. Each fall he would find a general store and buy himself a stout looking coat and an extra blanket. He reached a finger up and rubbed his front teeth. Something else he was going to need to replenish was his tooth powder. He usually went through two small cans a year, one lasting maybe five months. A man who lives out of two saddle bags really doesn't have room for much, but tooth powder was something he had used his entire life and wasn't about to stop now just because he had taken up the life of a trapper and mountain man. He hoped his pay for the month of deputy work would be enough to get the few things he needed for winter, which was assuming he wasn't eaten by monsters first.

Cecil and Zeke made it to the judge's house and hurried up the steps to knock on the door, the air felt colder now that the evening was getting late. Within seconds Preston answered and ushered the two into his study.

"Have a seat while I get something to take that chill out of your bones," the judge said.

Cecil knew the judge liked Old Grand-Dad whiskey and hoped that was what he was getting. Preston came back from another room and in his hand was a full bottle of Old Grand-Dad. He grabbed three glasses from the credenza behind his large reading desk and filled each half full. "Gentlemen, let's have a drink to the safe return of Zeke." Each man tipped his glass and took a sip.

Cecil then added, "And to the success of our little hunting trip." Again the three men took a small sip.

"Zeke, when I heard the knock at the door I hoped it was you. How is Ben? Did he enjoy his train ride?"

"Ben is fine Judge. We got into town a couple of hours ago and he has already had two suppers. We left him over at the sheriff's office for a while. I think he's planning on running for the job unless he finds work more to his liking," Zeke said. "And as far as the train ride, I think he might want to apply to be a conductor if he turns down the sheriff job." Cecil and Preston laughed.

"You say Ben has already ate twice, how about you, have you had a chance to get supper?"

"No Judge I haven't. To tell you the truth I'm flat broke," Zeke said.

The judge smiled. "See there Cecil, I told you Zeke here would make it to Rapid City alright. Come on in the kitchen you two and let's fix us up some supper."

Cecil and Zeke gladly followed the judge into his kitchen. It was of a nice size and had everything needed to prepare whatever you wanted. There was a big white enameled cook stove, a tall ice box stood to the right of the stove, and against the outside wall was a double basin sink with a hand pump. There was a small square table with four chairs in the center.

"Hope you boys like cold food; I really don't want to fire up that big stove this late in the evening." Preston said. "And I don't usually drink coffee this late; it has a bad tendency to keep me up most of the night if I drink it too late. You two pull out a chair and I'll grab us some food, won't take a minute."

Cecil and Zeke grabbed a chair as the judge started gathering food for their supper. He opened the ice box and pulled out a platter which contained roast beef. He put a big loaf of home baked white bread on the table beside the roast. On the stove was a pot with a lid on top. "These green beans and potatoes are probably still warm," he said as he sat that on the table. Zeke and Cecil were getting hungry just looking at the roast beef.

After the judge poured three tall glasses with sweat tea he put out plates and silverware. With everything on the table he smiled at his two dinner guests and took a seat himself.

"Zeke, why don't you ask the blessing?" Preston said.

Zeke gave a quick thanks to the Almighty for the food and reached for the platter that contained the beef. Cecil noticed how fast the blessing had been asked and knew it was because Zeke was so hungry. The food was good, even cold. Roast beef was one of the best foods for a quick snack, cold or heated it always tasted good.

"I bet when Ben smells this roast beef on your breath Zeke he'll regret not coming along," Cecil said.

"Probably, I wonder how much he could eat if the food kept coming," Zeke said.

"What have you figured out about our expedition Judge?" Cecil wanted to know.

"Savage is having trouble rounding up the ammunition we need. Everything in town has been hoarded up. People been scavenging around for anything that will fire a bullet. Once the regular stuff was all gone then they starting buying old black powder guns. I have never seen such a run on guns and ammunition. People think that once everyone in the outlying areas is taken then the monsters will descend on the town."

"If we can't get more ammunition and a few heavier caliber guns then what do you plan to do Judge?" Cecil asked.

"I still think Wiley will have inventory. He trades with mostly people from out that way and from what I hear no one is left out there to buy anything, including guns. Everyone has come to town for safety's sake," Preston said. "Anyway, we leave first thing Thursday morning. That gives us all day tomorrow to prepare."

"What are you going to do about being a judge and the courthouse work that you're expected to do here?" Zeke asked.

That's done been taken care of. I sent a wire down to Langley and asked Judge Lester if he would mind coming here two days a week to keep everything moving along. He gladly agreed. We get a lot more cases here in Rapid City than they do down in Langley. And anyway, the way I see it he owes me a favor."

"Well Judge, if you get eaten by them monsters did you make arrangements for him to continue coming here two days a week or just pack up and move here permanent?" Cecil asked.

Preston put down his fork and looked at Cecil. "You know deputy; you can be a real smartass sometimes."

"Thank you Judge, I always like it when somebody of your station in life calls me smart." Cecil winked at Zeke as he said this. It was apparent the judge and the town deputies like to dig a spur into each other from time to time.

"You got a place to stay tonight Zeke," the judge asked.

"I plan on staying over at the Sheriff's Office. One of them bunks in that side room has been calling my name for the better part of an hour now. Ben will probably just stay curled up in front of that big stove."

"That sounds good. You take real good care of that big dog. When we head out Thursday morning I plan on him leading the way. If things get dicey out there on the trail, I for one want that big dog on my side."

Cecil agreed. "That is a good idea Judge. The way they were piling on top of Ben when we found him and Zeke the other night I think he can account for himself really good in a fight. Plus, it would be harder for them varmints to sneak up on us with Ben along."

"That is something we need to consider when we stop at Wiley's Thursday morning. We need food for Ben. I want that wolf-dog to be well fed on this trip. If he is at the top of his game then it increases the odds for the rest of us," Preston said.

Zeke stood and stretched. "Judge, I want to thank you for the drink and also for this fine supper. Maybe if there is any of that big roast left you can bring it with you Thursday. We can have it for lunch and Ben will call dibs on the bone."

Preston stood and said, "Good idea, if I leave it here it will just go to waste anyway. You boys head on over to the jail and get some rest. I'll be there around seven-thirty in the morning and we can go for breakfast. If you see Savage between now and then tell him breakfast will be furnished by the town of Rapid City."

"Sure will Judge," Cecil said as he sliced off another piece of beef and then shoved it between two pieces of the baked bread. "And thanks again for this fine meal Judge."

The men parted company as Preston quickly cleaned up the dinner dishes and put the remainder of the roast in his ice box. That was a pretty good idea about taking the roast on the trip. He knew beef lasted pretty well, especially now that the weather was getting colder. He decided to get the restaurant that fixed his roast to have another big one baked and ready to go Thursday morning. Preston thought it was funny how a man who is heading into trouble could be thinking so much about his stomach. The judge liked to eat and even if he was going to be roughing it for a few weeks it was no reason to not eat well. It was nearly ten-o'clock when the judge finally turned in. He found the prospect of heading off into the wilderness to be exhilarating indeed. Maybe he had spent too much time on the bench. Exercise and fresh air was what he needed, even if there were monsters involved.

On the way back to the jail Zeke thought about the trip ahead as well. Cecil never really thought about anything other than the roast beef sandwich he chomped on. Zeke's ribs were still tender and he wondered how much longer before they were completely healed. If the judge wanted Ben at a hundred percent then Zeke wanted to be in good shape too. He felt sure he would be fine in a few days. When he pulled the trigger on that big .45.75 Winchester he didn't want to feel any pain.

The door to the Sheriff's Office was unlocked. Cecil pulled his Colt from the holster and motioned for Zeke to keep quiet. As he slowly eased the door open he saw Savage standing by the stove pouring himself a cup of coffee. Cecil quickly holstered his gun and stepped on in. Savage looked up from the coffeepot.

"Evening Cecil, who is that you got tagging along behind you there?"

"You remember Zeke, you two met once before I believe," Cecil said with a laugh.

Zeke barely remembered the marshal but something in the back of his mind told him he and Savage hadn't hit it off very well. Zeke walked over and stuck out his hand, "Pleasure to meet you Marshal. I don't really remember you but heard what you done for Ben and me."

The marshal shook Zeke's hand. "My pleasure. When we made it to where we found you it looked at first like we might have been too late."

"I heard it was some kind of fight. Ben done pretty good all by himself, I was mostly unconscious."

"You were at that. You came to as we were putting you on your horse," Cecil said hoping Savage wasn't going to pursue the argument he and Zeke had when he tried to abandon Ben.

"You were right to make us take Ben along. I was wrong to try and leave him," Savage said as he took a sip of coffee.

This surprised both Zeke and Cecil. It was a special kind of lawman who could admit when he was wrong. As of now Savage had both men's respect.

"You find anything out about where we can get ammunition Savage?" Cecil asked.

"Not a clue. I've checked everywhere in town and every last round has been bought up. Most of it was purchased ten or twelve bullets at a time, a few people even bought just two bullets. That tells me that most folks are just buying what they can afford. All these people coming in from the outlying areas are about to break the town. Most folks have spent what little money they had and now it looks like Rapid City will need to find a way to feed them. Nobody I've talked to is going back out there with those monsters roaming around."

Cecil said he had to make one more trip around town to check things out. Savage said he would go with him, which Cecil appreciated. Even though they were in town he was still leery of the dark. Zeke headed for the bunkroom, he was exhausted. It looked like Ben hadn't moved a muscle since earlier; he was sound asleep by the stove.

Zeke slept through the night and didn't remember waking even once. At a little after six he heard someone stoking the big stove in the front office. When he came through the door the first thing he saw was Ben sitting by the stove warming his hide.

"Well look who is back from the dead Savage, old Zeke," Cecil said.

Savage and Cecil looked fresh as if they had both slept well themselves.

All three men sat and sipped coffee waiting for Judge Preston to arrive at seven-thirty. They didn't need to wait long, Preston walked through the front door at fifteen after.

"Good morning gentlemen. You three ready for a little breakfast?"

"I don't know about these other two Judge, but if they ain't hungry then we can go without them," Cecil said.

As the four men made their way to the Lolli Pop Restaurant, Ben followed and gave the town a good look over. Ben himself was getting more than a few stares. People stopped whatever it was they were doing and just stood in amazement at the size and color of the dog, some of the women actually held their hands over their mouths they were so startled. If it hadn't been for the three lawmen and the judge then most people would have probably ran for safety. As it was Ben was just an attraction, maybe as if he had landed in town with the circus.

The Lolli Pop was doing a hefty business by the time they arrived. The only table available was right at the front door. Preston and the three lawmen always liked the back in order to observe the crowd. Preston wanted to wait until a table in the back became available.

"Why don't we take this table by the door Judge? Ben can sit out under the covered porch," Zeke said.

"That's good thinking Zeke. To tell you the truth I was going to see if they would allow Ben to sit by our table but on second thought that might be a bad idea. Lots of people don't allow dogs in their house and I doubt if they would want to have breakfast with one either," Preston said.

The three men took a chair as Zeke motioned for Ben to sit on the porch. He wondered if Ben would protest but to his pleasant surprise Ben eased up against the front wall beside a long bench and sat down Zeke went back inside and took his own chair. When one of the ladies who worked the tables came by the four men ordered biscuits and gravy along with bacon and eggs sunny side up. As the women turned to head back to the kitchen Zeke reminded the judge about Ben.

"Excuse me miss. Would you have anything back there we could feed another one of our group?" Preston asked.

"Well what does your friend like; we can make almost anything for breakfast your friend would want."

"Oh he isn't very picky, almost anything will do. He's sitting right outside and didn't want to come in, he's a bit bashful," the judge said with a sly smile on his face.

The woman turned and looked at the door but didn't see anyone. "Oh, now that just won't do, I'll ask him to come inside." She opened the door and peered outside. She suddenly screamed and slammed the door.

"Oh my gosh Judge, a bear has come into town and is sitting right outside this door," the woman said as she held a hand to her chest and tried to calm herself.

Everyone in the restaurant heard her scream and was looking in her direction.

"Oh, that's no bear miss, that's the friend of ours that is too bashful to come inside," Preston said as he began to laugh.

It was apparent the woman must have been accustomed to the musings of the judge. "Well Judge, I wouldn't have guessed he was a friend, he looks more like family. You both share a striking resemblance. I'll see what the cook has in the back." She slapped the judge on the shoulder as she walked past.

Cecil burst out laughing and before long everyone else at the table did too. Ten minutes went by and two women came back with four plates and a bucket. The woman who had been so scared at the sight of Ben sat three of the plates in front of Zeke, Cecil and Savage. She then sat the bucket in front of the judge and started toward the door with the fourth plate. Before she opened the door she turned back to the judge and said. "I'm sorry Judge Preston; I must have gotten these two orders mixed up." She picked up the bucket and then put the plate down in front of the judge.

To show the men that she wasn't afraid of the dog she opened the door and sat the bucket in front of Ben. The big dog looked in the bucket and then stood. The woman took a step back. Ben took a step closer and then licked her on the hand." After that he sat down and began eating. She just stood and looked at the dog; he had shown her a kindness. The woman stepped back inside and stood looking out the glass door watching Ben eat.

"What did you give Ben in the bucket?" Zeke asked.

"Oh he got the same thing you four got; I just didn't want to put it on one of the china plates. Wouldn't want people thinking a dog might have eaten out of a plate they may use tomorrow."

The woman stood at the door for another minute and then turned back to the men. "Is that dog part wolf?"

"We don't really know. He is what he is, I guess," Preston said.

With that the woman seemed satisfied. She went into the kitchen to wash her hands so she could continue serving.

As the men enjoyed their breakfast they talked about the day ahead. Preston was disappointed that Savage wasn't able to acquire any ammunition in town. Between the four men and what there was at the Sheriff's Office, they had maybe a hundred rounds of Colt .45 and another seventy or eighty for a Winchester. Zeke still had the stash of .45.75 ammunition for the big gun and hopefully it would be enough for that particular weapon.

"We can't go out with only that little stash of ammunition, if we get in trouble that much wouldn't last an hour," Cecil said.

Judge Preston didn't understand this. Savage explained it to him.

"If the four of us get jumped by whatever it is out there and let's say each of us is firing maybe five rounds a minute, that's twenty rounds total and that is just one minute. The way I see it we got just enough ammunition to last us eight minutes or there about. After that we die."

Preston sat down his fork and knife. He took the cloth napkin from his lap and wiped his mouth. It was apparent the judge had just lost his appetite.

The three men looked at the judge and asked what he was thinking.

"We load up as planned and leave bright and early in the morning. We should be at Wiley's store by nine-thirty or ten o'clock in the morning. We buy whatever he has there and then we proceed to hunt down whatever it is that has been killing folks around here."

This was the first time the judge had used the word killing. Up until now he had said disappear or vanish, he had always held out hope for the missing men, until now.

"And if Wiley has had all his guns and ammunition cleaned out Judge, what do you intend to do then?" Cecil asked.

Preston finished his coffee and sat down the cup. He looked at the three men and said, "We go anyway."

"Zeke, I say you and me head on back to the jail and count every last bullet we got. If we are going to be light on rifle ammunition then how does it sound if each of us takes a shotgun? I know the sheriff keeps at least two boxes of ammunition for them Greeners. That's forty rounds. Even if they ain't good at long range they will at least make a little noise," Cecil said. And it was a pretty good idea the other three men thought.

After breakfast the judge put the bill on the city's tab and all four men headed for the jail. As they walked out the front door of the Lolli Pop they found Ben sitting on the front porch with an empty bucket in front of him.

"What do you intend to take on this trip for Ben to eat Zeke. He can't eat biscuits and bacon the whole way," Preston said.

"I think biscuits and bacon would suit that dog just fine. Maybe throw in an egg or two every now and then," Zeke told him.

"You really plan on taking a few eggs along Zeke?" Preston asked.

"I sure do Judge. The weather is getting cool, maybe even cold, and eggs will keep a few days."

Cecil added, "This is sounding like a one way trip if you ask me, I say we at least eat good, what do you say Ben?"

Ben looked up at the deputy and licked his lips. "You know, that is about as good an answer as any," Cecil said as he laughed.

The four men were at the Sheriff's Office inventorying the ammunition and firearms when a rough looking man wearing worn out buckskin britches and a homespun shirt walked in.

"Say, is anyone of you fellars the sheriff?" the man asked.

Preston, who had been counting shotgun shells, looked up from his work and addressed the man. "The sheriff isn't here, there anything we can help you with?"

"No I don't think so. When will the sheriff be back?" the man asked.

The four men in the room really didn't have an answer. "Well, the sheriff isn't in town right now. We don't really know when he will be back," Cecil said. "I am one of the sheriff's deputies, maybe I can help you."

The man rubbed his stubbly chin and then looked at Cecil. "Maybe you can at that deputy. I got two brothers, Delroy and Gervais and both are missing."

The four men all looked at the stranger at the same time. Judge Preston thought he would take over the conversation. "What is your name mister?"

"Names Hiram Reece, me and my two brothers are prospectors."

Cecil went over to the sheriff's desk and pulled out a few pieces of paper. He grabbed a pencil and began to sharpen it with his knife. "I better write this down Judge and add the information to the rest of the missing men."

Again Zeke was impressed by the organizational skills of the deputy. When he had first met Cecil and Bill he thought they were both just stupid deputies.

"Others you say, how many others?" Hiram asked.

The judge thought it might be best not to startle the man with the truth. "A few, we don't have an accurate count as of yet but it is a few. How about you start at the beginning and tell us what happened." As the judge said this he grabbed a cup and filled it with coffee and then reached it to Hiram. He then pulled over a chair and motioned for the prospector to sit and tell his story.

After all five men were seated Hiram began. "Well, it's a long story so I'll just tell you the highlights. 'Bout a year ago me and my two brothers staked us a silver claim between Mud Butte and Castle Rock. It's about seventy miles from here as the crow flies but maybe a hundred on horseback. I made it on foot in less than four days from there to here." Hiram was talking fast and seemed to be getting nervous. He took a sip of his coffee and then looked back at the men seated in in front of him.

"Anyway we were working our claim and were coming across some good color right after we set up camp, like I said, that was about a year ago." Again he stopped and took a sip of coffee. His hands had started to shake.

Preston had observed the man and pretty much figured he was shaking from hunger, not fear. "Say Hiram, how long has it been since you had anything to eat?"

Hiram thought a minute and finally said, "Maybe two days ago, might even be three. When I lit out of our claim I was traveling fast and light. I took what little food there was in camp and never looked back. I kept off any known trails and travelled through the timber and boulder areas. I know it was stupid, but I figured I could hide during the times I needed to sleep and move unseen the rest of the time." Again he took a long pull on the coffee. "Say, if it ain't a put out would there be any sugar around?"

Cecil knew the man probably needed the sugar more than the coffee, it was apparent the man was starved. "We got a sack in that wall cabinet over there by the gun rack, Zeke how about you grabbing it."

Zeke went over to the cabinet and found the sugar. As he brought it back he wondered why they didn't keep it near the coffee pot, if they had he would have been using some himself. He never bothered with a spoon, he just tilted the sack and filled Hiram's cup to the top. Hiram never bothered to stir he just held the cup up and took a long drink.

"Zeke, how about you heading over to the Lolli Pop and grabbing this man some food, get whatever they got that can be carried in a sack and hurry on back. Just tell them to put it on the town's account. Tell them Judge Preston sent for it."

Zeke really didn't want to miss any of the story but didn't protest. Whatever the judge wanted was fine with Zeke. "I'll hurry Judge. I'm going to bring back whatever is already prepared so there won't be any wait." With that Zeke was out the door and ran up the street at a trot. Ben, who was still lying by the stove, saw the door open and just before Zeke closed it he ran out and went up the street with Zeke. When he realized they were heading back in the direction of the restaurant he thought he might get another bucket of food.

Zeke went inside as Ben sat in his same spot outside the front door. He saw the same woman who had waited on them earlier and approached her. "Excuse me miss, the judge sent me back to get something for a man that just stumbled into the sheriff's office and hasn't eaten in a few days. If you got anything back there that can be put in a paper sack then he said for me to bring it right back. Put it on the same tab as earlier."

She had her arms full with dishes she had just removed from a table. "I think the fastest thing would be some biscuits and maybe a couple of pieces of pork chop. Would that be okay? If it is then it won't take a minute."

"That will be just fine. I'll be out on the front porch with Ben."

The woman hurried to the kitchen as Zeke went back outside. When Ben heard the door open he hoped it would be by someone carrying a bucket, it was only Zeke. Maybe the bucket would be next. Wasn't long before the door opened again and the same woman came out with a brown paper sack in one hand and a thick slice of bacon in the other. Ben knew the sack was probably not for him but the bacon was a different story. Before Zeke could reach for it Ben stepped in front of him, blocking his path. The woman reached the piece of bacon to Ben who then stepped aside so Zeke could proceed. "Thank you kindly Ma'am!" With that he took the bag and hurried back in the direction of the sheriff's office. Ben walked along with the big piece of bacon in his mouth. He would just enjoy this once he was back by the stove.

As Zeke and Ben re-entered the sheriff's office Cecil was refilling the coffee cup that Hiram had been drinking out of. He filled it with a good portion of sugar and reached it back to the man. Ben immediately went to the stove and sat down. "Here you go Mister Reece. See if this suits your needs."

Hiram took the sack and said, "Much obliged. Right now anything will suit me. Whatever it is sure smells good though." He peered inside and took a long pull on the smell. "Oh my goodness, biscuits and pork chops. I thought when I finished my last morsels on the way here it would be my last supper."

Zeke had a puzzled look on his face. "Your last supper, was someone after you out there Mister Reece?"

Reece took a huge bite of a cathead biscuit and looked at Zeke. "Something was after me and it weren't no man. And by the way, you can just call me Hiram." He said this as he took another bite of biscuit.

Zeke then realized this man was probably talking about the same things that he had encountered. Hiram decided to talk as he ate. "Anyway, as I was telling these here fellars, me and my two brothers had us a good situation. Our claim was in an area of big boulders. Our camp and silver mine was concealed from view pretty good, you could walk past within a hundred yards and not know we were there. Color we found was strong and we knew there would be some mining involved. Silver is a funny metal. It doesn't lie on top of the ground like gold does at times, it likes to play hide and seek. If there is any silver about hiding under the ground then it will leave you a few clues. We check the rock until we find what we're looking for. Usually some really dark spots on the rock or some thin veins that look no more than a pencil mark." Hiram stopped and took a big bite of his pork chop.

"Is that what you mean by color?" Preston asked.

"That's it. We found some really good color and hurried to Rapid City to stake out our claim, that was about a year ago."

"You been working that claim for a year? What did you three live on?" Cecil asked.

"That's the best part. Me and my brothers had just enough money to file the claim and get us maybe a month's worth of supplies. After that we figured we could kill us a deer or maybe even an elk. That might do us a few weeks but we knew if we didn't find us some silver fast we would need to abandon our claim and head off in search of some paying work. We were nearly out of grub after that first month and decided that one of us would need to do a little hunting if we were going to survive.

"We drew straws and Delroy drew the short stick. The next morning at first light he set out in search of big game and wouldn't you know he bagged a big mule deer before noon. The three of us field dressed that critter and brought the meat back to camp. We jerked most of the meat; you know, cut it into thin strips, salt it a little and let it dry in the sun. Meat like that will last a while. We fried up the rest over the next couple of days. Delroy said he saw more deer and even came across elk sign. I hadn't ever tasted elk before and looked forward to bagging one of the big bastards." Again Hiram stopped to work on his pork chop and biscuits.

"What happened after that?" Cecil asked, anxious to hear more of the story.

"Well, we knew we were set for at least another week. The more we dug the stronger the sign got. We were within feet of finding silver. After we were maybe fifteen feet under the mountain we decided we better start propping up the roof of that mine. The first fifteen feet were solid and not a worry, really hard digging. But then it got a little gravelly and we knew we were close. Problem is, where the silver is hiding is a widow maker. You don't take precautions you might just find yourself buried alive. We couldn't just start cutting down trees and leave a trail to our camp, other prospectors might come to investigate, and worse than that is the injuns. We hadn't come across anybody the month and a half we had been there and we didn't want to neither. The last thing you need is some hungry prospector snooping around. We were more afraid of that than we were of the injuns.

"Anyway we decided to head off away from camp to get our roof braces. There is a spot about a mile and a half from camp where a bunch of trees had been knocked down, probably by one of them devil twisters. We never had us a horse or even a mule, we had walked to our claim, just poor old down and out prospectors. The three of us took one entire day and carried wood on our backs, careful to leave as little sign as possible.

Me and my brothers fought for the South during the war. The three of us were scouts and we were good at it. Once I even sneaked into a Yankee camp and stole their skillet of cornbread and pot of beans. Not only did we eat good that night but we had acquired us a good skillet and one of them cast iron Dutch Ovens. The three of us still use that skillet and pot to this day. It was that same pot we threw in the fire and made us a deer stew. Potatoes was about the last thing we had left before the deer gave its life so we could eat. Deer stew in a Yankee Dutch Oven is about as good a eating as a man could want." Hiram stopped talking as he remembered happier days spent with his two brothers.

Preston needed some of the coffee sitting on the stove. He poured the last of it into his cup and sat the empty pot back on the stove. Savage decided he needed to get up and move around a bit. He made himself busy refilling the pot to make fresh coffee. Cecil had used the time to catch up with his notes, Ben snored by the fire.

By now Hiram had finished everything in the poke and sat it down on the floor by his ladder back chair. "Anyway, after we spent that day gathering stout wood to brace the roof we went back to digging. It was nearly two weeks since Delroy had shot that deer and it was just about gone. We drew straws again and I'll be dogged if Delroy didn't draw the short stick again that time, same as the first. I told him if there was ever a contest for drawing short straws he would be world champion. We had one more day of digging before he was to go hunting and wouldn't you know it, we struck pay dirt.

"Gervais was underground swinging the pick while me and Delroy was toting out the spoil." Hiram could tell by the looks on the four men's faces that they didn't know what spoil was. He figured right then and there the big dog sleeping by the stove was probably the smartest one in the bunch. He neglected to share this with the other men. "Spoil is the dirt and rock you dig out of a mine." That seemed to satisfy the confused looks on the four men's faces.

"Anyway, he came running out of the mine and he was holding a small rock. When he made it to the sunlight it gleamed like the heavens themselves. It wasn't the sand bearing silver, it was a solid nugget. Now solid silver is rare, real rare. The three of us all ran in the mine, which is something you should never do. If there is a problem you always need a man on the outside so he can try to dig you out. I guess in our excitement we just plum forgot that little rule. Lady Luck was smiling on us that day though, we had hit a good strike and the roof held."

Hiram held up his coffee tin and drained it. He stood and headed for the pot, which was about ready. As he poured the sugar and coffee into his cup he continued his story. "We couldn't believe it. We had struck hard silver, not the stuff that is referred to as silver ore which needs to be processed. This was silver that could be held in your hand. It was soft stuff that you could just about bend between your fingers. By the end of that day we probably had somewhere in the neighborhood of a good pound of the stuff and we hadn't hit that vein until after lunch. It was decided that night over a meager supper that we would use the next day to see what else we could find and then pull out of camp and head north. We were broke and wanted to cash in on the silver we had in order to buy some badly needed supplies. We were down to two worn out shovels and the pick we had been using for the last month and a half was worn down to just a nub. Our prospectin days were just about gone by the time we hit that vein."

Judge Preston knew the story was taking a long time but really didn't care, this was extremely interesting and he wanted to hear it all. "Go ahead Hiram, tell us what happened next."

Well, the next day we continued to dig. If we thought the vein was going to be good on that first day then let me tell you that by the end of the second day we figured we might have found something that would rival the Comstock Load. The silver was there in chunks, each weighing maybe an ounce. We worked into the night on that second day using the last of our candles to light the way. The next morning we gathered our guns and with what few bites of deer jerky we had left we headed north with our silver."

"Why did you go north Hiram, the bank in Rapid City buys gold and silver," Cecil said.

"Well, we contemplated that but didn't want to come to Rapid City for two reasons. First is we didn't want anyone here to know we had struck silver, we know a little trading post north that will give us a fair price. Maybe not as much as we could have gotten here but we had a secret that we planned to protect." He stopped and sampled his coffee.

"What was the second reason?" Preston asked.

"Oh yeah, the second reason was I didn't want to do no business with that Shafer Bank here in town, they're the only bank in Rapid City that buys gold and silver. I don't like that bank and I don't care for the owner either."

Preston couldn't help but admire someone who hated the Shafer's as much as he did. "Where was your destination if it wasn't Rapid City then?" he asked.

"Prairie City, about another seventy miles north of our claim. It is a small place but they do buy silver there. There is a few business establishments about and nobody asks any questions. Prospectors can go there and know the bank won't ask anything about where you got your silver. Train stops once a week and they got a telegraph if you need to send any messages. On foot it took us three days. We camped outside of town on the last night because we were broke and couldn't afford a room. Anyway, first thing the next morning the three of us went to the bank.

"They took our silver and gave us nearly five hundred dollars. It was more money than any of us had ever seen before. We took the money and bought us a mule, stout looking animal but small. It would suit our needs. We went to the General Store and got the supplies we would need to last a month. Bought us a rifle too, Winchester .40.65 and she was a beauty, even if she wasn't exactly brand new. We put down thirteen dollars and sixteen cents for that little purchase. Shells to fit it cost another five dollars. Up till then all we had was two old black powder rifles and one pistol, which was also black powder."

"How much did the mule cost you Hiram? Cecil asked as he continued to write down the story.

"Gave fifty dollars for the mule. Along with our other supplies we bought a hundred pound sack of grain for the critter. We didn't want it eating everything for a mile around our hidden claim and figured the grain would limit the amount of grass it would need."

"If mules were going for fifty dollars apiece then why didn't you buy three, one for each of you to ride?" Savage asked.

"Three mules would have been nice and we had the money too. We decided in order to keep our trail narrow and our camp hidden we could only risk taking one mule back. Three would have made the place look eaten down, plus the smell would have been hard to hide; three mules would have made quite a stink unless we tied them far from camp. We just didn't want to take the chance.

"We left out of Prairie City two hours after we got there. As bad as each of us wanted a shave and fresh haircuts we couldn't take that chance either. We needed to be getting back to our claim. We were real cautious when we left, didn't want anyone following us and no one did. We made it back to our claim three days later and everything was just the way we had left it. The three of us decided to mine and make the trip back north once a month. Only one of us would go leaving the other two to guard the claim and continue to pull silver out of the ground. We knew about how much silver we had taken on the first trip and it was agreed to take about the same each time. We were pulling a lot more than that out of the ground and thought it would be best to stash it around and not try and take too much in. Delroy being the one who had some schooling figured by what we took on that first trip and it bringing five-hundred dollars we was probably pulling ten-thousand dollars a month out of that mine."

The other four men in the room let out a collective sigh. "You mean you and your two brothers were stashing ninety-five hundred dollars' worth of silver every month?" Cecil asked. As a deputy he could barely afford to eat.

"That's right deputy. We figured that once the mine played out we would take all the silver in at once. At that point who would care where a played out claim was located. After a month we decided to let Gervais make the trip to Prairie City by himself. Just an old gray bearded man and a skinny mule shouldn't draw any attention. He was to sell the silver the same as before and buy enough supplies to do us another month. We decided to pick up another gun on each trip. The claim was paying off and we wanted some modern firepower to defend it with. He was gone six days and came back with the supplies and another hundred pound sack of feed for the mule. This time he brought us a Smith & Wesson .44 caliber five shot double action revolver, brand new, paid a steep price for her though, twenty-three dollars. Boy she was a beauty. Bought sixty rounds of ammunition to fit the gun and forty more rounds for the rifle. We were acquiring us quite an arsenal."

Savage thought about all the guns he and his posse carried when they went to the rescue of Zeke and Ben and knew three old black powder guns along with one revolver and one rifle was nothing. "Did Gervais make the trip alright Hiram?"

"Made it just fine. As we worked the mine it kept getting better. Delroy figured we was stashing fifteen thousand dollars' worth of silver every month, maybe even twenty. Everything went fine until maybe a month ago."

Hiram stopped to sip his coffee. The others in the room could tell that he was troubled and knew he was about to get to the part where his brothers went missing. "Go ahead Hiram, what happened next?" Cecil asked.

"Well, Gervais left out with the mule but no silver. We had been accumulating a little cash and decided in order to draw less attention to the claim we would use up the cash to make it look like we had played our claim out. We hadn't taken any silver to town in over four months. Hell, it don't take five hundred dollars a month for three prospectors to live out in the wild. We were stashing everything, not in the same place mind you but in different spots. We can hide stuff where even an injun can't find it. Anyway, he left out with two hundred dollars cash and the mule. He was well armed too, two revolvers and a Winchester. We had two more Winchesters and two more revolvers in camp if we needed them along with lots of ammunition. The time we had spent in the war had left each of us with a great appreciation for firearms."

Again Hiram stopped to sip his coffee. The other men in the room knew he was struggling with the memories he was telling. They decided to let him tell the story at his own pace. Cecil was glad for the break; his writing hand had begun to hurt. "Go ahead Hiram, tell us what happened next," Preston said.

"Well, me and Delroy continued to work the mine. It was slow going with only one man at the face of it and the other outside in case something happened. Anyway, the six days went by and no Gervais. We weren't out of food yet and probably wouldn't be for another five or six days. We didn't worry much, figured he was just traveling a little slower on this trip. By the evening on the seventh day worry had settled in on the two of us. Gervais was nearly sixty-four years old and we began to suspect he might have taken sick on the way back. It was agreed that one of us would go the next morning and track him down. We each knew the way so either me or Delroy would go, not both of us. It was a risk to leave the claim unprotected and for that matter we had probably in the neighborhood of a hundred thousand dollars' worth of silver stashed, maybe even a lot more. No one wants to walk away from a treasure like that.

"At daylight the next day we flipped a coin and Delroy won." Hiram stopped for a second and then added. "I guess though I was the one who won because I made it here alive. Anyway Delroy took a Winchester and one of the revolvers and half the ammunition. I promised I wouldn't go back in the mine without anyone here in case I got into trouble. He took enough food for three days and some money in case he needed to buy supplies for his trip back. With only me in camp I had enough food for the six days he would be gone but nothing after that. I spent the next six days waiting for my two brothers to return, hoping it wouldn't take that long. It was possible Delroy would meet up with Gervais on his way back with the mule and have a good reason for his delay. With that in mind I hoped the two would show up any one of those six days, it didn't happen. Neither showed up.

"I spent the seventh day breaking down our camp and hiding everything. I even erased my tracks as I headed out of camp for at least a quarter mile and made very little sign after that. I stayed to hard packed ground and streams. After a couple of miles I was certain no one could follow my trail back to the claim. I had been real stingy with what little food that was on hand and figured I had enough to nibble on for two more days. I also had the last Winchester and an Army Colt with plenty of ammunition. I felt I was safe from about anything and then it dawned on me that both my brothers were heavily armed themselves. That made me real cautious. I slept at night without a fire, just my blanket pulled over me. Some of the nights that far north and at that elevation can get pretty cold.

"Gervais had described the two locations he had bedded down at during his trips to Prairie City and also the ones he used on his way back. I knew the spots; they were the ones we had used on that first trip when all three of us went. They were good spots, water close by and lots of cover. You don't ever want to make camp where someone can walk right in on you. Both spots were on high ground and hidden by trees and timber. No one could find you unless they were just plain lucky."

Hiram stopped talking. Preston looked at his pocket watch and saw that it was nearly one-o'clock in the afternoon. He was starting to get a little hungry and suspected the other men were too. Hiram, although he had eaten soon after getting to the sheriff's office, was probably hungry again himself. He had been talking for nearly two and a half hours.

"How much more of the story is there Hiram?" Preston asked.

"Not much, it's nearly at the end," he said.

"You go ahead and finish and then let's go and have some lunch," Preston said. Ben woke and raised his head, he was looking at Preston. It was uncanny how that hound could tell when someone mentioned food.

"Well, I kept a close eye out both in front and behind me. After the second day for some reason I felt as if I was being watched and maybe even followed. I took the time to circle back once and proved my suspicions correct," again Hiram stopped.

"What was it you found when you circled back Hiram?" Cecil asked.

"I don't know," was all he said.

These three words were enough to send chills over the other four men in the room. "What can you tell us?" Cecil asked.

"All I know is there wasn't just one, there were several, couldn't tell for sure how many. Never did see anything but they were there. Me and my brothers knew how to track and we know how to keep from being tracked. I picked my spot and lay in wait. I never saw who it was and they were never able to track me down completely but they were there. This slowed me down quite a bit and by the third day I was out of food. On that third day they set a trap for me, they could tell I was heading for Prairie City and were waiting between me and there. I figured both my brothers were done for and knew if I continued in the direction they had gone I would be a goner too." Again Hiram stopped as he processed his memories.

"What happened then Hiram?" Savage asked.

"Well, when you are dealing with someone who is a good tracker and you want to get away then the best thing to do is head in a different direction all together and you do it with all the speed available to you. If your adversary is good then he will continue for a few hours and wait if he knows you are coming his way. He knows your speed and the general direction you will take. While he is waiting to spring his trap then you are putting some miles between you and him. By the time he figures he's been tricked it will be a while before he can pick up your trail again. Once you have given up on your original direction then you can most likely lose your pursuers."

"Did you lose them Hiram?" Cecil asked.

"I thought I did. I moved with all possible speed back south. The ground was hard packed in places and rock in others. I left as little sign as possible and began to feel safe by that second day after I turned south. I thought I had lost them but they were still back there.

"I always travelled at least an hour after it got dark not wanting to stop until I had moved away from any daylight sign I might have left. I picked a spot and settled in for the night. Bout three or four in the morning I heard something that was out of the ordinary. Being in the war had taught me to be a very light sleeper. Anyway, I had the Colt in my right hand and the Winchester in my left. I had my back to a big rock so whatever found me would have to come at me from the front. I sat quiet as a mouse and listened. They had found me and were closing in. I had a decision to make." Again Hiram stopped talking and just looked at nothing in particular.

"What was it Hiram? What was the decision you had to make?" Preston asked.

"Back in the war I was in some territory that was unfamiliar to me. Yanks were about and I was trying to make my way back to my own side. One night they found me. It was pitch black and somehow they had tracked me down. I did something that night that seems foolish to most. I jumped to my feet and fired two shots. As I fired I also took off running. The Yanks were close enough that the shots had the desired effect; they were momentarily deafened by the noise. As I ran I doubt anyone heard my footsteps. Unless I ran right over one of them I might be able to escape, and that is exactly what I did. I laughed for a week at my good fortune.

"Well it worked once, maybe it would work again. One thing for sure, if I stayed where I was at I was going to die. I jumped to my feet and fired two shots with the Colt in the direction I thought one was hiding and then took off like the devil himself was after me. I ran in the direction I had fired and damn near ran over one of the damn things. I had hit it with at least one bullet maybe both. Had to jump over it. I ran and didn't stop until my lungs were on fire."

Preston had caught onto something Hiram had said and wanted clarification. "You described what you saw as 'It' or 'One of the damned things,' don't you mean 'He' or Him."

Hiram looked up at Preston, "No sir, I mean it."

Again the other four men felt a collective chill invade their souls. "Can you describe what you saw Hiram," Cecil asked.

"It was something I have never seen before. It was pretty dark but my eyes are good in the dark. What I saw was a monster. It wasn't moving but just a little. Wherever I hit it must have been a fatal shot because the movement it was making was what you might see after shooting a deer or an elk. It was death twitches.

"It took me two more days of hard traveling to get here this morning. I never ate and I don't think I slept. After that night I decided to sleep in the trees."

Cecil looked up from his notes. "You slept in the forest instead of in the fields Hiram?"

Hiram looked at Cecil. "No deputy, I picked me out a good stout tree and climbed as far off the ground as I could. If something was going to kill me and eat me then the only way it was going to get at me was to climb. I spent two nights way up in the trees and it worked. I could hear them down there but they never made an attempt on me while I was up in the trees. Seems they never bothered me during daylight, just followed me was all, but back far enough that I couldn't see them."

Zeke had been listening intently and was impressed with Hiram's solution. It wouldn't have worked for him personally because he travelled with horses and couldn't take the chance of something killing Rusty or Hazel. This was good information, whatever it was didn't like heights or maybe just couldn't climb very well.

"Is that all of it Hiram?" Cecil asked.

"That's it deputy. My brothers must have been killed by the same things that almost got me. As sad as I feel for the loss of Delroy and Gervais, may they rest in peace, I'm glad I got one of the beasts. After I get myself replenished here in town for a few days I plan on heading back there and settling the score. I've got sixty-five dollars left of the cash and that is all I need. I figure this is a one way trip and sixty-five dollars is enough to provision for one way. Maybe I can kill another one before they can kill me," Hiram said.

Savage knew the prospector would be a welcome addition to the four man hunting party they were putting together. Preston, Cecil and Zeke thought the same thing. Cecil laid down his pencil and paper and began to rub his right hand. He had written more than twelve pages of notes.

Preston stood and looked at his pocket watch again. It was after two-o'clock. "Hiram, I am truly sorry for your loss. You made it to town and found your way to this office and as fate would have it this is the very place you need to be. These three men here you see along with myself are preparing to head out first thing in the morning on a little hunting trip."

Hiram scratched his stubbly chin. "What are you hunting, if I might ask?"

Preston's chin stiffened as he said, "Monsters."

After a few minutes, as each man sat and pondered the answer Preston had given Hiram, it was decided to head back over to the Lolli Pop Restaurant for some lunch.

Hiram, I know you are probably getting a little hungry after your forced three day starvation. How would you like to join the four of," before Preston could finish Ben looked him straight in the eye, "Pardon me, five of us including Ben for a little lunch over at the Lolli Pop. The city will be glad to pick up the tab. What do you say?"

Hiram looked down at his filthy prospecting clothes and said he probably should decline the invitation. "I doubt if they allow someone like me in a place like that."

Preston considered what Hiram had just said and had to agree with him. His clothes were torn to pieces no doubt from climbing trees and running away from monsters. Preston also noticed that the prospector and Cecil were about the same size.

"Say Cecil, weren't you and Bill pretty much the same size; wouldn't each of you wear about the same in clothes?" Preston asked.

"Sure was Judge. At times we got our shirts and pants mixed up and wore each other's stuff. I know what you're getting at and I think that is a good idea. Got a pair of denims and a shirt in his trunk back in the bunk room and I'm positive if Bill was here he would want to share." Without another word Cecil jumped up and went into the bunkroom where he and Bill kept extra clothes for the times they had to work extra hours. A minute later he came out with a pair of denim overalls and a gray and red checkered shirt, kind of like what a lumberjack would wear. "Here you go Hiram. This ought to fix you right up. Head over to the livery and jump in that big rain barrel. There is a cake of soap on a shelf nailed to the side of the barn."

With the thought of a real meal in the works Hiram jumped up and grabbed the clothing bundle Cecil held and he nearly ran down the street for the livery. After he left it gave the four men a chance to talk about the story Hiram just told.

Savage got up and put his coffee cup on the sheriff's desk. "That was some kind of story. It kind of narrows down the direction we need to head in tomorrow. Due south is the route Hiram took to get here so we head due north to see what we come across."

Preston stood and stretched. "Due north is fine but not before we make a trip to Wiley's Trading Post. We provision there and then start our hunt." All the men agreed.

Within fifteen minutes Hiram was back and he was clean. The clothes Cecil had given him were a pretty good fit. The man still needed a shave and a haircut; he had the makings of the mountain man look.

"Thanks for these here clothes. After we eat is there a place where I can get a shave and haircut. I don't want to be buried looking like a wild animal." The other men took it to mean that Hiram felt it really was a one way trip.

"After we eat you can head over to Ondaloues, he is about the best barber in town. After that you can stay here at the jail either in a cell or on one of the bunks. We plan on leaving pretty early in the morning and we'll start from here," Cecil said.

"What will I do for a horse?" Hiram asked.

Preston broke in. "What do you say we head over to the Lolli Pop and order some supper. We can talk about all the particulars over there."

The five men ate and talked about the trip to come. Ben got his usual bucket and enjoyed it immensely sitting on the front porch of the restaurant. He liked the wilderness but with the excitement of the snare and monsters he felt he could lie on this porch a month and not ever move as long as someone gave him food. He watched the people of the town as they walked from place to place. He particularly liked to watch the young children as they romped and frolicked. He really wanted to join them for some fun but decided he better stay on the porch. Never know when another bucket might land at his feet. Wasn't long before he put his head down and fell sound asleep. Ben dreamed of his youth when he had played and romped not that much different than the children on the street. Ben was a good natured dog and dreamed pleasant dreams.

With supper over the men hurried back to the jail. Along the way a few of the children wanted to pet Ben. Zeke agreed but stayed close. As Ben got his head patted and his neck stroked he began licking the children. "Oh his breath smells just like bacon," one of the boys said. Ben marched on to the sheriff's office holding his head high and wagging his tail to beat the band. With all the trouble he had experienced in the last month it was nice to hear laughter and receive the attention of children.

The guns and ammunition were finished being sorted and counted. Bedrolls and packs were prepared. Ammunition was still a problem and a few more guns would be needed but every man knew if nothing else could be acquired then they would proceed anyway. What had been going on was destroying the territory. Rapid City had taken on the look of a refugee camp. People were sleeping anywhere they could find a bed. The livery had no less than five families staying there.

One thing Preston was glad to see was a food bank. Every farmer in the valley who had anything extra from the fall harvest was bringing it to town. People had to be fed and the mayor saw that no one went hungry. This was all well and good but if the situation lasted into winter then things were going to get tough.

Once everything was finished at the jail Preston said he was tired and heading home.

"One last thing Judge, what does Hiram ride in the morning?" Cecil asked.

"I've given that some thought deputy. We got Hazel extra but I think she would be handy as our pack animal. How about going to the livery and see if he will rent us a horse and saddle for a few weeks, maybe even a month?"

"You really think it will take a month Judge?" Cecil asked.

"At least, Hiram told us the trail we will be using and I don't want to leave a single stone unturned until we find what it is we're looking for."

"Oh, I don't think it will be a problem finding what we're looking for. It'll probably find us first," Cecil said as everyone enjoyed a nervous laugh. Ben heard the laughter and tried not to let it bother his sleep. He just wished they would all shut the hell up. Silly people!

Thirty minutes before day break the next morning, Preston kicked the door to the jail open and stomped in. He figured to find everyone still sound asleep but to his pleasant surprise they were all bright eyed and ready for the day. "Well, don't you men look ready for an adventure?"

Ben went over to the judge, he was hoping for another trip to the Lolli Pop but it wasn't to be. The judge informed the men that once the horses were loaded they would proceed straight to Wiley's. "We'll stock up there and also have us some breakfast, shouldn't be any later than nine-thirty or ten when we get there." There was a little grumbling but everyone agreed that it would be better to leave town before folks were out and about. No need to broadcast the groups every move.

Cecil had managed to get a horse for Hiram at the livery. It was a short looking mount, more suited to the likes of an Indian than a white man. Hiram even walked over and checked to see if the horse was shod. He knew Indian pony's went shoeless. It was a horse and definitely not an Indian pony because it did have shoes.

"Hiram, I think that horse is so short one of them monsters can look you eye to eye even at a full gallop," Cecil said.

Hiram had been looking the little horse over and started to see some advantages in the smaller mount. It could maneuver in timber better than a big horse and it was undoubtedly fast by the look of the frame. "I believe this little horse will outrun those overweight horses you folks will be riding. Never did put much stock in a fat horse." It was apparent Cecil and Hiram were cut from the same stock, both had a sassy side.

Once everything was loaded they headed out of town at a trot. Ben was in the lead and Zeke wondered how the dog knew where they were going. He pulled up beside the judge and asked a question.

"Judge, Ben might look fit as a fiddle but he still needs to go easy. If we get in a bind I for one want him rested and ready for a fight."

Preston had already thought of this. He knew what kind of shape the dog was in just a week before. "I've given that some thought myself Zeke and just as you say if there's trouble I want Ben rested. How would it be if we let him ride part of the way on top of that pack Hazel is carrying? I don't think we need to tie him up there anymore. He can jump off and lend a hand if we get in a situation. Let him run a while and the first sign of fatigue we fix up that pack so he can ride on top."

Zeke was impressed by the way Preston was always thinking one step ahead of everybody else. Preston was smart; he had to be if he was a judge. Zeke wondered when the time came and all the chips were on the table how a man of Preston's age would do. Deep down he felt the old riverboat captain was trying to prove something to himself. He wanted to see if he was still any good in a fight, time would tell.

By the time the group got to Wiley's, Ben was starting to slow. Zeke was proud of the distance he had traveled and knew it would improve with time. When they pulled out of the Trading Post Ben would be stationed on top of Hazel's pack. A little rest and he would be good as new.

As the five riders were tying up out front Wiley stepped outside, he was carrying a shotgun. "Judge Preston am I glad to see you!"

"Well Wiley, it's good to be here. Why the shotgun?"

"Ain't safe out of doors anymore Judge. Been some mighty strange things going on since you came through here two weeks ago, mighty strange things."

"That is what me and these young men are about to investigate. We're heading into the territory and we ain't coming back until we have us some answers," Preston said.

"Well, you boys come on in, I spect you're hungry." Ben had walked over to the porch and sat down. He suspected if you sit on someone's front porch then before long they brought you food. "This animal sitting in the shade I reckon belongs to you?" Wiley asked as he looked at the judge.

"Wiley, an animal that big don't belong to anybody but if you feed him then he will probably become your lifelong friend. Oh, one other thing, if you don't feed him and he wants to lick your hand he's most likely just seeing how you taste," Preston said with a sly smile.

"Well then let me get him some grub. Right now I could use a friend that size." Wiley and the five men went inside as Ben looked over the horses. He knew when horses were involved it was part of his job to see to their safety, Hazel could vouch for that.

Preston had made a list the night before after he had gone home He found sleep difficult so he used the time to think about what might be needed for the journey ahead. He knew they would only have one pack animal, which was the green eyed Hazel. Five men in the wilds for possibly weeks would need a substantial amount of supplies. With only one spare horse he would first make the list and then go back and thin it down as much as possible. He now held that list as he stood at Wiley's counter. Judge Preston, being the amateur outdoorsman, was so concerned with the food situation for the trip that he had forgotten completely about the shortage of firearms and ammunition.

"Preston, how 'bout you coming over here and look at this gun rack," Savage said.

Wiley had a good assortment; it was apparent his store was off the beaten path and hadn't been overrun by scared folk trying to purchase anything that would shoot. Preston, also being an amateur in the gunplay business, looked over the stock and didn't have a clue as to what should be purchased.

"This place has everything we need and then some Judge, lots of ammunition too," Savage said.

"You know more about this stuff than I do Marshal. Pick out what we need while I go over this grub list with Wiley," Preston said.

This was music to the ear for Savage. He was a man who knew his guns. He grabbed two 10 gauge Parker Shotguns and thirty shells for each. There was one Winchester Model 1886. Savage looked over this gun and discovered it was of a .45.90 caliber which was more powerful than the .45.75 Zeke carried. He chose that gun as well along with all the ammunition Wiley had to fit it, twenty rounds. Each man carried a revolver so with the two shotguns and additional Winchester he felt he and his companions were now as well armed as was needed. He knew to a shell how much ammunition they had and went about adding more. An additional one hundred and fifty rounds was laid on the counter with the three guns. As he stepped back to look over the purchase he wondered if Preston would object.

Wiley not only ran a trading post but he also sold lunches and dinners of whatever he happened to make that day. There were three small tables to the side of the trading post and this was where his customers could sit and eat, or just sit and talk, didn't matter to Wiley.

"Preston, were you interested in breakfast this morning?" Wiley asked.

"We are. Left town bright and early this morning expecting to eat here."

"I got a pan of biscuits and a big pot of bean stew, if that sounds alright this morning."

Preston walked over to the side of the trading post where Wiley done the cooking. "Never heard of bean stew before."

"Oh, I think you'll like it Judge. My old pappy was famous around these parts for his soup beans. He taught me how to make 'em just like he did right before he passed. He would take soup beans and put 'em in this very same cast iron Dutch Oven and let them start to cook. As they cook he would add chunks of beef or buffalo or just about anything else on hand and let it simmer for a few hours. He then added some spice and a bunch of diced up potatoes and let that simmer some too. It's more like chili in some ways but different in other ways. It may sound strange for breakfast but I think it suits. You and these other fellars want to try a bowl?"

Preston had to admit the smell was enticing. "I think we do Wiley. I believe cornbread might go better with the chili though if you have any."

"As a matter of fact I do, got two pones out just before you all got here. There is a ladle hanging to the right and bowls are on the shelf. You boys help yourself while I take these scraps out to that big dog sitting by the horses." As Wiley walked by and headed to the door Preston noticed he had made another stew of some sort for Ben. When Ben saw Wiley heading his way carrying a small bucket he knew it was breakfast time.

With breakfast over and the supplies gathered up Preston asked the other men if they thought all was in order. Zeke remembered the Light Toss sticks they had bought the first time through. Wiley had a few more and this was added to the rest of the supplies.

"Wiley, I know we got us a pretty good tab going but the town will pay. It you have everything written down then let me sign and we'll be on our way," Preston said.

As the men rode away Preston was pleased with the way the trip had started. Not only were they well provisioned but he had also purchased two bottles of Old Grand-Dad. He looked forward to evenings sitting by the fire and sipping his favorite whiskey.

Three days of steady traveling saw the group near the claim Hiram and his two brothers had worked for the last year. Hiram hoped his brothers were there and wondering where he had been for the last week, it wasn't to be. The camp was just the way he had left it; nothing had been moved or disturbed.

"Well, it was as I suspected Judge, no one has been here. Place looks plum deserted. You know, I figure it ain't right if I don't survive this trip to let the years hard work me and my brothers put in here to go to waste, somehow it just don't seem right," Hiram said.

"What do you mean?" Cecil asked.

"I've been giving this some thought ever since we left the trading post. I want to go and check on the hidey spots we got the silver hidden in. We all go and have us a look that way if I don't make it or if any of you don't make it back then who ever survives can have all the silver we got stashed. I think it is the way my brothers would have wanted it." After some thought Hiram added, "That is assuming it's still there."

That was probably a good idea and no one objected, who would in a situation like this. It took nearly three hours to look over all the spots where the loot was hidden. Hiram and his two brothers had done an excellent job of concealment. All the silver was just as they had left it.

"Well Savage, what do you think our plan of action should be now?" Preston asked.

Savage thought a minute and said, "Well Judge, we've been on the trail for three days and haven't seen a thing. I figured we would have been set upon by now. I say we let Hiram show us the way he and his two brothers traveled to get to Prairie City. Maybe between here and there we will find us some clues."

As the men rode they used a lot of caution. One thing they had in their favor was Ben. He was feeling strong after days of rest and plenty of food. He was getting healthier by the minute and was even putting on a little of the weight he had lost. It was agreed that the group of riders was strong and heavily armed and with Ben running everywhere it was doubtful if they would be attacked by the creatures during daylight hours. Still though, not a sign had been seen of anything at night either. It was again agreed that the party of travelers was just too strong and heavily armed. Another reason for the lack of attention from the creatures might have been the posting of two guards each night instead of one. While two men kept watch the other three slept. This went on in four hour shifts. At no time was anyone to be out of sight of someone else.

The next night spent after leaving Hiram's claim was anything but peaceful. At a little after two o'clock in the morning Ben, who had been sleeping near the fire, raised his head and perked his ears. Within seconds the horses became restless and the two guards, Cecil and Preston knew something was about to happen. Preston silently went to each of the three other men and roused them awake. They were to stay in their blankets and pretend to still be sleeping but be ready to rise at a moment's notice. Ben also played along; he was wide awake and very still but ready to charge into the darkness to battle with his enemies again.

Preston and Cecil each carried one of the new Parker Shotguns. Cecil was anxious to try out the big caliber Parkers but Preston wasn't. He was afraid of the kick a ten gauge shell would deliver. All five men were alert and ready for anything that might happen.

Ben had spent his time watching the six horses. He would play along for a while but once he saw movement heading in the direction of the six horses he would make his move. Hazel was peering into the darkness and standing still as a statue, the other five horses were fidgeting and looked ready to break from their leads and bolt.

As Preston and Cecil strained to listen and look for whatever it might be in the dark, Ben had no problem at all determining that it was the same creatures he had battled with before. He also knew how many there were and where each was hiding. He remembered the battle in the road the previous week and that little lesson had taught him a lot.

When he advanced into the darkness that night he crippled and maimed anything that got in his way. When he was stationary near Zeke while the man was knocked out he was overwhelmed and nearly killed.

This time he would do all his fighting in the darkness where he could do the most damage. He waited for the creatures to advance. When the time was right Ben bolted upright and charged in. At this Zeke and the other men came out of their blankets and stood. Knowing which way Ben went meant no one could shoot in that direction. Savage instructed the other four men with him to each fire one shot into the timber but be careful to stay above and away from the direction where Ben went. Five men each fired one round and waited. Preston was now satisfied he could handle the kick of the big Parker 10 gauge.

Ben wasn't surprised by the gunfire. The creatures he was advancing on stopped and stood for a second. When they realized the five men were all up and holding guns they started stepping back. When they realized the big dog was attacking they each retreated into the more heavily wooded portion of the forest and waited in ambush to kill him. Ben knew where they were and knew they were all bunched up. They were waiting on him. He stopped and started easing back toward the light of the campfire. This time the creatures could slip away but he knew he would soon get another chance.

When Ben strolled back into camp to lie down near the fire the five men knew the danger had passed. The rest of the night went off without incident.

The next day dawned cold and cloudy. As the five travelers moved north a lone wagon was spotted in the distance. Savage produced a spy glass and extended the barrel, as he peered at the wagon he told the others what he was seeing.

"Heavy wagon pulled by a six mule team. Five armed riders on horseback. Wagon has four men, two in front and two in back. The team is pulling hard but the wagon appears to be empty."

Hiram asked if he could take a look. "I used to drive a mule team a few years back," he said.

"Those mules are pulling hard. Whatever is in the back of that wagon is heavy but not the least bit bulky. It don't even come to the top edge of the side rails." He reached the scope back to Savage. The five riders were well hidden in the timber and were slightly elevated compared to the trail the wagon was using.

Savage looked at Hiram and asked, "What's you're take on that wagon Hiram?"

"She's a heavy built rig, a wagon like that being pulled by six stout mules is probably carrying three or four thousand pounds."

"What could weigh that much and not be big enough to even come to the top of the side rails?" Cecil asked.

Hiram looked at the men and said, "Silver, the stuff is heavy and don't take up much space."

The five men stayed concealed as each took turns looking at the riders and mule team as it disappeared over the next rise. It was a little after noon and the group decided to have some lunch without the aid of a fire.

"My guess is there is another silver mine nearby. If me and my brothers found such a rich strike then I'm sure there is more silver around here."

It was decided to move through the timber for the rest of the day and proceed in the direction the wagon had come from. About three that afternoon the men came to some rugged low-lying hills and with the spyglass they spotted the trail used by the wagon earlier. It was decided that Zeke, Hiram and Savage would proceed on foot. Cecil and Preston would stay with the horses. Ben was left behind too.

It only took thirty minutes for the three to get to a position with a good vantage point inside the small valley. What they saw was not what they would have expected. The valley was completely surrounded by rugged outcroppings of rock. There was a small stream which went through the opening that wasn't much wider than the width of the wagon that had just come out of it a few hours earlier.

Inside this valley were some tents and a few horses, no more than ten or twelve. About halfway up the opposite slope was the opening for a mine. Men were pushing handcarts of dirt and rock to the outside and pouring it over the side. These men were dressed in rags and looked thin, extremely thin, as if starved. Six or seven, dressed in warm clothing much better than anything the workers wore, were standing around with shotguns and rifles. These men weren't starved as the workers were, they actually looked well fed. It was Hiram who spotted the most troubling sight of all.

"Well, if I'm not mistaken one of them men is my brother Gervais." He took the spyglass from Savage and then looked again. While both excited at the sight of a brother he had given up for dead he was also angered that he was nearly naked, his clothes were torn and ragged. He was also thinner than he had been when Hiram had last seen him.

"It's definitely my brother. Those men are being forced to work and it looks like they aren't being fed, if they are getting any food then it is very little," Hiram said through clinched teeth as he handed the spyglass to Zeke so he could have a look.

The three men stayed maybe ten more minutes as they took in everything they could see before heading back. Back at the spot where Cecil and Preston waited they shared what they had found out.

Preston, having a mindset for figuring out motive after hearing all the facts, told the other four men what he suspected.

"I believe if what you have seen and described to me is correct then we may have most of this puzzle of the missing men figured out. Let's look at the facts. For the last several months men have been going missing without a trace. As of yet the number stands somewhere between forty and fifty men. Now if these men had met their deaths then with so many missing surely a body would have turned up. That hasn't been the case.

"You have just found a hidden mining operation and by what you have told me the men working that mine are doing so against their will. They are being used as forced labor. An operation of that size would require quite a few men and that many men would spread the word unless those same men were in fact prisoners. It is my guess that the mine is being kept secret and the silver doesn't belong to the men who are in control." Preston stopped to ponder some of what he had just said.

Savage added, "Well, we must make haste back to Rapid City and get word to the authorities. The five of us need more men. We come back here and bust up that operation and arrest everyone in charge."

"That won't work Marshal." Preston said. "From what you have described those men are in bad shape. The weather is turning colder and by the time we make it to Rapid City and get the help we need and then get back here it would take at least ten days. Some of those men would die, either of exposure to the elements or starvation. It's my guess that the mine must be about played out. If they planned on working through the winter then they would be furnishing those men down there with better clothing. My guess is we got here at the end of the operation."

"The end of the operation. If that is so then what will they do with all those poor souls?" Cecil asked.

Savage stood and with his back to the other four men said, "I agree with what the judge has just said. When the mine is played out then it's my guess they will march all those men inside the mine and then blow it down on top of 'em. No witnesses to talk and no bodies to raise suspicion."

Hiram had been quiet during this time. He stood and looked at the others. "I can't ask any of you to go with me." He then picked up one of the Parker Shotguns and loaded his pockets with shells.

One by one each of the other four men began loading up on shells and picking the weapons they would use. Zeke knew the men at the mine wouldn't be alive if they went to Rapid City for help. He was mad as Hell and wanted to help those starving men in the pit. "What's the plan?" He asked through gritted teeth.

Now Savage done the talking. "By the time we get back there it will only give us about an hour of daylight. We pick our spots and when the time is right we blast Hell out of the guards with Winchesters. If each of us hits a target then we just eliminated five men. That will leave at least six or eight more but they won't know where we are or how many of us they are up against. We continue to make our way through the timber until we have killed every last one of them or we are all dead ourselves. Either we succeed or we die. Those men down there got no other hope."

All five of the men knew the plan wasn't the best but it was all they had. Catch the outlaws by surprise and go in with guns blazing. Hiram seemed anxious to go. He had one brother still alive for sure and he wanted to help him. Even if he died trying his brother would know that Hiram had done his best.

When all the men were ready they headed back toward the small valley. Once there, Cecil and Preston saw what the other three had seen earlier. As they scanned the area it was decided to break into three teams and spread out. Savage and Hiram went left; Cecil and Preston went right leaving Zeke and Ben in the middle. Ten minutes later and all five were ready. Each of the men could see the others and it had been worked out that when Savage thought the time was right he would raise his right hand and then at the appropriate time he would drop that hand. This was the signal for each of the five to pour fire into the guards who numbered at least a dozen maybe even fifteen. Each man picked out a target and waited.

Savage needed as many of the guards out in the open as possible. It didn't take long before he got what he wanted. Two of the guards were lined up talking and from the position Savage had he could, with a little luck, get both men with the powerful Winchester .45.90. At the right moment he gave the signal and then squeezed the trigger on the big Winchester. The roar was enormous but Savage was congratulated by the sight of two men knocked to the ground by his shot. Neither of the two moved again.

The other four men fired and kept it up as the guards ran for cover. Their captives ran for cover too. Ragged looking men jumped into ditches or behind boulders, some even ran back inside the mine. These first few minutes were productive with at least ten men accounted for by the murderous fire from Savage and his friends.

Preston was extremely pleased; he knew he had accounted for at least two of the bad guys. Within two minutes it looked like the fight was about over. The shooting from Savage and the other four men was starting to dwindle; there weren't that many more targets.

Ben had sat watching all this when he sensed something to the rear. He turned to see the creatures advancing on him and Zeke. He turned and howled in anger as he ran toward them. Zeke turned just in time to see Ben go airborne and take two of the ugly beasts down. They were too close for a Winchester. Zeke drew his Colt and fired at two more that were advancing on him. This was the first time he had seen any of the strange animals in full daylight. They were actually running as if they were human but the fur they were covered with was that of any number of animals. The face was the thing that was the most terrifying of all. It looked as if it were raw bone with large eye sockets. This was what he aimed for. He hit both squarely between the eyes. They went down and thrashed around from their injuries. Ben was tangling with the two he had bowled over and actually had one of the ugly beasts by the throat. Blood sprayed everywhere. Zeke leveled the Colt and shot the other one. He had killed three with three shots and Ben had killed the forth.

Cecil and Preston had also thought the fight was won when they too were jumped by more of the creatures. The two men were about a hundred feet from where Ben had just made his kill and the big dog could see, and hear, that they were both in trouble. Zeke had just finished shooting the third creature when he saw Ben break and run toward the position he knew the judge and Cecil were holding. Zeke ran that way too.

When Ben came through the tree line he saw both Preston and Cecil on the ground and each had at least two of the ugly things on top of them. He knew Preston was the older of the two men and decided to clear the creatures off him first. He raced toward Preston and when he got there he tore and bit anything that didn't look like the judge. Within seconds the judge was free and scrambling to his feet. His face was bloodied but he was still in the fight. As Ben tangled with the two he had gotten off the judge Preston went to the aid of Cecil. Just when he got there Zeke came through the trees and also went to Cecil's aid. When the deputy managed to scramble free Zeke shot those two as well. Ben was tearing Hell all to pieces with the other two.

As the three men and Ben, who had now killed a total of three of the beasts, looked over the situation it was apparent a few of the guards were still alive and had started firing back at the rescuers. Off to the left gunfire could be heard as Savage and Hiram were dispatching the creatures from their position as well. By the time Zeke, and his crew made it over there they found both men alright and two more of the things dead on the ground.

Savage stood and wiped blood from a bad cut over his right eye. "Is everybody alright?" he asked.

The other four men had only scrapes and minor injuries with Preston being the worst.

Savage looked back down at the mine. Alright then, let's get down there. Everyone look sharp, I think there might still be a few bad guys alive down there. As the five men hurried down the hill they spread out and started looking for anything that presented itself as a target. There were none. By the time they got to the mine they found several of the miners had killed the remaining guards with picks and shovels, anything they could use.

One of the men holding a shovel that was bloodied on the end was none other than Sheriff Coleman. Cecil walked over to get a better look. "Sheriff is that you?" The man had lost a good thirty pounds and his clothes were nothing more than rags.

The man stepped forward and tried to straighten himself up. "It's me Cecil, over there next to the tunnel is Bill."

Cecil looked in that direction and there stood his friend. He too was thinner. Bill hobbled over and stood by the sheriff. "We made it Sheriff, we really survived." Cecil grabbed both men by the shoulders, he couldn't believe his eyes.

Sheriff Coleman looked at the badge Savage wore and asked, "How many men you got with you Marshal?"

Savage looked at his bloodied companions and said, "There's just the five of us Sheriff."

Coleman looked past the marshal at the entrance to the valley. "Ain't enough, they'll be back a little after dark."

Preston stepped forward. "How many are coming Sheriff?"

"Twenty, maybe twenty five men in all. You got here just in time. They plan on leaving this place tomorrow. Weather is getting bad and they don't want to be trapped in this country all winter. They have taken all the silver this mountain has to offer except what little we got out today."

"If they were leaving tomorrow what were they going to do with you and these other men?" Cecil asked.

"They told us they would transport us to the railroad up near Prairie City and turn us loose, but we knew it was just a lie. They were going to kill us. There might be forty of us left now and those outlaws couldn't let that many witnesses live. I figure we had until first thing in the morning and that was it. With twenty five men coming here in a few hours it still might be the end of the road," Coleman said.

"Cecil, you and some of these men that are still able to walk gather up the guns of the outlaws we killed. Pass out the extra weapons we got and let's get a defense set up. When those twenty five men get here I say we give them a hot welcome," Savage told him.

Some of the miners that were in better shape quickly gathered the available guns and passed them out. The rest of the men tore into the tents the outlaws were using and found food. All the miners were devouring whatever they found. Ben sat and watched, he knew starvation when he saw it.

Within thirty minutes, Savage had more than twenty men positioned around the camp, each with either a Winchester or a Colt, weapons either spared by the rescuers or taken from the bodies of the slain guards. Both of Hiram's brothers were among the twenty men. Delroy and Gervais, being recently captured hadn't experienced as much of the backbreaking work and starvation as the other men. Sheriff Coleman seemed to take charge even though he was only a shadow of the man he had been only months earlier.

The urgency of setting up a strong defense was very apparent to the sheriff. Only a few hours earlier he was certain that each and every one of the miners would meet their fates at the hands of their captors. Now there was a chance. He took the most able bodied of the miners and positioned them in spots that gave them a little cover and also afforded good positions to ambush the men he knew were on their way back.

When all was finished Coleman hoped it would be enough. He sat down beside Preston and sipped water from a canteen he had found beside one of the guards.

"Say Sheriff, how did they capture you? The last I heard you were going out to get some answers about all the missing men," Preston asked.

"Coleman put the lid back on the canteen and sat it on the ground between his feet. "I don't know, I just laid down in my blankets one night and woke up here. I've thought about that a lot since then. Other fellars here say the same thing, nobody really knows for sure."

Zeke came out of the trees followed by Ben. "Judge, I found something you might want to look at, you too Sheriff if you feel up to walking."

Both men stood and headed in Zeke's direction. They went up the hill to where Ben had killed one of the creatures. When Preston and Coleman got there it was apparent the sheriff had never seen one of the shaggy things before. "What in hell is that thing?" Coleman managed to ask.

Zeke already knew, he had looked over the one he had shot about fifty yards to the left. He pulled a big hunting knife from his belt and bent over the beast. He then cut into the fur and separated it. He sliced the pelt from the neck to the lower legs. When he spread the skin apart Preston and Coleman could only look in astonishment.

Coleman leaned down beside the body, "Why that's a man in there."

Zeke finished cutting the hide and pulled it away from what was inside. "That looks like an Indian, although I've never seen one so short," Preston said.

It was true, the body was shorter than any of the plains Indians they were familiar with. What it lacked in height it more than made up for in strength. The body was well muscled. As the three men looked at the body Savage came through the trees, he was carrying a brown bottle.

"I see you found out what was inside those ugly hides. I cut one open that me and Hiram killed and found the same thing along with this bottle." Savage reached the bottle to Preston. "Take a smell of that Judge, but you better make it a small one.

Preston took the bottle from Savage and uncorked the top. With great caution he took a small sniff and he immediately felt his senses leaving him. He quickly put the cork back on the bottle as he felt his legs get rubbery. "I better sit down before I fall down," the judge said.

After the judge sat for a minute he looked at Savage and with a harsh tone he asked, "Why didn't you tell me that bottle contained ether?"

Coleman grabbed the bottle and looked it over close but didn't dare uncork it. "Now why would these Indians be dressing up as monsters and carrying around this stuff," he asked.

Preston was slowly getting over the effects and had the answer. "My guess is they sneak up on unsuspecting victims and cap a cloth of some sort over their mouths that has a bit of the ether on it. After this stuff puts you to sleep you're transported to this valley and as soon as you come to they add you to the mining crew."

Zeke looked again at the dead Indian and the hides and furs he was dressed in. "So the creatures that have been terrorizing this region are responsible for capturing and transporting workers for this mining operation. If that's the case then who's behind all this, someone must have put this scheme together."

Before the men had a chance to finish there was noise from below. The four men hurried to the mine and found out that a lookout had spotted a wagon along with several riders on horseback. Marshal Savage and Sheriff Coleman got everyone quiet and told them to hold their fire until the last minute.

As the wagon entered the mine site the riders fanned out on either side. The men on horseback knew something was wrong when they didn't see any of the guards or workers. They began drawing weapons from holsters and scabbards. When the driver of the wagon saw a miner hiding nearby he raised his gun and fired. What happened next was nothing less than a small scale war. The other riders began firing at anything that moved. It was apparent they came back to kill every miner in sight.

This was a chance for the miners to get even. Everyman with a gun laid into the outlaws. It was a perfectly laid ambush. Within less than a minute the only men still standing were the miners and the rescuers. Savage and Coleman ran forward to capture any survivors before they were beaten to death by the miners.

Of the fourteen men who had ridden in on the wagon and horses, six were dead and five more were injured. Three had thrown their hands up in an attempt to surrender. It was all the marshal and sheriff could do to keep the miners from finishing the job they had started. Once the outlaws were separated into three groups, the dead, the wounded, and the living, Coleman assigned four men to watch over them with orders to shoot anyone that moved.

Just as darkness set in Preston looked at Coleman and Savage and asked, "Do you intend to start for Rapid City tonight? I for one think we better hole up here until morning."

Both the sheriff and marshal agreed. To leave out at this hour might be to invite another ambush. It wasn't known if any more outlaws were about and it was anybody's guess if the Indians masquerading as monsters had all been killed or not, more might be about.

"Zeke, how about you and some of the miners that are up to it find something to eat from the back of that wagon. It looks like it's going to be a cold night too, if you can stomach it, how about taking the clothes from some of them dead outlaws and distributing them to some of these men, especially the ones that are nearly naked." Preston asked. "Let's light a couple of fires and try to make everyone as comfortable as possible."

Zeke asked for some of the miners to help with what the judge wanted and they were eager to do so. The wagon did have some food in the back. With twenty guards it was obvious the wagon returning from a shipment would bring back food. Even the starving men required something to eat.

After all the miners and the men who were stationed as guards were fed and everyone was settled in for the night, Preston broke out both bottles of Old-Grand Dad and passed them around. Two bottles allowed each man only a small swig but it was much appreciated by the miners.

Zeke, Preston, and Cecil, wanted to interrogate one of the men they had captured. Once a few questions were asked of the prisoners it was determined that a man named Simian Judd was in charge of the mining operation. Judd was separated from the other prisoners. Preston sat in front of the man and introduced himself as the judge for the territory. He said once the prisoners were transported to Rapid City a trial would be held. Simian suddenly had a desire to talk. "If I tell you everything will you promise to go a little easier on me Judge?"

Preston hoped this would be the man's response. "I can guarantee you only that you will get a fair trial."

This seemed not to satisfy the man. "If you promise me that I won't hang then I will tell you who the man is that's backing this operation."

Now this had the judge's attention. He at first suspected Simian as the ringleader. "Tell you what, you give me the name of the leader of this outfit, and I'm assuming you got proof of what you say, then I can promise you that a noose won't be part of your punishment." Preston could always have the man shot but he wouldn't share that little piece of information.

"You got a deal Judge. I only work for the man who put this operation together. It all started back in February. Me and some of these other fellars you got tied up here were offered a job. The job involved running this silver mine. We were told if we oversaw the operation and never asked any questions we would be rewarded with a big bonus at the end of November. Said the job wouldn't last any past that. All of us agreed and I was put in charge, any of these other men will tell you the same thing," Simian said.

"How did you manage to snag all these miners Simian?" Preston suspected he knew the answer but wanted to hear it firsthand.

"That's the best part. It seems Wes worked out a deal with a tribe of Indians from way up north. They come down here and masquerade as monsters to keep anyone from coming in here snooping around. The other thing they did was to find unsuspecting men, slip up on them and render them unconscious with that stuff in them bottles. You know how easy it is for Indians to sneak up on a white man. Before long we had us a big crew of miners."

Preston pushed him further. "Who was in charge? You mentioned a man named Wes, would that be Wes Branham, was he in charge?"

Simian thought about his answer. "Well I was told, along with all these other fellars, that if any one of us talked we would pay for it with our lives. None of us cared about that at the time; we were only looking toward the end of the job and that big bonus. I guess I can tell you now since the man is dead. His name was Wes Branham."

The judge looked at Simian. "Is this the Wes Branham that was shot by Lloyd Shafer a week ago?" Preston asked.

You could see the blood run out of Simian's face. "I didn't say that. It was Wes Branham and you can't be putting words in my mouth like that."

It was obvious Simian was afraid of Lloyd Shafer. Preston decided to dig a little further. "I didn't say anything other than Shafer shot Branham a few days back. Did you tell me Wes Branham was in charge knowing he was already dead? Is the real mastermind of this operation someone other than Branham?"

By the look and mannerisms of Simian it was apparent he didn't want to answer.

"I can tell you right now Simian, if Wes Branham is the only name you can furnish then our little deal is off. I'll see that you hang if it's the last thing I do."

Simian could feel the rope around his neck; he could see the trapdoor under his feet falling away and his body falling through the newly created opening. When the rope ran out of slack he could only imagine what it would feel like as the noose broke his neck.

"Lloyd Shafer is the man Judge. He is the one who stole this claim from a family that filed the paperwork almost a year ago. Shafer was the attorney who prepared it. When he found out how rich the claim was he had the man who filed the claim killed. He knew he couldn't refile the claim in his own name, someone would figure out he stole it. The man he killed has family back East and knew they would come out here to find out what had happened sooner or later. He had to work fast and get this mine cleaned out of all its silver, that's where we came in. He gave us eight months to get the job done and told us he didn't care how we did it as long as there were no witnesses." Simian suddenly got an angry look on his face, something had just dawned on him.

"Go on Simian; tell us the rest of the story," Preston said.

"It's all clear to me now. Shafer said he had done this before, said whenever he filed the right claim for some poor soul if the claim proved rich he would do away with the real owner and have the claim worked for himself." Simian looked up at the judge. "That son of a bitch had the entire crew killed after each claim was worked. Wes Branham and his bunch of gun hounds did the dirty work. The other claims he took over were small potatoes, just took a few men to mine it dry. This strike was so big it took forty men to work it. He was going to kill all those men and us too, no witnesses. I knew we weren't going to let any of these miners go but it just now hit me, he wasn't going to let us go either."

Preston pushed further. "How do you know he was going to kill you and your men Simian?"

"Because we saw him, he came out here four times over the course of six months and he never tried to hide his identity. He knew he didn't have to, we were all gonna be dead except for Wes and the three or four men that worked for him. That sorry, banking, son of a bitch!"

"Can any of these other men identify Shafer?" Preston asked.

"Damn right we can. All of us who were on the payroll and most of the miners. We can all identify him."

"One last question Simian. When were the miners to be killed?" Preston asked.

"Tonight. The mine is all finished; we got all the easy silver out of there, nothin left but the small stuff. We were supposed to herd all the miners inside and blow the mine down on top of 'em with dynamite. It just dawned on me; they never brought enough horses for me and my whole crew to ride out of here on. We were going to be herded into that mine and buried alive along with the miners. No witnesses."

Preston had Simian taken back to where the other guards were being held. Once he was gone Preston stood and looked at the miners and realized he and the other rescuers had arrived within hours of their murders. God must have had a hand in the rescue. There was no other way to explain it.

Cecil said, "Well Judge, you always wondered how Shafer managed to climb up the ladder of life so fast, now you know. He's been stealing silver mines from unsuspecting men for years."

Preston looked at the deputy. "I was just thinking that same thing Cecil. As much as I'm going to enjoy being there when you arrest him I can't help but feel sad for all the people he has destroyed. Maybe we can take solace in the fact that he will now be put out of business."

Cecil added, "Put out of business, and then hung."

The next morning all the dead outlaws, along with the dead Indians dressed as monsters, were put in the silver mine and then the opening was sealed up. The lone wagon was used to haul the wounded and also the weakest of the miners. There weren't enough horses for the rest of the men so it was decided to let some of the thinnest miners ride two to a horse. It took nearly four days to travel back to Rapid City. On the last day a rider went in ahead of the group and told of the rescue of the men and also to not be afraid anymore of monsters; if any of the refugees wanted to head back to their outlying farms, it was now safe to do so.

Word traveled fast and ten miles from town the group of miners were met by families looking for lost loved ones. There were quite a few happy reunions. A mile outside of town Martha Ellen and the two little boys were waiting to see if any of the men were her two missing brothers. They had taken the train from Langley and made the trip to Rapid City two days prior, they wanted to be there if the rescue party was successful. Keene spotted them first. A happier reunion has never been witnessed as that of little Keene running to his two uncles. Martha looked at Zeke as he rode up and could only nod her approval.

Ben, who had been lagging behind the group saw Keene and his mom and came bouncing. A bigger smile was never to be found as the one on Keene's face as he grabbed Ben around the neck and shouted for all to hear, "Ben, you did it, you did it."

Ben licked Keene in the face but the little boy didn't seem to care. In his mind the big dog had rescued his uncles and that was all that mattered.

The End

Haunted West

Made in the USA
Las Vegas, NV
13 March 2023